T

CRITICAL EXPLORATIONS IN SCIENCE FICTION AND FANTASY
(a series edited by Donald E. Palumbo and C.W. Sullivan III)

1. *Worlds Apart? Dualism and Transgression in Contemporary Female Dystopias* (Dunja M. Mohr, 2005)

2. *Tolkien and Shakespeare: Essays on Shared Themes and Language* (ed. Janet Brennan Croft, 2007)

3. *Culture, Identities and Technology in the* Star Wars *Films: Essays on the Two Trilogies* (ed. Carl Silvio and Tony M. Vinci, 2007)

4. *The Influence of* Star Trek *on Television, Film and Culture* (ed. Lincoln Geraghty, 2008)

5. *Hugo Gernsback and the Century of Science Fiction* (Gary Westfahl, 2007)

6. *One Earth, One People: The Mythopoeic Fantasy Series of Ursula K. Le Guin, Lloyd Alexander, Madeleine L'Engle and Orson Scott Card* (Marek Oziewicz, 2008)

7. *The Evolution of Tolkien's Mythology: A Study of the History of Middle-earth* (Elizabeth A. Whittingham, 2008)

8. *H. Beam Piper: A Biography* (John F. Carr, 2008)

9. *Dreams and Nightmares: Science and Technology in Myth and Fiction* (Mordecai Roshwald, 2008)

10. Lilith *in a New Light: Essays on the George MacDonald Fantasy Novel* (ed. Lucas H. Harriman, 2008)

11. *Feminist Narrative and the Supernatural: The Function of Fantastic Devices in Seven Recent Novels* (Katherine J. Weese, 2008)

12. *The Science of Fiction and the Fiction of Science: Collected Essays on SF Storytelling and the Gnostic Imagination* (Frank McConnell, ed. Gary Westfahl, 2009)

13. *Kim Stanley Robinson Maps the Unimaginable: Critical Essays* (ed. William J. Burling, 2009)

14. *The Inter-Galactic Playground: A Critical Study of Children's and Teens' Science Fiction* (Farah Mendlesohn, 2009)

15. *Science Fiction from Québec: A Postcolonial Study* (Amy J. Ransom, 2009)

16. *Science Fiction and the Two Cultures: Essays on Bridging the Gap Between the Sciences and the Humanities* (ed. Gary Westfahl and George Slusser, 2009)

17. *Stephen R. Donaldson and the Modern Epic Vision: A Critical Study of the "Chronicles of Thomas Covenant" Novels* (Christine Barkley, 2009)

18. *Ursula K. Le Guin's Journey to Post-Feminism* (Amy M. Clarke, 2010)

19. *Portals of Power: Magical Agency and Transformation in Literary Fantasy* (Lori M. Campbell, 2010)

20. *The Animal Fable in Science Fiction and Fantasy* (Bruce Shaw, 2010)

21. *Illuminating Torchwood: Essays on Narrative, Character and Sexuality in the BBC Series* (ed. Andrew Ireland, 2010)

22. *Comics as a Nexus of Cultures: Essays on the Interplay of Media, Disciplines and International Perspectives* (ed. Mark Berninger, Jochen Ecke and Gideon Haberkorn, 2010)

23. *The Anatomy of Utopia: Narration, Estrangement and Ambiguity in More, Wells, Huxley and Clarke* (Károly Pintér, 2010)

The Animal Fable in Science Fiction and Fantasy

BRUCE SHAW

Foreword by Van Ikin

CRITICAL EXPLORATIONS IN
SCIENCE FICTION AND FANTASY, 20

Donald E. Palumbo *and* C.W. Sullivan III, *series editors*

McFarland & Company, Inc., Publishers
Jefferson, North Carolina, and London

LIBRARY OF CONGRESS CATALOGUING-IN-PUBLICATION DATA

Shaw, Bruce, 1941–
The animal fable in science fiction and fantasy /
Bruce Shaw ; foreword by Van Ikin.
[Donald Palumbo and C.W. Sullivan III, series editors]
p. cm. — (Critical explorations in science fiction and fantasy ; 20)
Includes bibliographical references and index.

ISBN 978-0-7864-4783-1
softcover : 50# alkaline paper ∞

1. Science fiction — History and criticism. 2. Fantasy fiction — History and criticism. 3. Animals in literature.
I. Title.
PN3433.6.S53 2010
809.3'876209362 — dc22 2010008713

British Library cataloguing data are available

On our front cover: Cover art from the November 1939 *Startling Stories,* artist unknown (Wood River Gallery)

Manufactured in the United States of America

McFarland & Company, Inc., Publishers
Box 611, Jefferson, North Carolina 28640
www.mcfarlandpub.com

Contents

Foreword
by Van Ikin

Animals are aliens, of a kind. Some of them see in a different spectrum than we do, some hear different wavelengths, some derive nourishment from substances that would be toxic to us. They're aliens, but they live in our midst and we interact with them — often happily, sometimes even lovingly. So it's not surprising that science fiction and fantasy should often deal with these aliens-among-us.

It would be tempting to say that Bruce Shaw's study of animals in speculative fiction arises from a lifelong passionate commitment to animals. But that's not wholly true. Dr. Shaw informs me, for the record, that there were three dogs in his family at different times during his early life, and a dog (Whiskers the Terrier) and a cat (Rufus the Cat) were both present when he began his study. But he is not a fully-fledged animal rights activist (though agreeing with the ideas in principle), and it was actually an intellectual fascination with Clifford Simak's *City* that propelled him into the 12-year process of writing this book.

Animals are a stronger, richer presence in speculative fiction than all but the most avid readers may realize. According to Brian Aldiss in *Trillion Year Spree* (1986), the novel *Sirius* (about a sheep dog which has the brain and perceptions of a human) "is the most human of Stapledon's novels." "Love is a rare thing in Stapledon's world," notes Aldiss, but "here, reaching across species, it finds the warmest and most touching expression, to live on even when the mutated dog is killed" (198). If animals brought out the warmer side of Stapledon, they elicited the deeper worries of Orwell in *Animal Farm* and of Mikhail Bulgakov in *The Heart of a Dog*— though at least Bulgakov sees room to provide a happier conclusion to his allegorical fable. On a much lighter note, Philip K. Dick's short story "The Little Movement" (1952) combines stuffed toys, conspiracy theory and Hans Christian Andersen motifs when mechanical toys take over the minds of children, only to be defeated by panda bears from the plush toy forces.

Animals in speculative fiction often receive nothing but brutality from our supposedly "superior" human hands — think of the hapless creatures in Kirsten Bakis's *Lives of the Monster Dogs*, or William Kotzwinkle's acerbic *Doctor Rat* (1971), which Shaw regards as "one of the strongest anti-vivisectionist texts in the field," or the satirical novella *Play Little Victims* (1978) by Kenneth Cook, in which the fate of a mouse civilization becomes a moving allegory of human destiny. Cordwainer Smith's animal underpeople endure great suffering and barbarity, yet when we see "the face of a weeping child, bewildered by hurt and shocked by the prospect of more hurt to come," this response is on behalf of the soldier putting the underpeople to death: The author is revealing the effects of cruelty on the perpetrators themselves.

Dire things happen to animals in some works, but in other works there is humor and playfulness, and Bruce Shaw is fascinated by this juxtaposition of light and dark. He has a real knack for describing humor in a way that keeps the funniness alive, and you'll grin at his account of the antics in Mikhail Bulgakov's *The Heart of a Dog*. This novella may once have been described as "a fierce parable of the Russian Revolution," but its ferocity is based upon the take-no-prisoners humor that arises when social engineers replace glands in the dog Sharik with those from a petty criminal. The dog unexpectedly becomes human in intellect and appearance — he gives the impression of "a short, ill-knit human male" — but behaves like an uncouth, street-wise lout, wearing loud clothes, drinking excesses of vodka while playing the balalaika badly, acts lewdly towards women servants, and has an irrational hatred for cats.

Bruce Shaw's study will help to renew the focus upon better-known writers like Bulgakov, Orwell, and Cordwainer Smith. It will also draw wider international attention to lesser-known gems like *Play Little Victims*, or potentially controversial works like Peter Goldsworthy's novel *Wish* (1995), which deals explicitly with sexual (as well as spiritual) love between a human and a gorilla, or Will Self's irreverent and hilarious romp, *Great Apes* (1997), in which a disaffected artist awakes to discover that he is the only human in a city of chimpanzees ... unless he is an ape with a singular neurosis believing himself to be human and consequently in need of intense psychiatric help?

In a delightfully clear and readable prose style, Bruce Shaw demonstrates the significance of the themes explored through speculative fiction's "animal tales," setting out their literary pedigree as an extension of the tradition of the animal fable, and exploring how such tales might be approached using the apparatus of literary theory. There is renewed and growing interest in animals throughout a number of disciplines (environment, ethics, social sciences, as well as in the humanities) and this book contributes enthusiastically to numerous aspects of these developing debates.

Van Ikin is a professor of English and cultural studies at the University of Western Australia.

Preface

Animal studies became of academic interest in the late 1990s and remained relevant into the present century, although that was not the reason I chose the topic. I like animals and enjoy reading science fiction and fantasy stories about them. My contribution became part of the general movement towards greater awareness of animals and so remains apposite today.

Works using animal intelligence as a foil against the intelligence of humans figure widely in the comparatively recent literary inventions of science fiction and fantasy. The appeal of using animals goes back to the early fables of ancient India, Persia, Greece and Rome, and present-day animal stories are written with much the same motives as in those fables: to amuse and to instruct, which introduces a mix of humor and seriousness, of tragedy and the comic. They entertain and instruct while at the same time unsettling us.

Many theoretical approaches assist our understanding of this genre. One way of interpreting what happens when we read a story of this kind is through Mikhail Bakhtin's concept of Carnival — more appropriately, the carnivalesque. This involves upsetting the status quo: overturning or inverting the serious through the use of satire and parody and other comic devices, with an overlay of the earthy or bodily so that we can find a good, though not exact, match between, for example, Roland Barthes' use of *jouissance* and the carnivalesque of Bakhtin's theorizing. However, Bakhtin is not unique. Many other scholars draw attention to the uneasy alliance between seriousness and humor, and use other means to point to what Bakhtin identifies as the regenerating power of laughter. What Bakhtin does is to give the "theory of laughter" another context.

Writers of science fiction and fantasy whose work is inspired by the animal fable of old reflect the societal fears of their socio-cultural milieux, as well as drawing on their personal troubles. It could scarcely be otherwise. Their output is nearly always interesting, whether the stories are weak in quality or belong to the literary canon, because there is an intrinsic connection between humans and animals whose world one shares with the other. We have an uneasy fellowship with animals, especially those with which we are often in contact in the domestic or nearly wild spheres.

Like the stories told using animals as foils for humans, there is at the same time affection and unease. Such stories are good to read. In the right hands a foil in its martial sense offers both protection and a means of offense. Laughter, especially that generated by the carnivalesque, acts as a conduit for social critique and as a means of regeneration (following Bakhtin), and helps to buoy us from the anxieties of the world.

Works of merit in the genre on animals are profiled in this book. Notable entries on short stories include Clifford D. Simak's "The Big Front Yard" (1959), Cordwainer Smith's "The Game of Rat and Dragon" (1975), and Daniel Keyes' "Flowers for Algernon" (1959). In the chapter on novels and novellas I survey Kirsten Bakis' *Lives of the Monster Dogs* (1997), Anatole France's *Penguin Island* (1908), William Kotzwinkle's *Doctor Rat* (1971), Kenneth Cook's *Play Little Victims* (1978), Poul Anderson's *Brain Wave* (1954), Walter Miller's *Conditionally Human* (1952), Stephanie Johnson's *The Whistler* (1998), and many others.

Some chapters or chapter sections come from book reviews written during the research. Early theoretical argument first appeared in the *Australian Journal of Comedy* (6.1 [2000a]: 99–131); and Bulgakov's *Heart of a Dog* was also published as a review article in the *Australian Journal of Comedy* (7.1 [2001a]: 71–92, editor Gerry Matte). A revised version is forthcoming in *Science Fiction: A Review of Speculative Literature* (editor Van Ikin). *The Whistler* review was first published in *Science Fiction: A Review of Speculative Literature* (16.1 [2001b]: 57–60). Peter Goldsworthy's novel *Wish* was reviewed in *Science Fiction: A Review of Speculative Literature* (15.2 [2000b]: 27–38). Sections of the chapter on Clifford Simak's *City* were published as a review article in *Extrapolation* (46.4 [2005]: 488–499, managing editor Javier A. Martinez). I thank those editors for permissions to reprint from the articles.

The elements of the animal tale in science fiction and fantasy short stories include three prerequisites for stories about animal intelligence, namely: speech, the use of or compensation for hands, and the acquisition of intelligence itself—hence the title—together with a statement about the appeal of this mode to readers as entertainment (the carnivalesque) and instruction (for example, political allegory).

I am indebted to Peter Morton, associate professor of English, Flinders University, South Australia, who asked relevant questions and reminded me to avoid over-compression. I acknowledge gratefully the counsel and encouragement of Van Ikin, Professor, English and Cultural Studies, the University of Western Australia; also to Dr. Michael Tolley (Adelaide University 1995) for permission to audit his lectures on science fiction that year.

University libraries consulted include Murdock University (Western Australia), Adelaide University, the Flinders University of South Australia, the University of Western Australia, and Curtin University of Technology.

Whiskers the Terrier and Rufus the Cat in their daily lives gave initial inspiration.

Introduction: Why Choose Animals?

The characterization of animals that speak, reason, use artifacts, have reciprocal dealings with humans, and in their behavior mimic or reflect that of humans has produced several impressive narrative forms. They explore moral and ethical principles and reflect upon societal and historical issues of the day. That is part of their appeal. But why choose animals? What do animal characters permit that may be denied to human characters?

Writers have often been predisposed to seeing the species *Homo sapiens* from without, and have made use of tropes from the beast fable and the fairy tale, techniques of reflecting and highlighting human vagaries through the eyes of animals with intelligences on a par with humans: *Canis sapiens* or *Felix sapiens.* Such works can deal with personified spiritual qualities like faith or innocence, as in Bunyan's non-beast allegory *The Pilgrim's Progress* (1678), or in the guise of guardian fairies, such as Mrs. Bedonebyasyoudid in Charles Kingsley's *The Water-Babies* (1863)—a "perfect Menippean" satire "influenced by Rabelais" (Northrop Frye 310) imparting Victorian morality. There is the well-known imagery of pigs as men or men as pigs in George Orwell's *Animal Farm* (1945).

Northrop Frye (309) observes that the Menippean satire deals with mental attitudes more than with people: "rapacious and incompetent professional men of all kinds, are handled in terms of their occupational approach to life as distinct from their social behaviour." Think of the experiences of Lucius in Apuleius' *The Golden Ass* and the stock characters through whose hands he passes: bandits, farmers, priests, a miller, a soldier—although I would have thought their social behavior to be just as important, reflecting as it would their approach to life.

Animal-human allegories frequently emphasize philosophical dichotomies: whether or not there are differences between the human and non-human, the domestic and the wild, the human and the beast within, intelligence and feelings, intelligence and personality, consciousness (mind) and spirit, and the wider question of what it is that makes us human. Animal tales appear in a number of genres: children's literature, fables, fairy tales, folktales, mythology, and science fiction and fantasy.

We are entertained by the humor they often contain. Consequently, animal-human allegories that have serious messages are frequently filled with satire, parody and irony (the carnivalesque) at one level, descending to dreadful puns at another level (which, too, is carnivalesque). We enjoy, as well being entertained by, mystery, horror and the macabre, and by tragedy, which can often be interwoven with humor. Animal characters have roles as companions and protectors, protagonists and antagonists; and as literary creations they often evoke powerful archetypal images and emotions.

Familiarity is one factor behind our choice of animal protagonists. Dogs, cats, horses, the primates, and cetaceans (dolphins and whales) have a long and close association with humans. It may have something to do with our hunter-gatherer past that led to animal domestication and a corresponding acknowledgement of animal intelligence, at least among the higher animals. This is purposely ambiguous: do I mean human acknowledgement of intelligence among the higher animals; or do I mean the higher animals, other than human, acknowledging human intelligence? Moreover, many domesticated species become animal companions ("pets"), a factor that helps cement close interaction and emotional ties. The theme has been the subject of several popular works of non-fiction since the last decade, such as Elizabeth Thomas' *The Hidden Life of Dogs* (1993) and Jonica Newby's *The Pact for Survival: Humans and Their Animal Companions* (1997), and reflects a heightening of debate since the beginnings of the animal liberation movement led by Peter Singer in the 1970s.

A moral point may often be better received if it comes from the jaws and snouts of cuddly domestic animals with which readers can believe themselves to more easily identify, though such beasts are not always harmless and friendly. We humans ascribe certain qualities to our animal *dramatis personae* that are reflections or extensions of how we perceive them popularly in everyday life, as well as being reflections and extensions of ourselves, and this includes the comfortable and the dangerous, which, as I have said, often permeates the same tale.

Frequently an accompanying effect is that of defamiliarization whereby familiar acts or words are made unfamiliar. In a controversial passage often cited, Victor Shklovsky (20) observes:

> The technique of art is to make objects "unfamiliar," to make forms difficult, to increase the difficulty and length of perception because the process of perception is an aesthetic end in itself and must be prolonged. *Art is a way of experiencing the artfulness of an object; the object is not important* [his emphasis].

Shklovsky (226–27) associates defamiliarization with such techniques as euphemism (for example, in riddles) and the creation of disharmony from apparently harmonious contexts, or the use of what he calls parallelism ("to transfer the usual perception of an object into the sphere of a new perception") or the satisfaction to be had from poetic language. The emphasis on pleasure in a text does not rule out the challenge it might pose for a reader.

In the animal fable and its offshoots, human failings are described afresh through the experiences of non-human characters. It is a form of defamiliarization to attribute almost-human viewpoints to animals and by so doing to present social issues — that is, moral issues — in different ways. In other words, paraphrasing C.S. Lewis' biographer A.N. Wilson (214): "make-believe [is] really another way of talking about the reality of things." Orwell does this in his novella *Animal Farm* (1945), writing against the Russian totalitarian political system; also Mikhail Bulgakov in his first novel, *The Heart of a Dog* (1925/1968), from within that same political régime. Another trick of defamiliarization is to introduce a Candide-like figure (as in the second example), a non-human through whose eyes the alien human society is laid bare.

In general, we like to be reminded of moral principles, such as our responsibilities to others, so long as we are not too embarrassed about our lapses; and the animal allegory reminds us of these things by making human thought and behavior stand out in relief without being too challenging. But this is not always the case. It introduces a wide range of themes, such as good and evil, the beast in humankind, Jung's archetype of the Shadow, Olaf Stapledon's "darkness and light" (the title of one of his books), and opposites like friendship and companionship versus loneliness, isolation, alienation, or xenophobia. It raises questions such as: What does it mean to be human? How might animal consciousness-of-being manifest itself? Are we alone in the cosmos? Where does humankind stand in relation to the animal world and the natural environment? What is friendship? In Brian Aldiss' words (5): "Can we be better than we are?"

I choose the genre of science fiction and fantasy and not fantasy works *per se*, such as *The Wind in the Willows* (1908), which belongs to a different branching of the animal fable. Another policy is to restrict the range to terrestrial species, such as dogs, cats, apes, and amphibians, and not to extend it to exotic extraterrestrial creatures except in passing. An assumption on my part is that it is unreasonable to expect readers to be familiar with some titles that are not mainstream in the generally accepted use of the term, or no longer in publication and so not read as frequently (many good works get lost in this way); hence it is necessary to convey sufficient detail on some works to facilitate understanding. Another policy is to use close reading as a tool for an appreciation of the texts and their relationship with their authors' biographies, paying attention to the narrative techniques they apply.

Many authors are impelled to impress the anxieties of their socio-cultural milieux into their fiction, especially in time of war or a similarly grave social upheaval, such as a natural disaster, and Modernist fiction necessarily includes confrontations with violence, nihilism, and despair, and a corresponding fascination with, and fear of, the unconscious. This, I think, is as true of the present decade as it was in the early twentieth century. That is, post-structuralism (and whatever fashion will arrive next in literary criticism) is concerned with much the same issues. Our understanding of a work is improved if we apply to it not only a close reading but also look at it through the author's biography. By this means we link public issues (history) to personal troubles (biography), following C. Wright Mills (248). Stapledon and Linebarger argue that love and spirituality are to be heeded; they warn about the consequences of one-dimensional power politics, as do Čapek and Simak, and Linebarger too in his far future authoritarian world.

There is more than power in our lives, though I should not be equally reductionist by saying that all you need is love. The works I discuss point to a number of qualities among which love holds a dominant place, but where the political and psychological are not denied. Some of these qualities are amenable to the carnivalesque and other cognate concepts, and that is the path I follow.

Common Themes in Animal Tales

Animal stories inspired by the ancient fables draw upon virtually every major genre and cliché in science fiction and fantasy. They include post-apocalyptic worlds and the cozy catastrophe; the Gothic, which subsumes the Frankenstein theme, the ghost story, and the tale of revenge, including the mad professor stereotype; space opera and the associated epic heroic tale; romance, including sexuality and love; the detective and mystery genre, with the stock character of the religious sleuth; also, the allegorical or cautionary tale. Within these lie an array of other stock situations and stock characters, including mutants, symbiotes, telepaths and clairvoyants, first contact tales, parallel worlds, interstellar police, transformations (metamorphoses), barroom tales, dream sequences, enclosed worlds, feudal and tribal societies, extraterrestrials secretly observing humanity, folkloric allusions, and the themes of rebirth or reincarnation and life after death.

Among the different narrative forms available, animal tales are allegorical to the core if we accept Baldick's (5) definition that allegories give human shape to abstract qualities, extending a metaphor into a "structured system," making "a continuous parallel between two (or more) levels of meaning in a story," and, by so doing, extend their implications to circumstances well outside the frame of the narrative. Allegories are often subversive of the status quo — turning it on its head — and so have a touch of the carnivalesque because they play on hidden meanings, with an expectation that readers will recognize the intent behind those meanings. For this reason they are often political in nature, though allegory has its origin in religious beliefs, and they invariably pursue easily recognizable social issues.

One issue is the misapplication of human science, exemplified in tales that harken back to Shelley's *Frankenstein.* Stories on this theme often include parodies of science, and a parody is a form of overthrowing, of the carnivalesque. Another issue is the critique on racial prejudice, which can include descriptions of human exploitation of another species equally or exceedingly more intelligent. Often related to this is a lively "as others see us" theme in which the world is presented from animal points of view. I say misapplication of human science because in one tale, Kenneth Cook's short fable *Play Little Victims,* sentient mice attempt to emulate humankind with disastrous results — heightened warfare, overcrowding, and cruelty — by misapplying an animal science derived from that of humans. Harry Harrison's Eden series concerning evolved dinosaurs confronting early humans is another rare example of this approach, for the science is almost exclusively in saurian hands.

Other common themes include the witnessing of humankind's faults and the decline of their civilization, as in Lester del Ray's short story "The Faithful" (1938). This theme is occasionally depicted through social realism (cf. Ellison's "A Boy and His Dog"). Another frequently recurring theme is that of an intelligent animal experiencing human duplicity, betrayal, and an accompanying loss of childhood or child-like innocence, as in John Christopher's "Socrates." The theme of child-like helplessness and appeal is strong in Walter Miller's classic novella *Conditionally Human.* On the other hand, commentaries on pride and an accompanying anthropocentrism are often depicted, with a matching *amour propre* on the part of non-human species when they perceive human minds to be hopelessly confused. This can include reversals of role, as in William Tenn's delightful short satire "Null-P." Reversals are a major ploy in satire and the carnivalesque, as when the members of humanity are depicted as slaves while believing they are the masters, a touch of double irony when the intelligent animals are rats, as in Bertram Chandler's "Giant Killer" or F.L. Wallace's "Big Ancestor." In the end, however, in those tales it is the rats that are self-deceived.

Another theme is the "animals fight back" scenario, which operates at several levels. At one level a sentient creation does little more than ask awkward questions, such as: "Why did you make me?" as in the novel *Sirius* or in Howard Fast's "The Mouse." At another level, visiting extraterrestrial intellects open social intercourse with alternative terrestrial intelligences, such as dolphins, or *vice versa*, to the exclusion of humankind, as in John Jakes' "The Highest Form of Life" or Gordon Dickson's "Dolphin's Way." On the other hand, at one extreme, total warfare can erupt between humans and animals, as in Wallace-Crabbe's *Dogs* and Kotzwinkle's *Doctor Rat*, discussed in the next chapter.

These numerous examples of inversions, often presented through modes of fun, such as parody, satire, and irony, are carnivalesque in nature and usually have a serious underlay. They possess the quality that Bakhtin calls the carnivalesque in their power to unsettle through comic crownings and uncrownings; probably more uncrownings than the former when we consider how often irony plays a part, usually at humankind's expense.

CHAPTER 1

The Beast Fable

The animal or beast tale is often found in science fiction and fantasy and, like the traditional fables that have survived for us to appreciate today and from which it springs, contains a mix of humor and serious intent that marks the best works in the genre. They reflect social and personal issues, such as violence, despair and fears of the unconscious, and for these reasons they can also belong to a literature of dissent. In the twentieth century such tales often have mixed attributes: they may be allegorical, contain wit and humor, be cautionary (that is, have underlying serious purposes), and are often skillfully crafted narratives. As David Lodge observes (137): "Popular science fiction, for instance, is a curious mixture of invented gadgetry and archetypal narrative motifs very obviously derived from folk tales, fairytale, and Scripture, recycling the myths of Creation, Fall, Flood and a Divine Saviour, for a secular but still superstitious age."

One way by which we understand such works better is to look at the biographies of those who write the tales. In a sweeping statement, Martin Amis observes: "Writers are now accorded their biographies whether or not anything ever happened to them, on the principle ... that such studies help explain why they wrote what they wrote," including in parentheses that this principle is a long-exploded one (245). On the contrary, I think we can indeed understand better why some, perhaps a great many, writers wrote what they wrote. A lot happened to the authors chosen for special attention below.

I read everything I could lay my hands on in science fiction short stories and novellas that drew upon the animal fable. For example, Karel Čapek (1890–1938) parodies narrative styles when writing about newts. Olaf Stapledon (1886–1950) writes a dog's biography. Clifford Simak (1904–1988), through gentle satire, emphasizes with dogs, robots and humans the theme of degeneration. Paul Linebarger (1913–1966) taps into the themes of love and rebellion in his underpeople stories. Those four authors were responding to pre-war fears, wartime realities, and post-war disquiet. For an earlier era, that of the 1920s, there is a novel by Mikhail Bulgakov with a dog protagonist. The late twentieth century is represented by one of Peter Goldsworthy's novels about an ape, and a post-apocalyptic novel by Stephanie Johnson narrated by a dog.

These narratives by which animal characters are created are "good to read" because they entertain while at the same time instructing the reader. Paradoxically, they entertain by challenging the reader in a variety of ways. They give pleasure but also defamiliarize us, elicit *jouissance* (from time to time I shall refer to mad French philosophers) and provoke laughter, while exploring moral questions by means of a variety of literary forms. On the whole, entertainment and instruction (political effectiveness) are complementary, but they receive varying emphases in the hands of different authors. This central idea that comedic works of fiction entertain but also challenge and disturb has a strong literary tradition. In *Consciousness and the Novel,* David Lodge discusses Evelyn Waugh's early works that "disturb and challenge as well as entertain the reader" (163):

> In combining elements of comedy, often of a robustly farcical kind, with satirical wit and caricature, in order to explore social reality with an underlying seriousness of purpose, Evelyn Waugh belonged to a venerable and peculiarly English literary tradition which we can trace back through Dickens and Thackeray, Smollett, Sterne, and Henry Fielding [164].

The tradition is not only English, for "comedic devices" such as slapstick, mistaken identity, and puns (Wikipedia 2008a), as well as many others that engender these mixed receptions of the pleasurable but also unsettling, can be traced back to classical times. The more recent tradition of which Lodge speaks is not only English but, in one instance, Russian or central European. As a foil against what might now be the waning fashion of mystification called deconstruction, I refer to Mikhail Bakhtin's theories about the novel, in particular that of Carnival and, by extension, the carnivalesque. I interrelate Bakhtin's insights with social history (public issues) and biography (personal troubles). But I also take into account other literary theories that appear to be complementary to that of Bakhtin.

The Beast Fable

In the contemporary genre of science fiction and fantasy, an experimental approach taken by some authors is to fall back upon the traditional fable or beast tale by writing imaginative stories about animals endowed with intelligences equal to or greater than that of humans. They appear as present-day beast fables, their protagonists — cats, dogs, foxes, lions and others — representing human stock characters by speaking and behaving like them in order to exemplify abstract moral principles.

The beast fable has an extensive lineage going back beyond the Graeco–Roman world to the Middle East and South Asia — Aesop (sixth century B.C.), tales of metamorphosis by Ovid (first century) and Apuleius's *The Golden Ass* (c. A.D. 158) — and continues in the bestiaries popular in the Middle Ages and such animal tales as those beginning with Pierre de Saint-Cloud's *The Romance of Reynard the Fox* (c. mid–1170s) and continuing with Jean de la Fontaine's *Fables* of the seventeenth century. But these works drew from what was already a very old tradition. Preceding these literary and folk traditions, there was the Indian *Pancatantra* (c. 300 C.E.). According to Patrick Olivelle (xliii):

> The *Pancatantra* influenced Arabic and European narrative literature of the Middle Ages, most notably *The Arabian Nights* and La Fontaine, who in the second edition of his *Fables* (1678) states expressly that much of his new material was derived from the Indian sage Pilpay, perhaps a corruption of the Sanskrit Vidyapati ("Lord of Learning") or of the common Brahmin title Vajapeyi.

Several themes from the ancient fables persist in twentieth century popular writing. Maya Slater's Introduction to a translation of Jean De La Fontaine's *Selected Fables* is a good starting point (vii–xxvii). She talks about the paradoxical diversity and duality of La Fontaine's approach, identifying such modes as pessimistic *and* light-hearted irony, the subversive new versions of classical Greek and Indian fables as reworked by La Fontaine (for example, social comment against kings), the different layers and shifts in perspective among the tales in the collection, and La Fontaine's avowed intent to both instruct and please the reader. Slater then lists five principal interconnected elements. First, the fable "tells a story, whose point is outside the story." That is, it has a moral or cautionary instruction. Second, the characters in a fable are chosen specifically "to demonstrate a truth to listeners or readers outside the story." That is, we might say it is allegorical in nature. Third, the characters traditionally are animals, which, Slater says, helps to emphasize the message directed towards humans. This quality of emphasis is a weak point in Slater's model. Perhaps she regards the usefulness of animal characters for emphasizing a story's moral to be self-evident. She might have followed up the thread by discussing the phenomenon of animal appeal.

These are the three traditional elements in fables, but Slater adds two more — namely, (fourth) La Fontaine's characteristic wit and humor in the making of (often deadly) serious points, and (fifth) another characteristic of La Fontaine's, to compose his versions not only as fables but also "as beautifully crafted poems" (Slater xv). In other words, there is a great deal of aesthetic pleasure taken in their preparation, in their reading, or in their recital. These elements suggest not only Bakhtin's ideas about *heteroglossia* and the subversion of authority, key elements in Carnival and the carnivalesque, but they also bring strongly to mind other factors such as *jouissance* and defamiliarization.

I think that we can see in some forms of twentieth century writing a process unfolding that recasts the animal romances of those earlier centuries into the genres we recognize today, including science fiction and fantasy. In this new form, intelligent animals such as dogs, dolphins or apes become major protagonists whose experiences reflect the anxieties of our century. Of course, it is really humans looking at themselves, for we cannot know easily how our species is perceived by another, so such works are frequently allegorical. That is, they are a means of stating "an abstract moral thesis or principle of human behaviour" by means of personifying the non-human as human (Baldick 6). Tales of this nature elicit reader interest and sympathy, first because they are moral narratives appealing to our sense of right and/or injustice, and, second, because they often contain a strong element of tragedy. Animal tales also appeal to our sense of fun by containing satire, parody, burlesque, comedy and humor. They are often good-natured in tone. Yet satire in particular is a potent weapon of dissent, and there is serious intent behind the fun.

As I have indicated above, the animal fantasy in broad terms is a phenomenon that does not belong to European literature alone, although the reader would be forgiven for thinking it was uniquely European. I have not attended to other parts of the world outside England, continental Europe, and the United States. But animal fables are an intrinsic ingredient in the mythology and folklore of the Middle East, China, Southeast Asia and South Asia. At least one of the authors in my list, Paul Linebarger, is strongly influenced by Chinese and south Asian (Indian) narrative forms. I have not chosen Asian fables because science fiction began as a distinctively western European genre, though it might draw some of its inspiration from Asian cultures. Most Asian literature concerning animals as moral exemplars resonates with that of early Graeco–Roman forms like Apuleius's *The Golden Ass* because it has a spiritual overlay. In the present day this has been lost, or remains as a palimpsest, partly submerged beneath modes of writing that are not necessarily religious, such as satire or parody, which Bakhtin says were indeed subversive of organized religion in Medieval times.

However, the objective of making social comment, if not social change, is to be found in those earlier forms. It appears sometimes implicitly, as in the close relationships between animals and humans in the Indian epics *The Mahabharata* and *The Ramayana.* In the latter, Hanuman the monkey god-king leads his cohorts against the monster Ravana in support of King Rama's military campaign to rescue his consort Sita. In the climactic battle the monkey warriors are pitted against Ravana's demons, the *rakshasas.* The sixteenth century Chinese novel *Monkey* (1942/1979) by Wu Ch'eng-en (c. 1505–1580) has a more satiric vein, especially in the hands of the Japanese actors in the BBC series that ran in Australia during the early 1980s. In the back-cover blurb of the Arthur Waley translation, the work is hailed as a "comic novel," and is described as combining "beauty with absurdity, profundity with nonsense, Folk-lore, allegory, religion, history, anti-bureaucratic satire and pure poetry" (7). The anti-bureaucratic satire is most evident in the pronouncements of the heavenly saints, a vehicle for satire used also by Anatole France in *Penguin Island* (1908/1968). In the Chinese hierarchy, the structure of government in heaven replicates that found on earth (Waley 7). In many of its episodes, the novel is carnivalesque in nature.

A celebrated present-day novel of south Asia that belongs without a doubt to the fantasy genre of today is R.K. Narayan's tale *A Tiger for Malgudi* (1982). The novel is a first-person account of the experiences of a tiger among a variety of humans, making it similar to *The Golden Ass* except that no metamorphosis takes place. Aside from that, the vehicle of social comment and satire is the same as in Apuleius's story: an animal is placed in a privileged position to observe human follies.

Bakhtin and the Animal Fable

Two formative eras, the Hellenistic and the Medieval, provide the inspirational sources for many of Mikhail Bakhtin's insights, in particular his ideas about dialogism versus monologism, polyglossia, and carnivalization. Yet Bakhtin accords very little attention to the tradition of the beast fable in either *Rabelais and His World* or *The Dialogic Imagination*, although one would expect that tales from Aesop's Fables, such as that of Reynard the Fox, and La Fontaine's reworking of many of Aesop's stories were ideal subjects. Bakhtin does, however, acknowledge Apuleius (c. A.D. 123–180), who is listed fifteen times in the index to *The Dialogic Imagination*, his work *The Golden Ass* seven times.

Polyglossia results when several cultures, and therefore their languages, intersect — a phenomenon that enriches any literary languages in use during such a time in the history of civilizations. In the Hellenistic world, Greek was written and spoken by the urbanized people (the upper classes with a literary education), and Latin was the language of administration and law under Roman rule. Other languages, such as Aramaic and those of Mesopotamia, Persia and India, contributed to and "interanimated" one another (cf. the *Pancatantra*). These were in sharp contrast, Bakhtin (64–65) says, to the "naive," "passive," "monoglottic" world of myth that existed before this era. Bakhtin associates the development of polyglossia with "the birth of novelistic matter-of-factness," and so traces the origins of the novel as a form that carries within it most other genres preceding it, such as Greek epic, lyric, and drama. We may compare this with our present literary world, which has become increasingly polyglot, with the frequent appearance in novelistic and academic discourse of words and expressions borrowed from other languages: Greek and Roman still, but also French, German, Italian, Spanish, Indian, Chinese, and so on. This is exactly the point Bakhtin is driving at, and I think he does not refer to such forms as the animal fable because he is mounting an argument at a higher level of abstraction concerning the rise of the novel.

Bakhtin (111–112) does, however, consider the folktale and "folkloric narratives," which include the animal fable, among other forms, and he discusses Apuleius's *The Golden Ass* as an example of the "second type of ancient novel" characterized as "an adventure — everyday novel" whose plot revolves around the hero Lucius' life, with the themes of identity and metamorphosis exemplified by his transformation into an ass and the wanderings he is forced to undertake. In another essay, Bakhtin (391) refers to this as the Helleno–Roman novel of trial, with its complementary elements of crisis and rebirth. The wanderings take Lucius, transformed into an ass, from owner to owner and place him at first in unenviable situations where he witnesses human perfidy and cruelty before the happy ending of an epiphany experienced during Lucius' initiation into the cult of the Egyptian goddess Isis that was highly influential in Greek society at the time. That is, social issues stand alongside or are accompanied by biography. Concerning "the extraordinary variety of folkloric narratives," these, says Bakhtin (112) elsewhere, are always ordered around the "motifs of *transformation* and *identity*" (his emphases), and are "distinctive features of popular-folktale time," which he considers later in a discussion of Rabelais.

Mikhail Bakhtin is one of many essayists who discuss the narrative styles of satire, parody and irony. His contribution to what might be called the theory of humor lies in his interpretation of Carnival and, by extension, the concept of the carnivalesque. Most of his writing, though voluminous, is comparatively easy to read because it contains so much repetition. Bakhtin limits Carnival to one particular epoch and a certain author, claiming that Rabelais is unique and that all writing after Gargantua and Pantagruel employs corrupt forms of humor. According to his view, Rabelais has no peer: his works stand solitary, and all works that follow are flawed. Humor, in Bakhtin's terms, reached its apogee with Rabelais and declined from then on. In my opinion, this is a narrow view of what is a great tradition in human letters, that of humor, satire, parody, and so on. But whether Bakhtin is correct or not by singling out Rabelais and Carnival as unique author and unique social theory is beyond the point, for the idea of Carnival suggests the subsidiary and, I believe, more useful concept of the carnivalesque.

Bakhtin is not unique either, as far as other developments in literary theory are concerned. His ideas, even that of Carnival, are not new. The concept of the dialogic, for example, is as old as the myth of the Tower of Babel, a myth, incidentally, that has elements of the carnivalesque in its themes of overturning and confusion. Authors who are rediscovered, especially those who experience great hardship in their personal and political lives, tend to be eulogized by the generation of students and scholars that rediscovers them, and to be critiqued somewhat more searchingly by those students who follow next. People tend to elevate them to genius on the basis of their private experiences and the societal fears mirrored in those experiences. They are great men or women because they did it tough. Literature has many notable examples: Bulgakov, Pasternak, Mary Wollstonecraft, Mary Shelley, Virginia Woolf. Their fame can be a reflection of the political correctness of the students' day. But we need not take the critique to the opposite limit. Those authors' lives and contributions to art invite new perspectives. Mikhail Bakhtin is important for a cluster of seminal ideas, all of which have been touched upon by other theorists at some time.

Bakhtin (454) appeals to the use of irony in Rabelais, saying that his statements are not so much direct as coming from, or expressing the spirit of, the people. The laconic nature of folk humor, of understatement and irony, appears to have been a survival strategy in Rabelais' time, as it is now:

> Rabelais ... never exhausts his resources in direct statements. This, of course, is not romantic irony; this is the broad, exacting spirit of the people which was transmitted to him with the entire system of the images of folk humor.

Bakhtin (141) cites L.E. Pinsky (174) with approval when that writer says of Rabelais' sort of laughter that it "is not a satire in the precise meaning of the word, it does not express indignation about vice or anger at evil in social and cultural life." It reveals instead two principles that Bakhtin holds dear in

Rabelais: "the element of knowledge ... and its link with truth." Laughter is a great antidote to sadness, and it is one of Bakhtin's principle arguments that, through Carnival, laughter — and, by implication, the carnivalesque — we become renewed, regenerated (78): "Following the days of lenten sadness he [the priest] could incite his congregation's gay laughter as a joyous regeneration." This appears in the context of Bakhtin's discussion of Apuleius' *The Golden Ass*, where he notes how this animal symbolizes traditionally "the material bodily lower stratum, which at the same time degrades and regenerates."

Those observations echo the theme that science fiction and fantasy stories using the tradition of the animal fable are at the same time unsettling and satisfying. The comparatively new genre (nineteenth through the twentieth century to now) has tendrils that go back to the animal fable and its traditions. To borrow from two culturally different lexicons, they juxtapose *jouissance* and *angst*. This is very close to a broader view about what the contemporary philosopher Alain de Botton (238) calls, paraphrasing Ruskin, "the twin purposes of art: to make sense of pain and to fathom the sources of beauty."

The Fairy Tale

Another genre ("genre" is literally a mode of delivery) that has a close kinship with the animal fable is the fairy tale. In Abrams' (69) definition, fables and fairy tales are subsumed under the folktale, a categorization followed also by Baldick (85). What the two forms have in common, along with myths, legends, tall stories, anecdotes and jokes, is their transmission via a culture's oral tradition. In course of time they are often transposed into a written medium and thus find their way into the culture's literary tradition, and in that form they are probably more amenable to analysis. The fairy tale itself is closely associated in the definitions with the German oral form of the *Märchen*, "tales of enchantment and marvels" (Baldick 129), with the observation that, strictly speaking, they rarely include fairies as their subject. Baldick points out that the *Märchen* can be subdivided into two categories — folktales such as those collected by the brothers Jacob and Wilhelm Grimm (1785–1863 and 1786–1859, respectively), and literary creations, "art tales" that can have an element of the uncanny, as in the tales of Ernst Theodor Wilhelm ("Amadeus") Hoffman (1776–1822).

As well as drawing upon two sources for a representative coverage of the beast fable (Maya Slater and Bakhtin), we can refer to a handful of high quality studies on the fairy tale: three essays by Karel Čapek (1931), a seminal essay by John Ronald Reuel Tolkien (1939), and Vladimir Propp's celebrated catalogue on the *Morphology of the Folktale* (1958).

Vladimir Propp (1895–1970)

According to Alan Dundes (xi), Vladimir Propp's study of the folktale was completed in 1928. However, although Propp's work predates that of Čapek and Tolkien, it was published in an English-language edition much later, in 1968, fifteen years after the publication of Tolkien's essay. Dundes does not indicate why it took so long for Propp's *Morphology of the Folktale* to reach a European readership, much less an English-speaking one. But I suspect it had something to do with the Stalinist censorship that was becoming established in 1928 and which hampered fellow members of the Russian intelligentsia, such as Mikhail Bulgakov (*The Heart of a Dog,* 1925) and Mikhail Bakhtin. Propp was himself a prominent member of the Russian Formalist school, according to Svatava Pirkova-Jacobson (xx–xxi), who observes that "the formalist trend was already in a state of crisis" when the book first arrived in 1928. Perhaps the structural analysis of seeking out motifs ("the smallest narrative units") and their functions ("what the *dramatis personae* do") that Propp pioneered were somehow inimical to the social realism favored by Stalin, and by the censors in the Russian art world who were under Stalin's thumb. Propp's typology did have influence in Europe, for, as Pirkova-Jacobson says, the French anthropologist Claude Lévi-Strauss makes extensive use of the approach in his analysis of mythology. Propp (119–127) is perhaps best remembered for his detailed listing of 151 elements of the fairy tale. Dundes (xii) notes that a weakness in Propp's work is that he considers the structure of texts in isolation from their socio-cultural context, a fault of other literary folklorists of the time, though I would have thought that preparing a marriage (element 131), equipping for a journey (element 65), or the use of intermediary characters (element 52) have within them socio-cultural indicators. However, Propp supplies no further analysis.

Karel Čapek (1890–1938)

Vladimir Propp is not the only scholar to organize the genre of the fairy tale according to dominant motifs and character types. Karel Čapek follows similar lines of enquiry in his transition years from the 1920s to the early 1930s. Čapek's three essays are a particularly happy discovery. Although first published in a 1951 English-language collection titled *In Praise of Newspapers* (49–73, 74–82, 83–89), they predate Tolkien by roughly eight years, and

Propp by almost thirty years. The first and longest of Čapek's essays is "Towards a Theory of Fairy-Tales," which, though undated, may have been produced in the same year as — or a couple of years earlier than — the other two essays, "A Few Fairy-Tale Motifs," and "Some Fairy-Tale Personalities," both published in 1931. Čapek also wrote "On the Natural History of the Anecdote," possibly between 1925 and 1928, on popular humor (1928), and on detective stories in 1924. All of these essays would have appeared initially as feuilletons in a Prague newspaper.

In the first of his essays, "Towards a Theory of Fairy-Tales," Čapek (54) would almost certainly have acknowledged Propp's work if he had known about it, for he at once sets the scholarly context by summarizing a number of antecedent movements and persons. Prominent among these are eighteenth-century Romanticism; Indian, Celtic, Greek, Oriental, African, Arabian, even Malayan sources; the work of the ethnologist E.B. Tylor (1832–1917) and the Scottish man of letters Andrew Lang (1844–1912), and the work of the philologist and Orientalist Max Müller (1823–1900). Čapek proposes that "there is no theory which would explain the fairy-tale entirely as a literary species *sui generis.*" Fairy tales are not unique genres ("species") standing in isolation, but they contain elements from other genres, such as "folk stories, legends, mythological fragments, epic poems of chivalry, fables, moralities, aetiological fables [causal or creation fables], anecdotes, jokes..." This is well accepted today in such definitions as those of Abrams.

What Čapek (59) was interested in were the motifs and subject matter certainly, but also the functions of the fairy tale, and its origins in another sense. On the origin of fairy tales in the spoken word around the campfire, Čapek emphasizes the element of narration by beginning with the prosaic statement that fairy tales are first and foremost stories or tales. But when he immediately introduces the concept of "narrative continuity" he elevates the idea of the fairy-tale-as-story to another level:

> The story is the product of the narration: as soon as I begin to tell a story I am compelled to bring narrative continuity into my ideas.... When I begin to tell a story I have not got it deployed beforehand in my head in its entirety; only a few more or less clear ideas which not till I have been carried away by my narration do I bring within the dynamic whole of a continuous story.... I destroy the continuity of the factual events, replacing it by the epic continuity which is created directly and immediately by the very act of narration. Every narration is a creative and superlatively free story-telling activity [62–63].

A few pages later, Čapek (66) says, "the creative achievement of the story is not in the subject, but in the very act of telling." The *joie de vivre* behind

Čapek's use of oral forms of narrative in his fiction, and especially in his novel *War with the Newts*, reflects these principles.

On the telling of fairy tales, Čapek (67–68) makes another distinction, that between short anecdotal tales and the "long fairy-tale," which has its own (we may guess, more complex) "psychological and formal laws" by which the listeners' "amount of satisfaction and amusement is sustained not only by the final point [as in the short fairy tale that concentrates on one point, what Čapek calls 'the intellectual fairy-tale'] but by the whole progress of the story." What he then gives is a worthy framework for his own use of fairy-tale narrative elements, as well as in the work of many other authors in our list of science fiction and fantasy works inspired by the animal fable. The framework, of course, can appear in other genres:

> So the teller of fairy-tales uses all kinds of tricks to slow up the progress of the story; he allows himself detours and deviations, he repeats always three times the theme of obstacles, of questions, or of the tasks, he links up heroic deeds and adventures, he piles one theme on top of another, and he weaves several stories into one action which becomes slightly confused, but at any rate complex and spacious [72].

The other two essays by Čapek are considerably shorter than "Towards a Theory of Fairy-Tales," and comprise relatively sketchy listings — of motifs in one essay and of personalities (what might be called, more accurately, stock characters) in the other. In "A Few Fairy-Tale Motifs" (1931), Čapek (74–82) lists: the wish come true, the gift, chance, the find, the magic wand, the often magical provision of help, the setting of obstacles and vicissitudes, success or the happy ending, surfeit (by which he means exaggeration of number, as in barrels of riches or thousands of enemies), the idea of other worlds beneath the waters of a lake or beyond the horizon, and the performance of a good deed. In "Some Fairy-Tale Personalities" (1931), he (83–89) does the same with the stock characters met in fairy tales: the hero (nowadays we include heroines), the princess, Cinderella, the Frog Prince and a magic spell that can include metamorphosis (frog to prince), evil creatures (such as magicians and dragons), the "sharp fellow" or trickster figure, and the simpleton.

Čapek's sketchy typologies are forerunners of Vladimir Propp's painstaking typology. J.R.R. Tolkien's essay "On Fairy-Stories" (1939) can fairly be regarded as the most seminal work.

J.R.R. Tolkien (1892–1973)

J.R.R. Tolkien's (109–161) essay "On Fairy-Stories" was originally a lecture that he gave at the University of St. Andrews in March 1939. It appeared in two anthologies after it was first published in 1947. In the best of scholarly convention, Tolkien begins by defining his subject. The fairy tale or fairy story has two broad connotations, somewhat along the lines by which mythology can be viewed. This follows what I call (1) a tale defined in its loose popular sense, and (2) the tale as defined in a more strictly literary (or social) sense. Tolkien (110) sums up the fairy story as "a tale about fairies, or generally a fairy legend," which then has what he calls two "developed senses," which are the equivalent of the colloquial or popular sense of a fairy tale. That is, the fairy tale may be received in the popular imagination either as something unreal or incredible, or as untrue, a falsehood (as in the popular though inaccurate usage of the word myth). A little later, Tolkien (113) is at pains to correct the common misconception that fairy tales are about fairies. They are instead tales about Faerie, which is an imaginative or mythical realm in which not only fairies abide, as we conceive of them, but where live also a host of other beings: dragons, giants, elves, dwarves, trolls, witches, and so on. The physical cosmos bounded by the sun, moon, sky and earth remains present. Hence, "a fairy-story is one which touches on or uses Faerie, whatever its own main purpose may be: satire, adventure, morality, fantasy." This is the more complex, literary sense of the fairy tale.

One of the functions of fairy stories is that they satisfy "certain primordial human desires" (116), which include what is readily identifiable as a *sine qua non* in science fiction, the desire to explore the depths of time and space. More suggestive for our purpose, however, is the desire "to hold communion with other living things." This function of the fairy story looks to one of the linchpins of our study. That is, one reason why we engage in writing and reading tales of animals that are sentient and almost (or more than) human is that *we are seeking in a roundabout way to hold communion with the real animals and the real natural world around us.* We do this because we are conscious, perhaps no more than at a subliminal level for some of us, of our close kinship with animals, a kinship which is not indissoluble but which we sever at our cost.

Tolkien (117) indeed draws attention to the close relationship between fairy stories and the beast fable, pointing out that animals often speak like men in what he calls "real fairy-stories." He recognizes too that the desire for communion with other living things that lies at the heart of the fairy story is also present in the beast fable. But the beast fable has another element that makes it distinct from the fairy story. It is a mark of the beast fable that it is a tale where animals are the only characters, or where humans play bit parts to the animal heroes and heroines, or where animals merely mask human faces, the better to satisfy satiric purposes. He cites such tales as *Reynard the*

Fox and *The Nun's Priest's Tale*, *Brer Rabbit* or the *Three Little Pigs*, as beast fables, and includes *The Wind in the Willows* as a beast fable (118). On the origins of the fairy story, Tolkien (125) digresses briefly into classical Greek and Norse mythology, pointing out that fairy tales (like mythology) have "three faces": "the Mystical towards the Supernatural; the Magical towards Nature; and the Mirror of scorn and pity towards Man." Magic he sees as "the essential face of Faerie."

Tolkien (132) also has useful insights into reader-response. In a section concerning children, he writes that the idea of "willing suspension of disbelief" is an inadequate description of what happens:

> What really happens is that the story-teller proves a successful "sub-creator." He makes a Secondary World which your mind can enter. Inside it, what he relates is "true": it accords with the laws of that world. You therefore believe it, while you are, as it were, inside.... This suspension of disbelief may thus be a somewhat tired, shabby, or sentimental state of mind, and so lean to the "adult." I fancy it is often the state of adults in the presence of a fairy-story. They are held there and supported by sentiment (memories of childhood, or notions of what childhood ought to be like)...

I take it that Tolkien is using the word "lean" in the culinary sense, as thin or perhaps depleted.

What Tolkien a little disparagingly calls sentiment I suggest is part of another linchpin in my treatment. Sentiment might be a weak way of putting it, but later in his essay Tolkien (138–139) discusses factors that appear closely allied to sentiment, the ideas of Imagination, Art and Fantasy. Imagination, he notes, is not merely "the mental power of image-making." More is involved in the concept behind the image — namely, one's "perception of the image" and one's "grasp of its implications." Imagination and its ultimate result, Sub-Creation, are linked together by Art, whereby "the inner consistency of reality ... which commands or induces Secondary Belief" is achieved. "Fantasy," as "a higher form of Art," is the term upon which Tolkien settles to embrace Sub-Creation, Art and Expression — the last-named including "a quality of strangeness and wonder."

It is a tall order to create a Secondary World in which the sun is green, and so on, but when it happens to any degree, Tolkien (140) would hail it as "a rare achievement of Art: indeed narrative art, story-making in its primary and most potent form." I argue that what appeals to us in such narratives is the mixture of pleasure and unsettlement that they elicit, and that these affects are conscious creations of the authors done through a variety of narrative techniques, plus, of course, good plots (which are, in a sense, part of narrative technique).

In the penultimate section of Tolkien's essay — on Recovery, Escape, Consolation — he returns to his emphasis on sentiment. Those three elements of the fairy story are concerned with the reader's/hearer's emotional responses. By Recovery, Tolkien (146) means the regaining of a clear view, which implies also "return and renewal of health," not "'seeing things as they are,'" so much as "'seeing things as we are (or were) meant to see them' — as things apart from ourselves." One way by which we do this is by the "fantastic tricks" that can be played with our "*familiares.*"

I think Tolkien is taking this word from the Italian *familiare*, which means the member of a family or household, or an intimate friend, with the additional meaning in translation of intimacy or familiarity. It seems there is no escaping the idea of the familiar in contrast with its reversal, defamiliarization. It keeps on reappearing in different but related contexts. In one example, Tolkien cites the neologism "Mooreeffoc" from the reading of the words "coffee-room" backwards, as seen from the opposite side of a glass door. This is attributed to Dickens' observations during a dark day in London, but it is also associated with Chesterton's remark about "the queerness of things that have become trite, when they are seen suddenly from a new angle."

To play on the word coffee-room in this way is an example of what Tolkien (147) calls "creative fantasy." But he says too that a large part of fairy stories, particularly the best of them, are based on "fundamental things" or "simplicities ... made all the more luminous by their settings." This is where Tolkien "first divined the potency of the words, and the wonder of the things, such as stone, and wood, and iron; trees and grass; house and fire; bread and wine." I suggest that it is where narrative technique enters in. Appealing to the familiar and then recasting (defamiliarizing) it in different terms, so that we perceive it in a different light, appears to be intrinsic to the factor of Recovery, in which Fantasy plays its part as well.

Tolkien's (148–151) next factor, Escape, is accompanied by other factors — more properly, emotions — such as Disgust, Anger, Condemnation, and Revolt, and is therefore unsatisfactory as a clearly descriptive concept, he says, because it stands for so many different things. One may be confused by the escape of a prisoner as contrasted with that of a deserter, or by escape from modern technology — introducing the notion of Reaction here, where one might wish to act the Luddite by tearing down street-lamps — or an escape into archaism by favoring knights and kings above factories and bombs. Fairy stories often have an escapist aspect. They also offer other "escapisms" of a more serious nature: "things more grim and terrible to fly from ... hunger, thirst, poverty, pain, sorrow, injustice, death." At this point Tolkien (152) returns to his favorite theme, that of "profounder wishes: such as the desire to converse with other living things [upon which] is largely founded the talking of beasts and creatures in fairy-tales, and especially the magical understanding of their proper speech," all founded, in their turn, upon "a vivid sense of ... separation [that] is very ancient ... a strange fate and a guilt [that] lies on us."

There is a marked shift in Tolkien's (153–154) train of thought here to the idea of Consolation in fairy stories—"the imaginative satisfaction of ancient desires," he says, that involves at one level Escape from Death (*vide*, the theme of immortality in many fairy tales) and, at another level, the Consolation of the Happy Ending. Tragedy, says Tolkien, is the "highest function" of Drama, but in the fairy story the highest function is the opposite of tragedy, which he describes by coining an oxymoron, "Eucatastrophe," from the Greek prefix meaning good or well. The word itself is not in the *Oxford Concise Australian Dictionary* or in Abrams' *A Glossary of Literary Terms*, but it appears in the *Wikipedia* (2008), where it is correctly attributed to Tolkien, and in other entries on the internet. Put another way, this is "the good catastrophe, the sudden joyous 'turn'" that elicits in us "a catch of the breath, a beat and lifting of the heart," says Tolkien. The tale gains its effect—a piercing glimpse of joy—through looking backwards, by which I infer, following Tolkien, that this "eucatastrophe" comes towards the tale's end and throws all that preceded it into a new context; just as today literary critics refer to the epiphany that comes, for example, at the end of Kipling's greatest novel, *Kim* (Sandison 12–21), or when we consider the joyous going to death of the underpeople in Cordwainer Smith's "The Dead Lady of Clown Town." It is another of those concepts that is not really new.

Near the close of the essay, Tolkien (155) calls joy "the mark of the true fairy-story (or romance)," and says that we should look at it more closely because, by apprehending it in what he calls "successful Fantasy," we are afforded sudden glimpses into truth or reality, certainly in the sense that if a writer's alternative (fantasy) world is well-built, "it is true in that world." That is, a good Fantasy partakes of reality in some fashion (while the willing suspension of disbelief is also at play). This seeming paradox contains within it momentous things. Tolkien (156) is referring to the Christian message in which "the Resurrection is the eucatastrophe of the Incarnation," and that the Art in it is Primary Art, or Creation, the rejection of which "leads either to sadness or to wrath." It is, he says (155), "a serious and dangerous matter." With this ideological (Christian) underpinning, Tolkien concludes what is ostensibly an apologia for tales of Fantasy. However, I think that we do not have to embrace Christianity in order to appreciate the idea in the penultimate sentence of Tolkien's essay (156) that "in Fantasy [we] may actually assist in the effoliation and multiple enrichment of creation." ("Effoliation" equals "cosmetic cleansing of the face," *Babylon Online Dictionary*.)

Tolkien believes that a tale is not an entire failure if it gains some degree of success in eliciting joy and enrichment, whatever other flaws it might contain. What he calls "serious" tales of Faerie have this quality, contrasted against the more sophisticated courtly tale known as the *Conte*, which is characterized by twists of mocking satire. Interestingly, Tolkien pairs these two sorts of tales together. Mocking satire is part of the carnivalesque, and the poignant uplifting joyousness of the eucatastrophe or the epiphany should call immediately to mind Roland Barthes' concept of *jouissance*. In Tolkien's essay on the fairy tale I find the same play-off between high spirits, joyousness, and seriousness in the beast fable.

Chapter 2

Philosophies of Laughter

Carnival and the Carnivalesque

In the early years of the twentieth century authoritarian and fascist states were on the rise, and the moral climate was changing, especially after the First World War and the Russian Revolution, although the foundations were laid earlier by empire-building and the growth of technology among the European powers. Artists, critics and other members of the intelligentsia responded to what was taking place within their own countries or on their countries' borders by producing an identifiable literature of dissent against totalitarianism. It is questionable, however, whether the efforts of these persons, while many of them were seminal thinkers, had much effect within their own lifetimes. Some experienced strict censorship and the confiscation of their work. Others died before their time, ground down by the war machine sweeping through their country. Many were minority voices scarcely heeded by those in power; while some, on the other hand, were not only controversial in their lifetimes but were also effective in their writing, and left a mark on their contemporaries. We can read and appreciate today the messages they were attempting to communicate to their own time. The rediscovery of some of these thinkers is one of the literary phenomena of recent years.

The Russian scholar Mikhail Bakhtin (1895–1975) is a case in point, for his work was not published in the West until the mid–1960s, after which, with the dissemination of his ideas, he posthumously became one of the leading twentieth century theorists in literary criticism. As David Lodge says (124–125), Bakhtin accords comedy and the novel central importance in poetics, rather than a peripheral place, and offers "an attractive theoretical alternative to traditional humanist, orthodox Marxist, and deconstructionist approaches."

Bakhtin's concept of carnivalization is particularly attractive because of the ways in which it enriches our understanding of humor by providing complementary insights into such literary modes as satire and parody, and their application in social criticism. Carnivalization, whereby rules are relaxed and authority subverted, has many applications and overlaps with other middle-range theories, such as defamiliarization or the uses of laughter. As noted already, in his study of Rabelais, Bakhtin drew from Graeco–Roman literature and Medieval sources, which belong to the same time frames as the genesis and development of the animal fable.

Carnival, a word derived from the Italian, which in free translation means "to leave off eating meat" (*carne* = meat; *vale* = farewell — that is, "goodbye to flesh food") is associated with the popular Medieval festivals that took place immediately prior to Lenten fasting. During such festivities the authorities allowed a relaxation between the traditional social hierarchies so that commoners might make fun of their lords, kings and clerics without fear of the severe reprisals they could expect at other times of the year. Hence Carnival is associated with a relaxation of taboos, the dissolution of inequalities, and the subversion of authority that is brought about by turning accepted modes of conduct on their heads. Kings become commoners, the sacred becomes profane, and opposites, such as heaven and hell, fantasy and fact, are mingled (Selden 18–19). In Bakhtin's words (10–11):

> One might say that carnival celebrated temporary liberation from the prevailing truth and from the established order; it marked the suspension of all hierarchical rank, privileges, norms, and prohibitions. Carnival was the true feast of time, the feast of becoming, change, and renewal ... it [the experience of carnival] demanded ever changing, playful, undefined forms ... of numerous parodies and travesties, humiliations, profanations, comic crownings and uncrownings.

Bakhtin uses the term carnivalization when describing the presence of these elements in literary genres, especially the novel, tracing them back to the dialogues of Socrates as reported by Plato, and the satires ascribed to the Greek cynic Menippus, third century B.C. (Warrington 344), as well as to customary Medieval life. Graeco–Roman origins, more correctly called Hellenistic in Bakhtin's scheme, are discussed by him in part II of his essay "From the Prehistory of Novelistic Discourse," and a treatment of parodic-travestying literature of the Middle Ages in part III of the same essay (51–83). This is discussed also in his dissertation on Rabelais where, in a chapter titled "Rabelais and the History of Laughter," Bakhtin observes that "for the medieval parodist everything without exception was comic. Laughter was as universal as seriousness; it was directed at the whole world, at history, at all societies, at ideology" (21). It has also "indissoluble and essential relation to freedom" (84). These insights about parodic-travestying literature have obvious bearing on modern novelistic discourse.

A word of caution, however: One can search out banqueting imagery, imagery of the grotesque, and the "bodily lower stratum" discussed in the other chapters of Bakhtin's study of Rabelais, and elements of these indeed are present in certain of the novels and short stories in science fiction and fantasy that gain their impetus from the animal fable. But they are not as important to my argument as are the more general ideas about subverting the status quo and the accompanying risks and uneasiness this entails. For one thing, Rabelais' oeuvre appears in Bakhtin's terms to be virtually unique phenomena. They represent a literary form that marks a watershed between the rigid ecclesiastical authoritarianism characteristic of the latter half of the Middle Ages, that took life seriously and eschewed laughter (allowing humor and high-jinks only during carnival times), and the emergence of the modern novel, when by the nineteenth century "the satirical or merely amusing comic literary genres ... of reduced laughter" (120) had come into their own (one imagines with Swift and Sterne in particular). By "reduced laughter," Bakhtin means irony, humor and sarcasm. These three "stylistic components" appear to emerge from "the disintegration of popular laughter" after the Renaissance.

For these reasons it is not a good idea to try to make twentieth century satirical and parodic literature fit the procrustean bed of Bakhtin's definition of carnivalization. Bakhtin himself states that he is not concerned with examples of reduced humor in nineteenth century literature, so much as with "tracing the major tradition of popular-festive laughter which prepared Rabelais' novel." Similarly, I am not interested in searching out one-for-one concurrences between Bakhtin's ideas about carnivalization in the works of science fiction and fantasy using animal characters. I think it is highly unlikely that an exact fit would be obtained.

Having said that, the adjectival form of the word, namely the *carnivalesque*, "signifying an attribute of the thing" (*OED*), is another matter entirely. Elements or traces of carnivalization—that is, the carnivalesque—are frequently found in the various works that I trace through subsequent chapters. To take a few examples in passing, there is the ritual beach dancing of the Salamanders described in *War with the Newts*, the dog Sirius cocking his leg in church in the novel *Sirius*, the mischievous imparting of sentience to the ants in one of Clifford Simak's *City* stories, and the almost carnival atmosphere of rejoicing and love on the part of the victims during their massacre in Cordwainer Smith's "The Dead Lady of Clown Town." This may be the age of reduced humor, to paraphrase Bakhtin, but I do not think we should be unduly worried about it. It is probably more realistic to think of humor as an evolving social artifact. That is, codes of humor and laughter change over time according to the changing nature of society, or according to its zeitgeist, if one prefers such a clichéd term.

Humor in twentieth century animal tales utilizes virtually the whole comic repertoire, including irony, satire, parody, puns, slapstick, transformations and ambiguous identities, and many other literary devices, including the contrarieties of the carnivalesque. This is a key part of the entertainment value of twentieth century animal fable mediated through science fiction and fantasy. Another aspect of entertainment is the way in which a text, while giving pleasure, may also challenge, even disturb, the reader, and lead ultimately towards an engagement with social issues. This, I argue, explains some of the appeal of the best works, wherein the pleasure resides in being shaken as well as stirred. Or, to take up Aristotle's point, the reader experiences an apparently perverse pleasure in the catharsis or purging of the emotions. Not all of this has to be directed at social issues, although they do insist on reappearing, often in unlikely contexts. Bakhtin's study of Rabelais and Medieval society exemplifies the idea that humor and its concomitant, laughter, mean different things to different people at different times.

Bakhtin in Perspective

Grand theories, "theories of everything," are suspect. They suggest closure but have illusive explanatory power. There is a tendency for scholars whose ideas taste of grand theory to be given unusual prominence by their students. Bakhtin's carnivalization is not a grand theory, nor is Bakhtin, strictly speaking, a grand theorist, although he does develop an interesting way of looking at the rise of the novel as a form. The fate of grand theories over the years testifies to their inability to provide final solutions. For the search fails as new theoretical models are invented, and while the students of a particular school of thought stand on the shoulders of their mentors, *their* students — the next generation — often turn rebellious (think of Freud and Jung; think of Sontag and Paglia). The current re-thinking of French and North American deconstructionist theory is a case in point. But using Bakhtin on carnivalization and the carnivalesque, Barthes on *jouissance*, Maya Slater on La Fontaine, and so on as heuristic models are useful exercises because they are more properly perceived as explanatory devices and are more modest in their aims. A heuristic model is literally a procedure for discovery. The term only sounds impressive because it derives from classical Greek.

Using modes of writing such as the carnivalesque, parody, satire and burlesque is dangerous. Many works had considerable political persuasion in their own time before, or in spite of, being suppressed by the authorities. For instance, some of Bakhtin's ideas were published clandestinely under the names of his students because, although he was not a writer of novels like Mikhail Bulgakov, Bakhtin wrote *about* the freedom (*heteroglossia*) of the novelistic form at a time when the comparative liberalism of the Second World War years was being replaced by a post-war "anti-cosmopolitan campaign" under Stalin, where artists were expected to produce ever more stylized portrayals of real life (Holquist xix–xx).

Consequently, although he was a literary theorist and not a novelist, Bakhtin experienced the same sorts of restrictions imposed on many Russian novelists and playwrights. These appear to be among the reasons why Bakhtin is celebrated as something of a hero. He was a survivor, and his work in literary theory was "rediscovered" towards the close of his life, and some of it published posthumously. It might appear that Bakhtin carried out his teaching duties and his theoretical writing almost within an intellectual vacuum, where the cross-fertilization between different literary schools in the West nearly passed him by. But there were many western influences at work on him, including Freud and Marx, as well as the intellectual ferment of the Russian formalist school and the Prague school of linguistics.

Michael Holquist (x) observes that readers respond to Bakhtin in a number of ways: "primarily as a literary critic; others have seen him as social thinker; still others value him as a philosopher of language..." and, of course, these roles are facets of the one person. For our purpose, I invoke Bakhtin chiefly as a literary critic and social thinker, just as authors like Karel Čapek or Olaf Stapledon are themselves social thinkers. The works of such authors, including Bakhtin, have come down to us irrespective of whether they were recognized in their own era, and that, it can be argued, is political effectiveness of a sort. My chief point is that we can appreciate their artistry and their messages — entertainment *and* instruction at the same time — because they speak also to our era, so short is the span of one century in human affairs.

The sorts of novels in which the carnivalesque may be found are typically many-voiced (*heteroglossia* in Bakhtin's lexicon) and multi-layered so that no one single authoritative (authoritarian) view is privileged. Roger Webster (40–41) cites Dickens' *Hard Times* as an example where the rigid emphasis on "facts" and capitalistic exploitation of the utilitarian ideology are offset by the "locus of comedy, play and the imagination" of the circus people. Insights from other literary theories, such as defamiliarization (Shklovsky) and *jouissance* (Barthes), overlap here and are useful additions to Bakhtin's conceptual tool-kit.

In point of fact, Bakhtin was not the first, nor will he be the last, to discuss such modes of writing. Nor is he the first to appreciate Rabelais, for as early as 1875, and twenty years before Bakhtin was born, Henry James (88) wrote an appreciation of Honoré de Balzac, referring to:

> That robustness of temperament and those high animal spirits which carried him into such fantastic explorations of man's carnal nature as the ... *Contes Drôlatiques* [literally "funny" or "strange" tales]—that lusty natural humour which was not humour in our English sense, but a relish, sentimentally more dry but intellectually more keen, of grotesqueness and quaintness and uncleanness, and which, when it felt itself flagging, had still the vigour to keep itself up a while as what the French call the "humoristic"—to emulate Rabelais, to torture words, to string together names, to be pedantically jovial and archaically hilarious...

Rabelais was appreciated for his carnivalesque writing long before Bakhtin came on the scene.

In the last decade of the twentieth century, Martin Amis makes very similar points without deferring to Bakhtin, although because his observations were published in 1992 it is reasonable to suppose that Amis knows about Bakhtinian carnivalization. In his Introduction to the Everyman's library edition of Vladimir Nabokov's *Lolita*, Martin Amis (xxi) says:

> What makes human beings laugh? Not just gaiety or irony. That laughter banishes seriousness is a misconception often made by the humourless—and by that far greater multitude, the hard of laughing, the humorously impaired or under-gifted. Human beings laugh, if you notice, to express relief, exasperation, stoicism, hysteria, embarrassment, disgust and cruelty. *Lolita* is perhaps the funniest novel in the language because it allows laughter its full complexity and range.

A few pages earlier, Amis (xvi) observes: "Great novels are shocking; and then, after the shock dies down, you get aftershocks." (See in its full context Amis' 1992 *Atlantic Monthly* review where he first wrote those words [488].)

This is another independent example of an idea sympathetic to that of Carnival. It echoes Barthes' elicitation of crisis and the uncomfortable, and Shklovsky's (20) note about laughter as a corrective to accepted notions of reality. These ideas, not new, reappear so often in so many different contexts that they must, I think, reveal some profound aspects of the human psyche.

Another approach is suggested in David Lodge's (270–285) entertaining structural analysis of Harold Pinter's three-page comedy sketch "Last to Go," first published in 1990, where at one point he talks about the presentation of "poetic messages." Almost as an aside to his application of phatic discourse in Pinter's sketch, Lodge (280) poses the question: "What is it that poetic messages, or messages capable of being received as such, have, that other messages do not have?"

The phatic itself does not appear especially important for our discussion. The term applies to speech which functions to prop up contact between persons for the sake of that contact alone rather than to convey a more weighty meaning (Lodge 275), although the phatic often masks deeper underlying emotions (Lodge's example in *Consciousness and the Novel* [173] of Evelyn Waugh's use of a telephone conversation in chapter eleven of *Vile Bodies* [1930]).

Lodge draws upon a weighty observation of Jakobson's (66): "The poetic function projects the principle of equivalence from the axis of selection to the axis of combination." Mercifully, Lodge (280) amplifies the point:

> In effect it means that discourses which are either designed as works of verbal art, or capable of being read as such, are characterized by parallelism, symmetry, repetition, contrast, and other kinds of binary patterning. The most obvious example is the metrical and phonological patterning of regular verse, which is not required for the referential, emotive and conative [*OED*: desire to perform an action; voluntary action] functions of the message. In prose fiction and "prose drama," the system of equivalences is more difficult to spot, because prose and realistically rendered speech do not exhibit the overt formal patterning of verse, and because the variety of discourses and voices in these forms obscures what patterning there is. Nevertheless it can usually be discovered.

Especially, it must be said, if the artist employs the metrical and phonological patterning and tropes of the fairy tale or folk tale, usually, though not always, conveyed in prose, as Cordwainer Smith and several others do to varying degrees.

My question about what moves us in a good tale, such as that of a thinking and feeling dog like Sirius, which answers itself in terms of enjoyment, recognition and a *frisson* of unease, appears compatible with Lodge's discussion of poetics. Those elements of enjoyment, recognition and a *frisson* of unease may be elicited for the reader by the use of parallelism, symmetry, contrast, and so on. They are all found in the narrative technique of the animal fable and its close cousin the fairy tale. Tricks of narrative technique are one means for understanding the pleasures and shivers to which we expose ourselves by reading such texts, and we do well to remember such warnings as that of A.N. Wilson (45):

> Reading is not a simple exercise. Very often, the "simplest" understanding of a text would turn out in another person's eyes to be a "misreading" of it. Reading is a creative exercise, an exercise in the imagination. It constitutes an experience in itself. Perhaps there are many imaginative, religious or

> emotional areas where it actually makes very little sense to distinguish between "real" or "personal" experiences, and things we have "only" read about in books.

This may be no more than to say that we respond psychically to various narrative techniques, subject matter, and storylines (plots) in ways that are difficult to arrive at in any final analysis, because no final analysis may be possible (just as a theory of everything is not tenable). But the main paths, and the byways that leave those paths only to reconnect with them again further in the journey, are often of great interest, and are pleasurable in their own right. The idea of the poetic is very close to any reading of Cordwainer Smith's science fiction and fantasy, and poetic messages are found in the other readings too. Lodge's observations add to our understanding of the crafting of those works which, because they employ the patterning and tropes of the folk tale — originally told in the lively medium of the spoken word — are full of the imaginative, the religious, and the emotional.

Bergson (1859–1941)

Bakhtin recognizes that in the philosophy of laughter (or humor) there are two opposing meanings or functions. He, or his translator, uses both words. One meaning is optimistic (positive) and the other pessimistic (negative), and, when one reads his literary commentaries, there is evidently for each of these interpretive views a very old tradition. Bakhtin mentions Henri Bergson (1859–1941) as one example of conceptualizing laughter in largely negative terms (71). He might easily have had in mind this statement of Bergson's: "The absence of feeling ... usually accompanies laughter ... laughter has no greater foe than emotion" (63). This is at first puzzling because one would have thought that laughter in particular has claims on our emotions. But Bergson's point appears to be that one aspect of laughter involves a suspension of pity, where, for instance, we gain pleasure from witnessing someone taking an awkward and potentially dangerous tumble.

Baudelaire (1821–1867)

The French poet and essayist Charles Baudelaire (1821–1867) takes a similar position when writing about "the essence of laughter." After talking of people falling down, he observes that the comic is in one instance "barbaric," in another violent, and that it leads us to entertain ideas about our superiority over others (140–161). His translator, P.E. Charvet, sees this essay as proof of "Baudelaire's belief in original sin," because laughter is a sort of vanity and is therefore "satanic" (21). Baudelaire's "strange reflections on the *comique feroce*" are noted too by Richard Holmes in his biographical essay on Jean-Gaspard Deburau, who redefined the character of Pierrot in nineteenth century French pantomime (86).

Voltaire (1694–1778)

Voltaire (1694–1778) has a unique approach to these difficulties which stands in contrast with Baudelaire. His translator, Roger Pearson, in the 1990 edition of *Candide and Other Stories*, says that the combination of entertainment and education is handled in such a way by Voltaire as to make those two qualities indistinguishable. The two elements, he adds, are present in the genre of the fable too, but the fable's "old-style" hallmark of speaking animals is "not quite the thing for a modern" (xxxix).

That the animal fable still has a place in discussions like this is evidence of its far-reaching influence. Through it, the theme of entertainment mixed with instruction has a very long history. Voltaire's satirical stories appear to be almost as important in the development of the carnivalesque form of literature, if we accept Pearson's view, as those of Rabelais in the eyes of Bakhtin. Voltaire's position, as Pearson paraphrases it, is that "The story civilizes us, knocks us about, turns us from brutes into men: it effects a metamorphosis." Or, put a little differently, "the Voltairean tale is the more real for being unreal. It defamiliarizes the familiar, renders the world and its inhabitants strange, ready to be seen and judged afresh" (xxxviii–xxxix).

The relationship between Voltaire's engagement with the social issues of his day and his use of the fabulous, setting humans apart from the beasts, is touched upon also by the "Romantic biographer" Richard Holmes in *Sidetracks* (2000). In his brilliant essay "Voltaire's Grin" (1995), Holmes observes:

> For Voltaire, the essence of intellectual freedom was wit. Wit — which meant both intelligence and humour — was the primary birthright of man. The freeplay of wit brings enlightenment and also a certain kind of laughter: the laughter that distinguishes man from the beasts. But it is not a simple kind of laughter: it is also close to tears. Voltaire's symbolic grin ... contains both these elements when he surveys the human condition. Life amuses him and delights him; but it also causes him pain and grief [348].

Holmes (348–349) goes on to cite a passage from Voltaire's *Questions sur l'Encyclopédie* (1772):

> Anyone who knows precisely *why* the type of joy which excites laughter should pull the zygomatic muscle (one of the thirteen muscles in the mouth) upwards towards the ears, is clever. Animals have this muscle like us. But animals never laugh with joy, any more than they weep tears of sadness ... they never weep for their mistresses or their friends, as we do. Nor do they burst into laughter at the sight of something comic. Man is the sole animal who cries and laughs.

The point here is that, for Voltaire, an enquiry into human laughter straightway suggests a comparison between human and non-human animals. His distinction between humans and animals may not be fully persuasive in the face of present-day observations that animals do indeed manifest cheer and sadness. Vets refer to dogs as smiling; elephants weep in dire situations, such as captivity, and appear to show emotion when inspecting the bones of their dead. Be that as it may, Voltaire's "satire on systems" in *Candide*, for instance (Pearson xix), is like that of twentieth century satirists such as Karel Čapek. They use animal protagonists in their social critiques.

Today I think we are more likely to associate the "negative" tradition about laughter, the comic, and so on with the unsettling, challenging, disturbing functions, and their appeal. The stories "knock us about," but they also make us more human. Certainly the images of people (including animals) sustaining hazardous pratfalls in such productions of popular television culture as "Australia's Funniest Home Video Show" (still running after six years) or, more seriously, "World's Wildest Police Videos," often evoke involuntary shudders, as some poor blighter bounces off a tree or a child falls into a pond, to be hauled out immediately by an anxious parent. The staple of the first-named show is people and animals falling over. This is unintentional slapstick whereby nobody is hurt. A slapstick refers literally to the harmless laths in combination used by clowns to strike other clowns with a loud noise (*The Macquarie Dictionary*). The relief that comes with hindsight — that no injury is, in fact, sustained — must be another factor in our enquiry into what it is that makes us laugh. A potentially tragic situation is transformed to a happy ending, and audience laughter must reflect the relief this brings about.

It is easy to drop the pretense of academic discourse and lapse into a colloquial style when drawing upon such examples.

Unlike Baudelaire, with his theory about the suspension of pity, but more like Voltaire, with his delight and amusement in life, Mikhail Bakhtin (71) is an apologist for the "regenerating, creative meaning" of laughter. In one of his more striking passages, Bakhtin (66) says:

> Laughter has a deep philosophical meaning, it is one of the essential forms of the truth concerning the world as a whole, concerning history and man;

> it is a peculiar point of view relative to the world; the world is seen anew, no less (and perhaps more) profoundly than when seen from the serious standpoint. Therefore, laughter is just as admissible in great literature, posing universal problems, as seriousness. Certain essential aspects of the world are accessible only to laughter.

Was the television audience renewed substantially? It is tempting to become skeptical. But if we stop to think, those popular programs may serve useful social and psychological functions. They impart a little basic wisdom about safety first in the home and the recreational environment, while at the same time creating feelings of sympathy, if not empathy, towards other beings, human and non-human. We use ourselves as test subjects, gauging our reactions and extrapolating guardedly to the likely reactions of others. It seems appropriate when writing about humor that the "high culture" of literature, as represented by Bakhtin, and the "low culture" of popular television meet.

Humor, laughter, the comic, and so on take a variety of philosophical directions. They invite us to see the world afresh and to experience different realities. They stand in contrast to seriousness and are not only admissible, they also appear defiantly in literature, great and minor. They unsettle and discomfort us, and for this reason appeal to us, paradoxically. These generalizations we can make about the carnivalesque, but they seem to apply equally well to other theories of dissent and resistance, to other definitions, such as those of satire and parody, and other works, aside from the Rabelaisian novel. Parody imitates "serious" writing — the work itself or an author's style — but in a different, more light-hearted setting, what Abrams (18) calls, "a lowly or comically inappropriate subject." Satire aims at making a subject ridiculous by means of derogating it or diminishing it, and is used "as a weapon" against a work, a person or an ideology outside itself (Abrams 166). Parody can be employed as a weapon in much the same way. The similarity of these two arts to the overturning and ribaldry of carnivalization should be no surprise; they belong to the same family of narrative approaches that give rein to dissidence, resistance, and paradox. They discompose.

Barthes and Shklovsky

Complementing such ideas are Roland Barthes' observations on textual *jouissance* (as opposed, one imagines, to *jouissance* in real life). But by rendering *jouissance* as "bliss," his translator, Richard Miller, is misleading, because Barthes in playful mood would have us equate reading with the altogether different (and stronger) experience of orgasm, which I think one must admit is unsettling as well as pleasurable.

> Text of bliss: the text that imposes a state of loss, the text that discomforts (perhaps to the point of a certain boredom), unsettles the reader's historical, cultural psychological assumptions, the consistency of his tastes, values, memories, brings to a crisis his relation with language [Barthes 14].

Susan Sontag (71–72) observes that in his later writing Barthes cultivates a more "personal" voice performed "in an affable register" in which he compares "teaching to play, reading to eros, writing to seduction," and was not as aggressive in approach as Nietzsche, for example. For Barthes, writing is "a kind of happiness." Certain texts are "good to read," as I note later for Robert Darnton. What we learn from Roland Barthes is that texts also are "good to write." There is a mutual pleasure in reading and in writing.

What Bakhtin says about the shared purpose in the world of parodic-travestying tales recalls Shklovsky's ideas about defamiliarization — namely, that it serves

> to provide the corrective of laughter and criticism to all existing straightforward genres, languages, styles, voices; to force men to experience beneath these categories a different and contradictory reality that is otherwise not captured in them. Such laughter paved the way for the impiety of the novelistic form [Bakhtin 59].

Sontag (66) refers to Shklovsky and his concept of making familiar things unfamiliar as the "pristine phase" of formalism. Bakhtin lived during this formalist period and was substantially influenced by it. The overturning, etc. of carnivalization is an aspect of defamiliarization.

Tzvetan Todorov (1939–)

Many scholars have tried to unravel the comic and the carnivalesque. Tzvetan Todorov observes that carnivalization suited the purposes of those in power to permit occasional licence. But to me the underlying cynicism of this safety valve argument is challenged by the perception held by many authorities that such writing represents a threat to their power, and the steps they sometimes take to curb the authors responsible without worrying themselves with Machiavellian acts of indulgence. Bakhtin experienced persecution, censorship and exile during the Stalinist regime. Karel Čapek was on the Nazi SS death-list. Olaf Stapledon came under fire from Tory commentators for his socialist sympathies. On the other hand, Clifford Simak's personal life appears not to have been touched by such political discord, and Paul Linebarger drew on his knowledge of the Pentagon for his depiction of a future authoritarian human Instrumentality without incurring displeasure. He worked for that organization for many years as an expert on Oriental affairs and may well have had mixed feelings about his role. If we grant for the moment that carnivalesque license is not much more than a sociological safety valve offering little real opposition to those in power, in effect supporting the status quo, its presence in the works of those writers proved dangerous.

Sigmund Freud (1856–1939)

Sigmund Freud wrote a lot about humor, in particular the social and psychological functions of jokes and the comic. His *Collected Papers*, Volume V, published in 1928, contains a short essay on "Humour" (Strachey 215–221) that stands as a synopsis of a monograph he wrote more than twenty years earlier, *Wit and Its Relation to the Unconscious* (1905), which is longer, constituting Volume VIII, a 250-page book renamed (perhaps by the editors) *Jokes and Their Relation to the Unconscious.* In the short essay, Freud (215–217) reiterates one of his key ideas: that pleasure taken in humor "proceeds from a saving in expenditure of affect." A page later he says: "Like wit and the comic, humour has in it a *liberating* element [his emphasis]. But," he continues, "it has also something fine and elevating," meaning that the ego becomes victorious because "It refuses to be hurt by the arrows of reality or to be compelled to suffer." Freud appeals to gallows humor, adding that this sort of humor is rebellious and a means of warding off suffering — the triumph of the "pleasure principle" in the face of adversity.

This seems to be another way of referring to the safety valve idea in laughter, and it does appear to fit neatly with Bakhtin's emphasis on the liberating qualities of carnivalization and the carnivalesque. But in its emphasis on individual psychological factors, Freud's explanation, I think, misses the importance of social elements outside the psychic life of any one individual. Carnival takes place in a group setting, as does the carnivalesque. Humor, laughter, and burlesque are social phenomena. Saying that the humorist takes on an adult, fatherly role vis-à-vis others, who are children, is unsatisfactory. It seems dangerously close to taking a reductionist approach when so much else has to be taken into account. Our understanding improves when we look at Freud's longer document in which he refers to social factors, for example "...jokes as a social process" (140–158) in the title of one chapter.

In his introduction to that book, Freud (10) talks about comic contrast, saying, "The comic is concerned with the ugly in one of its manifestations," and he refers to the element of caricature. There is also the idea of play in jokes, and the freedom (of mind, I think) that such play produces. This is an aesthetic attitude of mind because it involves the contemplation of something while not asking anything of it. Freud (11–14) cites Jean Paul Richter (24): "Freedom produces jokes and jokes produce freedom.... Joking is merely playing with ideas." Joking is defined by Richter as "the ability to bind into a unity, with surprising rapidity, several ideas which are in fact alien to one another ... Joking has a number of qualities, including contrasting ideas, sense in nonsense, bewilderment and illumination," the ability to deceive us for a moment, and brevity. Jokes play with ideas by means of "technical methods" (puns and play on words) and their use in speech.

In "Pleasure and the Genesis of Jokes" (119–122), Freud discusses the idea that "the techniques of jokes are themselves sources of pleasure," which are related in turn to his idea of "economy in psychical expenditure." The pleasure taken in a joke, Freud suggests, derives from the bringing together of two (or more) quite disparate "circles of ideas" that for the individual "short-circuits" the usual train of connected (logical) thought. This relates specifically to plays on words. Another group of technical methods, which seem to employ plays on words, are similarities of sound, multiple use, the modification of familiar phrases, and allusions to quotations, all of which appeal to our "rediscovery of what is familiar." (If "rediscovery," then the familiar had been defamiliarized.) Freud cites Aristotle's idea that our joy in recognition lies at the center of our enjoyment of art: "rhymes, alliterations, refrains," the pleasure of remembering and our rediscovery of the familiar. These are elements intrinsic to the fairy tale and the beast fable.

Robert Darnton (1939–)

The cultural historian Robert Darnton, at one point in *The Great Cat Massacre and Other Episodes in French Cultural History* (91–92), observes that just as Lévi-Strauss declares some animals "good for thinking," so too might some animals be "good for swearing," and cats in particular "have ritual value"—they are "good for staging ceremonies." He appeals to human fascination with cats, the "quasi-human intelligence" that lies behind their eyes, the way their night-time howls are often mistaken for human cries, and their appeal to artists. In this context, Darnton (99) acknowledges Bakhtin's study of Rabelais and Carnival: "Mikhail Bakhtin has shown how the laughter of Rabelais expressed a strain of popular culture in which the riotously funny could turn to riot, a carnival culture of sexuality and sedition." I argue that narratives which make use of the carnivalesque (or whatever cognate term one likes to employ), and its accompanying inventory of satire, parody, humor and the like, are essentially "good to read" because, as in La Fontaine's fables, they entertain and instruct, and are subversive in their hidden intent. Conversely, as in Sontag's critique of Roland Barthes, the process is also "good to write." I find it "good to argue" that such models as those of Lévi-Strauss or Bakhtin do not have final, elegant consummations, and probably were not intended for those ends by their creators.

CHAPTER 3

The Lineage of the Animal Fable

So the beast fable has a lineage that goes back to the folk tales of India (brought together in the *Pancatantra*), to the Graeco–Roman world in the fables and metamorphoses of Aesop, Ovid, and Apuleius, and continues into the Middle Ages with Pierre de Saint-Cloud (*The Romance of Reynard the Fox*, mid–1170s) and in the seventeenth century to Jean de la Fontaine's version. The history of the fable continues in Joel Chandler Harris' (1848–1908) Uncle Remus tales, from which time a new sub-genre of children's stories appears to have split off from the main trunk. One thinks of such classics as Charles Kingsley's *The Water-Babies* (1863), Beatrix Potter's animals (beginning in 1902 with *The Tale of Peter Rabbit*), Kenneth Grahame's *The Wind in the Willows* (1908), A.A. Milne's *Winnie the Pooh* (1926) and *The House at Pooh Corner* (1928), or Lewis Carroll's *Alice's Adventures in Wonderland* (1865) and *Through the Looking-Glass* (1872). For a useful reference source listing books about speaking and thinking animals in mainstream English literature, see Cotton and Glencross, who list seventy-two titles about cats and 150 concerning dogs.

Another branching of the lineage is the development of science fiction and fantasy. In the science fiction commentaries and the general encyclopaedias and indexes, listings of animals are comparatively rare, and when they do appear they are usually subsumed under broader categories. For instance, Brian Ash (197–203) uses two double-barreled categories—"Animal and Vegetable Mutations" and "Mutants and Symbiotes"—in six pages of entries (with illustrations), that include Lester del Ray's "The Faithful," Clifford Simak's *City*, Stapledon's *Sirius* (mentioning allegory), and Andre Norton's *Star Man's Son*. H.W. Hall's (617, 801) reference index contains one entry under animals, one for dogs (which is La Faille's bibliography, see below), and one for dolphins. Pierre Versins' (47–48) French language encyclopaedia contains an entry titled *Animaux Intelligents*. Most reference works cover broader themes such as aliens, devolution, evolution, and fabulation, as in Peter Nicholls' encyclopaedia. I found seven higher degree dissertations listed under such headings as "science fiction: animals," "Stapledon" and "Simak."

The source list appears modest, but the overall range of animal-human tales in science fiction and fantasy is surprisingly large. Eugene La Faille's (2–3, 76) bibliography "Pawprints Across the Galaxy: Dogs in Science Fiction" lists fourteen novels in print, including authors such as Orwell, Simak and Stapledon, five out-of-print novels, and fourteen short stories. The only bibliography of greater comprehensiveness, to my knowledge, is one published on the Internet by Dan Lorey of Cornell University. Lorey (1–2) finds what he calls "furry novels"—that is, novels "containing at least one major furry character/plot thread." He subdivides these, making "three categories of furriness ... Animals behaving intelligently ... Intelligent Animals ... Intelligent Animalmorphs." In this scheme, animals who behave intelligently are represented in such works as *Bambi* (Felix Salten), *The Hundred and One Dalmatians* (Dodie Smith), Richard Adams' *Watership Down*, Kenneth Grahame's *The Wind in the Willows*, or Rudyard Kipling's *The Jungle Book*, to name some of the most familiar. When talking about the effects that the Disney studio's adaptation of Salten's *Bambi* had on that industry, the author and film historian John Culhane says, "They worked out the essence of Disney animation on Bambi that continue to this day, which is: animals who are caricatures of human beings, and at the same time move and behave like animals."

Lorey lists thirty-two authors and sixty-seven works in this category. (Several authors wrote more than one book, some producing up to seven titles.) This corresponds roughly with the branching into children's moral tales. Lorey's second category he describes as: "animals in their natural form who, through methods scientific, magical or other, are able to express their intelligence in interactions with humans and/or other 'intelligent' species." They include David Brin's "Uplift" series, C.S. Lewis' Narnia series, A.A. Milne's *Winnie the Pooh*, and Olaf Stapledon's *Sirius*, a mix of what I call the first and second branching of the lineage. Lorey names forty-one authors and eighty-nine works in this category. His classification of "Intelligent Animalmorphs" refers to "anthropomorphic species"—the leonine beings in C.J. Cherryh's Chanur series, for instance—and so belongs fully to the second branching, that of science fiction and fantasy.

There is a short lineage we might call a third branching of the tradition of the animal tale. Chaucer (present-day translation, 1951/1977), Cervantes (1613/1615), Chekhov (1887), Anatole France (1908), Saki (1911), and Kafka (1917) are all in Harold Bloom's list (548–567) as canonical, although the short stories and one novel relevant to the animal theme are largely minor creations within the total *oeuvre* of their authors and are not in themselves canonical, with the exception of Anatole France's *Penguin Island* (1908). They are just good examples of their creators' output.

Geoffrey Chaucer's "The Nun's Priest's Tale" (216), which stands as the eleventh offering among the twenty-four of *The Canterbury Tales* (1386–1387), looks back directly to the tradition of Aesop, by which Chanticleer the rooster, Pertelote his favorite hen, and a fox are used as stock characters to make a moral point: "In those far off days I understand/ All birds and animals could speak and sing."

> ... And if you think my story is absurd,
> A foolish trifle of a beast and bird,
> A fable of a fox, a cock, a hen,
> Take hold upon the moral, gentlemen [231].

The "moral" or didactic purpose of "The Nun's Priest's Tale" revolves around an injunction not to accept poor advice, especially from women. Chanticleer took his wife's advice that it was safe to walk in the yard, whereupon he was taken by the fox. The idea of not following advice rests also on philosophical questions about the efficacy of dreams in foretelling the future. After chiding her husband for cowardice, Pertelote gives an example from the classic writer Cato (the Elder?), who advised us not to take dreams seriously. Chanticleer responds by drawing examples in the affirmative from other authorities: St. Kenelm, the *Book of Daniel*, a story about Croesus (from Herodotus) and the dream of Hector's wife Andromache foretelling her husband's death at the hands of Achilles (from Homer's *Iliad*). Aesop-like elements appear prominently in the final events of the tale. Chanticleer is persuaded by the fox's flattery to close his eyes when singing, at which point the fox takes him upon his back and carries him off. Chanticleer, in turn, tricks the fox by urging him to shout defiance at their pursuers — a motley collection of farmyard animals and human villagers — and flies free the moment the fox opens his mouth. The story warns against pride as well as the taking of bad advice.

Miguel de Unamuno's (Cervantes') dialogue "The Dogs' Colloquy" (1613) — contained in the volume *Exemplary Tales*, published between parts one and two of his monumental work *Don Quixote* (1605, 1615) — is generally regarded as Cervantes' best work, second only to *Don Quixote*, according to his translator C.A. Jones (14). Jones (15) hails "The Dogs' Colloquy" as providing not only a rich psychological study of Cervantes' Spain (sixteenth-century to early seventeenth-century), but also a fine example of style, containing "clarity, rhythm and richness of vocabulary." The dog Scipio's disarming explanation why he and his companion Berganza can talk must be one of the earliest rationales to assist readers to suspend their disbelief. This and another canine trait — alternatives for paws — appears frequently in the literature:

> This miracle is greater in that not only are we speaking but we are speaking coherently, as if we were capable of reason, when in fact we are so devoid of it that the difference between the brute beast and man is that man is a rational animal, and the brute irrational.... What I have heard praised and extolled is our good memory, our gratitude and our great loyalty; to such an extent that they often depict us as the symbol of friendship [195].

"The Dogs' Colloquy" is constructed as a critique of society in its author's day, just as *The Golden Ass* was for Apuleius, who, in fact, is mentioned during the colloquy (231).

Leaping ahead to the nineteenth century, Chekhov (1860–1904) in 1887 published a short story using a dog as central character observing human activities, but with little understanding of them or the part she plays. The eponymous dog Kashtanka becomes separated from her drunken master, a carpenter, who, with his son, regularly mistreats her. She is adopted as a stray by a vaudeville clown who trains a small menagerie consisting of a gander, a cat and a pig to perform simple acts. In contrast to Kashtanka's old masters, the clown is a gentle man who feeds her and treats her well. When the gander dies as a result of being stepped on by a horse, Kashtanka is trained to do tricks. But at the first show in which she appears her old masters are in the audience, and she returns to them. This modest plot is a vehicle for Chekhov to sketch Russian character types against a background of poverty, as in many of his stories. Kashtanka appears to be a borderline example because a high degree of sentience in the animal is missing. There is speech on the part of the gander, but it is incomprehensible to the dog. However, social comment revealed by the experiences of an animal as innocent witness goes back to the traditions exemplified already — in *The Golden Ass*, for example. Such tales nearly always include an element of human cruelty.

A strong touch of mystery, with a strain of the Gothic, is present in works of the nineteenth century. Shelley's *Frankenstein* and Wells' *The Island of Doctor Moreau* represent early speculative fiction that contrasts domesticity with wilderness, and depicts sentient, intelligent creatures as protagonists in two very different environments. Those works ask questions about individual responsibilities contrasted against communal or societal values, and, to some degree, attempt to hammer out moral codes underpinning those responsibilities. It is Victor Frankenstein's failure to take responsibility for his Creature, who becomes an outcast in the wilds, and the repercussions this has on the cherished family and friendship circle to which Frankenstein belongs and from which the Creature is excluded. Shelley's novel is saturated with images of wilderness, which are compared implicitly with the comfortable domestic circles lost to Victor Frankenstein and denied to his creature.

The second case, Wells' short novel, is a moral tale pivoting on a similar responsibility, though the animals made into quasi-humans through vivisection techniques belong to a society, and have a rudimentary culture of their own, that reflects human values.

The short story "Lokis" (1905) by Prosper Mérimée (who wrote *Carmen*) has in it the elements of wilderness, a castle, and a man's transformation into a bear (or vice versa)—the suggestion in the tale being that he is, in fact, a rikscha (*rakshasa*) from Indian mythology—in which form, it is implied, he has sexual relations with a young woman who he/the creature subsequently kills by biting on the neck, prefiguring Bram Stoker's *Dracula* (1897), published a few years earlier. Mérimée's translator, Nicholas Jotcham (xxiv), observes that "The tale spells out the message that in each of us there is a latent animal nature, normally held in check by reason and morality; that bestiality lurks beneath the civilized veneer."

Fine exemplars of satiric cruelty can be found in the works of Hector Hugh Munro (1870–1916), who, under the pseudonym of Saki, wrote stories that the *Chambers Biographical Dictionary* (1053) describes as "humorous and macabre, which are highly individual, full of eccentric wit and unconventional situations." There had to be an animal story in his huge output, if only to satisfy the criterion of unconventional situations. We find it in "Tobermory" (1911/1986), a whimsical tale about a domestic cat who discovers the power of speech and, along lines similar to those of Pamela Sargent's "Out of Place" (1981), proceeds to embarrass the humans around him by revealing publicly their foibles and misdemeanors. In Sargent's tale telepathy is the vehicle for human embarrassment; in Tobermory's case it is speech, coupled with a disdainful attitude towards humans.

Tobermory (17) is elevated to the state of "a 'Beyond-cat' of extraordinary intelligence" by an amateur scientist, Mr. Cornelius Appin, who has "discovered a means for instructing animals in the art of human speech." Tobermory's revelations to a drawing-room crowd—as a cat he is privy to their marital infidelities and spiteful gossip—motivates a plan to do away with him. Nature, however, does the job for them when Tobermory falls beneath the attack of a neighboring Tom. Some of the main elements of satire and the carnivalesque can be identified in this slim story: human embarrassment at finding themselves on equal terms with an animal, the idea that animals are not necessarily sympathetic to human ways, and the privileged position of animals as witnesses during our worst moments. Like many of his other stories, Saki's tale of Tobermory closes on a suitably ironic note when Cornelius Appin is reported as being killed by an enraged zoo elephant because he insulted the animal.

Animal tales are often employed for political satire. Franz Kafka (1883–1924) does this in "A Report to an Academy" (1917), using the ape-into-human metaphor. Kafka's "The Transformation," in which a young man finds himself gradually being transformed into a cockroach, is another of his stories with an animal theme. The form of an academic lecture is used in this (and other) genres, most notably by Karel Čapek in *War with the Newts*, a far more extended parody than that of Kafka.

In "A Report to an Academy" an ape recounts the circumstances under which he was taken from the Gold Coast. The psychological and ironic content appears briefly at the beginning—when the ape remarks about his loneliness during the transition from his origins to humanness—and at the end where the satiric carnivalesque overturning between ape and human nature occurs. Speech is a hallmark of being human. Upon exclaiming "Hullo," the ape "sprang with this cry into the community of men" (194). As in the life of the dog Sirius, the ape is allowed to have a sexual companion of his own kind: "a little half-trained chimpanzee" (195). But the real satirical blow against humanity lies in what the ape has learned in order to become human:

> By dint of exertions as yet unequalled upon this earth I have attained the cultural level of an average European ... [which is] ... With my hands in my trouser pockets, my bottle of wine on the table, I half lie, half sit in my rocking-chair and look out the window.

Science fiction addresses many philosophical questions by setting the human condition against that of the Other, whether they be robots, androids, aliens, intelligent evolved animals, or devolved humans. We seek to establish what it is to be human by comparing and contrasting ourselves with others, deemed correctly or incorrectly as not fully human. In a chapter titled "The Icon of the Monster," Gary Wolfe (204) observes:

> A writer may avoid monster imagery while exploring the notion of an alien intelligence by imparting natural intelligence to familiar animals, either through mutation or through discovery of their secret "language." Stapledon's *Sirius* (1944) provides one of the most thoughtful explorations of a non-human intelligence in all science fiction simply by focusing on a superintelligent dog. Dogs as alien intelligences ("alien" only by virtue of its being different from that of human beings) are also featured in Pohl's *Slave Ship* (1957), Simak's *City* (1952), Anderson's *Brain Wave* (1954), Elli-

son's "A Boy and His Dog" (1969), and several other works. Cordwainer Smith is fond of exploring the intelligence of cats in his Instrumentality of Mankind stories, and Robert Merle's *Day of the Dolphin* (1967) does the same thing with dolphins.

The often very narrow gap separating the human from the non-human introduces a range of conflicts. Mary Shelley's *Frankenstein* (1818) and H.G. Wells' *The Island of Doctor Moreau* (1896)—arguably the foundations of science fiction—use this approach to raise moral questions about nineteenth century issues such as social isolation, and caution about the potential misuses of science. This search for the Other, with accompanying questions about what is human, is often part of formal definitions of science fiction and fantasy.

Twentieth Century Anxieties

These concerns remain as a substratum to twentieth century anxieties. The Czech author Karel Čapek wrote *War with the Newts* (1936) partially in response to the rise of Nazism in neighboring Germany. But he also condemned Communism, Fascism, and Capitalism, which, together with Nazism, comprised the four great "isms" of his day (Harkins 97). Concerning the anxiety of war, Olaf Stapledon's *Sirius* (1944) is a British story about an intelligent dog, human cruelty and war. Short stories and a novella by Paul Linebarger written between the mid–1950s and the early 1960s appear to have some bearing on Linebarger's Pentagon background. Some works are from the western world of the United States and Britain, and the "east" of Central Europe and Russia, and, as a consequence, they address oppression in four substantially different settings and the political ideologies they reflect: Stalinism, Nazism, the Pentagon, and British patriotism.

This reflects an historical watershed in utopian and dystopian writing in twentieth century science fiction. As Margaret Atwood says (299):

> As the optimism of the nineteenth century gave way to the Procrustean social dislocations of the twentieth ... literary utopias, whether serious or sardonic, were displaced by darker versions of themselves. H.G. Wells's *The Time Machine*, *The War of the Worlds*, and *The Island of Dr. Moreau* prefigure what was shortly to follow. *Brave New World* and *1984* are of course the best known of these many prescient badlands, with Karel Čapek's *R.U.R.* and the nightmarish fables of John Wyndham running close behind.

Parody and social and political satire (including the sardonic) within an allegorical frame are present in many human-animal tales. These include questions about individual freedom and conformity, group solidarity and identity, and teamwork contrasted against ("deviant") individual solitariness. Some protagonists have not only a non-human nature but also are the only ones of their kind. Such a state is often brought about through scientific meddling, as in *Frankenstein* and *Sirius.* We read similar cautionary tales, but this time on authoritarianism and war—and disillusionment—when we come to Mikhail Bulgakov's novel *The Heart of a Dog* (1925) and his last novel, *The Master and Margarita* (1967), which uses the "novel within a novel" technique. Both make strong political and moral statements against Stalinist repression.

Other works address aspects of evolution and Darwinian theory, such as themes of degeneration whereby humans devolve to the forms of apes or troglodytes, as in Huxley's *After Many a Summer* (1939), or, to the contrary, evolve from animal to human and back again, as in Wells' *The Island of Doctor Moreau.* Those works owe a lot to Mary Shelley, as well as to much older forms describing metamorphoses from animal to human and vice versa. Much the same might be said when such Candide-like innocent bystanders as dogs and cats gain privileged insights into human behavior because they are perceived as non-human and are therefore socially invisible, like Apuleius' character Lucius, who is metamorphosed into an ass and witnesses "squalid, brutal miseries" (Grant xiii). A similar complex of themes is a predominant plot device in Olaf Stapledon's *Sirius.*

Naomi Mitchison (43), feminist and prolific mainstream novelist—her output exceeds eighty works (Blain and Grundy 746)—and writer of several science fiction works, maintains that part of a writer's brief is to act as a moral voice: "The moral basis on which we build our lives, which for writers is essentially what we write" undergoes continual redefinition as changes in technology occur. That is, as I see it, morality has different meanings among writers of science fiction and fantasy living in different epochs. For Mary Shelley and H.G. Wells, writing in the *début de siècle* and *fin de siècle* of the nineteenth century, respectively, numerous social values changed with a rapid overturning of accepted wisdom and knowledge of previous eras, with particular respect to technology, biology and religion. Similar changes could be taking place right now in the first decade of the twenty-first century, or are they a continuation of this trend?

In the nineteenth century, authors like Shelley and Wells were responding to the dramatic changes in English society brought about by the industrial revolution and the religion versus science controversy. For later writers of the twentieth century the preoccupation is with war and its threat to human civilization, as well as with earlier nineteenth century anxieties. Writers of speculative fiction using the animal theme in the 1930s and 1940s were responding to the ferment of a worldwide depression, two world wars, and the Cold War years that followed. Like Mitchison, these authors pose questions about moral responsibility, the human need for companionship, the nature of mystic or religious experience, and Jungian individuation — namely, the "slow, imperceptible process of psychic growth" of the individual (von Franz 161). The quest for knowledge and a corresponding psychic maturing of the individual is a mainstay of the novel *Sirius*, which traces the biography of its isolated eponymous character, the dog Sirius, who says at one point:

> I must be given a chance to find out. I must be helped to look round at the world.... You see, I feel I have my own active contribution to make to — well to human understanding. I can't be just a passive subject for experiments [91].

Such questions are posed in the face of human inadequacy in the search for truth, because it is nothing short of a working philosophy of life that we are seeking.

The Cold War period is characterized by numerous animal-human novels, most prominently Clifford Simak's *City* (1952), Poul Anderson's *Brain Wave* (1954), Daniel Keyes' novelette "Flowers for Algernon" (1959), Robert Merle's *The Day of the Dolphin* (1969), William Kotzwinkle's *Doctor Rat* (1971), and others (many of them short stories). Simak's *City* (1952) depicts intelligent dogs and robots in partnership. *City* is, strictly speaking, a collection of eight short stories linked by common themes, written from 1944 to 1951, and rounded off by an "Epilog" of indifferent quality in 1973 (Tweet 516). A little later in the history of the animal tale in science fiction we find the genetically engineered "humanimals" of Cordwainer Smith's (Paul Myron Linebarger's) Instrumentality of Mankind series, in which "The Ballad of Lost C'mell" (1962) and "The Dead Lady of Clown Town" (1964), among others, pose questions about human prejudice, with real-world racial discrimination not far from mind. The sub-theme of humankind discovering too late their emotional and psychic debt to animals that by then are largely extinct appears in Philip K. Dick's novel *Do Androids Dream of Electric Sheep?* (1968), but this "animal contract" message was virtually lost in the film version *Blade Runner* (1982), which emphasized instead the wonder and mystery of life for androids.

The publication of several works in the last decade of the twentieth century suggests that we have come full circle to themes characteristic of the late nineteenth century: Peter Goldsworthy's *Wish* (1995), Peter Høeg's *The Woman & the Ape* (1996), Robin Wallace-Crabbe's *Dogs* (1993), Kirsten Bakis' *Lives of the Monster Dogs* (1997), Marie Darrieussecq's *Pig Tales: A Novel of Lust and Transformation* (1997), Will Self's *Great Apes* (1997), and Stephanie

Johnson's *The Whistler* (1998). Humans and apes, as well as dogs, go back a long way in the science fiction and fantasy branch of the animal tale. There may also be some splitting-off taking place between science fiction and fantasy into separate genres, the latter represented by many works that recall childhood, as in the fantasy animals of Kenneth Grahame's *The Wind in the Willows,* where there is no science worth mentioning, although cars and trains are important plot motifs in some chapters. The fantasy genre includes the Duncton Woods creatures and the heroic warrior archetypes of Brian Jacques' Redwall series for a young adult market.

Many works of science fiction that belong to the space opera mode depict humans conquering their fears of the hands, claws or suckers of threatening aliens by annihilating them. In one of the best recent examples of space opera, we have another concept, however, that of "uplift." This tutelary idea is found in several of David Brin's novels, including *Startide Rising* (1983) and *The Uplift War* (1987), which depict sentient apes and cetaceans for whom human society acts in a mentoring role. This means the recognition by humans that apes and cetaceans are self-consciously aware beings, and a corresponding willingness to live and work with them.

But there remain an intriguing array of aliens, several of whom fill the role of menace indispensable to space opera. There is another example in C.J. Cherryh's "feminist" lion-like beings, the Hani, in her series beginning with *The Pride of Chanur* (1981). These less extreme and more thoughtful treatments of space opera themes have the protagonists reaching amicable terms where sometimes merely establishing the existence and friendly intentions of extra-terrestrials is sufficient, sometimes expressed in the form, or sub-genre, called "anthropological science fiction."

This can quickly become clichéd, however, as in the homily "We are not alone" from the 1977 Spielberg film *Close Encounters of the Third Kind.* Important sub-themes include contact, close encounters of the first, second, third and fourth (that is, sexual or erotic) kinds, often followed by concomitant desires for communication, union, or reunion between species (and the questions they pose for animal sentience), conscious reasoning, language, and religion.

CHAPTER 4

Recasting the Animal Fable: Short Stories

The short story is more concentrated and, because of its restrictions in length, makes use of impressions and suggestions on the reader, often with an abrupt surprise ending. It is good for presenting a single idea but not as efficient for detailed or repetitive argument, or for character development (Hawthorn 338–45). On the brevity of the short story, Henry James (334) writes on

> two quite distinct effects ... the one with which we are most familiar is that of the detached incident, single and sharp ... the other of rarer performance, is that of the impression, comparatively generalised — simplified, foreshortened, reduced to a particular perspective — of a complexity or a continuity. The former is an adventure comparatively safe, in which you have, for the most part, but to put one foot after the other. It is just the risks of the latter, on the contrary, that make the best of the sport ... the large in a small dose, the smaller form put on its mettle and trying to do — by sharp selection, composition, presentation and the sacrifice of verbiage — what the longer alone is mostly supposed capable of.

A common criticism that science fiction by comparison with other forms is relatively weak in characterization but strong on ideas needs to be made in the knowledge that the short story, to some extent, shares the same disadvantage. A great deal of science fiction appears in the short story form, so the failing is not altogether surprising. However, the long short story or novella allows for more complex characterization — for example, in the psychological studies of Paul Linebarger or in Daniel Keyes' "Flowers for Algernon" (1959). There are also novels in science fiction and fantasy that contain an abundance of characterization, such as Stapledon's *Sirius*. The generalization, like most generalizations, has its exceptions, but it is accurate enough when we come to many short stories and some novellas.

Animal Protagonists and Antagonists

On the whole, animal companions are not as threatening as human protagonists or extraterrestrial aliens, but they nevertheless are treated with sufficient ambiguity for elements of mystery, even the macabre, to figure in many tales. To play the role of companions, a shared sentience or intelligence is a necessary prerequisite. Mutual understanding and self-aware communication are pivotal in the relationship, whether humans and animals are allies or antagonists. Many stories, then, have what Philip K. Dick (504) calls "obscure menace," sometimes facilitated by the masking of non-human intelligence.

The theme of invasion in one story brings together beloved nursery creatures as protagonists against supernatural peril. Philip K. Dick's short story "The Little Movement" (1952) is a tale of stuffed toys that combines conspiracy theory with Hans Christian Andersen motifs. A six-inch metallic wind-up soldier named My Lord is in the vanguard of an invasion force. Adults, "the ruling race," are too large, so the mechanical toys (precursors to Dick's malevolent androids and robots) attempt to establish mind control over the children. But their "little movement" has not reckoned with a resistance movement in the form of the children's plush animals: "It did put up quite a fight. It was tougher than this one. But we had the panda bears from across the way" (46). Stories of this sort combine elements from both science fiction and fantasy, with echoes of the more comfortable tales of Beatrix Potter and Kenneth Grahame (those pandas).

Extraterrestrial intelligence offering comfort and companionableness, and the pitfalls attendant on them, is the theme of F.L. Wallace's "Bolden's Pets" (ND) and Alan Anderson's "Strokie" (1959). In the former, a "pet" the size of a small dog but having the build of a slender bear is given to a human settler (Bolden) by one of the planet's indigenes. The animal cures a disease that attacks the human (and indigene) superficial nervous system, though it leads eventually to the death of the animal itself: "If you listed what you expect of a pet, you'd find it in this creature. Docile, gentle, lively at times; all it wants is to be near you, to have you touch it. And it's very clean" (85).

Alan Anderson's tale uses the familiar theme of a hidden danger in an apparently harmless species. Strokies are hamster-like, with pea-green fur and feeding tubes in their posteriors. They ride on the heads of the humanoid inhabitants of the planet Clantae, with whom they share a symbiotic existence, feeding on the bloodstream and giving pleasure in return. Wearing strokies catches on after they are imported to Earth, but the most serious side-effect — aside from growing a pelt of green fur — is the sapping of the human work ethic. Eventually an antidote is found in the smoking of tobacco. (In the 1950s the dangers of smoking were largely unknown or ignored.)

Pride in human uniqueness gets a drubbing in Robert Mattingley's "Discovering a New Earth" (1980). The President (of the United States of America one supposes) receives a briefing from his aides on the requirements of the extraterrestrials with whom first contact has just been made. These terms are that "all mentally superior beings" be represented in the new world government to create a "panomorphic civilization unit," which reveals unintentionally (but satirically) that aliens also indulge in bureaucratese and tend to impose benevolent but dramatic changes. To the President's consternation, the list does not stop with humans alone, as one by one other species are named: dolphins (their slaughter by tuna fishermen is mentioned), termites, the Abominable Snowman and Bigfoot, whales, mermaids, ion-creatures in the ozone layer, hollow-earth dwellers and, finally, elves in hiding (at that point one of the President's aides removes his face mask).

Tales about mutant animals range on a continuum from the aesthetic and lightweight to profound social comment. Kit Reed's "Piggy" (1961) is a gentle tale about a horse who possesses a form of telepathy that allows a boy, Theron, to recite or write poetry when mounted upon him: "Life is real, life is earnest / And the grave is not its goal / Dust thou art, to dust returnest / Black as the pit from pole to pole" (63). Towards the other extreme, Stanley Weinbaum's "Proteus Island" (1936)—a variation on *The Island of Doctor Moreau*—explores what might happen if species variability takes place not over centuries and millennia but with each generation. Like Victor Frankenstein and Dr. Moreau, the biologist's experiments in genetic engineering cause the anomaly.

Such propositions as these are pivotal to many of the tales. Does physical form distinguish humans from animals, or does intelligence mark the distinction? If it is the latter, it follows that a creature whose intelligence is on a par with that of humans is itself human, though its form may be that of a dog or a chimpanzee.

Dogs

Two divergent attitudes towards dogs are expressed in Arthur C. Clarke's "Moondog" (1962) and E.C. Tubb's "The Captain's Dog" (1958). Like the Strokie tale, these short stories do not quite fit my choice of earth-bound intelligent animals. However, Laika, the canine companion of the storyteller in "Moondog," is an ordinary dog whose warning bark awakens a scientist from his sleep on the moon's far side in time for him to don his protective suit prior to a moonquake — just as she had warned him years earlier on Earth when the San Andreas Fault shifted. But Laika is dead, having "lost interest in living" after being left behind. It is a faithful dog ghost story on the familiar theme of love and a warning from beyond the grave. The scientist dismisses it: "There is no mystery about it, no miraculous warning across the gulf that neither man nor dog can ever bridge" (194). But readers might know better.

Tubb's story "The Captain's Dog," on the other hand, is not about a dog but employs the canine analogy to an android that not only talks but reads and reasons: "It was as if a dog had suddenly commenced to talk. Its ability wouldn't make it human but, at the same time, it would no longer be wholly a dog" (7). In the end, Andy the android gives his life for the human crew of the spaceship and receives burial: "For the highest honour men can pay is to bury a stranger as one of their own" (22). The "stranger factor," the non-human Other, is the dominant theme of this story. Andy is still a stranger. The human protagonists have not quite taken that mental step beyond the human/non-human divide.

Philip K. Dick's "Roog" (1953) is written in the same spirit as "The Little Movement." It centers on Boris the family dog, to whom the men periodically collecting the garbage are frightening non-human beings with heads that wobble on their necks. They not only carry off the precious contents of the "offering urns," they also intend indefinable harm to the dog's human family. Though "Roog, Roog" appears at first sight an onomatopoeic rendering of a dog's bark, it is the generic name of the alien beings. As in "The Little Movement," there is a resistance organization unknown to humans, the neighborhood family dogs who are perceived by the Roogs as Guardians: "'ROOG!' Boris screamed, and he came toward them, dancing with fury and dismay. Reluctantly, the Roogs turned away from the window" (31–36).

This was Philip K. Dick's first short story accepted for publication, in *Fantasy & Science Fiction*, and in hindsight he says it was written in all seriousness because: "It tells of fear; it tells of loyalty; it tells of obscure menace and a good creature who cannot convey knowledge of that menace to those he loves" (504). He wrote it from Boris the dog's point of view, with the proviso that this protagonist's perceptions might not reflect actuality. He asked himself: "What must the world look like to that dog?" adding that one of the life-long objects of his writing was "the attempt to get into another person's head, or another creature's head, and see out from his eyes or its eyes" (505–506).

Dogs are protective heroes, but they can have more sinister aspects. Ray

Bradbury's "The Emissary" (ND), in a traditional surprise ending, has a literally ghoulish twist. Bradbury is a highly sensual writer in his use of imagery, evoking touch, smell, and hearing. "Dog" leads friends and acquaintances to Martin, a bedridden boy. Martin's beloved schoolteacher, Miss Haight, brings him cakes and books and board games. But Miss Haight has "the secret of signs, and [she] could read and interpret Dog" (569). In the next sentence she is dead, killed in a car accident. Martin rails at God and speculates that the dead might be playing at it, just as Dog plays "dead Dog." Then Dog, who has been acting strangely, disappears and returns several days later: "Dog was a bad dog, digging where he shouldn't. Dog was a good dog, always making friends. Dog loved people. Dog brought them home" (576).

The canine sidekick to young male protagonists makes another appearance in what have been called the "Scholar's Cluster" stories of George O. Smith. "History Repeats" (1959) and "Understanding" (1967) belong to the space opera sub-genre where canine intelligence takes second place to action, although, as with Cordwainer Smith's cats in "The Game of Rat and Dragon," they come together in a dog's combination of wits with speed. As the self-described "noble dog," Beauregarde says to a menacing guard:

> Dog and man, man and dog, have been together for about a half-million years. Once dog helped man in war and peace, and man gave dog food and shelter. Dog helped man rise above the level of the savage, and man has helped dog rise to the level of intelligence. But dog has one advantage. None of us has been intelligent long enough to really believe that dog has a soul, and those of us who do believe that also know that dog's soul is devoted to man [77].

These are some of the principle clichés of the genre, that dogs have been with humans for thousands of years and are devoted to humans. It is a stock idea, more so than the question whether dogs (or animals in general) have souls, which is not often raised. The heroic factor is important to George Smith. Beauregarde, or "Terrestrial dog" as he calls himself, is described as a "trained dog of war" (164), and few pains are taken to enter into canine depth psychology. Speech is touched upon at one point: "a well controlled whine and whinny, with chest sounds adding bass with a well modulated growl or a low rumble. The lips and tongue were sufficiently mobile to give fair articulation" (146). The dog is credited with "understanding," a trait shared with women. (Note the decade in which it was written.) Beauregarde says tautologically: "It is a dog's Understanding because, being a dog, I think like a dog" (174). At least Buregarde/Beauregarde survives. (There are two alternative spellings of his name.)

More superficially, the bloodhound protagonist Scorpio in Benford and

Eklund's juvenile space opera *Find the Changeling* (1980) is killed by a ray-gun after making rare appearances as a faithful tracker with few words: "Yes. I. Have. Vocab' ... Warm. Here ... I. Sleep" (76–77).

Where humor is concerned, dogs appear to figure more often than cats, perhaps because we perceive cats as loners, inscrutable, or fey. Richard Wilson's short story "Just Call Me Irish" (1958) is an extended pun on a salesman's spiel to the householder. It plays on the dog's Korean War service in the K-9 Corps, his "dogged persistence," the "dogma" of army regulations, and exclamations such as "Well, I'll be doggoned" or "You're quite a wag." In similar vein, Henry Slesar's "Speak" dates from the vaudevillian talking dog act whereby Manny, a failed showman, makes a suicide call to his wife Phyllis. It is not Phyllis at the other end of the line, however, but his dog Rex (185): "I don't know what came over me. When I heard the phone ringing, I just *had* to answer. I knocked it off the table with my paws and I started talking."

In Mack Reynolds' "Dog Star" (1956), a trading expedition to the second planet of the star Sirius meets sentient creatures resembling Airedales who ride octopus-like beings that they control through telepathy. The humans are chagrined to find that the dominant species is the "dog," not the "octopus," and that their ship's mascot, Gimmick, an ordinary dog, is thought to be the master species, a confusion explained by the inaccuracy of telepathy in pinpointing who is "talking." "We've got to continue pretending that the dog is Earth's dominant life form, and man his servant," says the Lieutenant (103), a development that will engineer a re-breeding program because dogs on Earth are now scarce (102): "Man was going through a period of wearying of his ages-long companion."

William Tenn has a reputation for works of biting satire against human follies. The title of his short story "Null-P" (1951) refers to an overturning of the Platonic idea that the most competent in a society should govern (that is, "Null-Plato"). In a post-apocalyptic United States the average, "normal" and mediocre is the sought-after condition—*Homo abnegus,* named after the quintessential norm who became the President. After a quarter of a million years a civilization of Newfoundland retrievers evolves:

> These sturdy and highly intelligent dogs, limited before to each other's growling society for several hundred millennia, learned to talk in much the same manner that mankind's simian ancestors had learned to walk when a sudden shift in botany destroyed their ancient arboreal homes—out of boredom [135–136].

The Newfoundlands domesticate those humans who remain so as to pursue the pastime of throwing sticks for them to fetch, until the humans become dispensable and die out when machines are invented that can carry out the stick-throwing function better.

Lester del Ray's short story "The Faithful" (1938) shares similarities with Clifford Simak's *City* (1952). "The Faithful" was published in *Astounding* in 1938, and Simak's short story "Census," which first introduces his Dogs, in 1944, eight years later. Certainly "Census" and the other stories in *City* elaborate on many of the same themes touched on by del Ray: the abandoned city, wilderness, reasons for Man's downfall (biological warfare), Man perceived as god by the dogs, the problem of having paws (in "The Faithful" this is overcome through a dog-ape partnership, and in *City* by a Dog-robot partnership). The dogs in both stories are left on their own with the death of the last human. In his more complex, but uneven, novel, Simak did a better job.

James Gunn considers del Ray to be a lesser light in American science fiction, though he makes his mark on the genre later in his career. Del Ray writes in a lofty narrative style. The human names of Roger Sten, the scientist who, through surgery, creates the first of the Dog-People, "Hungor," and his human character Paul Kenyon, are ordinary enough; but the names "Hungor Beowulf XIV" and "Ape-Man Tolemy" evoke ancient times. Perhaps this too obvious setting of themes through the naming of protagonists prompts Gunn to be critical of del Ray's work. In "The Faithful," as the title suggests, the Dog-People feel incomplete because they can no longer be partners with humans. As Hungor's name implies, they hunger for "the return of Man. The old order, where we could work together" (433). Kenyon, before he dies, suggests that a similar relationship might be developed between the dogs and apes, but warns that the apes should not be allowed to become too much like humans lest the calamities that brought humanity down be repeated. The replacement of humans by apes is one possible outcome, but another, voiced by Hungor, is that the dogs themselves in the far future may become virtually human. They have already, with the apes' help, built a civilization with monorail cars and factories:

> Perhaps in time to come, with their help, we can change our forepaws further, and learn to walk on two legs, as did Man.... The Earth would be peopled again, science would rediscover the stars, and Man would have a foster child in his own likeness [436–437].

The dogs want to emulate humans in physical form as well by recreating human technological culture.

In his short story "Socrates" (1951), John Christopher directly acknowledges Olaf Stapledon's *Sirius* (1944), published seven years earlier, by building a reference to that novel into the dog's characterization. A chance X-ray mutation produces a litter of large-headed, blue-eyed Airedale pups, of which only one survives. Jennings, the human owner, exploits the dog Socrates' abilities in a travelling show, refusing to sell him to a professor, who is the narrator of the story. However, Socrates and the professor become friends, and the dog regularly visits for reading and conversation. The eponymous dog "had reveled in Stapledon's works and drawn interesting comparisons between himself and Stapledon's wonder sheep dog" (186). The same theme of loneliness is present in "Socrates" as in *Sirius*: "Sad to think I might have had brothers and sisters like me. Not to be always a trick dog" (184).

Like Sirius, Socrates enjoys the company of Tess the golden retriever, though she is an ordinary dog. He reads philosophy and poetry, and he possesses canine abilities to perceive phenomena not picked up by human senses: "He spent nearly an hour one evening describing to me the movements of a strange spiral-shaped thing that, he said, was spinning around slowly in one corner..." (185). This is like the cobbly worlds sensed by the Dogs in Clifford Simak's *City*. Jennings continues to mistreat Socrates, and the dog, in turn, fears that he will turn on his owner. In a fight between the professor and Jennings, the latter falls into a swiftly flowing river. Socrates leaps in and attempts to save his master, but both are swept to their deaths.

Most of these short stories were published in the 1960s or earlier. There appears to have followed a hiatus of some thirty years before another animal story featuring dogs came on the scene. Ian McDonald's "Floating Dogs" (1991) is something of a misnomer, because the principal animal characters rendered sentient by means of electronic implants into their brains are a porcupine (Porcospino), a cat (Ceefer), a raccoon (Coon-ass, from whose point of view the tale is told), a bird (Bir-dee), and an ant-eater/pig (Peeg). They are an unusual array of animals to be made sentient. They travel with a guardian robot called Papavator who feeds them and sometimes changes orders through their circuitry. The setting is a devastated world in which war is still being waged between robots and animal species made sentient through human technology, long after the humans are gone, a world of warring machines much like that of Philip K. Dick. The humans are remembered as angels, representing deities to the animals. The group is on a quest to infiltrate enemy lines, and at one point are attacked by a horde of dogs also wearing "emplants." In the end, all are killed except for Coon-ass and Bir-dee. In a symbolic gesture, Coon-ass removes Bir-dee's emplants before removing his own, setting her free: "Go, Bir-dee, go. Be animal again. Be full of joy" (94).

Cats

Cats, like dogs, are often portrayed as possessing qualities of either protectiveness or menace. In her introductory note to the Andre Norton short story "All Cats Are Gray" (1971), Jane Yolen (105) says: "While humans and dogs have a long history of teamwork, cats have not always been our most cooperative friends. They have been worshiped as gods and cursed as devils." Andre Norton's story is pure space opera, telling how Bat helps save the life of his human companion, "Steena of the Spaceways," and her slow-witted business partner Cliff Moran. An alien creature enters their spaceship. Utilizing one of the clichés of the genre (cf. *Predator*), the creature's color lies beyond the range of the human visual spectrum except when it is juxtaposed against gray surroundings. Steena, who is color-blind and sees in shades, can perceive only a flicker. But Bat sees it clearly.

Roberta Ghidalia's "Friends?" (1973) has two elements common in folklore: the cat's association with witches and its supposed ability to take, or change places with, a child's soul. Like Martin in "The Emissary," Dorrie is incapacitated. She prevails on her mother to ask the witch-like neighbor Mrs. Stubbs for possession of the cat Sassy. Mrs. Stubbs grudgingly allows this but warns that the animal is evil. Dorrie and Sassy develop a strong emotional bond, reinforced by ritual: "'Friends?' Dorrie would say to the cat. 'Meowrr,' the cat would reply" (222). One night Dorrie and the cat kill Mrs. Stubbs. Later they perform their ritual: "'Friends?' said the cat. 'Meowrr,' replied the child" (225).

Sometimes protection and the macabre are combined, as in Fritz Leiber's delightful "Space-Time for Springers" (1958). The story is well written, with a light touch of humor, and contains many elements that we find in longer works. It is one of the few short stories in science fiction and fantasy that meets the standard of the second of the effects observed by Henry James (334): "the large in a small dose ... sharp selection, composition, presentation and the sacrifice of verbiage."

"Space-time for Springers" revolves around the relationship between a girl child and a precocious kitten, only this time the flaw lies in the child and not the cat. Like Philip K. Dick's canine character Boris, the Gummitch-kitten (Gummitch is one of the kitten's many nicknames) has inner reasoning and a unique view of the human world. "Space-Time for Springers" is the title of a book Gummitch plans to write when he is older, along with other works that parody human scientific treatises, such as "*The Encyclopedia of Odors or Anthropofeline Psychology*" (208). Touching on the Pinocchio theme, Gummitch, with an I.Q. of 160, believes that it is only a matter of time before he will metamorphose into a human boy able to speak in all languages, while the ill-starred sister to Baby, Sissy, who shows malevolent sibling rivalry towards Baby, will become a nasty she-cat. But Gummitch witnesses Sissy about to scratch Baby's cheek with a pin, and, in an act of desperation to protect Baby, he flings his spirit into Sissy. A transfer takes place and Gummitch is "enfolded by the foul black blinding cloud of Sissy's spirit" (220). In a compassionate but ironic ending, Sissy becomes an animated and happy child, but there are unforeseen tragic consequences for Gummitch:

> The spirit, alas, is not the same thing as the consciousness and that one may lose — sacrifice — the first and still be burdened with the second.... Gummitch knew very well, bitterly well indeed, his fate was to be the only kitten in the world that did not grow up to be a man [220–221].

Pamela Sargent's "Out of Place" (1981) illustrates the unusual repercussions of humans becoming suddenly gifted with the power to "overhear" and understand the thoughts of animals. Their telepathic abilities are one-way, however, for the animals are unable to understand humans. This gift begins satirically by juxtaposing a mood of wonder with that of irony. A Robin in poetic mode thinks: "Earth, yield your treasures to me," and goes on to exclaim: "I hunger, my young cry out for food." An earthworm says, "I create space ... the universe parts before me" (96), before it is eaten by the Robin. But it soon becomes apparent that animals do not share human inhibitions. They are, in fact, brutally to the point, often jealous, self-centered, and unconsciously troublemakers — like humans, of course, for the allegorical intent is obvious.

Using parallels from veterinary science, the animal point of view can also be reasonable, or at least very human. A dog hates cars because one killed a bitch he loved. Cows complain about the size of their stalls, the quality of feed, and their need for greater pasture. Humans become reluctant to slaughter animals for meat, veterinarians to put down sick or abandoned animals, and medical researchers discontinue animal experiments. There is more animal news on television:

> "I saw an interesting cat on Phil Donahue this morning," Marcia said. "A Persian. Kind of a philosopher. His owner said that he has a theory of life after death and thinks cats live on in a parallel world. The cat thinks that all those strange sounds you sometimes hear in the night are actually the spirits of cats. What's interesting is that he doesn't think birds or mice have souls" [60].

The embarrassment caused by domestic cats and dogs unwittingly broadcasting their owners' private thoughts and misdemeanors to their spouses and neighbors finally triggers a backlash. As she walks home, Marcia passes dead cats and dogs. She tries hopelessly to tell her cat Pearl that she has to stay indoors for her own good.

Ron Goulart's "Groucho" (1981) is a modern version of the supernatural revenge tale. It is one of the few science fiction/fantasy stories to use the theme of rebirth. Buzz, a hack scriptwriter, arranges through a spiritualistic medium for his partner Warren's reincarnation in the form of a talking cat named Groucho. Groucho realizes an ambition from his earlier life — to be a close companion to the beautiful secretary Panda Cruz. Jealousy erupts between Buzz and Groucho, and Buzz kills the cat. Five days later, a trifle early for rebirth to take place, "Standing half inside the screen door was a large gray police dog.... 'I'm back again, old boy,'..." (93). This short tale has a Gothic touch, for one of Buzz's acquaintances is Otranto, the salad chef at Udolpho's restaurant.

In Terry and Carol Carr's "Some Are Born Cats" (1973), two adolescents, Freddie and Alyson, observe that the movements of Alyson's cat Gilgamesh are self-conscious, as though he is playing a part unsuccessfully. They speculate idly that he is really a shape-changing being from Arcturus or Procyon, a fancy that many of us have who know cats. Gilgamesh appears to be a normal cat until under the anesthetic for an X-ray he begins to talk. But that is not all. Alyson's second cat George is the other alien, on the run from Gilgamesh, who is a policeman. After Alyson insists on giving George sanctuary, Gilgamesh departs in disgust, saying (135):

> Tell him he's dumb lucky he happened to hide out as a cat. He can be lazy and decorative here, but I just want you to know one thing: there's no such thing as a decorative amoeba. An amoeba works, or out he goes!

Randall Garrett's long short story "A Little Intelligence" (1958) takes the theme of a terrestrial pet mistaken by aliens to be fully sentient. Unlike Mack Reynolds in "Dog Star," Garrett draws upon the classic detective genre whose deductive sleuth is a religious, somewhat in the tradition of the Father Brown character. Sister Mary Magdalene — it is hinted more than once that her choice of monastic name is a reflection of a worldly past — solves the murder of her cat Felicity. The crime was carried out by one of four peace delegates, Pogathans from the Capella IX system:

> Vor Gontakel saw me talking to the cat, and Felicity meowed back. How was she to know that the cat wasn't intelligent? She knew nothing about Terrestrial life. The other two did. Felicity was murdered because Vor Gontakel thought she was a witness [243].

"Afternoon at Schrafft's" (1984) employs situational slapstick based on the theme of magical transformations gone awry. Because it takes place in a restaurant, it belongs also to barroom tales. A wizard's cat familiar — who emulates Dodgson's disappearing Cheshire Cat — withdraws his magical assistance when the time comes for the wizard to pay his bill. There follow disconcerting transformations as the wizard assumes the form of a herbivorous dinosaur who unintentionally breaks furniture; the quiches are transformed into large frogs; and when the cat at last returns the wizard to his proper form, they leave a restaurant whose clientele have become dinosaurs.

Another barroom tale, "The Kit-Katt Klub" (1962) by John Shepley (whose name is not listed in Clute and Nicholls), shows how transformative chaos can be done better. In a play-off between a dream sequence and social realism, a young boy, Tony, waits for his down-at-heel mother in a bar: "a beautiful lady with greying hair and tired eyes ... drinking an old-fashioned..." (59). After retiring to their hotel rooms, Tony slips out — evidently the beginning of the dream sequence — and wanders the back streets until he comes upon the Kit-Katt Klub. The proprietress residing over the cash register *is* a cat, Mrs. Kit-Katt: "grey with tabby stripes" (61). A black and white ex-vaudeville fox terrier touches Tony for the price of a drink and repetitively tells his hard luck yarn. The interlude ends abruptly with a police raid. When the boy returns to his hotel, things do not appear to have changed. What marks this otherwise forgettable short story are the barroom stereotypes in animal form: the worldly Mrs. Kit-Katt, the self-pitying terrier, the old turtle who sits in a corner for hours, the battle-scarred bartender, the game-playing friends. It is a gentle tale about childhood naivety and growing up.

"Gorilla Suit" is another gentle story from Shepley's pen. According to Anthony Boucher (152), this was Shepley's first short story, published in 1956 in *The Best American Short Stories*, edited by Martha Foley. Boucher included it in his anthology for *The Best from Fantasy and Science Fiction* a year later. "Gorilla Suit," like "The Kit-Katt Klub," takes as given the gorilla's abilities to read book reviews, magazine articles and local news, solve crossword puzzles (aside from one frustrating clue), and to consciously perform "a recognized social function" (157) as a zoo gorilla. Toto reads in the classified advertisements of the Bali-Bally Department on Broadway: "a job opening for a man with a gorilla suit *or a gorilla* [Shepley's italics] to help publicize Dorothy Lamour's latest picture" (153–154). The job is attractive. It would be fun to be photographed with the star. This protagonist is characterized as cautious and a bit of a worrier. Much of the humor of the story revolves around Toto's agonizing over the decisions he makes as he moves apparently unremarked in the human world. He puzzles over the semantics of the advertisement: "Perhaps what they wanted was a man with a gorilla suit or *a man with* a gorilla — in which case, there was no point in *his* applying" (154), and, "suppose *other gorillas* [Shepley's italics] applied?" (155). In the end Toto makes his way to the Broadway address in the company of a rag-tag group of down and out costume actors — an erstwhile Santa Claus, a former Easter Bunny — like the barroom stereotypes of "The Kit-Katt Klub." Toto almost passes muster in the line-up when (169):

> In all its horror — the door opened, and in came another real gorilla, an arrogant creature carrying a shining aluminum suitcase ... and — to Toto's stunned mortification — took out a lustrous gorilla suit, into which he proceeded to zipper himself.

Rick Rubin's "The Interplanetary Cat" (1961) is a hyperbolic fantasy about an antisocial Siamese called Sumi whose trait of chewing everything that comes her way is exaggerated in a grand manner. Rocketed into space en route to Mars, Sumi "was a kitten where no kitten had ever been, and she could eat anything, hot electric sparks, solid rocket fuel, red dust of Mars" (26). Sumi becomes larger than the planet until she is floating in space and begins swimming towards the sun, attracted by its warmth. Viewers from the Earth "stared at the vast furriness of Sumi, the interplanetary cat, swimming hungrily toward them" (28).

Another story dealing with felines in space is Cordwainer Smith's "The Game of Rat and Dragon" (1975). Smith (Paul Linebarger) structures his short story along the lines of a game with playing cards, titling each of the episodes "The Table," "The Shuffle," "The Deal," "The Play," "The Score." Underhill is a "pinlighter," a member of a select group of humans who by means of a "pin-set" can "see" far ahead on a spaceship's interstellar route. That is, the machine augments the pinlighters' natural telepathic range so that they can foresee dangers that lie ahead. Cordwainer Smith's physical environment for space travel is hazardous. He describes it using concepts that are original even for science fiction and fantasy: "the pain of space," "planoforming," and "entities something like the dragons of ancient human lore ... tenuous matter between the stars" (71). The malevolent entities can be destroyed with massive flashes of light within the nuclear fission range. But they are so quick in their attack that the human pinlighters need to work in concert with specially chosen cats who also have telepathic abilities. "The Game" begins with the mental pairing between human and feline, and "The Shuffle," or drawing of lots, at the commencement of each journey. "The Deal" describes preparations for travel. "The Play" and "The Score" are recognizable as the standard plot sequences of climax and dénouement.

The action is narrated briefly but imaginatively, another rare example of the more complex short story form described by Henry James. Human pinlighters are connected mentally with feline partners by means of the pin-sets. The partners travel in football-sized containers towed behind the spacecraft. Contact is made with the malevolent forces in deep space, whereupon the cats "pounce," triggering the flash devices attached to the exterior of their pods. The long journey, "skipping" between the stars in planoforming sequences, is thus made safer.

The psychological framing of "The Game of Rat and Dragon" is all-important, as it is in most of Cordwainer Smith's work. Here it is explored through the close ties of affection between paired human and feline pin-lighters, a relationship not entirely condoned by society (like sexual/companionate love between species), hence the drawing of partners by lot. Cordwainer Smith produces some delightful imagery of cat and human interactions not unlike those in Fritz Leiber's two tales of Gummitch the kitten:

> The partners seemed to take the attitude that human minds were complex and fouled up beyond belief, anyhow. No partner ever questioned the superiority of the human mind, though very few of the partners were much impressed by that superiority [74].

This is the appeal to a reader's affection for animals that we find in many other tales.

Rats

Although we are not as fond of rodents as we are of the higher animals like dogs, cats and dolphins, they are well represented in the genre, and we can identify commonly applied perceptions about them in a handful of stories. One popular ploy is to attempt a surprise ending by not revealing the identities of the rodents. I say attempt because an observant reader will tumble to the ruse early in the tale, even if it was not sometimes given away by the accompanying artwork. For instance, in F.L. Wallace's "Big Ancestor" (1954), "mankind is descended from rats which escaped from some interstellar vessel putting in at Earth" (125–126), a theme Brian Aldiss (35) identifies as belonging to the class of "horrid revelations" that owe a lot to the Gothic tradition. Another common theme is that of the enclosed world in which rats and mice create short-lived civilizations facilitated by natural selection (mutation). Biologically-driven behavior derived form such circumstances is another theme, giving rise to inter-breeding, overcrowding, warfare, and tribal or feudal rat societies, such as in Avram Davidson's "The Tail-Tied Kings" (1962).

One of the earlier generation of Australian science fiction writers, A. Bertram Chandler, depicts a similarly enclosed tribal society in "Giant Killer" (1945). Its fairy-tale provenance (Jack the Giant Killer), including a blend of fairy story motifs, is also found in "The Tail-Tied Kings" and "Big Ancestor." In Chandler's scenario, humans are referred to as Giants. Mutated newborns, called Different Ones, are put to death on the orders of a Judge of the Newborn as part of their Law. There is a Cave-of-Food, a Place-of-Green-Growing-Things, and so on. Within this tribal society are waged continual struggles for power between leaders. Mutation includes a degree of clairvoyance, as well as obvious physical differences, revealed in such names as Three-Eyes and No-Fur, and there is a common history. The People are (of course) living within the hull of a spacecraft.

While they are competently written, these rat tales are disappointing because they do not go beyond tribal bloodletting. Their authors' clear intention is to have them stand as allegories for the human species.

In an introductory comment on Daniel Keyes' (1927–) "Flowers for Algernon" (1959), Eric Rabkin (371) notes an important distinction between intelligence and personality:

> Here science manipulates with mixed success the intellect of a man, but the story seems to argue, in keeping with one main branch of science fiction ideology, that the essence of humanness is not intelligence at all but some aspect of personality, some child-like and innocent generosity and selflessness. Science is granted great power, but not the power to break the human spirit.

"Flowers for Algernon," in its original short story form, is an indictment of "man's inhumanity to man." In Brian Aldiss' view (257), the story proved weaker when enlarged to the proportions of a novel, but (he says) it retains its strength in the film version *Charly* (1968), directed by Ralph Nelson. The Algernon of the title is a white rat whose intelligence is enhanced parallel to but slightly ahead of that of Charlie Gordon's. This is important because the first signs of retrogression in the rat alert Charlie to his own predicament, which he cannot reverse, though he attempts to do so to the limits of his superhuman genius. The human, as well as animal, tragedy lies in Charlie's consciousness of his waning powers. In his autobiographical tracing of the gestation and growth of "Flowers for Algernon," *Algernon, Charlie, and I* (1999), Keyes (90) says, "It never occurred to me that a developmentally challenged person — in those days they called it *retarded*— would be aware of his or her limitations and might want to be more intelligent."

Mice

Smaller forms of the genus *Mus*, such as *Mus musculus* (house mouse) or *Mus sylvaticus* (field mouse) are usually characterized as far less malevolent than *Mus decumanus* (common brown rat) or the more rare *Mus rattus* (black rat). Comparatively smaller size and cuteness are probably factors. Generally speaking, stories about mice are sentimental, cautionary, or comic. The first is exemplified in the motherly homebody Wee Widow Mouse of Walter Wangerin's novel *The Book of the Dun Cow* (1980): "What does mice do? Mice cleans in the spring. Mice wears aprons and sweeps" (188). These are the words of John Wesley Weasel, an archetypical warrior type who idolizes Wee Widow Mouse for the nurturing, mother image she projects. Described as a fable on the flyleaf, the novel is emotionally powerful because it is packed with many archetypes in a cosmic battle between good and evil. This makes it a delightful read for young adults as well as their elders.

Coming ten years after "Flowers for Algernon," Howard Fast's sensitive short story "The Mouse" (1969) similarly addresses the theme of self-consciousness. Isaac Asimov (106) describes it as "cautionary in nature," but I think it goes beyond being a cautionary tale because of the way in which Fast, like many other writers in the genre, values the idea of mind. In the tradition of the eavesdropping animal, a mouse can, with the grace of newly imparted intelligence given by visiting alien scientists, act as their eyes and ears:

> As much as the space people, he was a stranger to the curious ways of mankind, and he listened to them speculate on the mindless, haphazard mixture of joy and horror that was mankind's civilisation on the planet Earth.... And so it went, question and answer, while the mouse lay there in front of them, his strangely shaped head between his paws, his eyes fixed on the two men and the two women with worship and love ... [112–113].

Eventually, like the dog Sirius in Stapledon's novel, the mouse begins to ask questions. He pleads to return with these beings to their home of music, beauty and peace, and no killing of the weak by the stronger. But this is impossible because of the crushing gravity of their Jupiter-like planet, whereupon the mouse raises that central of all moral questions posed by uplifted beings: "Did you ask me whether I wanted to be like this?" Part of their reply is that "life is good and beautiful — and in itself the answer to all things" (114). Unable to reverse their surgery, and with regret (the cautionary note), the scientists depart, leaving the mouse, at his request, in the yard where he was found. Before he intentionally walks into a trap to end it all, the mouse experiences a moment of epiphany:

> He knew now ... the space people ... had given him the ultimate gift of the universe — consciousness of his own being.... He saw the wholeness of the world and of all the worlds that ever were or would be, and he was without fear or loneliness [115–116].

In an act of unawareness — the opposite to that of raised consciousness — a human throws the dead mouse into his neighbor's garden. Such ideas appear often in various ways and with differing degrees of artistic competency in the work of many writers in this genre.

Humor in mouse stories can be similar to that of some dog tales. In "Star Mouse" (1942), by Fredric Brown, a scientist sends a small grey mouse towards the moon, but the rocket lands on an asteroid whose tiny inhabitants raise the mouse to self-awareness and speech with a machine that taps into subconscious memories. Back on Earth the mouse pursues his newly found ambition to change his fellows into super-mice. He suggests to the professor that the continent of Australia be given to the mice because it has a comparatively small human population who can be resettled in other parts of the world, a nicely ironic touch considering that country's colonial history. In exchange, the mice will sign a non-aggression pact with the humans, exterminate the rats, and live in peace in their new country. The professor agrees to act as intermediary, but not without misgivings. However, before this can be put into effect the mouse enters a cage without bars to join his mate, only to have the transformation reversed by the electrified floor.

The plot is simple and follows a recognizable formula. An animal is raised to self-awareness by some means. With an equivalent or greater than human intelligence it confronts questionable human values, such as war, killing and cruelty (these *are* values if we stop to think about it). Finally, by choice or mischance it returns to its former intelligence and/or dies.

What makes the difference in Brown's story is that "Star Mouse" is broad satire. Herr Oberburger, a genial aspect of the mad professor stereotype, speaks in fractured Germanic English, which in turn becomes the speech style of the mouse Mitkey, the style then being passed on to the Prxlians on their asteroid. When they suggest to Mitkey that he be clothed for his return to Earth as a civilized being, he chooses the costume of his cartoon namesake:

> Bright red bants mitt two big yellow buttons in frondt und two in back, und yellow shoes for der back feet und a pair of yellow gloves for der vront. A hole in der seat of der bants to aggomodate der tail [173].

The strength of Brown's humor lies in the ridiculous play on language and the perpetrating of bad puns. Mitkey's mate is, of course, Minnie. Australia is to be renamed Moustralia, Sydney to become Dissney. But there is a serious undercurrent. Mitkey's insistence on a "non-aggression pact" has echoes of the Second World War, which was well under way the year the story was written, and his plans to create super-mice and exterminate the rats suggests that Mitkey has vague Nazi sympathies, no doubt explaining the professor's unease about human willingness to support a future mouse civilization. This apparently light satirical tale has a cautionary subtext. In its humor and surprise, even cruel, ending, "Star Mouse" is representative of Fredric Brown's oeuvre (Clute and Nicholls 163–164).

Sea-Going Mammals

Seals, sea lions and cetaceans (whales, dolphins and porpoises) have been close to humans for hundreds of years. We think of legends from the Mediterranean about dolphins rescuing shipwrecked mariners. But the cetaceans are not domesticated. The different medium in which they live distances them geographically and emotionally from humans. For more than a hundred years they have been exploited for their fur, their blubber and other body parts, just as with many land animals. See, for instance, Rudyard Kipling's story "The White Seal" (1894), in which the protagonists find safe breeding beaches far from human hunters, or Vincent Smith's more recent but indifferently written *Musco — Blue Whale* (1978). Both stories are heavily anthropomorphic. Tales figuring cetaceans, it seems to me, have an underlay of human guilt in the telling. I find three very similar short stories on this theme.

John Jakes's "The Highest Form of Life" (1961) is a first contact story with a difference. The occupants of a U.S. Navy submarine engaged in dolphin experiments pick up an alien broadcast. The school of dolphins to which the broadcast is directed reply: "We are the highest — you are the highest — we seek you" (16). The crew in the submarine soon realize that neither the advanced intelligences in the spaceship nor the dolphins with whom they are communicating wish to make contact with them, because humans are considered "egocentric" and "pitiably brutal." The same moral lesson is the theme of Gordon Dickson's "Dolphin's Way" (1964): "The dolphins had known, perhaps for centuries, that it was to them alone on Earth that the long-awaited visitors from the stars would finally come" (206).

The premise (some would say cliché) behind such moral tales is that extraterrestrial civilizations observe human society critically and find it wanting, because its level of spiritual sophistication has not kept pace with technological sophistication. Contact with Earth, followed by an invitation to join a pan-galactic civilization, cannot therefore be made. The bite to these tales is that while humans do not qualify, other species — often those that humans hunt, exploit and whose intelligence they belittle or of which they are unaware — appear as more advanced in the qualities that matter. Sometimes it is as simple as the dolphin culture itself rejecting humankind after having experimented on them, as in George Annas' "Dolphin Mission" (1979):

> I have been placed off limits by the dolphin community, and the experiment has been declared a miserable failure. The decision to teach me in the first place was one that badly divided the dolphin community ... communication with humans has been shelved for at least another century [111].

The dolphin community had witnessed one of the humans kill a dolphin and then being killed in turn by the human narrator/protagonist.

Poetic Imagination

Most of the short stories surveyed above are run-of-the-mill tales that fit Henry James' one foot after the other category in their effect. The tales that stand out as belonging to James' second type, more considered and in their narrative structure able to condense important themes and feelings more usually communicated by the novella and novel, include Cordwainer Smith's "The Game of Rat and Dragon," Daniel Keyes' "Flowers for Algernon," and Fritz Leiber's "Space-Time for Springers."

Style and voice in the best of the stories reminds us that poetic imagination is frequently found in animal tales. This includes sensory imagery, such as touch, smell and hearing. Some stories contain a lyricism suggestive of children's poetry. Other stories draw upon traditional human affection and fancies about animals, such as addressing them as though they could reply in words, or indulging in the conceit of thinking of them as extraterrestrials. There can be an aesthetic sensibility and literary conceits in the characterization of animal protagonists. For example, dogs and cats (and in one case a horse) may compose poetry and engage in philosophical speculation. Some stories contain rare intertextual allusions, such as mentioning animal protagonists from other well-known tales, or they may indulge in quasi-classical allusions and style. The use of surprise endings, especially in short stories, is another feature of style and voice in this genre, where the religious or numinous is often a factor. In some conclusions the protagonist experiences an epiphany.

The tragic element in animal tales often hinges upon differences between human and animal points of view, and the misunderstandings that can result. These include incompleteness and loneliness (for example, when dogs can no longer be companions to humans), rebellion against authority, and innocence betrayed. Many tales conclude with the animal's death or with other unforeseen repercussions (for example, the pitfalls in apparently advantageous developments such as uncontrolled telepathic broadcasting). Another source of tragedy is the protagonist's self-awareness of waning consciousness. Finally, biological needs and drives can manifest in "atavism," whereby the animal protagonist slips back into the ways of the wild. They are another source of tragedy: the theme of the beast within.

Animals can appear as a threat to humans via elements such as mystery, ambiguity, conspiracy, eavesdropping, and dangers hidden behind harmless appearances. (On the physical plane this includes natural camouflage.) There are traditional associations of some animals with the supernatural. Cats have solitary habits and are sometimes associated with witches and the stealing of human souls, while dogs may have intuition and perceptions of unseen worlds. The ghost story (supernatural revenge tale) fits in here. In order to have its impact, the Gothic draws upon the strangeness of animals because they do not share human feelings, a feature that can add point to a tragic tale.

Beneath these lie philosophical issues concerning the meaning of intelligence and sentience and how "being human" can be defined. The literature frequently raises a number of key propositions that writers explore with varying artistry and different degrees of success.

CHAPTER 5

Recasting the Animal Fable: Novels and Novellas

Animal tales can be typed according to the classic narrative genres of the romance, tragedy, comic, and Gothic. The romantic view sees animals as allies, implying a mutual understanding and affection between them and humans. This carries with it a variety of emotions and archetypal relationships, including companionableness, the giving of comfort and caring, empathy, compassion, gift-giving (bringing things home, a feline as well as canine trait which can have undesirable consequences, as we have seen), and unselfish love, which can go together with sentimentality and innocence. Animal figures are also protectors, the common archetype of the faithful dog or (less usually) cat sidekick, the link that of a shared human and canine (or feline) history over millennia. As well, humans may be held in awe by animals. The trait of devotion or faithfulness in dogs may lead to another stock idea, that of humans as gods, to which is added sometimes a theme of mutual respect and understanding between animal and human.

A variety of philosophical propositions lie at the heart of science fiction and fantasy tales drawing upon the tradition of the animal fable. Physical form does not correlate with intelligence. Hence, if intelligence is the mark of being human, one does not have to possess a humanoid form to qualify as human. For example, one can be a dog with a human mind. Intelligence and personality are not the same thing. One can possess intelligence, yet not be human if feelings or spirit are left out. Do animals have souls? There is an argument that animals do not share human feelings. Having feelings includes emotions and "spirit," and the ability to compose poetry and engage in philosophic discourse. Being human is often defined as possessing self-awareness/ self-consciousness and communicating through language that is either spoken or telepathic, or both. Being human is sometimes defined as having the ability to make and use tools and exploit fire, an archaeological definition. If a being's intelligence *exceeds* that of humans is there a point beyond which it ceases to be human?

Novels and novellas, because of their length, provide more opportunities in which to explore such propositions. As noted above, the novel is a good vehicle for plot and character development, an advantage it holds over the short story.

Surdity

Stephanie Johnson's fifth novel, *The Whistler* (she has also written plays, short stories, and television and radio documentaries), continues the tradition in speculative fiction of projecting conditions and social issues from the present into the future. Her depiction of a technological world rapidly gone adrift, descriptions of a future time extrapolated from the anxieties of the twentieth century's final years, belongs to those novels of exemplary warning, such as Aldous Huxley's *Brave New World*, George Orwell's *1984*, and a host of other post-apocalyptic tales both well- and poorly-told. *The Whistler*, in my opinion, is one of the better-told treatments of the theme.

Sydney in the year 2318 is a microcosm of the future world, sullied by the combined effects of global warming, nuclear war, and depletion of the ecosystem. The urban environment is dominated by crowded tower blocks and shanty towns. Public spaces, such as Centennial Park and racecourses, house refugees from the war-ravaged countries to Australia's north, following the Greater Asian Wars around the year 2096. Heaps of rubble are so commonplace that "there are over a hundred words for defining different types of it" (132), a play on the anthropological cliché about Inuit perceptions of snow or Nuer classifications of cattle. It is a time of "cold immorality," where even to step outside one's door to visit a neighbor is to face extreme danger. Social attitudes have hardened against what were once desirable human qualities. Belief in originality is no more; fatherhood is meaningless; knowledge is almost a monopoly held by the Corporations, with reading and learning pursued by only a few outsiders; the poor and outcast wear clothing of plastic fiber; human minds are impoverished; the seaboard is heavily polluted, though the fires of the burning oil-wells have since died out. It is a future world different from that of the present day only by degrees.

The society of this world is fragmented into various combinations of haves and have-nots. Sydneysiders in 2318 live according to a siege mentality under a social and political system characterized by different variants of feudalism. In some parts of the city the large corporations hold power, and life there for wealthy executives has perhaps not changed so much from Sydney 2010. Here, near the sea, "buildings stand to the edge of the land, the homes of the wealthy, the Corporation management" (228). Elsewhere the tower blocks are controlled by "kings" living in luxurious penthouses. In between are the streets and individual homes. Society is broadly divided into two impoverished classes, the Flickers, who hardly ever leave their small apartments but fill their leisure hours with "mind-numbing computer games" provided by the Corporations, and the Drens, people of the streets eking out an existence as best they can outside the control and protection of the Corporations or the tower kings. From the safety of their apartments, the Flickers gain vicarious amusement by watching Dren daily life on their television sets.

The underlying mood is one of deep pessimism characterized by the word "surdity"—that is, deafness or voicelessness, an unusual term that appears to have been coined from an obscure dictionary reference (surd = "of a sound uttered with the breath and not the voice"; from the Latin *surdus* = "deaf, mute"; in turn mistranslated from the Greek alogos = "irrational, speechless" *OED*). The narrator says: "This is an era when, in most respects, one would welcome surdity" (172); "human nature just repeats itself, over and over, through the centuries" (26); "metaphors ... soften the truth and illuminate it" (53). People do not talk about "things that matter ... their lives, their homes, their desultory work..." (59). The feeling is claustrophobic, close, expressed in another unusual word not found in the *OED* (or on the Internet): "proximitous" (75). As well as surdity, absurdity is not far from mind. The image of Drens moving about a busy intersection presents "a fable for a senseless world" (161). "Few care about the world, fewer are interested in what has gone before" (174). One community's adaptation within a woman-only society a century after 2096 is that Faith comes before Truth (185).

The Whistler is just one of many other science fiction and fantasy novels on the post-apocalyptic theme, and so a tad boring for that reason? Or is there something that makes this novel different from others? Johnson's speculations are very close to the bone, for we can recognize in them many social conditions prevailing today; so what better than to create the character of a genetically altered dog to provide the outsider's view? This protagonist is named Smooch. His physical condition is such that he can ingest food only in liquid form, a product with the superbly nauseating trade name of Tux. (There are no bones in this tale.) Smooch has been genetically engineered for his combined roles of companion lapdog and storyteller. Storytelling is the chief motif that helps unify the novel.

There is a light undertone of humor in some of this but, in the main,

Johnson's novel is appropriately bleak for its subjects of world pollution and the real possibility of human extinction. The associated theme of degeneration dates back to H.G. Wells' *The Time Machine*, but extinction is another matter. That theme seems not to have been in evidence much in science fiction and fantasy for most of the twentieth century until comparatively recent decades. Perhaps people were a little more optimistic earlier in the century.

Johnson does not make the mistake of thickly laying on the puns that others sometimes do who use canine protagonists. The best is probably Smooch's speculation that, given the opportunity, he would have written "The Book of Dog" for the Bible. But in Smooch's characterization there are deeper qualities concerning dogs that writers before Johnson have put to use. Emphasis on a canine's olfactory powers is one example, contrasted with the weak apparatus possessed by humans. So Smooch in a previous life picks up the "pungent legs" and "caressing traitor's voice" of Mary Queen of Scots' male secretary, who is a spy for the English queen (58). Human mating behavior is likewise unsettling for the dog, who perceives "peculiar smells and furniture may misbehave" (209). In association with the olfactory sense is another that appears frequently in dog narratives. Dogs rely on "instinct and sensation" (107), have "antique sensibilities and artful conversation" (198), and (in Smooch's case and by his reckoning) are sagacious creatures (210). But dogs are also different from humans. Dogs of old do not have imaginations (24), and Smooch — who can relive in his imagination his own past lives — lacks "the capacity to recognize the human soul returned" (52).

Another commonly found characteristic of such stories is "the empathy that many humans have for canines" (51). This element plays upon the folk belief that dogs (and cats) possess supernatural qualities (which most human companions of dogs and cats know to be true). They have a touch of humor about them, and the human pessimism in this novel is offset by the subdued humor and optimism of Smooch's inner world, though he, too, is a troubled being. Smooch's ability to remember past lives appears to be explained by the scientifically-controlled breeding programs that produced dogs like him, but there are enough uncertainties to suggest that there is something other than pure science in this changing world. The discovery of a natural ability to communicate telepathically between dog and humans at the end of the story is further evidence of the fantastic in the novel. There is a hopeful outcome in *The Whistler*, as the metonymically eponymous dog returns to the sea (explaining his mutation to flippers).

Penguins

Penguins are counted among animals chosen to exemplify human frailties, which is not so unusual when we remember their humanoid image in the popular imagination. They stand upright, walk on two legs, congregate in large groups, and have feather colorings that remind us of dinner jackets. In fact, a great many animals chosen to allegorize the human condition are humanoid in appearance, though not all. Four-footed animals such as dogs, cats, and rodents have been known to stand upright. Birds do so as a matter of course, as do the salamanders of Čapek's *War with the Newts*, and apes are the most humanoid of animal chosen for allegorical effect.

Anatole France (Anatole-François Thibault, 1844–1924) wrote several allegorical works, including *L'Île des pingouins*, published in his native country in 1908 and a year later in an English translation. In *Penguin Island*, the monk Saint Mael is blown off course from the southern Irish coast in his stone coracle into the "fabulous seas" of the North. He effects landfall on a rocky island and, because his eyes are blinded by the glare of the ice, mistakes a group of penguins for humans: "animated forms grouped in rows on the rocks, like a crowd of people..." (30). Taking them to be "men living under natural law," he first preaches the Gospel, then baptizes them. This is disconcerting to the saints and other worthies in heaven, who debate the human-animal thesis. Saint Catherine observes that "the separation between man and animal is not a complete one, as evidenced by monsters which issue from both of them" (39). Lactantius points out that angels, a combination of human and bird, "are purity incarnate" (41). In the end, God decides that, in keeping with His eternal plan, the penguins should become human. But He adds a warning:

> I foresee some disadvantages. Many of these men will find fault with themselves that they never would have as penguins. It is certain that their fate will be much less desirable as a result of this change than it would have been without baptism and assumption into the family of Abraham [42–43].

The monk is told by the archangel Raphael to change the penguins into humans in God's name, and the transformation is done accordingly:

> Their foreheads broadened, and their heads rounded into domes.... Their oval eyes opened wider on the universe; a fleshy nose decorated the two slits of their nostrils; their beaks turned into mouths from which came words; their necks shortened and thickened; their wings became arms and their paws legs; an anxious soul inhabited their breasts [44].

In succeeding chapters the penguins wear clothing, invent states, governments and laws, and adopt human customs, all of which provide Anatole

France with many opportunities for allegory and satire. In the introduction to the 1968 Belle Burke translation of the novel, David Caute (v–xvi) writes on the nature of allegory as it relates to France's two themes of "guarded optimism and guarded skepticism." Caute says that allegorical novelists convey principally pessimistic messages, as Anatole France does, but that in France's case there is also guarded skepticism because he is moderate in his views, and he entertained "hopes for a better, socialist future" (vi).

France's "elegance of style and sureness of touch" masks these conflicting tendencies, because France—like George Bernard Shaw—possesses "a fiercely logical intelligence, caustic wit, a flair for paradox and irony, independence of mind, a deceptive simplicity of style..." (vi–vii). These qualities we find to varying degrees among many authors in the sub-genre. Certainly Caute's list applies in full to Karel Čapek. Olaf Stapledon's approach is different, gentle without the verbal pyrotechnics of Čapek; and so, too, is that of Clifford Simak. Paul Linebarger's light touch, while dealing sometimes with horrific issues, is a different case again. This can be said of the short stories reviewed earlier. But the same tension between optimism and pessimism is there, a bipolar thesis that suggests the presence of entertainment versus insecurity in the carnivalesque.

Space Opera

Space opera gets its name by analogy with the soap operas of radio and television, which themselves received the label because such programs were often sponsored by the manufacturers of soap products. Once scorned because of these associations, present-day space opera is "now more commonly accepted as a legitimate label for the upbeat space adventure narrative that has been the mainspring of modern science fiction," writes Jack Williamson (433). In common with its genetic cousin, the American western ("horse opera," "oat opera"), and its precursor, the early heroic saga or folk epic (*chansons de geste*), space opera has simplicity characterized by a sharp distinction between good and evil, grand themes, innocence, raw courage, ingenuity, occasionally the displaying of supernormal powers, and more often technological expertise and power held by its heroes and heroines. Among its mythic themes is "the optimistic assumption of future human expansion across the galaxy" (Williamson 434).

Norton's cozy catastrophe novel *Star Man's Son: 2250 A.D.* (1952) has an element of space opera because abandoned spaceships lie in the countryside, and the star man's son of the title is an adolescent named Fors (a pun on "force") whose father was one of the last astronauts in this post-apocalyptic world. The faithful animal sidekick is a cat named Lura. Dogs have died out from radiation sickness, but cats survived: "Small domestic animals of untamable independence had produced larger offspring with even quicker minds and greater strength" (11). Lura is telepathic in the sense that she knows Fors' thoughts, but in all other respects she behaves like an ordinary cat. *Star Man's Son* follows the predictable pattern of these adventure yarns: a trek through radioactive terrain, the discovery of a ruined city, capture and narrow escape from mutated "Beast Things" that infest the land, meetings with tribal groups whose model is Native American culture, and climactic battles between allied human groups and Beast Things.

Alien animals with intelligence, or terrestrial animals possessing intelligence but transplanted into an off-world environment, figure frequently in space opera. David Brin's enthralling Uplift war series is a good example of the latter, where apes and cetaceans, their intelligence "uplifted" so as to place them within the ranks of consciously sentient beings, fight on other planets in alliance with their human partners against extraterrestrial cultures. Because I am limiting this survey to Earth-bound intelligent animals, such tales are not directly relevant except occasionally to illustrate a point. The same can be said for two otherwise excellent treatments of the alien species theme: C.J. Cherryh's Chanur series, in which the Hani are female lion-like farers through hyperspace who meet with an array of strange aliens, including one human man (Hani males remain on the home planet engaging in tomcat strife); also Alan Dean Foster's novel *Cachalot* (1980), named for an ocean planet refuge to which cetaceans have been transported by humans out of guilt for having brought the species close to extinction on Earth.

Features redolent of space opera, however, can be found in some science fiction stories with their plots planted on the earth. In Frederik Pohl's novel *Slave Ship* (1957), published originally in three parts in *Galaxy Science Fiction*, animals are employed for the purposes of war. This theme is present in a number of tales. In *Slave Ship*, the boisterous affability of dogs is the chief animal characteristic. Brian Ash (163) says the novel tells "of the training of animals to fight in wars," but, strictly speaking, this theme receives only passing mention in the second installment within a wider Cold War setting. A Western (United Nations) submarine is pitted against an oriental antagonist, although the real agent is later found to be a form of telepathic extraterrestrial life attempting to make contact. The animals, which are expendable — apes, a seal, and dogs — are trained to operate levers in an engine room close to the submarine's leaking nuclear reactors. The ethics of this policy are not explored beyond the fictional narrator's acknowledgement that the human submariners are "Judases," "living a lie" (88, 92), which, for a thoughtful reader, makes the concluding homily somewhat hollow: "we have learned to get along with our animals" (127)—so now we can get along with Them, it is implied. Pohl's dogs are diverting enough to elicit reader sympathy in spite of the fictional narrator's patronizing tone:

> Their main problem was garrulousness. You would explain to them, say, a complicated course-correction maneuver and they would bark, growl and semaphor the whole thing back to you. And they wouldn't repeat it just once; they would tell you the whole procedure two or three times, and then come up and put their forepaws on your legs and mention a couple of the high-spots, and tell you about the fire-control drill they had done the day before, with emphasis on how High-Shiny-Lever was not the same as Little-Thick-Lever, even though both of them had to be pulled sharply outward [91].

The same military expediency is questioned in deeper moral terms in Merle's *The Day of the Dolphin*, published a decade later when people were becoming more aware of such issues as animal—and human—rights (1967/1973). This lightweight "underwater space opera" was very likely aimed at a young adult readership, so perhaps we should not expect the kind of philosophic angst of other examples in the genre. However, whether they are facile, as in *Slave Ship*, or more confronting, as in Merles' novel, they come under the general category of cautionary tales.

Cozy Catastrophe

What Brian Aldiss called in 1973 the "cosy disaster" or "cosy catastrophe" begins with H.G. Wells' *The War of the Worlds*, continues in Karel Čapek's *War with the Newts* (where humankind may at some future time descend from the mountains where they have been forced to retreat by the continent-undermining Newts), and, more appropriately for Aldiss' definition, in John Wyndham's novels. This idea of war between humanity and the Other, be it Martian, terrestrial plant, terrestrial animal in the wild, or domestic animal, is a popular theme. Clute and Nicholls (338) remark on "an obsession with the weather" among United Kingdom disaster authors, while their cousins in the United States are more anxious about disease. But war with animals is mooted on both sides of the Atlantic. The point about the cozy catastrophe is that the depiction of disaster, no matter how far-reaching, is never entirely serious. Through the efforts of the novel's heroes and heroines, humanity survives against all odds. There is often a tongue-in-cheek quality in these critiques. Aldiss (254) says: "The essence of cosy catastrophe is that the hero should have a pretty good time (a girl, free suites at the Savoy, automobiles for the taking) while everyone else is dying off." Catastrophe leavened with irony and satire in such fiction belongs to the carnivalesque.

Susan Sontag, in her seminal essay on "The Imagination of Disaster"—a relatively early contribution to narratology—refers to what she calls "the aesthetics of destruction." Her limiting of discussion to science fiction films and exclusion of novels does not quite come off because, in my opinion, the visual, though obviously more prominent in film, does have its novelistic counterpart in the imagination of the reader. It is not so easy to separate "intellectual workout" (novel) and "sensuous elaboration" (film), as Sontag (212–213) does. What Sontag calls "the peculiar beauties to be found in wreaking havoc, making a mess," I am sure are experienced by a reader of science fiction as well as a viewer of the same. This is not restricted to science fiction films. One has only to view such quasi-military dramas as *Rambo* or the detective genres represented by the "Dirty Harry" series to hold the suspicion that Americans enjoy, above many things, trashing their automobiles, with public buildings, usually monuments reflecting national prestige, coming a close second in the demolition. One of the satisfactions that Sontag reviews harks back to Aristotle's (39) concept of catharsis, when she states that the viewing of wholesale destruction "releases one from moral obligations" (215). Compare this against the temporary release from moral obligations in Carnival in Bakhtin's terms, and the more general (cathartic) release in the carnivalesque.

But disaster movies (and, by extension, novels on the same theme) have other functions. They are, first of all, morally simplistic, where the nature of the enemy is such that human cruelty towards them can be countenanced if not fully condoned, a partial overlap, Sontag says, with horror films. Paradoxically, horror movies are heavily moralistic, cautionary tales about the proper versus improper uses to which science may be put (the ubiquitous Frankenstein theme), and betray an ingrained distrust of the scientific person as detached intellectual. They also contain a lot of wishful thinking—for example, "hunger for a 'good war'" coupled inconsistently with a "yearning for peace," and, in the frequent depiction of technology as grand unifier against the enemy, they have a Utopian aspect. We see these factors played out in real world politics, where it is not difficult to relate the art of fiction with the propaganda of Realpolitik. Paul Linebarger must have been aware of this all the time when writing his pinlighter and underpeople tales.

Cozy catastrophes are, subconsciously, anxiety tales "about the condition of the individual psyche" (Sontag 220), and serve the reassuring purposes of mythology. But though films in science fiction may be perceived "as thematically central allegory, replete with standard modern attitudes" (223), they lack social criticism. This is where allegorical science fiction novels and short stories differ most markedly from popular films in the genre. The written text is a potentially strong purveyor of social criticism. In novels and other literature it is possible to find works representative of one or the other of the two extremes Sontag describes:

> One job that fantasy can do is to lift us out of the unbearably humdrum and to distract us from terrors — real or anticipated — by an escape into exotic, dangerous situations which have last-minute happy endings [the "cosy" aspect]. But another of the things that fantasy can do is to normalize what is psychologically unbearable, thereby inuring us to it. In one case, fantasy beautifies the world. In the other, it neutralizes it.... They inculcate a strange apathy concerning ... destruction which I for one find haunting and depressing [224–225].

Walter Miller's novella *Conditionally Human* (1952) is a poignant mutant story. In an overcrowded world, rigid birth control restricts the begetting of human children, but the emotional drive to give nurture is irresistible. Anthropos Incorporated specializes in creating mutant animals: cats, dogs, dwarf bears, chimpanzees, and others, genetically engineered so that their biological maturation does not go beyond childhood. For the protagonist Terrell Norris, "'intelligence' is a word applicable only to humans" (8). But as time goes by he begins to have second thoughts: "Anthropos feared making quasi-humans too intelligent, lest sentimentalists proclaim them really human" (40). Moreover, some mutants, illegally made in the laboratory by a disaffected scientist and sold on the black market, have the potential to exceed human intelligence.

Harlan Ellison's "A Boy and His Dog" (1969) is a post-apocalyptic tale set in a ruined city with violent, street-wise characters. At sixty-four pages it qualifies as a novella. Ellison implicitly criticizes American middle class life, now gone underground to perpetuate itself and its niceness, contrasted against the ruin above ground where gangs and loners fight continually for survival. (There is a film version.) In a floating, not quite conclusive, ending, Vic and his dog Blood move on without the company of Quilla June. Vic nurses Blood until he recovers from his wounds, both well fed by now, although hitherto desperately in need of food:

> It took a long time before I stopped hearing her calling in my head. Asking me, asking me: do you know what love is?
> Sure I know.
> A boy loves his dog [15].

Aldous Huxley's *Ape and Essence* (1949) has the features of a cozy catastrophe, but is less cozy than other works of its kind. Its theme of degeneration is one of the psychological anxieties of the twentieth century, as it was for the nineteenth century. The theme can also be traced through other texts, notably in the dog Sirius' emotional wrestling with the wolf-nature within him. Compare this against the metamorphoses of pigs and humans in *Animal Farm*, but it is most striking in *Ape and Essence.*

Animal Farm draws directly from the traditions of the Graeco–Roman and Medieval beast fables, and Orwell's political intentions are the most obvious. As Robert Welch (49) says: "Orwell's adaptation of the convention of the animal fable is fundamental to almost any discussion of the book as a whole." The two interlocking themes of entertainment and explication enter in, with greater emphasis on the novel as a cautionary tale, suggesting comparisons with *War with the Newts* and *Sirius.* Orwell's political allegory *Animal Farm* is more pessimistic than *Sirius*, and just as pessimistic as Čapek's *War with the Newts.*

J.T. McIntosh's *The Fittest* (1955) is an example of a poorly written cozy catastrophe. It is not nearly as well executed as John Wyndham's *The Day of the Triffids* (1951) or *The Chrysalids* (1955), but marginally important because it touches on animal intelligence and, as it says on the back cover, "an uprising of animals against the human race." The animals in question are mutated cats, dogs and mice, called Paggets collectively, and Padogs, Pacats, etc. individually, after the name of the scientist Paget, a Frankenstein-like figure who discovered the genetic process that made them into animals with attitude:

> animals whose brains have been forced a few million years further along the evolutionary highway, while their bodies remain very much the same as their ancestor's bodies ... *animals*, with animal motivations, savagery, tradition, and temperament [18].

Just like humans.

In the tradition of this genre, as in *Star Man's Son*, the male protagonist experiences a series of violent adventures, picking up beautiful women along the way in the 1950s style. The survival of the fittest is the main theme: "Human beings, after all, are the natural enemies of any other intelligent life form on this planet. We brook no competition" (44). Ordinary dogs, however, sometimes remain the friends of humankind and fight alongside them against the paggets, and in the end even padogs and humans form an alliance. Therein lies hope for the future.

The novel belongs to the tradition of pulp literature. It is written in a racy style, male chauvinist to present-day tastes, and evocative of tabloid journalism, explained partly, I think, by McIntosh's background in journalism and teaching. But Baird Searles (119) finds McIntosh's work pedestrian,

> reasonably ingenious science, but often bland in characterization and written with a kind of pedestrianism that dulls the essential sense of wonder. His people and their thoughts are one-dimensional, but they act in complex and often interesting frames of reference.

Robert Merle's *The Day of the Dolphin* (1967) belongs to the same class as that of George Annas covered in the last chapter, but there are no extraterrestrials. Instead, the action takes place between humans and dolphins. The novel has interwoven themes that reflect three major genres — espionage, romance, and animal story. Human reactions to the dolphins' amicable intelligence and speech following a press conference are similar to those burlesqued by Karel Čapek in *War with the Newts.* As in Čapek's work, a philosopher expounds on dolphin intelligence without fully understanding the issues. In another Čapek-like touch, human reactions include dance crazes (the "Dolphin Roll"), fan clubs, new slang expressions, changes in human religions, and, a practice familiar to us, dolphin logos on beverages, toys, and clothes. In those respects, the two novels are so similar that I wondered whether Merle had read *War with the Newts.*

The dolphins are characterized by friendship, good humor and trust, qualities inimical to human realpolitik. One dolphin, Fa, likes watching westerns on television, and his favorite reading is Kipling's *The Jungle Book*, in which he recognizes associations between the dolphin (himself) and Mowgli, a human child who grew up among wolves (Fa was raised among humans). The novel is a form of cozy catastrophe, with the Cold War soon to become "hot." The resolution takes place with the two dolphins accompanying the humans in their escape from the intelligence operatives who have bombed their island. The humans are, of course, gods:

> It was a game, and the best game of all, this long unexpected journey through the open sea at night wit.h Ma and Pa, they understood the importance of their mission, they were helping the good gods escape from the bad gods, everything was clear again ... [328].

William Kotzwinkle's acerbic novel *Doctor Rat* (1971) must be one of the strongest anti-vivisectionist texts in the field. It is sharp edged and fast-paced, with many narrative voices expressed in the stream of consciousness mode, each that of a species as it answers a spiritual call to rise against humankind. The multitude of animal voices — dogs, chickens, dormice, pigs, whales, eagles, apes, elephants, tree sloths, bears, deer, badgers — are linked together by a recurring narrative voice, that of the laboratory animal Doctor Rat, a quisling figure who assumes the persona of a mad scientist, hence satirizing not only that archetype but also the prison or concentration camp trusty. The scene shifts continuously between the enclosed spaces of the laboratory and the outside worlds of the city and the wild. In the laboratory, the pointlessness of animal experimentation, with its replicated tests of the obvious, are exemplified one by one in harrowing detail. The city immediately outside the laboratory is no less a prison for the domestic animals.

The movement for change takes place in the relative freedom of the wild spaces of nature — the plains, forests, seas and air. A meeting of all animals is convened by King Eagle on Vulture Peak, to which humanity is also invited because, as an over-optimistic young ape says to an oldster:

> The time has come for us to gather in great numbers so that we can merge our thought streams as one.... Once we gather this way, man will come too. He will realize that we are all one creature, and he will stop killing us. His realization will be sudden and wonderful [114].

When the mass migrations of animals from the cities and the wild bring them together at single points on each continent, human troops are sent in by fearful administrations, and there follows a massive slaughter, genocidal in effect. To the animals, however, it is not meaningless, and the dying thoughts of some are sublime as well as tragic. It remains for the old tree sloth to say almost the final words at the approach of the Soul of the Animals:

> A tremendous number of them died today, all over the earth. It has loosened the thread that ties us to our bodies.... Our great departure time may have come. All the signs indicate that it has, but nonetheless it's our duty to resist.... I'm drawn into the depths of the Soul, into its vast dream.... This path of my nature took so long to fashion and now — now it is undone, never to be found or fashioned again [212–213].

In Doctor Rat's words, "Humanity is still functioning. But no scurrying little feet in the grass.... Not a single meow, not a chirp, not a solitary bark.... You can feel the emptiness out there: the Final Solution gives you a sort of lonely feeling" (215). This is the most cautionary of tales, warning against the total destruction of animal life by humankind, with the lesson that nature, in the form of the One Animal, may some day take back the Soul of the Animals.

The conscious departure of an entire species (several entire species in *Doctor Rat*) to another realm re-enters contemporary myth with the migration of the Elvish folk in the film version of Tolkien's *The Lord of the Rings* (1954–1955), and occurs in Clifford Simak's *City* when first humans and then robots leave the earth for the stars. To depart is a sort of overthrow or inversion, though I do not think that it partakes fully of the carnivalesque.

Kenneth Cook's satirical novella *Play Little Victims* (1978), on the fate of a mouse civilization founded on remnants of human culture, is a transparent allegory of humankind, compared in the flyleaf a little extravagantly with George Orwell's *Animal Farm*. But it is a delightful book, an essay in cross-cultural misinterpretation, with a tragic end that rivals *Doctor Rat*. It is one of the few works to contain illustrations — Megan Gressor's black and white line drawings. (Illustrations are more often met with in the science fiction and fantasy magazines, such as *Galaxy*, *Analog* or *Amazing*.)

Two field mice, Adamus and Evemus, escape the extinction of all life at the wriggle of God's finger and, in an isolated valley, set about repopulating the world. Adamus gains access to the valley library where he becomes steeped in a disparate mix of works that range from Shakespeare, Freud, the Bible, and Bertrand Russell to Graham Greene, Mickey Spillane and the *New York Times*. These he calls collectively the Word of Man, and he sets out to model a society on that of humans, perceived as supermice that prepared the way for his own kind. He establishes a governmental Board, and mouse society irresistibly follows the course of human history as they dutifully apply human solutions to various problems. Against objections raised by Logimus — the unsuccessful voice of reason — overpopulation, resulting from a too-literal interpretation of the premise God is Love, is stemmed at first by the introduction of warfare. Motor vehicles become another means of reducing the population, with the result that wars increase in popularity — "because the battlefields [are] so much safer than the streets" (56). Mouse society soon has "war, the motor car, alcohol, tobacco, pollution and abortion," with "starvation and disease" to follow. What began as a beautiful and peaceful valley becomes "jam-packed with malformed drunken mice with cigarettes stuck in their mouths, racing around in screeching motor cars when they're not involved in the weekly war or taking time off to have an abortion" (79). Adamus realizes that their "faithful replica of what Man did" (82) has failed them. At a banquet he devises a Final Solution to overpopulation.

Poul Anderson's novel *Brain Wave* (1954) offers an unusual twist on the cozy catastrophe. The "catastrophe" is a sudden rise in the intelligence of all earth's creatures when the planet passes out of a radiation belt that until then had damped down the evolutionary processes that lead to higher intelligence. There are some echoes of Clifford Simak's *City*, first published a full two years earlier in 1952. Cities have no longer an economic justification (94), and in the end the more advanced humans leave the earth to populate the planets of other stars while animals and former mentally incapacitated humans remain.

John Crowley's novel *Beasts* (1976) has the more usual post-catastrophe setting, in a future America partitioned after undergoing another civil war. Mutated animals — the results of past human experimentation — travel the country. Chief among these are lions, the Leos, but a key protagonist is a fox appropriately named Reynard. Crowley (50) draws consciously from the tradition of the beast fable:

> There was no way for Reynard to conceive of himself except as men had conceived of foxes. He had, otherwise, no history: he was the man-fox, and the only other man-fox who had ever existed, in the tales of Aesop and the fables of La Fontaine, in the contes of medieval Reynard and Bruin the bear and Isengrim the wolf, in the legends of foxhunters. It surprised him how well that character fitted his nature; or perhaps, then, he had invented his nature out of those tales.

The novel is listed among a cluster of works studied by Jill Langston Milling (1985) on the theme of the "ambiguous animal."

When Animals Succeed

A great many animal tales end in tragedy or at least ironic failure. Rarely do we have the theme of animals succeeding against human cruelty and power, either collectively or individually.

Mikhail Bulgakov's *The Heart of a Dog* (1968)—originally titled "A Dog's Happiness"—closes on a note of ironic though happy failure. Two doctors change a stray mongrel Labrador into a human who becomes so disruptive that they are forced to reverse the process. This simple premise is the vehicle for satirizing Russia's totalitarian state and its effects on the lives of ordinary people. A "Frankenstein monster" has been created, for Sharik the dog becomes an uncouth lout combining human vices with his original street-wise canine character. He has become all too human. These circumstances allow for broad comic farce, a good example of the carnivalesque. In a gently ironic ending, Sharik, reconstituted as a dog, is thankful for his place in life. Unlike Sirius in Stapledon's novel, Bulgakov's canine character returns to normal and, by a dog's standards, is better off than he was before (see chapters 6 and 7).

Clifford Simak's novelette "The Big Front Yard" (1959) is a tale of successful first contact. It is descended from his earlier masterpiece *City* (1952). "The Big Front Yard" has most of the elements critics came to expect of Simak: a dislike of human bureaucratic folly, the isolated country house, a door opening onto another world (the "big front yard" of the title), affable aliens, slow-talking but canny neighbors, a village half-wit who possesses hidden talents, and a telepathic dog. Hiram Taine is the principal character who, through the mediation of the simpleton (Beasly) and the dog Towser (who does not figure greatly in the overall picture), successfully establishes a trade in selling paint to aliens.

In a chain of communication, Towser, who is an ordinary dog in so far as he cannot talk, brings home an alien who looks like a man-sized woodchuck. Beasly, who names this alien "Chuck," can communicate with it, and Chuck in turn translates for other aliens, who are black-skinned "cowboys" on horseless saddles that float in the air. Simak's quirky humor is in full flight: no space opera, no cozy catastrophe, but instead first contact between the human species and aliens mediated by a "dickering" (haggling) salesman (a mild version of the trickster figure) and described stylistically with tongue-twisting wordplay. These observations do not do justice to Simak's novelette, which is included in a list of his best works (the others are *City* and *Way Station*). Hiram's companion and protector, Towser, would be an ordinary dog if he did not possess telepathic ability.

For some animal characters to survive, the absence or irrelevancy of humankind is a prerequisite, as with the Dogs of *City* and in some dolphin stories. But there are three notable exceptions, Karel Čapek's *War with the Newts*, Robin Wallace-Crabbe's *Dogs* (1993), and Peter Hoeg's *The Woman & the Ape* (1996). Elements of racy adventure appear in these works. Tzvetan Todorov (157?) makes an apposite point when he says, "The thriller's tendency toward the marvelous and the exotic ... brings it closer on the one hand to the travel narrative [a feature of adventure stories too], and on the other to contemporary science fiction [that is, science fiction in the 1960s, when the article was written]." This helps to explain why we find elements of the adventure tale and the thriller in science fiction and fantasy novels, for there are interrelationships between the genres. (Karel Čapek wrote essays on the detective novel as well as on fairy tales.) Peter Høeg's *The Woman & the Ape* contains danger, pursuit and combat in fair measure, certainly the marvelous and the exotic, but does not emphasize strong violence, vile passions, or immorality as in a thriller. Robin Wallace-Crabbe's *Dogs*, on the other hand, opens with a mix of vile passions and the marvelous, while Michael Crichton's *Congo* (1993) is a light-weight adventure tale in the tradition of Rider Haggard or Conan Doyle. *Congo* belongs to the type of terrestrially-based adventure story that has a thin science fiction overlay. Crichton's characters are one-dimensional. In its synoptic style, the novel was amenable to a film script and was likely written with an eye to the cinema, a point I found since observed by Martin Amis (223) in his review of Crichton's *The Lost World*: "Recast those sentences in the present tense and you see them for what they are: stage directions ... a creative-input memo to Steven Spielberg."

Dogs, by Robin Wallace-Crabbe, contains themes and plot elements that parallel those found in *Doctor Rat* to such an extent that it is hard to believe Wallace-Crabbe was not inspired by Kotzwinkle's riotously chilling satire.

Wallace-Crabbe pays more attention to his characters, however, and though reader sympathy is elicited, as in *Doctor Rat*, by a catalogue of human cruelties to animals, it is reinforced by lightly drawn, quirky characterization. Wallace-Crabbe's treatment of his animal and human characters early in the narrative suggests that it will become a picaresque novel for dogs, comparable to Hollywood road movies such as *Bonnie and Clyde* (1967), which is recognizably the paradigm for the early chapters of *Dogs*. The ease with which an ordinary-seeming dog can stand on its hind legs, drive a motor vehicle, dress in fashionable clothes and remain undetected by humans as a dog, is treated matter-of-factly, which persuades the reader to suspend disbelief. Todorov (157?) defines fantastic literature as "deliberately designed by the author to leave the reader in a state of uncertainty whether the events are to be explained by reference to natural or to supernatural causes." In *Dogs*, Wallace-Crabbe moves effortlessly from the realist to the fantastic and back again.

Magic and the preternatural become more dominant in the character of Merlin Mandrake Houdini III and his companion Felix, "a tiny popeyed chihuahua" (35), which parallels Mikhail Bulgakov's remarkable last novel, *The Master and Margarita* (1967/1995, first and second publication, respectively). Beneath his various disguises, Merlin is a Pan-like figure that, in the tale's epiphany, is metamorphosed into his ultimate form, a giant Corgi. This transformation is a closure of sorts, because it satisfies earlier speculation by "some of the more intellectually inclined amongst the dogs ... that *the* great leader of the dogs was going to be a perfect dog" (96). One of the forms taken by the giant Corgi is that of "the wise horse called La Gitana [*gitano* = gypsy in Spanish] who galloped past from time to time, carrying messages between the species and searching for the wild herds of her own kind hunted out long ago" (16). He/she is a being like Bulgakov's devil who exists "in a thousand worlds" (110) and intervenes from time to time as a *deus ex machina* on behalf of the animals.

Dogs has many of the elements already noted for its type: magic and the supernatural, archetypal protective beings, and malevolent adversaries. Like other animal allegories, *Dogs* is a novel of social criticism, with themes such as compassion for the weak, a community of animals, and a "Dogocracy" modeled on human revolutionary working class principles. There are also moments of parody, such as when human linguists attempt to transcribe the dog language phonetically; or when Nancy, the canine equivalent of an Earth Mother, declaims to her audience, "how Canis familiaris had made the fatal mistake of getting along too well with Homo sapiens" (113). On the other hand:

> Nancy had long nurtured the romantic hope of a coming together of the two species, an end to this stand off, to this phony master-servant relationship; an end to exploitation as well. At her most utopian, she'd dreamed of quadrupeds and bipeds meeting as an inter-species parliament. And not just two- and four-legged creatures either, she had dared hope that every living thing which crawled upon the earth — or for that matter remained stationary — might have its say, be offered the chance to represent its species' interests [134].

Before this can take place, however, there is a general uprising against the humans. The television station is captured, and, in a reversal of the total genocide of *Doctor Rat*, all humans are driven off the island after a great loss of life among the animals, while a handful of humans remain who are sympathetic to the animal cause.

Apes

As the nineteenth century reached its close, the controversy surrounding Charles Darwin's *Origin of Species* meant that pongids caught the public imagination. Pierre Versins' encyclopaedia (48) says that "In the nineteenth century, especially since Darwin, through a kind of self-criticism, Republics of Apes multiplied." Much later, in the closing years of the twentieth century, many of the archetypes of the late nineteenth century return to haunt us: in the United States with Michael Crichton's *Congo* (1993), in the Australian novel *Wish* (1995), in a novel by the Danish author Peter Høeg, *The Woman & the Ape* (1996), and in England with Will Self's *Great Apes* (1997). Apes are making a comeback. It appears that allegorical fantasies about relationships between humans and animals, and, by extension, the natural environment, are under reconsideration following a hiatus since the 1970s. One of Peter Høeg's characters (224) may be voicing what most of us in the Western world know:

> People are forming closer attachments to animals than ever before. Dogs and cats sleep in people's beds, get kissed on the mouth, stroked between the legs. The media are overrun with animals. Children's rooms are chock-a-block with them. It's extremely interesting.

The Woman & the Ape is striking for its depiction of a strong female character. Superficially, the plot turns on the development of love and companionship between an alcoholic socialite and a large male ape mutant, a reversal of the sexual romance between a man and a genetically altered gorilla depicted in Peter Goldsworthy's *Wish*. Goldsworthy's treatment, by comparison, appears labored. In *The Woman & the Ape* Høeg uses what Murray Waldren (7) describes as "deft phrases, satirist's eye and scalpelled insight into the absurdities of human pretension [which] make the prose sing, while his lucidity and wit can make one gasp in recognition."

But Waldren is not entirely satisfied, for, while he advises that the novel is well worth reading, he finds weaknesses in aspects of its technical competence and theme. He notes that Høeg "still can't do endings" and calls the work a fantasy in preference to the publisher's description of it as a fable, stating that it is not an allegory so much as an exquisite Chinese feast that leaves one over-full and unsatisfied. What Waldren says about Høeg's earlier detective novel, *Miss Smilla's Feeling for Snow*, applies equally well to *The Woman & the Ape*. It has a "curious mix of exotica and idiosyncrasy, of the straightforward and magic realism ... not afraid to use emotion and intelligence, science or slapstick." *The Woman & the Ape* may not be Høeg's best work, but, in my opinion, it matches many other science fiction and fantasy novels about animals and humans.

Sexuality between human and non-human is a relatively unique theme, but Peter Goldsworthy, when he writes explicitly on it in *Wish* (1995), is not the first to have done so. The theme of sexual and companionate relationships and needs between the human and non-human can be traced back through a number of science fiction and fantasy works to Mary Shelley's *Frankenstein* and beyond. Such tales have at their best a mixture of humor (especially satire) and tragedy. When writing about animal-human sexuality there is a fine line between establishing reader empathy towards the protagonists and using narrative techniques that distance the reader from the actions of the main characters, because bestiality is a strong social taboo. On the other hand, beneath the sexual explicitness (*eros*) of the novel there are suggestions of spiritual love (*agape*) that, it might be argued, can be extended to cross-species intelligences (see Chapter 10).

Will Self's *Great Apes* (1997) is an irreverent and hilarious romp through London society. The premise of the novel at first appears simple enough. Simon Dykes, a disaffected artist, awakens one morning after a night of sex with his girlfriend to discover that he is the only human in a city of chimpanzees. Or is he an ape with a singular neurosis believing himself to be human and consequently in need of intense psychiatric help? The novel is a fast-paced inversion of the ape-human condition where, in true satiric style, it is the humans who are few in numbers, their species at risk, living in small enclaves in enclosed structures, subject to agoraphobia, and the objects of experimentation at the hands of chimp scientists. This situation is flagged from the beginning in the "Author's Note." The author is a chimpanzee.

Will Self keeps up the carnivalesque pace throughout four hundred pages because he writes in an easy flowing style and conjures up striking ideas and images. He is interested in creating distortions of scale in architectural space, among other things, and one of the most striking — and amusing — moments in the novel is his evocation of a scaled-down London, where the buildings and streets are lower and more narrow, and its inhabitants (dressed in suits, bowler hats and carrying briefcases) enter and exit through windows and brachiate from tree to tree, as well as walking the streets. The novel provides plenty of scope for satirizing the worlds of art, academia and psychiatry. Jane Goodall pursues work in Gombe observing humans in the wild. Her mentor is a chimp called Louis Leakey. The description of an orderly queue of male chimps patiently waiting their turn to service a female in estrus is one of many touches that evoke the carnivalesque. (It was never like that when I was in Victoria Station.) As part of his therapy, Simon sketches scenes from the daily lives of humans:

> In place of the chimpanzees who inhabited the finished works were the naked, zombie-like figures of humans. Humans running upright with their stiff-legged gait; humans walking in throngs, all separated by an arm's length; humans sitting with one another, not touching, not grooming, lost in the uncommunicative prison of their own meagre sentience, their own primitive cast of mind [220].

What helps to unify our ideas about authorship, biography, the socio-cultural frame, and the carnivalesque is what I call a basic decency in the characters of these authors, and the relationship that can sometimes be found between this and their choice of animal protagonists. It recalls the folk wisdom that a person cannot be all bad if he or she loves animals. Some biographers trace an author's choice of animal protagonists to childhood associations, as in Olaf Stapledon's life, or to periods of respite in those lives, associated also with animals, such as the interregnum Karel Čapek experienced. At the same time, critics have often ferreted out an author's weaknesses, both literarily and temperamentally, such as Stapledon's obsessive nature and his infidelities, or Karel Čapek's free experimentation with literary genres within the one work. We look at the lives of these authors in the next chapter.

Chapter 6

Author Biographies: Private Experience and Societal Fears

Contemporary anxieties are often expressed by playing off entertainment against socio-political issues, most of which are mediated through laughter of one sort or another, commonly through satire, parody and irony, and the carnivalesque. But what impelled so many authors to choose a genre based on the traditional beast fable (one of many literary traditions that a writer can draw upon to equal effect)? Questions about author intention, and the relationship between an author and the text, have given rise to the healthy industry of the literary biography. This involves what C. Wright Mills (248) calls the matching up of personal troubles in the individual life with public issues, a blending of biography with history, or what Donald Horne (xiii) calls "individual experience with surprises and oddities beyond stereotypes."

Mikhail Bulgakov and the Writing of The Heart of a Dog *(1925)*

Mikhail Afanasievich Bulgakov (1891–1940) was born the eldest of seven children in the Ukrainian capital of Kiev on May 15, 1891. His father, Afanasy Ivanovich Bulgakov, taught at the Kiev Theological Academy, receiving his Doctorate in Theology after 1906 when Mikhail would have been in Alexandrovsky High School, aged around fifteen. Afanasy's interest in religions influenced his son in later life—in *The Master and Margarita* (1938), for example. Mikhail Bulgakov's biographer, Nadine Natov (2–21), divides his life into several periods: childhood and youth (1891–1921), his "earlier period" in Moscow (1921–1925), his rise as a playwright (1925–1929), his time with the Moscow Art Theatre (1930–1936), and his final years (1936–1940). He died on March 10, 1940, aged forty-nine, of hypertonic nephrosclerosis, a kidney disease that had also claimed his father.

At the age of twenty-five Bulgakov became a physician, graduating from the University of Kiev in 1916. He treated wounded soldiers in city and country hospitals while applying often to the authorities for permission to move to Moscow. Back in Kiev he opened a small practice where he treated venereal diseases. From 1917 to 1919 Bulgakov witnessed various military and political contests over possession of the city. Subsequently he travelled south to the Caucasus with the Third Kazak Regiment as a field physician, hoping to be reunited with his brothers Nikolay and Ivan. But he missed them. Wounded, they had moved on to Rumania. Instead, Mikhail left the military and began work as a journalist in Vladikavkaz with the newspaper *Kavkaz* ("Caucasus"). Bulgakov gave lectures to citizens and soldiers on literature, music, the theater and drama (like Olaf Stapledon in England during the same period). He began to craft plays. He wrote comic sketches for the newspapers and started a novel. Bulgakov also ran afoul of the Department of Arts and, together with a fellow writer, was expelled from that body, the first of many disputes he was to have with the authorities (Natov 3–7).

The photographic portraits of Bulgakov reproduced in Nadine Natov's and A. Colin Wright's biographical studies (two portraits in the latter) show a man in his mid- to late-thirties, with bushy eyebrows and straight dark hair neatly cut, receding a little at the temples. He is a handsome man. There are telltale laugh lines at the corners of his eyes. Stronger natural lines etch either side of his mouth. His gaze appears calm, steady and searching, though we must remember he was asked to pose for the camera. He wears a white shirt and tie, and a conservative jacket that in one photograph appears to be a light color, possibly brown, twill or serge. He is clean-shaven. In one photograph there is a pronounced vertical indentation between the nose and upper lip, highlighted by the lighting. His chin and jaw-line are firm. It is a strong face in alert repose. One can easily imagine it being expressive of passion, laughter, and compassion.

Natov (iv–vi) tells us that Bulgakov's journey to Moscow in 1921 with his first wife of eight years, Tatyana Nikolaevna Lappa, marked the turning point in his career when he began to devote his energies to literature. His *oeuvre* includes *A Country Doctor's Notebook* (1921), which is partly autobiographical; a novel, *The White Guard* (1923–24); a novelette, *The Heart of a Dog* (1925); a collection of five short stories titled *Diaboliad* (1925); a series of plays, beginning with a production of *The Days of the Turbins* (1926); *The Crimson Island* (1927); *A Cabal of Hypocrites,* renamed *Molière* (1931); *Bliss* (1933); *Alexander Pushkin (Last Days)* (1935); and *The Master and*

Margarita (1938). Most of these dates designate the same years in which Bulgakov wrote those works. Many of them were suppressed, their publication or performance delayed or cut short by the authorities: "Bulgakov was doomed to struggle against editors and censors until the end of his days" (Natov 7).

In Natov's scheme (9), *The Heart of a Dog* belongs to the end of Bulgakov's "earlier period," and particularly to 1925 and 1926—years she says, "were the best in Bulgakov's publishing career," with his first short story collection (*Diaboliad*) and parts of *The White Guard* appearing in *Rossiia* ("Russia") magazine, though *The Heart of a Dog* was refused publication. During the three years that led up to the completion of *The Heart of a Dog* in 1925, Bulgakov continued writing light sketches for newspapers and magazines (feuilletons) in Moscow. Sam Lundwall (957–958) ranks Bulgakov as one of three "revolutionaries" of his time, the other two being Evgeny Zamyatin, who wrote the dystopic science fiction novel *We* (1920), and Vladimir Mayakovsky, who wrote a similarly futuristic dystopian novel, *The Bedbug* (1929).

Natov (44) cites from the memoirs of Bulgakov's second wife, Liubov Evgenievna Belozerskaya, whom he married in 1924:

> Bulgakov's second wife has recalled in her memoirs the "beautiful evening" when two "investigators" visited the Bulgakovs, and spent all night looking through books and manuscripts. When they found *Heart of a Dog* and Bulgakov's diaries, the "guests" confiscated them and left immediately. Only two years later, at Maxim Gorky's insistence, was the manuscript returned to the author. The story was first published in 1968, and only in the West.

Wright (59) notes that the work was dedicated to Lyubov Yevgenievna. In fact, we are told (Natov 125) that the novelette came out in 1968, first in *Grani* ("Facets") magazine in Frankfurt, in *Student* magazine in London, and in book form in Paris the next year. Hence there is a gap of forty-three years from the time when it was first written before this work became known in the West. The bibliographical page (reverse of title page) in my copy of the 1989 edition of the Michael Glenny translation notes that *The Heart of a Dog* was first published in Great Britain by Collins and the Harvill Press in 1968, and that the copyright in the English translation lies with the Harvill Press and Harcourt, Brace and World, also for that year. There seems to have been another hiatus, this time of twenty-one years, before the book was re-published. Bulgakov once again is rediscovered, not only by English readers. An Italian language film version came out in 1975, and a Russian language version faithful to the written work from Lenfilm in 1988.

Nazism and the Writing of Karel Čapek's War with the Newts *(1936)*

The Czech author Karel Čapek wrote *War with the Newts* as a *roman feuilleton* in response to the rise of Nazism in neighboring Germany. The satirical, multi-layered novel that resulted, dealing with intelligent amphibians (the newts or salamanders of the title), is a fascinating work because of the mix of styles and thematic inconsistencies it contains. In its parodic-travestying form it contains good examples of the carnivalesque.

The title that Harold Bloom gives to our era, "The Chaotic Age," is apt for Karel Čapek because the general subject of *War with the Newts* is the gradual onset of worldwide chaos as the Newts literally undermine the continents by extending the coastal shallows in order to create living space for themselves. *War with the Newts* was written when Nazi Germany began casting its net eastwards, first to Czechoslovakia, then to Poland, the latter move igniting World War Two. One of the functions that defines canonical works, says Bloom (526–527), is that they refuse to free us from "cultural anxiety." "Rather," he adds, "it confirms our cultural anxieties, yet helps to give them form and coherence." This is a little like my theme that animal tales, with their roots in the tradition of La Fontaine and Classical Greece, at the same time amuse us while posing uncomfortable issues. When he wrote *War with the Newts*, Karel Čapek did both those things: diverting the reader while at the same time confirming many cultural anxieties and, by giving them form and coherence, exhorting his countrymen to engage with them.

War, of course, generates great anxieties at both personal and historical levels. The novel *Valka s Mloky* (1936), in the Ewald Osers translation, is titled *War with the Newts* (1985), and is *The War with the Newts* in Alexander Matuska's "essay" (330). But it is more correctly translated as *War with the Salamanders*, according to Darko Suvin (276). The front covers of three translated editions have *War with the Newts* as the preferred title. Matuska's rendering, one might argue, is a little more accurate because calling the novel *the* war contains the seed of the popular phrase "war to end all wars." This is how the First World War was perceived until the Second World War came along. Čapek's intention in writing about war with the newts (or salamanders) arguably had this sense of final war in mind, because the novel's outcome is almost (but not quite) that of a war to end all wars (until perhaps the humans descend from the mountains). What seems indisputable is that the novel's dominant theme is war, from amicable but exploitative beginnings to the build-up of hostilities, to actual engagement and its results. *War with the Newts* is a parable or allegory of what was going on in the real world as Čapek watched and wrote.

Karel Čapek was born in 1890 and died in 1938, a year before seeing his prophecy of a second world war become a reality. Over the forty-eight years of his life he produced a large volume of work in various genres: journalism, eight works of prose fiction (novels, travel writing, essays, and science fiction), and five plays (Clute 583–589). His *oeuvre* includes plays: *R.U.R.* (1920/1923), *The Insect Play* (1921/1923); novels: *The Makropoulos Secret* (1922/1927), *Adam the Creator* (1927/1929), *Power and Glory* (1937/1938), *The Absolute at Large* (1922/1927), *Krakatit* (1924/1925), *Meteor* (1934/1935), and *War with the Newts* (1936/1937); and short stories: *Money and Other Stories* (1921/1929), *Tales from Two Pockets* (1929/1932), *Fairy Tales* (1932/1933), and *Apocryphal Stories* (1945/1949).

Karel and his brother Josef received an education that encouraged humanitarian values. Their father was a physician who took an active interest in cultural matters, and their mother, who is described by Clute (584) as "an hysteric"—presumably subject to emotional disturbances such as convulsive weeping or laughter (*OED*), a condition which today we might identify as manic-depression or bipolar disorder—clearly passed on her interest in oral folklore and music, in spite of her psychological difficulties. The brothers' maternal grandmother is also a key figure. William Harkins (2–3) reports that "Josef Čapek believes that her fluent folk speech, rich in proverbs, bywords, and rhymed phrases, helped form the 'rich, pithy, flexible and, at the same time, simple language of Karel Čapek.'" This middle-class family provided stability and intellectual enrichment to its sons without losing touch with the common people, and folk art remained important to the brothers as they pursued their careers in later life. Karel Čapek's childhood is described by Harkins (3) as "sunny," although he was often in poor health, having been born prematurely.

From 1919 into the 1920s, which was the early period of his professional life, Karel Čapek often collaborated with his brother Josef (1887–1945). As well as introducing science fiction into "meaningful drama" (Moskowitz 100), the two brothers hold a special place in science fiction history for having introduced the word "Robot" into the English language. In 1923 their play *R.U.R. (Rossum's Universal Robots)* was first published. Sam Moskowitz (102) says that Karel Čapek conceived the idea of writing a play about artificial beings when observing crowds of people from a car (his robots are more akin to androids). It was Josef who used the descriptive term "robot," from the Czech *robititi/robata*, which meant "to work." Brian Ash (63) notes that the Czech word "robot" means "compulsory labor," and that in Polish it refers to a "worker." Darko Suvin (270–271) refers to this period in Karel Čapek's life as his "first SF phase."

After their collaborative work, the brothers followed separate careers. Josef became a Cubist artist of repute, and also wrote short stories and critical essays. Karel Čapek moved from play writing to lyric poetry, short stories and the commencement of novel writing (Moskowitz 109), and by the close of the 1920s his career was established. The next period in Karel Čapek's life, the early 1930s, is characterized as "a gracious period" by Moskowitz (111), "good years" when he wrote short stories and travel letters, as well as

> books on dogs and cats, gardening, fairy tales, newspapers and the theatre. It is Karel Čapek's period of respite. Those volumes were filled with a charm, wit, humanity and sagacity that can only be compared to Mark Twain.

Harkins (14) paints a similar portrait:

> Čapek's favorite subjects were flowers, dogs and cats (which he kept as pets), or simple objects, such as old shoes or a pair of scales. He used his photographs to illustrate one of his books: *Dashenka; or, the Life of a Puppy* [1932].

Čapek's humanitarian character is compared with that of other authors in science fiction and fantasy. Brian Ash (64) observes: "Čapek ranked with Stapledon and Wells" as a humanitarian. Clute (589) infers that authors such as John Brunner, Doris Lessing, and J.G. Ballard might owe something to Čapek for the *roman feuilleton* approach in their own work, while the Polish writer Stanislaw Lem might owe "his human breeziness" to having read Čapek. Clute explains *feuilleton* as the practice by some newspapers to fill the bottom unused section of a page with essays, fiction, poetry and the like. Darko Suvin (282) goes a little further by claiming that Čapek "is the missing link between H.G. Wells and a literature which will be both entertaining (which means popular) and cognitively (which means also formally) avantguardist [sic]." Suvin also finds in Čapek echoes of Wells' *Island of Dr. Moreau*, the *Lost World* (1912) of Arthur Conan Doyle, Aesop's fables, later Wellsian stories, and Anatole France's *Penguin Island.*

Other biographers are over-zealous in finding literary and philosophical influences on Čapek. William Harkins cites a string of philosophers and British authors, and Alexander Matuska (22–24, 59–60, 306–307) exhaustively itemizes Čapek's literary and philosophic roots. This does not appear to acknowledge adequately Čapek's intellect. Certainly some generalizations about Čapek as a writer can be made from inventories such as these. They include a close alignment between philosophy and literature; a strong element of the poetic imagination; a preponderance of nineteenth century English authors in the lists (Čapek was clearly an Anglophile); and links between Čapek's *oeuvre* and that of other writers of speculative fiction, often utopian and dystopian. But we need to look at his work in its own right.

The reader has the sense of a humane and gifted man addressing the social and philosophical issues of his day through his literary arts. Matuska (376) refers to Čapek as "a true and honourable man and writer." There is an animal connection in Čapek's writing, with his own illustrations in a children's book about the life of a pup. As remarked, he was raised on traditional fairy stories, and in later life was greatly attracted to colloquial narrative and used it in his writing. These facts are sufficient to rank him among the twentieth century authors who took the tradition of the animal fable and reworked it to their own purposes.

War with the Newts began as a broad-ranging satire, but something happened in world political events while the episodes were being written which impelled Čapek to change tack, so that the novel ends on a note of pessimism and warning. As Darko Suvin (276) says, "A limit was found beyond which the pseudo-human became clearly evil; that limit is reached when the new creatures ... *grow into an analogy* to the Nazi aggressors" (my emphasis). In other words, in the novel's second half it becomes an allegory on Nazism. It grows as one would expect of a work written in the first instance as a *feuilleton*, and takes its particular direction from a mid-point after Hitler's intentions became painfully clear. John Clute (587) tells us that the novel was first published in the newspaper *Lidove noviny* from 1935 to 1936. It appeared in book form in Čapek's homeland in 1936 and came into English translation a year later.

Hence Čapek wrote *War with the Newts* in the mid–1930s when Europe was experiencing anxieties brought on by the Great Depression and the rise of Fascism. His countrymen looked askance across the border at their uncomfortably close neighbor Germany, which, under Hitler's Nazi regime, was in the business of armament manufacture and clearly getting on a war footing. Čapek saw the conflagration was near at hand, and, in *War with the Newts*, he accurately forecast the onset of war in three years. The novel transparently parodies the arms race between Germany, France and Britain. But it goes further to shoot strongly satirical barbs at many western European cultural mores and practices, mercilessly parodying them one by one. Colonialism, business entrepreneurship, the motion picture industry, scientific taxonomical method, zoos and sideshows, journalism, the scientific report, sexuality, the arms race, evolutionism, gun-boat diplomacy, patriotism, racial superiority, Hitler and Nazism — none of these are spared. Nor are we spared the socio-cultural anxieties they represent.

This variety of targets in Čapek's satire has led at least one critic to claim that in *War with the Newts* Hitler and his Nazi Party were not the only objects of ridicule and dire warning. William Harkins (98–99) reiterates the point that Čapek singled out capitalism for criticism, as well as "national socialism ... and communism," and all other forms of "absolutisms":

> There is nothing in the story of the discovery of the newts or the trade in newt slaves to parallel the formation of the Nazi Party or the rise of Hitler. The novel cannot be read as an allegory on Nazism alone; it is an allegory of contemporary civilization, of which Nazism is a part.

Harkins appears to be having it all ways, for while it is certainly correct to interpret *War with the Newts* as an experiment in mixing genres, and in the process satirizing almost everything under the sun, it seems equally valid to argue that Hitler and the Nazis were notable objects of satire. To claim that the novel is so general an allegory as to take on most absolutisms is to blunt Čapek's warning message. An answer to this question of degree lies in attempting to explain more specifically the sharp thematic shift at the novel's mid-point.

From the mid–1930s, Karel Čapek became increasingly concerned with Nazi expansionism, and in a radio broadcast from Prague on June 22, 1938—two years after finishing *War with the Newts*—he made a plea to deaf ears in Berlin for world tolerance (Moskowitz 112). This is the period that Darko Suvin (275) identifies as Čapek's second science fiction phase. Karel Čapek had built up *War with the Newts* as a premonitory novel from apparently minor beginnings with mischievous "satirical thrusts at human obtuseness," to end with a blunt attack on Hitler and Nazism. At this point, says Clute (588), the newts (salamanders) of the novel "become a kind of 'squirming, intoxicated, frenzied' protofascist '*Collective Male*'" (Clute's emphasis). Sam Moskowitz (112) does not miss the similar imagery of robotic goose-stepping armies entering Prague found in Čapek's earlier 1920s work *R.U.R.*

After the Nazis invaded Czechoslovakia on March 15, 1939, Josef Čapek was incarcerated at Bergen-Belsen concentration camp and died, possibly of typhus, during his repatriation in April 1945 (Suvin 282, Clute 584). But his younger brother predeceased him. Karel Čapek died of pneumonia, "inflammation of the lungs," on Christmas Day 1938. With his death he cheated by three months the Gestapo who came to arrest him (Clute 583). On a romantic note, some commentators suggest that Karel Čapek died "of a broken heart" (Suvin 291–292, Moskowitz 112). He had lived long enough to see the province of his birth handed over to Hitler's Germany by the Munich Accord of 1938, though the subsequent Nazi occupation of Moravia and Bohemia came in February 1939, after his death.

As noted, *War with the Newts* was first published in installments in the daily newspaper *Lidove noviny* from 1935 to 1936, though I am uncertain whether this was on a daily or a weekly basis. Considering the time it took and the divisions of the finished novel into approximately twenty-six chapters, it was very likely a weekly affair. The central part of Book Two, about the Newts' climb up the ladder of civilization, is long and may have been published in several shorter segments. This serialization gives the novel qualities not always shared by works written in other circumstances. Discursiveness and experimentation is allowed or circumscribed by the literary form chosen, plus the physical print space available. Čapek had not only to fill spaces and make a tale flow from one issue to the next, he had also to keep his readers' interest. The novel appears to have taken form in this way, which helps to explain why some parts are lengthy, particularly the central chapter on Newt and human history in Book Two, and why the novel's structure is anecdotal. It gave Čapek plenty of opportunity for experimentation.

But the form in which it is written also creates a central difficulty. William Harkins (96) observes that "there is some unevenness in the quality of different parts of the novel, but this is inevitable in a *roman feuilleton*. More disturbing is the frequent change in point of view." There might be a better understanding of this if we can suggest a solution to my earlier question: what happened in Europe between the years 1935 and 1936 that may have caused Čapek to take such a sharp swing away from his original allegory? The newts are first depicted as harmless humanoids subject to all manner of colonialist exploitation. Was Čapek allegorizing his own Czech countrymen? But later they are depicted as malevolent, thinly disguised Nazi storm troopers headed by a Hitlerian figure, the Chief Salamander, who speaks (220) in a "croaky, angry and heavy voice." Harkins' (20) general observation does not appear sufficient: "By the mid–1930s Čapek had become acutely aware of the threat posed to Czechoslovak independence by Nazi Germany, and more and more he bent his energies to inspire a will to resist in his countrymen."

I think we can infer this turning point more precisely. We are looking at approximately two years, perhaps less, from 1935 to 1936, so we may pinpoint with some confidence events that triggered Čapek's change of direction, remembering that in politics, if a week is a long time, two years is more than ample for dramatic changes.

Subsequent to the collapse of the Austro-Hungarian Monarchy, Czechoslovakia was proclaimed a Republic on November 14, 1918, under its first president, Thomas Garrique Masaryk, who was instrumental in founding the Republic at the end of the First World War (*The International Encyclopedia and Atlas* 194). One of the earliest mentions of Czechoslovakia for 1935 in

Keesing's Contemporary Archives (1647, 1658, 1907) is the report of a Czech protest on May 11 against the forcible removal by a Bavarian gendarme of a German refugee, very probably Jewish, from the Czech side of the border, infringing on Czechoslovakian sovereign rights. The entry that follows, under "Germany," tells us that by this time the Nazis had set up a concentration camp to "acclimatize" those Jewish and political refugees who unwisely chose to return. In the same month, the results of the General Election of May 19, 1935, report that the Sudetendeutsche Party (National Socialist Party), led by Herr Conrad Henlein, is now the second strongest party in Czechoslovak politics.

These two facts — the presence of Nazi concentration camps, and disputes over the southland (Sudetenland) — are probably interrelated. The latter became a contentious issue between Czechoslovakia and Nazi Germany that ultimately afforded Hitler the pretext to invade Czechoslovakia, and Poland soon after. However, another event occurred on December 14, 1935, that would have affected Karel Čapek personally. This was the resignation, due to ill health, of his close friend President Masaryk. Their conversations, taken down by Čapek, provided Masaryk's biographer Paul Selver (7) with invaluable material a few years later.

Nine entries in the Keesing Archives for 1936 may have a direct bearing on Čapek's writing of *War with the Newts*. They raise three major concerns: the gradual placing of Czechoslovakia on a war footing (two items concerning frontier defense); at the same time arguing strongly for peace in the region and/or claiming that war will not come (mentioned thrice); finally, continued diplomatic exchanges over Sudeten-German autonomy (mentioned five times) that reflect a growing level of desperation within the Czechoslovak government.

In 1936 the big political question was of territoriality, autonomy, or *lebensraum* for a minority national group, the German-speaking people of the Sudetenland. Territoriality is a dominant theme in *War with the Newts*. The personal tragedy of Masaryk's poor health and consequent ending of his career in December 1935 may have been the turning point, cementing Čapek's pessimism, but it seems more realistic to see the shift in the role of the newts from a harmless to a threatening entity as having taken place more gradually as 1936 unfolded.

Many of these events were taking place in the year the novel was published, or shortly after publication, but the circumstances leading up to them were bubbling away during the preceding years. The novel certainly becomes more pessimistic from its mid-point to its conclusion, and that seems to be a fair reflection of the contemporaneous developments in European power politics. Two years after 1936, when *War with the Newts* was published in book form, the shameful Munich Pact was made between Great Britain and France, ceding the Sudetenland to Germany. Subsequently, Czechoslovakia fell under German military control in March 1939.

Alexander Matuska (141) proffers a dual argument. In a broad sense, he notes that Čapek confronts what we might call the *zeitgeist* (in Matuska's words, the "spirit of the epoch" or "contact with the epoch") with "contact with infinity" (which, placed by Matuska in italics, are Čapek's own words). Matuska (155) goes on to claim that Čapek in his feuilletons directly addresses nature and concrete social questions, whereas his novels are more abstract: "He knows so much about social questions, about class stratification, about actual social relationships — in his feuilletons. In his novels and dramas, this knowledge becomes more abstract." But *War with the Newts* was written originally in the form of a feuilleton, and many of its episodes are far from abstract. We can argue on this basis that it contains some of the best of both genres, the immediacy of the feuilleton and the broader, abstract (if you like) province of the novel. Čapek was thoroughly conscious of these connections between literature and the real world. He said once that the writer's responsibility was to respond to social troubles, while at the same time, art "must have its own law, its own essential autonomy" (Matuska 140).

Olaf Stapledon's Sirius *(1944)*

Olaf Stapledon is best known in science fiction as the author of works such as *Last and First Men* (1930), *Last Men in London* (1932), and *Star Maker* (1937) that deal on cosmic proportions with human evolution. His *oeuvre*—profiled in Clute and Nicholls (1151–1153) — includes poetry, non-fiction philosophical treatises, and less well constructed speculative fiction: *Latter-Day Psalms* (1914), *A Modern Theory of Ethics* (1929), *Old Man and New World* (1944), *The Flames* (1947), *Worlds of Wonder* (1949), *A Man Divided* (1950, and, posthumously, *The Opening of the Eyes* (1954) and *Nebula Maker* (1976, written around the mid–1930s). But he is almost as well known for two psychological novels — *Odd John* (1935), about a human of far advanced intelligence, and *Sirius* (1944, published when he was fifty-eight), concerning a genetically altered dog with a human mind.

Olaf Stapledon's novel *Sirius* is a story about an intelligent dog, human cruelty and war. It uses the medium of a canine biography, and has depth and roundedness similar to what we find in the better non-fictional biographies. Many critics took the novel seriously, but Stapledon wrote much of it tongue in cheek — for instance, the punning title (Sirius = serious). Satire and the carnivalesque are found in many of its pages.

William Olaf Stapledon was born in 1886 and died in 1950, aged sixty-four. Brian Ash (185) tells us that Stapledon "was a British Doctor of Philosophy, born in Cheshire in 1886, who lectured in philosophy and psychology at Liverpool University, served in a non-combatant ambulance unit during the First World War, and remained until his death in 1950 an active and idealistic socialist."

The bare list of dates and events in the development of Stapledon's *oeuvre* gives little indication of his character. Like all of us, Stapledon was shaped in part by world events and by unique personal experiences. From World War One he espoused socialism, experienced the Great Depression, the rise of Fascism, and the Cold War years after the Second World War. In the personal sphere he had strong ties to the Welsh seacoast and countryside, and close, it is said, obsessive relationships with women: the Australian cousin who became his wife and, in Stapledon's later life, at least two other women.

The port of Liverpool straddles the River Mersey at the northeastern tip of the Wirral Peninsula, which forms an arm of Cheshire. Not far to the south of the peninsula lies Wallasey, the township near which William Olaf Stapledon was born on May 10, 1886. That locality and the region of northern Wales separated by the peninsula and the River Dee to its south, and the university city of Cambridge far to the east, form much of the physical setting of his novel *Sirius.*

By several accounts, Stapledon is a minor author, a loner who sought inspiration in the solitude of his study or the heights of the Welsh countryside. Stapledon scarcely mixed with like-minded peers. He belonged to no writer's set, though he was acquainted with H.G. Wells, and two of his warm friends were J.B.S. Haldane and Haldane's sister Naomi Mitchison, both persons of letters (Mitchison wrote science fiction).

There is a view that Stapledon is not only a minor writer but a mediocre one as well. Yet he is sufficiently important to be the subject of a competent literary biography by Robert Crossley, whose treatment is self-avowedly a labor of love. For this reason Crossley commits the biographer's sin of including much trivia, ironically in keeping with the turgid language that admittedly is present in a lot of Stapledon's work. Robert Philmus (110) takes Crossley to task for dealing mostly with "outward circumstances" and providing only glimpses of Stapledon's "inner mental processes" as he wrote each work, and I think he was a little wearied, too, by Crossley's minutiae:

> I don't mean to insinuate that Stapledon's life must inevitably appear boring.... My point, rather, is that life as a whole is not inherently gripping,

> and not easy to vivify without taking novelistic liberties.... Much of Stapledon's early life — the first 35 years or so of it ... hold very little interest of any kind.

Because I had the temerity to point out Stapledon's stylistic weakness, supported by reference to authorities such as Philmus, the editor of a well-regarded science fiction journal in the UK rejected a version of this chapter section out of hand. The editor admired Stapledon too much to allow criticism.

Elements of Stapledon's early life are important for a better understanding of the novel *Sirius*, and are interesting. I am glad that Crossley saw fit to give space to both Stapledon's childhood in Port Said and his involvement with the ambulance corps in World War One when he wrote so many letters to his future wife. For a minor writer whose books are often out of print, Stapledon receives a good deal of attention from scholars, and his life and work are not without controversy. Stapledon has a complex character behind the quiet exterior. He is also an engaging writer when at his best.

During his time in Egypt as a child, Stapledon's closest companion was a fox terrier named Rip, a canine influence said by him in later years to have been one of his inspirations for the character of Sirius. In his early adult years, Stapledon taught English Literature and Industrial History as a special lecturer connected with the University of Liverpool from 1912 to 1915. His contacts with working class people were formative experiences for his socialism, but the onset of the First World War interrupted this so far conventional career. David Mandelbaum (181) says that an individual's life passage is marked by important transitions he calls "turnings" (not turning points): "when the person takes on a new set of roles, enters into fresh relations with a new set of people, and acquires a new self-conception." The First World War was one of intense transition for Stapledon, both as a participant in that world event and in his personal life. For philosophical reasons Stapledon joined the Ambulance Unit operated by the Society of Friends (Quakers) and did tours of duty in France from 1915 to 1919 as a non-combatant.

By then he was twenty-nine. The personal change he experienced in this period was an intense correspondence with his Australian cousin Agnes Zena Miller. Stapledon is said to have fallen in love with her from their first meeting more than ten years earlier, when he was seventeen years old and Agnes nine, during Agnes' family's visit to England. Back in Australia, Agnes became a frequently bemused confidant to Olaf, receiving a great many letters from him during his ambulance service. Crossley (xiv) remarks:

> The more than two million words they exchanged amount to something very like a vast epistolary novel, full of crisis and introspection and meticu-

> lous attention to their own microcosm and to the world at large.... He felt [his love affair with Agnes] as the central psychological experience of his life, and it nourished his creative work.

Agnes reciprocated with letters that frequently contained much common sense. It was here too that Stapledon experienced another canine influence. He writes in one of his letters: "I should like to be Ginger, the Aberdeen terrier [the convoy's mascot], to feel the world as it is to him, and to relish all the thrilling smells that constitute his daily experience, and to explore the limits of his doggy mind" [Crossley 261].

The relationship between Olaf and Agnes grew more intense, perhaps in response to the hostility of Agnes' father, and they married soon after Stapledon's demobilization in 1919. Olaf Stapledon was by now thirty years old, and Agnes, eight years his junior, about twenty-two. They had a son and a daughter in the next few years. Stapledon again took up lecturing in psychology and philosophy in Liverpool, and in 1925 he gained his Ph.D. from Liverpool University.

The period between his marriage at thirty years and his first major science fiction work, *Last and First Men* (1930), at forty-four was, in Crossley's (156) words, a "crucial decade" during which "a desire for academic respectability was at war with irrepressible questioning of habitual modes and avenues of thought." During the early period of writing, Stapledon continued to earn a modest living teaching at the Workers Educational Association. He studied philosophy and wrote indifferent poetry. His Doctorate thesis was "no less opaque, prolix, and dull than most theses in any field" (Crossley 165). But when he wrote *Last and First Men* it was a breakthrough that foreshadowed dominant themes in his later writing. As Sam Moskowitz (263–264) says, "Stapledon deals in depth with every phase of human development, covering not only the scientific but also the social, cultural, sexual, psychological, and philosophical changes." This is what Stapledon does too in *Sirius*.

A photographic study of Stapledon reveals a short, slightly built but wiry man whose gnomish aspect is accentuated by a lined face and scrawny neck (Crossley 321, 377). He was physically active throughout his life, an inveterate mountain climber, hiker and swimmer, though this did not spare him the "massive thrombosis" that ended his days, attributed in part to "a lifelong weakness for cream, butter, eggs, and tobacco" (Crossley 396). A variety of formal and informal photographic portraiture reflects several aspects of Stapledon's character: energy, intensity and obsession, a sense of wonder, a sense of humor, an unassuming nature, and a degree of loneliness.

Stapledon's writing belongs to the period of science fiction that James Gunn (6–7) describes as post–First World War disillusionment, in contrast to the high optimism that characterized the late nineteenth/early twentieth centuries:

> In the first forty years of the twentieth century science fiction began to ask questions that had never before been asked: Will humanity progress or regress? Will its social forms change? Will humanity survive?

In his philosophical monographs and science fiction novels, Olaf Stapledon single-mindedly tries to make sense of a psychological condition common to his era, the mind divided against itself and in conflict with the Other, which we might describe as a search for the ambiguous mind or soul. It was one of his obsessions throughout life. But he is one among many thoughtful observers who put their misgivings into print, and who, like Karel Čapek, chose elements from the ancient animal myths and fables better to make his points. One theme is the search "to define humanity and to describe its prospects," a quest which led naturally to the working out of moral propositions. Lois and Stephen Rose (56–57) list several topics that identify some of the twentieth century's chief anxieties:

> aspects of man's evolution and destination, the centrality of improved communication, the ambiguity inherent in his intelligence and scientific knowledge, the problems of the will, and the need for some transcendent standard to counter the impulse toward totalitarian elitism.

The animal allegory theme in Olaf Stapledon's novel *Sirius* is one direction in which he bent his search; others are the superman theme and cosmic speculation, present also in *Sirius*, though in muted form.

Sirius is a unique literary work in the animal-human genre because it attempts within a biographical mode to describe in a lot of detail not only the feelings its protagonist experiences, but also that person's individuation from birth to death — in the fictional biography of a large dog. Until Stapledon wrote this fantasy, the closest we have to that approach is the nineteenth century classic to which Stapledon owes much, Mary Shelley's *Frankenstein or the Modern Prometheus*, in which Victor Frankenstein's Creature experiences a self-educational period so that he/it becomes a thinking and judging individual. Very few authors have attempted to imbue their works with such detail in the intelligent animal fantasy genre, certainly not before Stapledon's time. But he did gain inspiration from a number of literary forebears aside from Mary Shelley:

> The book Stapledon finally called *Sirius* (after rejecting the allegorical title "The Beast and Beauty") belongs among the modern achievements in the fantastic and satirical tradition. *Gulliver*-like, it skewers the vices of "normal" human society as experienced by a cultural and physical outsider.

> Investigating the ethos of the scientific imagination and the psychology of an artificial being, it aligns itself with *Frankenstein*. With Wells's *Island of Dr. Moreau* and David Garnett's *Lady Into Fox*, it redraws the boundary lines between the animal and the human. One of Olaf's favorite contemporary fantasists, Karel Čapek, used animal fables in *War with the Newts* and *The Insect Play* for biting political criticism [Crossley 292].

Stapledon himself calls the work a fantasy, but it is evident that in spirit it is close to the allegorical animal fable. Just as H.G. Wells is named as an influence on Karel Čapek, so too is Čapek reported by Crossley to have been among Stapledon's favored authors. The fairytale origins of Stapledon's decision to write *Sirius* are revealed by the discarded alternative title, "The Beast and Beauty." Social commentary in *Sirius* prompts Crossley to compare it with Swift's *Gulliver's Travels* (1726). The exploration of the divide between humankind and animals in Wells and Garnett (*Lady into Fox*, 1922) implies that the gulf may not be as wide as popularly supposed. Stapledon, in his turn, is said to have influenced many writers of speculative fiction, many of whom were his contemporaries.

Clifford Simak, City *(1952)*

Clifford Simak's novel *City* (1952) is a collection of nine short stories chronicling the degeneration and ultimate disappearance of the human species. Genetically uplifted "Dogs" have inherited the earth, along with their robot companions/helpers. The stories are linked by the observations and speculations of latter-day canine investigators, and while some of the tales are uneven, others have frequently found their way into anthologies. There is an overall unity when they are brought together into a single novelistic frame. This novel is by many accounts Simak's masterpiece.

Clifford Simak writes with a light touch about human relationships with a variety of non-human sentient beings: "first contact" stories about extraterrestrial aliens, butlers who are robots, and Dogs whose intellectual qualities are enhanced through human intervention. Sometimes a quirky amity, if not companionship, characterizes these contacts. There is occasional violence, but that is usually muted to little more than a suggestion of force. Instances of xenocide are rare. Simak does not have the same harsh element in his work as Cordwainer Smith in some of his stories, or the emphasis on war that is ever-present in Karel Čapek's *War with the Newts*.

But there is a darker side nonetheless: fears of human violence and nonhuman malevolence, a sense of entropy, and an element of despair. Clifford

Simak is one of the few science fiction writers of his era to have contemplated the gradual extinction of the human species *and carried it out* in his fiction. He does not do this through natural or self-imposed apocalypse (in *City*, at any rate), but through entropy and metamorphosis. In the "cozy catastrophe" genre that was given a head start by H.G. Wells' *The War of the Worlds* and was continued in Karel Čapek's *War with the Newts* and John Wyndham's novels, the humans "come back from the mountains" and reassert their presence, although in Čapek's novel the ending is ambiguous. But Simak's tales are directed towards different ends, towards a physical, intellectual and affective state of being substantially "better" than the human condition. As Brian Ash (179) says, in *City* the Dogs and other animals of the backwoods inherit the earth. It is left to them by the majority of humankind, who realize fulfillment in a totally different, non-human, form while a small number in *fin de siècle* exhaustion opt for indefinite suspended animation in the Sleep. It is salutary that two of his best works, *City* and "The Big Front Yard," are animal tales.

Clifford Donald Simak was born in Milville, Wisconsin, on August 3, 1904, and died on Monday, April 25, 1988, at the age of eighty-four (Weinkauf 494, Dickson 145). His first published science fiction story, "The Cubes of Ganymede," came out when he was twenty-seven, in 1931, after which his output became prolific. His best works are listed by Roald Tweet (513) as *City* (1952), which won the British International Fantasy Award; a novelette titled "The Big Front Yard" (1959); another novel, *Way Station* (1964), which, as well as "Front Yard," won the Hugo Award; and a short story, "The Grotto of the Dancing Deer" (1980), which won a Nebula Award. Tweet observes that "Simak's work has been remarkably consistent in quality," and he is a major figure in science fiction. But many of his other works are *not* consistent in quality.

In his obituary for Clifford Simak, Michael Bishop (141) sums up Simak's personal qualities in terms of "the palpable decency of the man behind the plots and prose." L. Sprague de Camp and Catherine Crook de Camp (77) quote Simak on his hobbies:

> Clifford Simak stated: "My interests include chess, stamp collecting, and rose growing, but I'm a mediocre chess player, have virtually given up stamps through lack of time, have decided you can't grow roses in the villainous Minnesota climate. Most of my spare time is spent at reading."

Gordon Dickson (142) remembers Simak as possessing "unusual strength and endurance," which is what one might expect of a man who had "grown up dirt-poor in the backwoods." Simak loved the outdoors. Unfortunately, as in

Olaf Stapledon's case, physical strength cannot shield one from serious health problems, and he was to die peacefully from leukemia after a long illness in 1988 (Dickson 145).

Simak might be compared with his British contemporary Olaf Stapledon, to whom some commentators attribute "niceness" with overtones of mysticism, mixed, paradoxically, with agnosticism (Philmus 107). Tweet (513) observes that Simak "has added to science fiction a singular, gentle — often mystical — voice that is recognizably his." Sam Moskovitz (86–97) dubs him a saintly heretic.

Like many other authors in this genre, such as Stapledon, H.G. Wells, Mikhail Bulgakov and Karel Čapek, Clifford Simak began as a journalist, in which occupation he remained for most of his life. Brian Ash (179) tells us that Simak did his studies in journalism at the University of Wisconsin, and Tweet (514) provides a brief history of the career that followed: 1929 with the *Iron River Reporter* in Michigan; 1932–1938 trouble-shooting for the McGiffin Newspaper Company of Kansas; 1939 working for the *Minneapolis Star*, where he became "chief of the copy desk," from which he rose in 1949 to news editor specializing in science news. Thereafter, from 1959, he became the writer of a weekly science column. He wrote science fiction as a sideline from 1931, but gave up journalism to work exclusively in that genre from about 1976 onwards. Simak retired in 1977, aged seventy-two, and died eleven years later (Dickson 144).

The period during which Simak wrote *City* and "The Big Front Yard" coincides with the development of his interest in writing science news stories for the *Minneapolis Star*, when he was aged between forty-eight and fifty-five years and clearly at the peak of both his careers in journalism and science fiction writing. Simak himself describes the "City" stories as a "watershed" in the development of his craft. Tweet (514–515) describes his style as that of a reporter: plain, direct, muted, but also poetic. Clifford Simak's work, however, went beyond his journalism. Gordon Dickson (143–144) notes his appreciation of nineteenth century essayists, such as John Stuart Mill, and Ruskin's "love for the order and control of the finely tuned essay," to which Simak brought the sensitivity ("emotion") of a writer of fiction. As Pringle (19) says:

> One of the most notable features of Simak's style is that a high proportion of his best narratives is taken up with such musing introspection. In such passages his prose is usually at its best, as it is generally when he is writing about old men and matters bucolic.

Simak frequently imparts information through dialogue between two or more speakers, for example between Richard Grant and Nathaniel in "Census," between Ebenezer and Shadow his robot in "Hobbies," or between Lupus and Bruin, Fatso the squirrel, and Lupus and Peter in "Aesop" (see Chapter 11). He characteristically divides his stories into episodes, called by Jill Milling (167) "rapid montage" (especially in "Aesop"), a film technique that is evidently his "use of artistic, literary, and architectural devices and images to inform the narrative structure and 'confuse' the separate scenes of earlier tales."

When Gordon Dickson (141) knew Simak as a fellow member of the Minneapolis Fantasy Society around 1940, Simak was comfortably off with his wife Agnes (nicknamed Kay) and a "black, curly-haired, friendly fellow called Squanchfoot," the dog on whom Simak modeled his canine protagonists in the "City" series and other tales. The common human foible of attributing literary intellection to animals enters in, for Squanchfoot the dog was, by Dickson's account, a fully-fledged member of the club who occasionally wrote pieces for local fanzines. But most editions of *City* carry the dedication "In Memory of Scootie, Who Was Nathaniel," and not Squanchfoot. Sam Moskowitz (94) affirms that "Simak's own pet scottie" was in mind when the stories were brought together in the 1952 collection. The character of Ebenezer, for example, is described in *City* as a "little black dog" (167), and as early as the December 1944 edition of *Astounding Science Fiction* (2), an unnamed graphic artist drew a sturdy Scottish Terrier for the header illustration of "Census." So while inspiration may have come from one particular canine, it is safe to assume that many dogs entered Simak's life. David Pringle (22) remarks:

> Simak's fondness for animals goes hand in hand with his love for the countryside. Animals of all sorts play a very large part in his stories — most notably dogs. There are the intelligent talking dogs in *City*, the friendly alien that takes the form of a dog in *They Walked Like Men*, Hiram Taine's mutt Towser in "The Big Front Yard."

In *They Walked Like Men* (1962/1975), Clifford Simak elicits the terror of the Other, as in a cozy catastrophe, on his protagonist's meeting for a second time with the Dog, when he discovers it can speak (telepathically) — only a few pages later to return to his trademark of gentle quirky humor in the matter-of-fact reaction of Stirling the scientist:

> I reached the car and swung open the door next to the wheel. Something stirred in the opposite side of the seat, and it said to me: "I am glad to see you back. I was worrying about how you were getting on."
>
> I froze in unbelieving terror.
>
> For the thing sitting in the seat, the thing that had spoken to me, was the happy, shaggy dog I'd met for the second time that very evening on the sidewalk in front of my apartment house! [Simak 77–78] ...
>
> "You have to get that dog out of here," he said. "There are no dogs allowed."

> "This isn't any dog," I told him. "I don't know what he calls himself, or where he may have come from, but he is an alien."
> Stirling turned all the way around, interested. He squinted at the Dog.
> "An alien," he said, not too surprised. "You mean someone from the stars?"
> "That," said the Dog, "is exactly what he means" [Simak 85–86].

Countryside is important, too, as a formative influence in Simak's life. The Wisconsin backwoods where he lived and through which he journeyed as a boy left a lasting mark on his psyche. As Simak says (in Walker 64):

> The impression made upon me by that country has stayed with me throughout my life. It is a picturesque country, with great high hills, deep wooded ravines, a couple of good size rivers, the Wisconsin and the Mississippi, and any number of smaller streams running down almost every hollow or valley. As a boy and young man I hunted the hills and fished the valleys and was never happier than when tramping through the woods. There was a peace and an understanding there I have found nowhere else.

Moskowitz (87) reports Simak as saying, "We hunted and fished, we ran coons at night, we had a long string of noble squirrel and coon dogs."

Not surprisingly then, the physical settings in Simak's fiction are often drawn from such localities, for which reason he is stereotyped as a pastoral writer. The pastoral is a genre that harks back to ancient Greek poetry. Its affect includes nostalgia, the valuing of rural peace and simplicity in contrast to an urban life of complication, an idealized rural environment, and often a belief in a past golden age. Its characters are frequently shepherds (the Latin *pastor* = shepherd), often found sitting or reclining in meditation or in friendly converse and song, their closeness to nature lending them a different perspective on life (Abrams 127–128).

In a chapter on "The Functions of the Pastoral," Andrew Ettin (54–55) analyzes Mary Shelley's less well-known speculative work *The Last Man* (1826) along similar lines, finding that "the pastoral world can be [both] disdained and envied." I suggest this is because there is a juxtaposition of affects. On the one hand there is personal freedom, "companionship with nature," innocence, and "friendship among equals"; on the other hand, when living in a pastoral setting one experiences loneliness, a reluctance to take action, and a distancing from human companionship. The pastoral, says Ettin (56),

> is not a simple phenomenon but rather a group of images and attitudes which may appear in any combination.... The pastoral might be contrasted with cities or wild nature or the bustle of business or the turmoils of unrefined passion or the sophistication of high society. Pastoral attitudes might be rejected at last, or embraced. The pastoral ideal might be already lost, or waiting for us in the future.

In his summation of pastoral influences in Evelyn Waugh's *Brideshead Revisited* (1945), Ettin (57) identifies the growth of friendship and affection between protagonists ("an artificial and playful society of almost carefree young men whose main interests are literature, entertainment, and comradeship"); a sheltered environment; the political background of the Second World War; nostalgia; and "a keen feeling of loss."

Most of these elements are found in Clifford Simak's *City*, where, in place of Waugh's university men, we have carefree young Dogs provided for by robots and living in the sheltered environment of an old country house. Unknown to them, there was a human diaspora from the cities to the countryside in the pre–Dog era. That exodus had two additional manifestations. In the first, humans metamorphosed through newly discovered technology to take on a non-human but incomparably advanced form living on the pastoral landscapes of the planet Jupiter. The second diaspora was via space travel "to the stars," a favorite phrase of Simak's. By the era of the Dog-robot civilization, there are no humans on Earth aside from those lying in suspended animation within a domed and sealed city in Geneva.

The time scale that Simak visualizes is uncertain, but it has to be immense. The human family dynasty that through its inventions founded the Dog-robot symbiosis extended roughly from 1920 to the year 2117 (47), so long past that the Dogs, from their perspective, ask whether humans ever existed. This speculation on the part of latter-day Dogs raking through their oral literature for clues hundreds and perhaps thousands of years past, in which they often call the humans Websters, epitomizes the sense of loss and canine speculation about whether there had once been a golden age.

Cordwainer Smith: "The Dead Lady of Clown Town" (1964)

In a novella titled "The Dead Lady of Clown Town," written under his pseudonym of Cordwainer Smith, Paul Linebarger experiments with stylistic forms taken from his wide knowledge of traditional Medieval and Eastern (Chinese, Indian, Japanese) oral narratives. In particular he explores themes of love and rebellion within a carnivalesque atmosphere. Linebarger's work appears heavily influenced by his Pentagon background and by ambiguous relationships with women in his personal life.

Paul Myron Anthony Linebarger was born in 1913 in Milwaukee, Wisconsin, and died in 1966, aged fifty-three. The photograph in John Clute's illustrated encyclopaedia shows a smiling and bespectacled man, slightly built, somewhat frail in appearance. Linebarger suffered ill-health all his life. By Gary Wolfe's (506) dating we see that Linebarger was a university academic, not a journalist, and that his career has two major patterns — university lecturing and work with the United States military intelligence service. Clute (146) describes Linebarger's tales as "autumnal, wry, poetic, sentimental, and grave." Like Karel Čapek, Paul Linebarger's writing is anti-war with dystopian touches. Brian Ash (182) describes Linebarger's style as almost "full-blown fantasy ... lyrical, bitter-sweet, elusive, surrealistic, violent," elements also shared with Čapek. Perhaps Linebarger's mature writing was a personal antidote to his experiences with the military mind. Clute points out that when he wrote one of his earliest stories, "Scanners Live in Vain" (1950), under his science fiction pseudonym of Cordwainer Smith, Linebarger was already aged thirty-seven.

These qualities introduce an element of ambiguity into Linebarger's works, as well as in his life. He wrote a seminal text on psychological warfare and is described by Baird Searles (160) as a propagandist, remarking that it is "a fact that may startle readers impressed with the tenderness of his writing." If we follow Wolfe's summaries, we find that Linebarger attended a string of universities where he studied and taught, including his chief employer and *alma mater* Johns Hopkins University (1935, and from 1937 to 1946). His academic work appears to have become interwoven with the Pentagon in the last twenty years of his life, from 1942 to 1966. But this double strand of the academy and military intelligence is present, too, when we fill in the wide gap left by Wolfe in his chronology — that is, the first twenty-seven years of Linebarger's life, covering his childhood and young adult experiences from 1913 to 1930 when he entered the University of Nanking. We must rely on other sources for information on these important years.

During his childhood Paul Linebarger lived with his parents in parts of China and Japan, and also in Europe. He became fluent in Japanese, Chinese and, later, French and German. His father was a judge who became a legal adviser to the new Chinese Republic, from which connection the man who was to become founder of the Chinese Republic, Sun Yat Sen, became Paul's godfather (Morgan 519). There is a story told by John Pierce (xii) that the Chinese characters on a tie Linebarger wore, Lin Bah Loh, meaning "Forest of Incandescent Bliss," designated a name given him by Sun Yat Sen. It is an appropriate prefiguring of Linebarger's use of exotic names in many of his tales, and, indirectly, is one of his first pseudonyms.

Another anecdote about Linebarger also hinges on a play on words. During his time in Korea, from 1950 to 1952, according to Wolfe's chronology, Linebarger persuaded Chinese troops to surrender by pointing out to them in a leaflet that there was no dishonor in reciting the words love, duty, humanity and virtue, which in that sequence sound like·the English words "I surrender" (Pierce xvi). These were perhaps *ai, ser, ren, tao*, but I am guessing. This principle is addressed by Linebarger himself (235) when discussing the use of surrender leaflets in his book *Psychological Warfare*, where he says: "Whole series of leaflets will teach the enemy soldier how to say, 'I surrender,' in the language of the propagandist." (Surrender leaflets continue in use as part of the United States' psychological warfare program in the Middle East.) Pierce says: "He considered this act to be the single most worthwhile thing he had done in his life." Love, duty and humanity are recurrent virtues in Linebarger's fiction.

Throughout his life Linebarger experienced poor health, both physical and psychological. According to Alan Elms (270–271), this included a "brilliant" but isolated and stressful childhood, "a fear of blindness" following the loss of an eye at the age of six, and accompanying "anxiety about being ugly." The importance of sight recurs in the visual imagery of his writing—for example, in "Scanners Live in Vain," though Elms (275) hastens to add that (loss of) sight was not so much a central theme as a device providing "a powerful set of metaphors and defensive reverse-metaphors" to deal with other anxieties. In "The Game of Rat and Dragon," the imagery of bright light is intrinsic to the tale, a *leitmotif* important for the destruction of malevolent entities in deep space.

It was mostly later in life that Paul Linebarger began writing science fiction and fantasy. His output in that genre dates from 1963 to 1979 (posthumous), with a scattering of short stories published in the 1950s (the exception being "War No. 81-Q" in 1928). But prior to the 1950s he not only wrote a series of psychological and political works under his own name, he also wrote two mainstream novels—*Ria* (1947) and *Carola* (1948)—under the pseudonym Felix C. Forrest (*vide* "Forest of Incandescent Bliss"). In those novels he explores a woman's psychology and addresses themes that today are identified as feminist in spirit. His interest in the feminine principle was longstanding. While there are insights into his uneasy relationships with women, there is no all-revealing correspondence available to fuel one's gossip like that of Stapledon to Agnes.

Linebarger was a very private man who may have enjoyed presenting a mysterious identity to readers. For example, the pseudonyms he was fond of inventing were not chosen haphazardly. He liked word play and literary allusions, and was strongly influenced by Chinese and Japanese storytelling techniques. The echo of Linebarger's Chinese name Lin Bah Loh is present in the pseudonym "Felix C. Forrest" that he chose for the novels *Ria* and *Carola*.

There is a bracketing out here: the use of his own name, "P.M.A. Linebarger," for the academic political histories and psychological manuals; the choice of "Felix C. Forrest" for his psychological novels; and the coining of the pseudonym "Cordwainer Smith" for his fantasy/science fiction.

When Alan Elms (280) writes about the psychologically therapeutic "process" in Linebarger's work, he acknowledges the great importance to Linebarger of literary craftsmanship: "He was too consciously a creative artist to have been writing for self-curative purposes alone." Hence it seems appropriate that Paul Linebarger should settle upon that particular pseudonym, "Cordwainer Smith." A cordwainer is a worker in leather, more specifically a shoemaker or cobbler, and literally a "worker in cordwain"—leather from goat- or horse-hide manufactured in the Spanish town of Cordova, from which the name is derived (*OED*). The alias might be regarded as a metaphor for the great care he took in crafting his fiction, as well as a pun on the idea of cobbling stories together, or hammering them out in the way of a metal worker.

Someone Who Likes Animals

Speculative writing of science fiction and fantasy, so well exemplified by writers such as Mikhail Bulgakov, Karel Čapek, Olaf Stapledon, Clifford Simak and Paul Linebarger, is essentially different from its precursors of earlier centuries. Nineteenth century anxieties did not include warfare of unprecedented magnitude. The two centuries have their parallels, *vide* the Napoleonic Wars in the nineteenth century, but the era of the nineteenth century saw also a flowering of industrialization, the rise of science as an ideology, and the new Darwinian theories of human evolution that challenged accepted religious dogmas. Speculative fiction about apes and animal metamorphoses to human form thrived around the end of that century. These were substantially different social forces from those of the Medieval era, with its established religious institutions that helped produce Rabelais, as well as to re-establish the animal fable from its earlier Classical roots. But by the time *The Heart of a Dog*, *War with the Newts*, *Sirius*, *City* and "The Dead Lady of Clown Town" were written, just before the mid-point of the twentieth century, the social ferment of the nineteenth century was over and the new ideas of that era had become generally accepted.

I think the societal preoccupations of the late nineteenth century had something to do with the splitting of the animal fantasy lineage inherited from the Middle Ages into the two branches we know today as children's animal literature (for example, *The Wind in the Willows*, with its pastoral setting) and science fiction and fantasy (such as *The Island of Doctor Moreau*, with its obvious debt to Mary Shelley). In each of these eras can be found echoes from the preceding eras. At the beginning of the twenty-first century we are still animated by animal fantasies because they have become part of our literary tradition. We build upon them, and, because of the fears and troubles characteristic of our time, there is always material available for satire, parody and the carnivalesque.

Tales founded on the tradition of the animal fable hold their appeal and are successful in harnessing a reader's imagination because there is something intrinsic to the animal fable itself, revealed by the works and philosophies so far discussed. The repertoire of narrative techniques reflects that tradition. We respond to animal characters, lovely and sometimes unlovely. We respond to tales that amuse and make us feel good, but we also engage in serious issues. The stories we read are not always comforting. A "good" tale, one that is effective and emotionally satisfying, must always demand something of the reader. It must impart unease as well as good humor, defamiliarization as well as the carnivalesque. Like the animal stories they write, the authors whose lives I have summarized are without exception men of good humor and goodwill, but they have dark sides as well. They are strong characters. They had to be to write the fiction they did. Satire and allegory, and the carnivalesque, are heady, demanding and dangerous forms.

There is some artificiality in singling out one work from an author's *oeuvre*, relating it to the short period during which it is written, and implicitly ignoring other works by that author and the life in full. Perhaps we get away with this because the time frame over which a single work is produced, and the social and personal anxieties of its period, can be measured against what biographers say about the life experiences preceding it. An author's formative years need to be taken into account if we are to understand satisfactorily their more polished output.

The major works on animal-human themes I chose are without exception mature products written after years of apprenticeship in the world of letters and against a background of momentous world events. They display various facets of the carnivalesque. On the one hand they draw upon laughter in different ways (especially satire, parody, irony and defamiliarization resulting from them) as a corrective to accepted views about reality, to use Shklovsky's terms. Complementarily, they address discomfiting issues and crises, as in Barthes' terms. One of Karel Čapek's biographers, William Harkins (38), describes as "burlesque" the "paradox of savage violence stemming from 'loftier feelings'" in Čapek's utopian fantasies, as well as owing something to Dostoevski and Nietzsche, referring particularly to the theme of dehumanization in the face of modern technology in *R.U.R.* and *War with the Newts*. Paul Linebarger is noted to have acquired inspiration from reading Huizinga's *Homo Ludens* (1949)—perhaps because of the "playing" with language that Arthur Burns (9) says is so evident in Linebarger's work. But many other factors influenced Linebarger.

We now look at those works in greater detail.

Chapter 7

Satire and the Carnivalesque 1: *The Heart of a Dog*

Long after his death, Mikhail Bulgakov (1891–1940) is rediscovered as one of Russia's great twentieth century authors. The English-language publication of his animal-satirical novel *The Heart of a Dog* came out in 1968, more than thirty years after its brief publication in the Soviet Union. Throughout his life as journalist, essayist, playwright and novelist, Bulgakov's work came continually under the jaundiced eyes of the authorities, who did their best to keep him in obscurity. He was often subject to censorship and his manuscripts confiscated, his plays cancelled. When they did make it to the stage his plays performed to packed houses until the end of their run. But, more often than not, after their first performance they were banned by the censors.

This is not surprising. Bulgakov's writings are savagely satirical, and in his time they lampooned Russia's post–Revolution political order remorselessly. The blurb to the Michael Glenny translation of Bulgakov's novelette *The Heart of a Dog* compares it with his final novel, *The Master and Margarita*, for their combination of "outrageously grotesque ideas with a narrative of deadpan naturalism." This I call "high satire," not so much because it shares with high comedy in touching our intellectual funny-bone as for its "boisterous display of nonsense," high spirits, and "sense of fun." *The Heart of a Dog* also has low comedy with carnivalesque themes — hence its appeal — but many of the questions it raises make for high comedy (see Abrams 29). It is, as the blurb goes, "a fierce parable of the Russian Revolution." But there is amiability behind it too. Unlike the grand tragedies that befall the protagonists of *Frankenstein*, *Sirius*, *Animal Farm* and *Wish*, Mikhail Bulgakov's *The Heart of a Dog* has a felicitous ending.

A Nice Little Dog

Two doctors change a dog into a human who becomes so disruptive that they reverse the procedure. This simple premise is the vehicle for satirizing Russia's totalitarian Communist regime and its effects on the lives of ordinary people. The seriousness of Bulgakov's message is mediated by broad comic farce. Doctor Philip Philipovich Preobrazhensky is experimenting with human rejuvenation techniques. He and his junior colleague, Ivan Arnoldovich Bormenthal, take in Sharik, a street dog, and exchange certain of the animal's glands for those of a recently deceased petty criminal. The experiment works but with an unexpected outcome. Instead of being rejuvenated, the dog becomes human both intellectually and in outward form. Sharik can read and converse. However, the two doctors have created a "Frankenstein monster" from this dog, for when Sharik is metamorphosed into human form he becomes an uncouth lout with a combination of human vices and the original street-wise character of the canine. He wears loud clothes, smokes, drinks vodka to excess, plays the balalaika badly, has appalling table manners, is destructive (especially towards cats), and behaves lewdly towards the two women servants, Zina and Darya, in Preobrazhensky's household.

These circumstances allow for broad comic uproar, beginning with the destruction of a stuffed owl in the doctor's study and progressing from that moment to one misdemeanor after another. The chasing of a cat and consequent flooding of the bathroom is a high point of slapstick in both novelette and film. However, Sharik, by now renamed Sharikov, for a time enters the human world. He is made Sub-Department Controller of the City Cleansing Department and spends his days strangling cats. This and his increasingly wild behavior lead to a final confrontation between Sharikov and the two doctors. They reverse the operation, and Sharikov becomes a dog again, living with thankfulness in the comfort of the hearth, having no memory of his escapades as a human. The novelette's original title was "A Dog's Happiness" (Wright 59).

Bulgakov uses a variety of narrative forms, called by Natov (44) "different narrative 'voices,'" including the dog's inner monologues. Wright (62) observes that there is a "nice balance between dog and man," an "unusual narrative technique, with the dog taking over the narration for much, but not all, of the story." One distinguishes also an omniscient third-person author's voice and brisk dialogue between characters, and there is a form that appears to belong to what Natov describes as *skaz*: "a stylized story utilizing the vocabulary and mentality of an ordinary worker" (Natov 38). See also David Lodge, *The Art of Fiction* (18): "vocabulary and syntax characteristic of colloquial speech ... this is an illusion, the product of much calculated effort and painstaking rewriting by the 'real' author." The language is colorful in the sense that it is highly colloquial, with witty and rapid dialogue, often argumentative and interlarded with comparatively mild scatology by present-day standards. Sam Lundwall (956, 958) notes that *The Heart of a Dog* is a "complex novel which nevertheless utilizes some of pulp fiction's techniques ... the entertaining magazine story technique." Bulgakov's experience as a playwright evidently informs his novelistic dialogue.

The Heart of a Dog has fantastic elements in keeping with science fiction, but they are interwoven with realism. The present-day expression "magic realism" seems appropriate. It is, in Natov's (44) words, a "multilevel narrative" in which "humour, biting social satire, bold political statements, grotesque images and situations exist alongside the mysterious world of scientific discovery." Wright says that the choice of a dog as self-aware protagonist has precedents in Russian literature [just as in English letters], and cites such works as Gogol's "Diary of a Madman" and Chekhov's "Kashtanka," but adds (60):

> What sets Bulgakov's story apart from these is the complete lack of sentimentality or idealization, his portrayal of the dog's limitations once he becomes a man, and the credibility of events that follow. This is the way a dog-become-man would behave, one feels. Clearly, he would have more in common with the lowest elements of society than with the civilized Preobrazhensky. Thus the story becomes a study in conflicting human attitudes which may be described as those of the intellectual as opposed to the uneducated masses.

I take issue with some of this, especially Wright's two points that imply the dog-made-human is an unsympathetic character and that there is a complete lack of sentimentality. But Bulgakov's clever mix of realism with the fantastic is indeed the driving force behind the writing.

Bulgakov uses variant speech patterns to help dramatize the differences between the social classes of bourgeois and proletariat while mapping the dog's metamorphosis from Sharik to Sharikov. The canine has rudimentary spelling skills. In an inventive stroke, Bulgakov depicts him spelling the shop sign "delicatessen" backwards and from an angle, as a dog from his lower height might perceive the letters. (See my note in chapter 2 on the use of this device by Tolkien, Dickens and Chesterton.) As Sharik's vocabulary grows it becomes a vehicle for Bulgakov's satire on Russian public life. His first utterances (62) are "liquor," "taxi," "full up," "evening paper," "and every known Russian swear-word." They reflect folk aspects of post–Revolution life, such as searching the papers for work, standing in long queues, and drowning one's poverty in drink. Sharik is a proletarian dog from the start, his thoughts those of a street-wise homeless person; and towards the end, as Sharikov, his speech remains ungrammatical: "Me and her's getting married. She's our typist" (117).

The science of Bulgakov's tale owes much to Mary Shelley, the Faust myth, and H.G. Wells. Natov (42) observes:

> H.G. Wells's science fiction was popular at the time, but there was genuine scientific research on problems of biology and medicine, on many obscure phenomena of living organisms, going on then. Both Bulgakov's uncles were physicians, as he was himself, which made the scientific ambience familiar to him. The image of the old magician-scholar Doctor Faustus, bent over his books and retorts, appealed to Bulgakov as a symbol of man's striving after knowledge. But this also entails the danger of unleashing forces that can escape the scholar's control and cause evil.

Frankenstein, in the tradition of English letters, and Faust in the Germanic dramatic tradition, both attempted, and were tempted by, the forbidden. Victor Frankenstein meddled with creation. Faust sold his soul to the devil for magical powers in one early tradition. But the Faust of Goethe's plays, in his struggle with the devil, epitomizes the conflict between the cynics who deny "goodness in the search for goodness, and the dedication of those who make the search" (Wynne-Davies 515).

Wells is directly mentioned in the 1988 Lenfilm adaptation of *The Heart of a Dog*, though not in the novelette, when plaudits are being passed around on the experiment's apparent success: "Congratulations colleague. This makes Wells pale into oblivion." The novelette has a characteristic Wellsian beginning insofar as the pituitary gland experiments are described only in sufficient detail to satisfy the reader, though the actual mechanics, the details, are not given.

Wells' 1896 vivisectionist tale *The Island of Doctor Moreau* comes to mind, but Mary Shelley's *Frankenstein* evidently inspired Bulgakov. There are distinct Frankensteinian touches in the scientific descriptions: horror, unnatural creation, misdirected experiment, and remorse. Some of these touches read almost like stage directions, a reflection of Bulgakov's skills in live theater:

> ... the horrors that lined the room.... Human brains floated in a disgustingly acrid, murky liquid in glass jars. On his forearms, bared to the elbow, the great man wore red rubber gloves as his blunt, slippery fingers delved into the convoluted grey matter. Now and again he would pick up a small glistening knife and calmly slice off a spongey yellow chunk of brain [47–48].

Later (77) Preobrazhensky tells Sharikov: "You are what you might call a ... an unnatural phenomenon, an artifact..." [ellipses his]. This sense of the unnatural is again evoked towards the end (123–124) when the operation is reversed:

> Silence filled the flat, flooding into every corner. Twilight crept in, dank and sinister and gloomy. Afterwards the neighbours across the courtyard said that every light burned that evening in the windows of Preobrazhensky's consulting-room and that they even saw the professor's white skullcap.

As in Victor Frankenstein's experience, the experiment (63–66) has an unwelcome outcome, with the two doctors realizing that the transplantation of the pituitary makes the non-human subject human both in appearance and self-awareness, rather than being a means of effecting rejuvenation. Moreover, the fact that the human donor was a petty criminal, a thief, and the recipient a dog means that the resultant being has an unfortunate mix of canine impulses, such as antipathy towards cats, exaggerated by the human cunning of the thief. At one point (69) Bormenthal asks, "Does it matter whose pituitary it is?" As the story (110–111) unfolds, it becomes all too clear that it does matter. Preobrazhensky replies:

> The pituitary is not suspended in a vaccuum. It is, after all, grafted on to a canine brain, you must allow time for it to take root. Sharikov now only shows traces of canine behaviour and you must remember this — chasing after cats is the *least* objectionable thing he does! The whole horror of the situation is that he now has a *human* heart, not a dog's heart. And about the rottenest heart in all creation!

This thematic declamation is a correction to Bormenthal's comment (110): "Just think of the way he goes for cats. He's a man with the heart of a dog." Frankensteinian remorse (108)—"This, doctor, is what happens when a researcher, instead of keeping in step with nature, tries to force the pace and lift the veil"— also contains, I think, an argument not specifically raised in Mary Shelley's novel, a reflection of Bulgakov's common sense (107–108):

> And now comes the crucial question — what for? So that one fine day a nice little dog could be transformed into a specimen of so-called humanity so revolting that he makes one's hair stand on end.... I, Philip Preobrazhensky, would perform the most difficult feat of my whole career by transplanting Spinoza's, or anyone else's pituitary and turning a dog into a highly intelligent being. But what in heaven's name for? That's the point. Will you kindly tell me why one has to manufacture artificial Spinozas when some peasant woman may produce a real one any day of the week? ... Mankind, doctor, takes care of that. Every year evolution ruthlessly casts aside the mass of dross and creates a dozen men of genius who become an ornament to the whole world ... what is its practical value?

This view is reflected in the film versions. It is remarkably topical considering the present-day debate over human cloning. Moreover, as in *Franken-*

stein, the doctor's creature talks back, questions the decisions and adds to the creator's sense of remorse (74): "'I didn't ask you to do the operation, did I?'—the man barked indignantly—'A nice business—you get an animal, slice his head open and now you're sick of him ... I bet I could sue you if I wanted to.'"

Comic Riot

Horror and remorse in *The Heart of a Dog*, however, are mediated between two other elements: comic, often farcical, situations and social comment. *The Heart of a Dog* is constructed from contrasts and balances between the serious and the facetious, and has an underlying good humor and sensibility. First of these contrasts is the character of the dog Sharik (translated as Fido in a film version) in his canine form and in human form, as Sharikov (Fidov). Initially (64) this newly created being "gives the impression of a short, ill-knit human male," but very soon the unsettling strangeness that could reinforce horror is replaced by vivid, evocative comic visual images (71):

> Leaning against the doorpost there stood, legs crossed, a short man of unpleasant appearance. His hair grew in clumps of bristles like a stubble field and on his face was a meadow of unshaven fluff. His brow was strikingly low.... His jacket, torn under the left armpit [through scratching for fleas], was covered with bits of straw, his checked trousers had a hole in the right knee and the left leg was stained with violet paint. Round the man's neck was a poisonously bright blue tie with a gilt tiepin. The colour of the tie was so garish that whenever Philip Philipovich covered his tired eyes ... he saw a flaming torch with a blue halo. As soon as he opened them he was blinded again, dazzled by a pair of patent-leather boots with white spats.

The description is so striking as to leave those after-images in the mind of the reader. They are faithfully reproduced in the film, though something is lost in black and white.

The sense of the absurd reaches high points of action, as when Sharikov embarks on a cat extermination program for the local Moscow council, or in the slapstick of the bathroom incident (82): "Two large fragments crashed into the kitchen followed by a tabby cat of gigantic proportions with a face like a policeman and a blue bow round its neck." Surreal scenes like this place *The Heart of a Dog* among the 1920s forerunners of the literature of the absurd, along with the works of Joyce and Kafka (cf. *Metamorphosis* in Abrams 1).

Satire and parody come into their own with Bulgakov's treatment of social issues, principally his poking fun at post–Revolution authorities through the conflict between Preobrazhensky and the housing committee, headed by Shvonder, and their demand that the doctor give up most of the rooms of his flat. It is a classic Marxist opposition between bourgeois and proletariat, and there are some very funny interchanges between the protagonists. This conflict becomes a medium for satirizing bureaucracies, including their obsessive requirements for documents, covering most areas of life: building management, residence, army reserve card, trade union papers, employment office (from the film). Hence, Sharikov says (75): "I can't manage without papers. After all you know damn well that people who don't have any papers aren't allowed to exist nowadays." Lundwall (957–958) likens Bulgakov's combination of humor and bitterness to Swift's parodic and sometimes picaresque novel *Gulliver's Travels*, and calls Sharikov a Dickensian character.

There is a more politically sensitive aspect — the question of freedom and the use of coercion by authorities to keep people in line. Lundwall (957) and Wright (61) independently paint a grim picture of Sharikov's character, associating the ironic situation of a former dog exterminating his own kind with Stalin's secret police (though it is cats and not fellow dogs who receive Sharikov's unwelcome attentions). I would have thought such a connection was closer to home (Preobrazhensky's in particular) in the guise of Shvonder and the rest of the house committee, with their secret meetings, reports to officialdom, and generally envious demeanor. Beneath what Wright (61–62) calls his "undisguised hatred of the revolutionary society" and contempt for the proletariat, Preobrazhensky has relatively enlightened views. He says (20) to Zina, his housemaid, on the question of controlling Sharikov: "People who think you can use terror are quite wrong. No, terror's useless, whatever its colour — white, red or even brown!" The "colors" must refer to the different politico-military groups in Bulgakov's first-hand experience — the Bolsheviks, the white army, etc. Again (44) the doctor tells Zina: "No one is to be beaten.... Animals and people can only be influenced by persuasion." When Dr Bormenthal (39–40) exclaims that the place where they live is going to ruin, Preobrazhensky corrects him:

> "You must first of all refrain ... from using that word [ruin].... It's a mirage, a vapour, a fiction," Philip Philipovich spread out his short fingers, producing a double shadow like two skulls on the tablecloth.... Ruin, therefore, is not caused by lavatories but it's something that starts in people's heads.

The same might be said of the idea of freedom, which Bulgakov probably had in mind. It must reflect Bulgakov's sensibility (110): "Never do anything criminal, no matter for what reason. Keep your hands clean all your life." Or perhaps it is a reflection of the doctor's bourgeois origins.

The Search for Identity

The Heart of a Dog can be interpreted as a search for personal and social identity, and a means of questioning the differences between human and animal. The importance of naming in establishing one's identity comes through satirically when the dog-man renames himself Poligraph Poligraphovich Sharikov, the first two names taken from the doctor's consulting-room calendar for the name day of the fourth of March. The third is his family name, Sharik/Fido. It is, as we know, a transliteration in colloquial English applied to dogs from a Latin word meaning "faithful."

I noted earlier that one prerequisite for tales of this genre is for the writer in some manner to endow the animal character with hands or a substitute for hands, such as a helpful robot, and with speech or a speech substitute, such as telepathy. Bulgakov overcomes these difficulties by causing his animal character to metamorphose into human form. Speech is one of the signatures of human sentience (I hesitate to say "intelligence"), though not perhaps for being human, which point Preobrazhensky (126) challenges at the end: "'Because he talked?' asked Philip Philipovich. 'That doesn't mean he was a man.'" But we must remember this is a ploy to mislead the authorities enquiring about the disappearance of Sharikov, now returning to his original canine state after the corrective operation.

Another factor frequently found in the intelligent animal genre, and present in *The Heart of a Dog*, is that of eavesdropping: the unsettling thought that our companion animals are observing us with human and therefore judgmental and enquiring minds. As Doctor Bormenthal (67) writes in his scientific report:

> All the words which he used initially were the language of the streets which he had picked up and stored in his brain. Now as I walk along the streets I look at every dog I meet with secret horror. God knows what is lurking in their minds.

The characterization of Doctor Preobrazhensky and the dog in his two forms as Sharik (Fido) and Sharikov (Fidov), and the relationship between them, reveal Bulgakov's humanity, though tinged also with hard irony. As mentioned already, Sharik is a proletarian dog, his mind honed to a sharp edge by deprivation and a continual struggle for survival in the Moscow streets, and as a result there is subterfuge in his nature. The first chapter (10–11) shifts back and forth between the doctor's coaxing and the dog's ironic responses:

> What can I do? I'm too young to die yet and despair's a sin. There's nothing for it, I shall have to lick his hand.... He's christened me Sharik too. Call me what you like. For this [a sausage] you can do anything you like to me.

Part of Bulgakov's irony lies in the doctor's perception of Sharik as a nice dog, while the dog is cynically availing himself of the food being offered. But a human castaway on the Moscow streets would harbor similar thoughts.

Sharik is like a member of the proletariat, though it is a class the dog hates (especially cooks and porters, who chase dogs), along with the bourgeois (of whom the doctor is a representative). Sharik is a true outcast, belonging to neither class because he is a dog. But he becomes proletarian when he is made human. At first (30) in their relationship the dog takes alternative sides for or against Preobrazhensky: "'What a man,' thought the dog with delight, 'he's just like me. Any minute now and he'll bite them.'" Or he plans (50) a typically canine revenge when locked in the bathroom: "Right. This means the end of your galoshes tomorrow..." There are other touches of class-consciousness, as when Sharik (46, 50–51) discovers the social value of wearing a collar:

> A collar's just like a briefcase, the dog smiled to himself.... I'm a gentleman's dog now, an intelligent being, I've tasted better things. Anyhow, what is freedom? Vapour, mirage, fiction ... democratic rubbish...

There are other notes of canine humor, as in the description of Zina chloroforming Sharik (52): "Then a lake suddenly materialized in the middle of the consulting-room floor. On it was a boat, rowed by a crew of extraordinary pink dogs." This belongs more to light fantasy, a touch of humor that reminds one of Fritz Leiber's short tales of Gummitch the kitten, or of canine good nature, as when Ebenezer in Clifford Simak's novel *City* (146) thinks, "*It had been such a nice rabbit!*" Similarly, Sharik admires Preobrazhensky. He uses Faustian imagery (42): "Now I know what he is. He's the wizard, the magician, the sorcerer out of those dog's fairy tales..." There is scope, too, for canine vanity (43):

> I am handsome. Perhaps I'm really a dog prince, living incognito, mused the dog as he watched the shaggy, coffee-coloured dog with the smug expression strolling about in the mirrored distance. I wouldn't be surprised if my grandmother didn't have an affair with a labrador...

These thoughts are re-echoed in the final passages that give traditional closure to the novel (128):

> I've been very, very lucky, he thought sleepily. Incredibly lucky. I'm really settled in this flat. Though I'm not so sure now about my pedigree. Not a drop of labrador blood. She was just a tart, my old grandmother, God rest her soul. Certainly they cut my head around a bit, but who cares. None of my business, really.

In the film the ancestral sire is a Newfoundland. The closure of the Lenfilm version compares faithfully with that of the novel:

> I'm so lucky. So lucky. Incredibly lucky. It looks as if I'll stay in this flat. I'm definitely not blue-blooded. There's probably some Newfoundland in me. My grandmother was a slut. May she rest in peace. I wonder why they cut up my head? Never mind. Time heals all wounds. It's best not to think about it.

In keeping with the novelette's riotous good humor, the central protagonists on the whole are characterized sympathetically and even-handedly, contrary to what I noted earlier about Wright's (60) view. This saves *The Heart of a Dog* from becoming a true Frankensteinian tragedy while still treating serious themes. Even Shvonder and the rest of the housing committee are objects of fun, though with an underlay of the sinister. They carry side arms, for example. So does Sharikov at the end, which is the final straw that impels Bormenthal to overpower him and Preobrazhensky to reverse the operation. True, Preobrazhensky at certain points in the novel has a Victor Frankensteinian/Faustian aspect: "...looking like a greying Faust in the green-tinged lamplight...," (98) to mix metaphors. However, he is agreeable to us as an irascible critic of petty bureaucracy at loggerheads with the housing committee who act as his foil.

This allegory is true to the broad spectrum of science fiction in that the ideas are more important than character development, and it can be argued that most, if not all, of the characters are one-dimensional. For example, Bormenthal the younger man seems prone to violence in his loyalty to the older man. But aside from his loyalty and quick temper we know very little about him. This is what Wright (62–63) finds:

> The main fault of the story is in the lack of characterization.... Bulgakov tends at this time [his early period] to give us stereotypes, with little development. Indeed, in the case of Preobrazhensky, he seems to use leitmotifs rather than character as a means of identification: constant snatches of song....

I do not agree entirely with Wright here, because behind the political comment and farcical scenes which are important for the working of the novel there are hints of a deeper characterization as far as the two protagonists, Doctor Preobrazhensky and Sharik/Sharikov, are concerned. The intertextual references, Wright's leitmotifs, can be interpreted differently as serving to give greater depth to Preobrazhensky's upper middle class (bourgeois) character. There are references to Isadora Duncan, Preobrazhensky's attendance at the opera *Aida*, his singing of snatches of song (19)—"From Granada to Seville...," and the last line of the novella (128): "...to the banks of the sacred Nile..." (from *Aida*). There are, too, the thematic references to Faust, a Germanic counterpart to Mary Shelley's Victor Frankenstein, and parody, as well, in quotations from shop front signs, official letters, and scientific reports. We remember that this is a novella of 128 pages. Within that frame Bulgakov writes a relatively dense, economic text with skillful and highly satiric use of dialogue.

The doctor's primary foil is Sharik/Sharikov. Their uneasy relationship is marked by a strong element of affection as much as exasperation. Early in the tale (46) the authorial narrator says, "The dog Sharik possessed some secret which enabled him to win people's hearts." Later (57), when Preobrazhensky fears that the experiment will fail and end with Sharik's death, he exclaims: "I feel sorry for the dog, Bormenthal. He was naughty but I couldn't help liking him." Just as Victor Frankenstein was reminded of his responsibilities towards his creation, so too Preobrazhensky (77) learns from Sharikov: "Much more of this, and he'll start teaching me how to behave, and he'll be right. I must control myself."

It is a short step from here to the development of a father-son bond between them. Several times Sharikov addresses Preobrazhensky as though he were his father, as, for example, during the farcical cat-chasing scene (85): "'Will you beat me, Dad' came Sharikov's tearful voice from the bathroom." As Sharikov's creator, fatherhood is, in a sense, the doctor's role. There is an additional element of pathos when Sharikov (102) attempts to shave himself:

> Taking advantage of Bormenthal's brief absence he got hold of the doctor's razor and cut his cheek-bone so badly that Philip Philipovich and Doctor Bormenthal had to bandage the cut with much wailing and weeping on Sharikov's part.

It is not stated explicitly, but the obvious explanation is that Sharikov, who still retains many of the traits of his former canine self, wants to become more human, very like the action of Peter Goldsworthy's (217) genetically altered female gorilla Wish in the 1995 novel of that name. Bulgakov is also drawing upon the example of a pubescent son copying his father's shaving technique.

Another element that arouses a sympathetic response in the reader is their shared loneliness. Sharik, both as dog and man, is an outsider. Preobrazhensky (105) is lonely because of his age: "You must forgive an old man's testiness. The fact is I'm really so lonely...," and also because he is rebelling against oppressive authority. Sharik needs a father. Preobrazhensky needs a son. The ambiguities in Bulgakov's characterization of Sharik the dog and Sharikov the man similarly may have distracted the critic Lundwall (958), who depicts him as "half-man, half-beast on the surface, but all upstart inside, a ruthless human animal fighting for survival, a latter-day Uriah Heep." I cannot agree, but Lundwall is right when he observes that the small novel presents a moral problem that merits careful consideration.

A reader's personal predispositions will almost always influence whether *The Heart of a Dog* is perceived as a satiric romp with a darker side, or as an even more cynical judgment of human nature where the main characters have few redeeming features. I favor the first view, chiefly because I cannot see the characters of either dog or doctor in a totally unfavorable light. But the moral and political difficulties Lundwall identifies are certainly present.

Preobrazhensky is a Victor Frankenstein figure, pursuing his medical researches into longevity and rejuvenation, and is not above actions condemned by the anti-vivisectionists. He is also a comfortably-off bourgeois with strong antipathies towards post–Revolutionary life in general and the proletariat in particular. Wright (61) says: "Sharikov immediately identifies himself with the proletariat, and a natural assumption is that in the author's view the proletariat is not very much different." On the other hand, the reader has to admire the doctor's stand against the authorities and his loyalty to those close to him: the cook, the housekeeper, the porter, Bormenthal and, in the last analysis, to Sharik/Sharikov as a quasi-son. His confessed loneliness evokes reader sympathy. Preobrazhensky is not immune from the finer feelings.

Sharikov the dog-man similarly has a mixed nature: at war with his animal instincts (compare Stapledon's Sirius), cynical as both dog and human towards those who can harm or assist him, and in a sense wanting to please, taking the adolescent role in his relationship with Preobrazhensky. His human actions, such as carousing at public houses, are recognizable proletarian traits and causes of conflict and comic riot. But other actions, such as bringing two drinking companions home and persuading the impoverished typist to marry him (through bullying, bragging, and the offer of a better life), bespeak his loneliness. In the opening scene of the Russian film, as in the book, the typist befriends the injured dog, calling him Sharik for the first time. Later it is the dog in human form who offers a better life to the girl, one of Bulgakov's means of imparting to the reader a sense of balance. Sharikov is not entirely honest in this, and his sexual interests are obvious, but he craves human company just as clearly, and this excites reader sympathy.

One answer to the Faustian moral problem about the search for goodness lies in the relationship between Preobrazhensky and the dog-turned-human. It may be as simple as saying that no person (dog or human) is entirely good, no one entirely bad. This is Bulgakov's realism and compassion speaking to us over the years. The contrast between the comfortable living of the middle classes and the daily struggles of working class people is a constant backdrop to Preobrazhensky's relationship with Sharikov. The third, mediating character of Shvonder is required here. For the opposition between classes is symbolized by conflict between our two principal characters, and is metaphorically a Faustian tug of war between Preobrazhensky and Shvonder for Sharikov's soul. The outcome is that the doctor triumphs, and the original balance, the status quo, reasserted. The authorities are confounded, the dog Sharik is happy in his new home, Preobrazensky is at ease, perhaps less lonely. The novella's closure has a traditional storytelling form. The two themes of comic riot and Frankensteinian and Faustian warning are united in the doctor's light-hearted snatches of song from *Aida* while he continues, literally, to probe the mysteries of the human brain. *The Heart of a Dog* might fairly be taken as representing an early example of Mikhail Bulgakov's search for good in the human condition.

Chapter 8

Satire and the Carnivalesque 2: *War with the Newts*

Carnival begins in high spirits but it can close in anxiety, sadness and disillusion. It sets up fantasies whereby commoners become kings for a day, and, because of the imbalance implicit in this state of affairs, there is nearly always a sobering movement back to harsh realities. *Sirius* ends in violence and the death of the eponymous hero. *City* closes on a note of loss with the disappearance of the humans so that the Dogs might inherit the world and there will be no more killing. "The Dead Lady of Clown Town" ends with slaughter and the immolation of "Dog Joan," but, as in *City*, there is a projection to a better future. There is a similarly hopeful outcome in *The Whistler*, as the dog returns to the sea. In *War with the Newts*, the transition from the depiction of the newts as sympathetic victims of human cruelty to thinly disguised Nazi storm-troopers further exemplify the sobering returns and often violent endings.

In its treatment of ridiculous situations, its parodic and satiric moments, its inversions and comedic overlays, serious intentions lie at the core of *War with the Newts*. It has been noted that within the two years of the novel's serialization as a *roman feuilleton* the political anxieties created by Nazi expansion at the cost of Czechoslovakian security brought about a shift in Čapek's original light-hearted, parodic and satiric treatment, overturning the element of play with a note of warning and pessimism.

Čapek's novel is a response to cultural anxieties, fears and preoccupations found in other science fiction and fantasy works written in the era of the Second World War. Olaf Stapledon reflects the English response to World War Two in *Sirius*, and Clifford Simak in *City* suggests a world no longer peopled by humans, reflecting more generally anxieties about post-war technologies. Like Simak's *City*, *War with the Newts* has a vision of alienation. In its heavy use of pastiche it evokes debilitation or exhaustion, dehumanization, and acceptance. As in Cordwainer Smith's (Paul Linebarger's) "The Dead Lady of Clown Town," *War with the Newts* has touches of horror. However, an overwhelming impression is that this novel stands in a class of its own; just as in Darko Suvin's scheme, it is midway between Wells' era and the era of popular or avant-garde science fiction, or between the reaction of the mid–1920s against authoritarian dictatorial regimes and the outbreak of war. The brothers Čapek were contemporaries of the equally talented and versatile Mikhail Bulgakov, whose plays and novels satirized the Stalinist régime in Russia.

Carnival and the carnivalesque are among a variety of ways by which we might identify this cluster of interrelated themes in Karel Čapek's novel. To make an apparently tangential comparison, Les Murray's (319) review of the convict Francis MacNamara's "A Convict's Tour to Hell" (c. 1839) at one point would have been just as appropriate if the terms carnival or carnivalesque were substituted for the word "genre":

> The Tour [read Carnival] is a dream-vision belonging, if we are of a classifying turn of mind, to the genre of the world-turned-upside-down, the Saturnalian and Medieval trope of Misrule, in which absurdities are revealed and the world refreshed by inversion.... There are compressed ironies ... it suspends the vision as a potent thought-balloon above the everyday ... it mocks the potential fury of the ridiculed penal authorities with a patently insincere repudiation of itself ... it undercuts seriousness and assists the lightness of tone necessary if so biting a wish-fulfilment is not to bog down in its own anger. And after all that, how sad it is too.

Murray might easily have been rehearsing Bakhtin's concepts. Saturnalia, festive and unrestrained merrymaking (Macquarie Dictionary), in Bakhtin's terms (11–12), is part of

> the complex nature of carnival laughter. It is, first of all, a festive laughter.... Carnival laughter is the laughter of the people. Second, it is universal in scope; it is directed at all and everyone, including the carnival's participants. The entire world is seen in its droll aspect, in its gay relativity. Third, this laughter is ambivalent: it is gay, triumphant, and at the same time mocking, deriding. It asserts and denies, it buries and revives.

Karel Čapek's work is grounded in folklore—*vide* his three essays on the fairy tale—and throughout *War with the Newts* he depicts a wide range of human types, from the common people to scientists, business people and politicians. The last three categories, it might be said, are prone to misrule. All of these stock characters (thinly sketched) become prey to Čapek's satiric moods. Satire and the carnivalesque (the overturning of images and expectations) are directed at every character, including the newts, giving the novel universality, for some of us may see ourselves in the characterizations. But because the subject matter concerns the gradual destruction of human land-based industrial civilization by the underwater industrialization of the Newts, the novel's humor is ambivalent.

The plot in its simplest terms follows the discovery of a colony of newts (salamanders) on a tropical isle by an adventurer, Captain van Toch, and the subsequent exploitation of the Newts as slave labor by a business entrepreneur. It is a matching of "the exotic adventure tale," as Darko Suvin notes (276–278), with the rise of world capitalism. The Newts, who are highly intelligent, walk upright, and are the size of small children (with little hands), become objects of scientific and popular curiosity among the humans. As time goes by, however, the Newts develop an underwater industrial civilization, and in the process begin to undermine the world's continents to create more room for themselves upon the shallow edges of the oceans. This means a gradual depletion of land resources for the humans, over which a war breaks out between humans and Newts. The Newts are led by a Hitlerian figure, and by the dystopic close of the novel the humans are defeated and forced to retreat to the high mountains.

The novel shifts and changes continually, depicting a world turned upside down. The discovery of the Newts on their island as another intelligent species suggests to business interests that they are a potential source of cheap labor, their role as slave labor hailed as introducing change and renewal to human industrial life. The prevailing ideology of capitalist enterprise receives Čapek's satiric treatment. Some commentators see the novel chiefly as an attack on world capitalism, but, as several others point out, it goes further than that to include different ideologies, fascist mentality in particular. In Bakhtin's terms (11):

> It demanded ever staging, playful, indefined forms. All the symbols of the carnival idiom are filled with this pathos of change and renewal, with the sense of the gay relativity of prevailing truths and authorities. We find here a characteristic logic, the peculiar logic of the "inside out" (*a l'envers*), of the "turnabout."

Accepted truth and authority are overturned, for example, when the Newts pose a threat to human enterprise after themselves becoming industrialized. Another example is the effect of Newt civilization upon human popular culture. That chapter is loaded with fashions of popular culture. The common people adopt Newt speech idioms, Newt dancing, and so on, as in Robert Merle's *The Day of the Dolphin*. Gradually the humans are colonized by the Newts, a reversal of the colonization and exploitation of the Newts in earlier chapters.

The Oddity of the Novel

The serialization of *War with the Newts* imbues the novel with qualities not always shared by works written in other circumstances. Discursiveness and experimentation is at one moment allowed or at another moment circumscribed by the literary form chosen, plus the physical space available in a publication like a newspaper. Čapek had not only to fill spaces and make a tale flow from one issue to the next, he had also to hold his readers' interest. The novel grew over two years, published in installments from 1935 to 1936 (Clute 587), which helps to explain why some parts are lengthy, particularly the central chapter on Newt and human history in Book Two, and why the novel overall is anecdotal in structure.

The first clue for the reader that different literary styles are being mixed lies in the words of Captain Van Toch (101), who was among the first humans to discover a sentient Newt colony in the tropic seas:

> I have too much taste to mix different styles. Captain van Toch's style was, let us say, the style of the adventure novel. It was the style of Jack London, of Joseph Conrad and others. The old, exotic, colonial, almost heroic style.

The racy dialogue ("*skaz*") and the tropical and colonial setting of the first chapter prompted me in a first reading to question whether the overt racism was intended for a later contrast between humans and Newts. It soon became evident that Čapek was indeed parodying different forms of discourse. He gives the game away in the last chapter of Book One, "The Salamander Syndicate," when, as a prelude to establishing a more aggressive capitalist exploitation of Newt labor, the entrepreneur G.H. Bondy distances himself from the now deceased Captain's "style" in his address to the general meeting of shareholders.

Clute (587) explains this conscious mix of literary styles in terms of Čapek's long experience as a journalist. He describes Čapek's mood as one of exuberance and pyrotechnics:

> Čapek in *War with the Newts* uses all the resources available to him to construct a *roman feuilleton* with no holds barred: photographs, footnotes, scholarly lectures, typographical shenanigans, indecipherable inscriptions, parodies of popular storytelling modes (from adventure tales a la Robert Louis Stevenson to Hollywood romances), facsimiles of spectacular newspaper accounts.

The novel is a relatively early example of intertextuality and metafiction (see Lodge 98–103, 206–210).

It has already been noted that a lack of in-depth character studies is a generally accepted weakness in the science fiction genre, which tends to focus instead on ideas and themes. *War with the Newts* contains a great many walk-on characters who have their day and are seen no more: ship's crew members, film producers, scientists presenting technical papers at conferences, or company shareholders. But there are a number of key characters important for the novel's dramatic tension and development, and there are a lot of ideas.

When they are discovered, the humanoid Newts are already endowed with intelligent thought roughly equivalent to that of humankind. Čapek (17) imbues their discovery with suspense worthy of the adventure genre he is parodying:

> They're about as tall as a child of ten, sir, and nearly black. They swim in the water and on the sea-bed they walk upright ... but they sway their bodies the while ... they've got hands too, just like human beings; no, they've got no claws, more like the hands of children ... and a big head, a round head ... they didn't say anything; they only seemed to smack their lips.

The depiction of the alien and non-human as childlike is one of two standard motifs in twentieth century science fiction, and comes from the frequency of such depictions in human race relations in the nineteenth and twentieth centuries. The prevalence of these folk myths nearly always invites satire and parody. It is reassuring if aliens appear smaller and weaker than us. Contrast the child-sized creatures of *Close Encounters of the Third Kind* (1977) or the toddler-sized *E.T.—The Extra-Terrestrial* (1982) as comfortable if not comforting first contacts with alien species against the less comfortable "Bug-Eyed Monsters" in the *Alien* (1979, 1986, 1992) or *Predator* series (1987, 1990, 2004). The two types are, of course, two different facets (among many others) of the human.

Donald Lawler (2424) lists seven principal characters in *War with the Newts*. There is Captain van Toch, who discovers a small Newt colony on a Pacific island and implements a strategy to sow other islands with the species for breeding purposes, his goal to make a fortune in pearls by training the animals to dive for them. J.H. Bondy, the entrepreneur, initially supports van Toch financially, and after the captain's death institutes more far-reaching exploitation of the Newts' labor as a captive market for human manufactures. Andrew Scheuchzer is the first Newt to be attributed with speech and intelligence. There is Bondy's chief factotum, Mr. Povondra. Captain James Lindley is the first human killed in an early skirmish, leading up to the war between Newts and humans. An English pamphleteer named X plays a prophetic role. The Chief Salamander is a Newt who rises to power and with whom the humans are forced to negotiate.

Captain van Toch, Bondy, the Newt Andrew Scheuchzer, Captain Lindley, X, and the Chief Salamander play their parts and are gone. The one character who, as a commentator, is a connecting link throughout the novel is Mr. Povondra, a point noted by Lawler and Suvin (279). This is aside from the authorial narrator who talks to himself in the final chapter about alternative endings.

Povondra is a sort of Victor Frankenstein figure, not because he is the creator/finder of the Newts — a distinction that belongs to Captain van Toch — but because he blames himself as the cause of the chain of events that leads to the literal crumbling of human society, as the Newts' subterranean engineering projects undermine the continents. Povondra, in his role of manservant, is persuaded to give Captain van Toch an audience with Bondy. The tragic remorse of an otherwise minor character is highly satirical, for Čapek's moral force extends beyond the actions of any one individual. The cause of the war with the Newts is human capitalistic greed and cruelty, not the action of a manservant doing his duty. The novel is a version of the old storyline of slaves or serfs who ultimately turn upon their human masters, as in the Čapek brothers' earlier play *Rossum's Universal Robots*. The individual is important, but human society at large is Čapek's target. Bondy and the Chief Salamander, who, like Hitler, had supporters and collaborators, were able to tap into the darker side of human and Newt nature.

John Clute (588) points out how *War with the Newts*, with its "narrative strangeness," makes a transition from a mood of almost lighthearted satire and parody, in which we feel sympathy for the Newts, to an increasingly impersonal tone presaging a darker outcome. Captain van Toch's romantic image of the newts (37), with whom he has a paternalistic relationship (like Preobrazhensky in *The Heart of a Dog*), is one of the best examples of the first of these moods:

> "They're very good and clever, those tapa-boys; when you tell them something they pay attention, just like a dog listening to his master. And most of all those childish little hands — you know, old boy, I'm an old chap with no family of my own.... An old man, you know, is rather lonely," the captain muttered, trying to control his emotion. "Very sweet those lizards are, dammit all. If only those sharks didn't hunt them so! When I began to throw stones at them, at the sharks I mean, *they began to throw stones too*, those tapa-boys."

This sympathetic albeit satirical narrative tone is then used to depict the reluctance on the part of human scientists to attribute intelligence and self-awareness to the Newts in the face of all supporting evidence. The science relies not upon surgical techniques, as in the Victor Frankenstein story, or in the creation of the super-dog Sirius or the "humanimals" of "The Dead Lady of Clown Town," but on social experimentation building on existing evolutionary potentialities. From this prejudiced beginning follows a resolute refusal to recognize Newt intelligence. Spoken language is the strongest indicator, but we are headed off by a vaguely speculated "elan" (spirit) as explanatory factor. Čapek (75–76) is satirizing the tendency in science towards mystification. Andrias Scheuchzeri is a *faux* scientific name given to the creatures by investigators such as Dr. Johannes Jakob Scheuchzer, using the convention of naming the newly discovered species after its discoverer (91–92):

> That Andrias Scheuchzeri could croak a few dozen words and learn a few tricks — a fact which to the layman seemed evidence of some kind of intelligence — was not, in any scientific sense, a miracle. The miracle was the powerful and vital élan which had so suddenly and extensively revived the arrested existence of an evolutionarily backward and indeed near-extinct creature.

Much later in the novel (143) — with an intertextual note touching on the animal fable — Newt intelligence is acknowledged by educators:

> The young fry of salamanders working at Marseilles and Toulon were taught French language and literature, rhetoric, social deportment, mathematics and the history of civilization.... She [their human teacher] would recite to us Lafontaine's fables...

The Newts, in fact, possess many human traits. They stand upright, have hands, use tools, and have speech and language: all preconditions for representing intelligent non-human species, which is among the principal motifs of the animal-human allegory. Čapek is clearly aware of this tradition, evidenced in his frequent references to the animal fable (see also his essays on the fairy story).

William Harkins (168) makes a somewhat surprising point about the elements of science and philosophy in Karel Čapek's *oeuvre*, writing in one instance: "Perhaps no one of his generation tried so systematically and consciously to express philosophical ideas through literature," and in another instance (169) using literature (art) as a means of discussing scientific and technological issues:

> The subject matter of science and technology is normally cognitive, and as such belongs more properly to the domain of science or philosophy than to that of art, which is partly irrational. In this connection one must ask whether Čapek is not one of these writers (such as H.G. Wells or Aldous Huxley) who are not really writers in the strict sense, but who are able to use literary forms, often with great success, for their own purposes.

This is interesting, and potentially controversial. If one is able to employ literary forms successfully he/she must thereby be a "writer." But it can be matched with the generally accepted view that science fiction deals with ideas more than with characterization.

The center-point of the book's second narrative mood, marking the transition from the comfortable to the threatening, is the human predilection for exploitation, warfare, and imperialism, whether directed against members of their own species or those of another species. The allegorical intention appears obvious. Book Two, "Up the Ladder of Civilisation," leads us step by step through the preconditions for all-out warfare between Newts and humans, which becomes the subject of Book Three. We follow at first the continued scientific debate about their intelligence, as reported by an eyewitness named R.D. This character (137) observes satirically how the scientists might themselves react to the kinds of experiments they are carrying out on Newt subjects: "How would the smiling Dr. Okagawa react if I stimulated him electrically?" The Newt laboratory assistant — "an educated and clever animal" (140) — despite his usefulness, is eventually eaten for the furtherance of scientific knowledge. This anti-vivisectionist satirization is taken to further lengths in other novels, such as Kotzwinkle's *Doctor Rat.*

It is hard to know where to stop, because Čapek's work is dense with examples of satiric and parodic moments. Every page calls for comment. The Newts are not wholly subjects of exploitation; they affect human society in a variety of ways. While scientists ignore them, the ordinary populace absorb aspects of Newt culture into their language and, later, in the emergence of Newt-oriented religions. Linguistically (146), "their neologisms [are] ... adopted by the dregs of dockside humanity ... and ... society." Gradually it becomes more difficult to relegate the Newts to the status of animals. It is argued that they deserve treatment as citizens because they are subject to taxation, rent, school fees, and so on. Criminal punishment for Newts is described in terms contrary to those to which humans would be subjected (153): "detention in a dry and well-lit place or even by depriving them of work for a lengthy period" — a neat touch of the carnivalesque.

Newt technological society becomes more strongly defined. They begin to order "various parts of machinery according to their own designs" (160); a generation gap becomes evident as young Newts aspire towards "progress" by adopting much of "dry-land culture," (164) including "flirtation, fascism and sexual perversions," while the older generation, meanwhile, clings "conservatively to natural Newtism"; and there is an uncanny parody of a 1990s fad: "Real, self-assured Newt Age people..." (166). The long section ends on a note of warning about the manufacture and sale of munitions to the Newts, and the creation of trained Newt armies by some European states.

Book Three, which carries the novel's title, completes the shift from comparatively light-hearted parody to grim satire. Čapek is watching the growth of Nazism in Europe as he writes, and by now he is allegorizing the Newts pretty obviously as Nazis, in savage parodies of Hitlerian dogma. The Teutonic super-race whose destiny it is to conquer all other inferior peoples becomes "Der Nordmolch" (194):

> Today the Baltic Newt is the best soldier in the world; psychologically perfectly brainwashed, he sees his true and supreme mission in war; he will go into any battle with the enthusiasm of the fanatic, with the cool reasoning of the technician and with the terrifying discipline of a true Prussian Newt.

There comes an interregnum of apocalyptic warning, followed by the emergence of a Hitler-style Chief Salamander.

Such ideas were troubling for some of Czechoslovakia's near neighbors. Harkins (20) reports that Čapek's wife believed that he was not awarded the Nobel Prize for literature because his satirical references to Hitler in the novel upset the Swedish judges who did not wish to sour good relations with Germany.

Donald Lawler (2424) claims that *War with the Newts* is not allegorical. But the salamanders' personification, mirroring humans themselves and, in particular, Hitler's Nazis, must surely qualify the work as allegory. That is, if by allegory we use Baldick's definition (5): "a story or visual image with a second distinct meaning partially hidden behind its literal or visible meaning"; or that of Abrams (5): "in which the characters and actions that are signified literally in turn signify, or 'allegorize,' historical personages and events [Chief Salamander = Hitler, Nazi expansionism in the Sudetenland]"; or that of Lodge (143): "the development of an allegorical narrative is determined at every point by its one-to-one correspondence to the implied meaning."

Satire and parody, which are intrinsic to the novel, do not invalidate its allegorical features but go hand in hand with them. The Newts become many things, and so reflect and embody different kinds of human ideology and motivation as the story unfolds. Lawler goes further by saying that, strictly speaking, *War with the Newts* does not qualify as a novel but rather as "an imaginary history or fictitious chronicle" in which the characters are pawns. But novels can be structured in the form of chronicles and other types of personal document, as in the wide use of the letter as novelistic discourse in the nineteenth century. Lawler's point may rest on the fact that Čapek is playing with a variety of narrative forms and range of thought, including "the heroism of ideas," as Darko Suvin (283) puts it in his closing passage; and for this reason the novel is puzzling if we are looking for characterization. Čapek *is* self-contradictory. This is why the novel is such a perverse read. As Suvin

(280–281) observes, Čapek "did not quite manage to overcome his permanent ambiguity of the inhumans being on the one hand a wronged inferior race or class (at the beginning) and on the other a menacing embodiment of the worst in modern humanity—both Nazis and robotized masses."

A constantly changing world and the need for us to solve its problems actively might be considered one of the philosophical underpinnings of *War with the Newts* and helps to explain the different shifts in tone. It was written over a period of two years, during which momentous events were taking place around its creator, and Karel Čapek responded to those changes with wide-ranging and biting satire. It is not surprising that the Nazi SS placed him and his brother on their wanted list. Čapek's satire is effective whether the novel is uneven or not.

Actions, once set in motion, acquire a life of their own and drive inexorably towards a conclusion inimical for the human species. Čapek's work is one of the few books that look beyond the cozy catastrophe where humankind stands bloody but unbowed. These anxiety fantasies or catastrophe tales are back in vogue, especially on the screen. By the last chapter of *Newts* it appears that *Homo sapiens* is on the way out. The potential ending of humankind is treated in a dispassionate mood, together with an inconclusive authorial speculation that, after an inevitable war of attrition between the Newts themselves, humankind might return from the mountains to reclaim the planet, a semi-cozy ending perhaps. The Newts (239) will have their own mythologies:

> The tiny island of Tana Masa. The cradle of the Newts. And there King Salamander reigns ... *their* Orient, see? That whole area is now called Lemuria, whereas that other region, the civilised, Europeanised and Americanised, modern and technologically advanced region is Atlantis.

Newts and humans remain apart. As Suvin (276) says, "there is no conciliatory happy ending."

Two Critiques

In his Introduction to the 1964 English translation of *War with the Newts*, Alexander Matuska (7) observes that the rediscovery of Karel Čapek—his "coming to the fore again"—was essentially because he was ahead of his time: "It is probably not because he 'solves' some of our current problems, but because he introduced them, in essence, before the Second World War." Matuska (64) is a commentator who notes extensively this element of social and political anxiety in Čapek's work, linking it with the influences that a host of other writers and thinkers had on Čapek:

> The Thirties: 1933, the entry of the Nazis; 1935, Ethiopia; 1936, Spain, the occupation of the Rhine Valley; 1937, the war between China and Japan; 1938, the Anschluss (of Austria) and Munich. At home, the intensification of the class struggle, strikes, demonstrations, armed clashes, unemployment.... Each of these eras has its own face, but all of them are marked with the stigma of war. Čapek scarcely has a book in which a war—current, past or yet to come—does not play a part.

This is not particularly surprising. All writers are influenced to some degree by virtually everything they read and hear. It is a more helpful insight to know that the critical appraisal of Matuska and other scholars notices many of the elements that are to be found in science fiction and fantasy stories that owe something to the animal fable.

Where Karel Čapek's narrative style is concerned, Matuska (69–70) makes two points, first that Čapek valued his feuilletons more than he let on, and made sure they were soon published in book form, and, second, that his prose work had something more about it than merely journalism:

> If his artistic prose stands somewhere on the edge of journalism, then his feuilletons move about some place on the border of art. And that is true not only linguistically, stylistically, but certainly from other points of view as well: viewpoint and composition, wealth of observation, pictures from life and reality.

Čapek was at ease with many different styles or, as we call them today, discourses: the far-fetched traveler's yarn, the scientific treatise, the newspaper report (of course), the telegram, the political tract, mock-ups (parodies) of ancient scripts, and so on. We find elements like these in the narrative technique of Cordwainer Smith (in, for example, the reportage of the Underpeople's revolt led by D'Joan via far futuristic television). Linebarger appeals openly to the storytelling mode of the folk tale. Both men were heavily influenced by childhood exposure to the traditions of the fairy tale and the folk tale, and this finds expression in their writing throughout their lives.

The whole writing enterprise that mixes the carnivalesque with serious social and moral comment is full of complexities at its best; "social problems are in fact moral problems," says Matuska (51), and so I think that a "good" story about sentient animals requires its readers to do some work on both fronts, to enjoy themselves but also to absorb the moral points. This is as true of the other authors as it is for Karel Čapek. The perhaps unlikely balance between the carnivalesque and a more serious mood continually manifests itself throughout *War with the Newts*, and in the appraisals of its critics. Matuska (110) writes:

> It is not merely in the fact that he wrote "jokingly" about serious things and seriously about minor ones.... It is in the complex relations between his intellectualism and his lyricism, between his intellectual caprice and his factuality, humour, satire, sarcasm.

In keeping with the carnivalesque, Čapek enjoyed "standing a thing on its head" and employing "the spirit of polemic and disagreement," parading "clichés and false opinions," illuminating triteness (Matuska 112–113).

Matuska (155) also finds two moods in Čapek's work that do not quite converge. On the one hand there is directness and "reality," attentiveness and explicitness, and on the other hand there is an element of the abstract and the withdrawn. The former, to do with "social questions, about class stratification, about actual social relationships," is found in his feuilletons; but the latter (the abstract) appears more prominent in Čapek's novels and dramas. Towards the end of his study, Matuska (291) remarks that "This dichotomy follows from the fact that Čapek's prose is, in its philosophy, on one hand strongly essayistic ... and on the other strongly colloquial, almost familiar." So we may argue that *War with the Newts* contains the best of both genres.

Alexander Matuska's treatment of Karel Čapek's era and oeuvre is often verbose, with a great deal of stress on a multitude of writers and philosophers who influenced Čapek one way or another, and it is for this reason heavy-going. The critique also leans towards hagiography, especially in the last chapter. But one of his summations (331) in an earlier chapter captures well what Čapek does in *War with the Newts*:

> *The War with the Newts* is, after its fashion, Čapek's "contemporary history," for it draws freely—as did few of his works—on historical reality, on the situation in the mid–Thirties.... Apparently put together accidentally, turning now here and now elsewhere, *The War with the Newts* is a novel that is in reality very carefully thought out. There is order, method in its confusion. It corresponds with the times. A view from many sides, interpreted by the rapid change of scene, newspaper reports, speeches, declarations, opinions and polls, is intended to express the variety of reality, the co-existence of the different and the diverse.... What used to be a source of joy of discovery has been transformed here into terror, which is only gently covered up by a film of irony.

Published two years before Matuska's literary biography of Karel Čapek, William Harkins' study might be expected to notice different things about Čapek, his oeuvre and the era in which he lived. Both critics, however, agree on the importance of Čapek for what C. Wright Mills (248) calls "[personal] troubles and [public] issues ... biography and history." Harkins (v) says that Čapek's main success "lies in his effort to give a philosophical definition to the individual and his relation to democratic society."

War with the Newts marks a watershed between Čapek's earlier and more youthful work (much of it done in collaboration with his brother Josef, such as *R.U.R.* and *The Insect Play* in 1923), and his later and — as some critics recognize — more pessimistic works. Harkins (39) notes "the conflict of nature and civilization within man" as the predominant theme in Čapek, a theme that unifies his "youthful pieces" with the writing that came later. *War with the Newts* was a variation of the earlier robot theme, and indeed combines robotic images with that of animals in Newt dancing, in a sense combining figures from *R.U.R.* with *The Insect Play*, although the Newts are amphibians and not arthropods. Harkins' best summation — alongside that of Matuska — also gives praise to the feuilleton approach. I would, however, call *War with the Newts* a dystopian novel, which is, in any event, part of "the utopian genre" of which Harkins (95) speaks:

> *The War with the Newts* is Čapek's greatest work in the utopian genre. Closer to Swift than to Wells, it has a satirical tone absent in *R.U.R.*, and is far less melodramatic.... The loose form of the *roman feuilleton* allowed Čapek great freedom for satire and parody. The novel is a brilliant pastiche of the most diverse kinds of writing.... Every conceivable typographic device is employed for comic or satiric effect; there is even an obscure historical note printed in the older Czech type (*svabach*), as well as an extremely blurred and tiny photograph of the giant newts.

The increasing pessimism of Čapek's later works is understandable, and has been discussed already. Over fifteen years the brothers Čapek witnessed increasingly grave political developments in Europe so that when *War with the Newts* was published, "the coming of a second war was almost a certainty" (Harkins 99).

Without a doubt, Karel Čapek wrote *War with the Newts* (1936) in response to the rise of Nazism in neighboring Germany. But his net was not cast only in that direction. As a long-time satirist with similar human-animal (and robot) works behind him, Čapek set out to poke fun at and parody many aspects of Western civilization. The satirical, multi-layered novel that resulted is at one moment fascinating because of its mix of styles and thematic inconsistencies, and at another moment somewhat dissatisfying, perhaps for the same reason. Its form as a *roman feuilleton* may be in itself a limitation, because an author employing such a form is tempted to go in those multiple directions and so cannot settle down to a compact and more focused sort of novel, developed in a handful of consistent styles.

CHAPTER 9

Companionate and Erotic Love 1: *Sirius*

Sirius is a psychological study, whereas most of Stapledon's other fiction deals with cosmic evolutionary events on a grand scale. *Sirius* does not have the galactic ambience for which Stapledon is better known, but in its own way it is quite as ambitious. Louis Tremaine (67) says, "Beyond their own separate achievements, *Odd John* and *Sirius* (and, to a lesser extent, shorter works like *A Man Divided*) develop an imaginative vision directly complementary to that of the more massive works." Crossley (351) cites Stapledon's belief that this novel, with its thematic subtitle *A Fantasy of Love and Discord*, is his best work, and many critics agree, pointing to its detailed and compassionate portrayal of the principal character's tragic life. Neil Barron (113) says:

> Perhaps better than *Odd John*, this also deals with the uses of super intelligence but has an ending of greater emotional impact. The writing is better, and the characters often seem well developed. The mutated dog, Sirius, becomes believably human and is far more interesting than the usual stereotypes used by authors attempting to allegorize the human condition. Probably this comes from Stapledon's concern with the evolution of mankind to ethical and mental supermen or perhaps from his focus upon an extremely short span of time. Always a writer of ideas, which are often central to his works, he is at his best when he deals with one-to-one relationships. Sirius and his human companions offer ideas but also the realization of human ideals of love and friendship.

Sirius is a comparatively long novel written in the third person by a fictional narrator consciously setting down the biography of the super-dog of the title. Brian Aldiss (7), writing about Stapledon's early novel *Last and First Men*, notes that his "delivery is always deceptively simple, his tone of voice level." I do not think we can say that of *Sirius*, a more polished work written by an older Stapledon. As Barbara Bengels (60–61) says regarding Stapledon's tone (or style):

> In *Sirius*, Stapledon has not only dispensed with much of his ponderous, pedantic musings, but he has also enriched the work with a somewhat lighter tone (thereby accentuating his darker moments when he wishes to) and more interesting human characters who feel as well as think.

Nevertheless, Stapledon is, if anything, a verbose writer, so the biographical form is a good choice. He used this form also in the earlier superman novel *Odd John*. Of the two works, Peter Nicholls (567) says, "Many critics argue that *Odd John* is the best novel about a superman, and that *Sirius* is the best book with a non-human protagonist." Eric Rabkin (238) calls the latter "perhaps Stapledon's most readable novel." Similarly, John Kinnaird (517) describes *Sirius* as "perhaps his most aesthetically satisfying fiction."

A Dog's Biography

It is now some sixty-five years since the publication of *Sirius*, and the novel will be unfamiliar to many readers.

The first chapter opens with Robert's love for Plaxy and her inexplicable disappearance from his life after her mother's death. In flashback Robert tells of Plaxy's mysterious letter, prompting him to seek her out in Llan Ffestiniog, where he meets the dog Sirius for the first time. While girl and dog are out of sight, Robert hears snatches of conversation and is puzzled by the "queer speech of whimper and growl" (8) that is Sirius' way of communicating: "Interspersed with Plaxy's remarks was no other human voice but a quite different sound, articulate but inhuman" (11). Plaxy and Sirius are discussing one of the relatively minor but nonetheless important plot elements — that Sirius has paws and not hands. Other crucial factors are introduced. After a physical description of Sirius, Robert's jealousy comes to the surface, and he debates within himself how best to free Plaxy from "inhuman bondage" (11). Towards the chapter's end, Sirius declares his love for Plaxy but adds he will not stand between her and human love. Robert prepares to piece together a biography of the dog by getting to know him better and by reading Plaxy's father's papers. From being a rival, Robert becomes ostensibly a chronicler and friend, although the theme of rivalry remains in the background.

In his use of the flashback (the scenes in chapter one come well after events still to be described), Stapledon employs a Wellsian opening gambit. He introduces the *ménage à trois* and evokes elements of mystery or strangeness, setting the stage for the novel's major conflict. Sexuality is hinted at with Stapledonian humor (12):

> Then Sirius made another remark with a sly look and a tremor of the tail. She turned back to him laughing, and softly smacked his face. "Beast," she said, "I shall not tell Robert that."

John Kinnaird (2089) says the fairy tale of "Beauty and the Beast" is archetypical for *Sirius*; indeed, Crossley (292) notes, "The Beast and Beauty" was an earlier "allegorical title" that Stapledon eventually rejected.

Unlike Wells, Stapledon takes more trouble over establishing scientific veracity in nine pages, whereas Wells often dismisses the scientific in less than a page, as in *The Time Machine*. Here Stapledon's debt to the Frankenstein theme, and his conscious adaptation of it, is exemplified in the relationship between Sirius' creator, Thomas Trelone, and Sirius. The science of the novel uses medical speculation about the workings of the brain and the endocrine system as understood in the first half of the twentieth century. Trelone's making of Sirius involves a hormone injected into the mother's bloodstream to stimulate brain growth in the fetus. This increases the size of the cerebral cortex and the fineness and number of nerve fibers. After birth, additional doses of the hormone are given the pup in its food, and surgical techniques delay the joining of the skull sutures while the brain grows. Early tests are not always successful. Trelone chooses dogs as his subjects because they have the right temperament, can move more freely in English society, and have bodies large enough to support the additional weight of the head. Sirius is a cross between a Border Collie and a German Shepherd, the breed called Alsatian in the novel by Stapledon (or his editor) because of the unpopularity of the word "German" at the time. Sirius is unique as the only survivor of a litter of four. The dogs from a second litter do not become like Sirius but mature into "super-sheep-dogs" who work for nearby farmers. Sirius' return to shepherding, sometimes working with them, is a recurring pastoral motif.

The novel *Sirius* thereafter breaks neatly into several parts.

The super dog's upbringing is in many ways modeled on the traditional Edwardian middle class family that Stapledon knew. Sirius' human family employ servants, send their children to boarding school and plan for a university education. Stapledon's *Sirius* contains many autobiographical echoes. In the third chapter, describing how Sirius and Plaxy grow up together, the main elements of the theme of discord are established in the changing relationships between Sirius, other dogs, and humans, and their differing abilities. The dog's poor sight, for instance, is compensated for through smell, good hearing, and sensitivity to mood. The dominant theme is that of Sirius' intellectual, almost human, nature at constant war with the beast within (27):

> the conflict between what he later called his "wolf-nature" and his compassionate civilized mentality.... Hunting now gripped Sirius as the main joy of life; but it was a guilty joy. He felt its call almost as a religious claim upon him, the claim of the dark blood-god for sacrifice; but he was also disgusted with the sacrifice, and deeply disturbed by Plaxy's horror.

These actions contrast against a love of poetry, music and singing, and an impulse to help his human family care for sheep, introducing an ambiguity of spirit that Louis Tremaine (74) notes:

> That spirit self lies persistently beyond his [Sirius'] individual reach, however, forcing him to seek the desired reconciliation through association with other beings. The claim is made several times that such associations come naturally to Sirius as a dog, that "dogs excelled in social awareness" [*Sirius*, 2:172]. That claim is not supported, however, by example. In *Sirius*, dogs pursue their social life by fighting, copulating, and serving man together — they do not form spiritual communities.

When Sirius claims a dog's social awareness in the face of contrary evidence, it is probably Stapledon's irony at play. Social awareness does not necessarily preclude doggish pleasures, and fighting, copulating, and serving others are also human traits.

On the other hand, there is the *communitas* of spirit between Sirius and Plaxy's family and close allies, the family being Stapledon's chief vehicle for the "individual-in-community" he envisaged. The same goes for Tremaine's critique that there is a contrast between wilderness and community. Sirius does not find "sustainable spiritual existence" in London or Cambridge, but puzzlement and conflict, even during the sublime periods of singing in church and discussing the nature of spiritual life with the priest Geoffrey. On the contrary, Sirius' family live on the edge of the wilderness, and from Robert's citified point of view they are part of it. Representing Sirius' character as an uneasy balance between canine and human traits against the mirror images of urban life and wilderness is one of the main points of the novel. Stapledon uses an urban-rural dichotomy similar to that of Clifford Simak's *City*.

By this point in the novel it becomes necessary to hide Sirius' true nature from outsiders. Two servant women are dismissed. Sirius and Plaxy are separated when Plaxy goes to boarding school, and Thomas Trelone plans Sirius' future around shepherding with the family's tenant farmer Pugh, followed by the dog's introduction to Cambridge scientists. Much to his distaste, Sirius is renamed Bran and becomes propertyless, putting away his toys in order to learn sheep-dog maneuvers. His experience of humans deepens in keeping with the tradition of the animal allegory that goes back to Apuleius. His first classification (53–54) divides humans into those who are indifferent, the sentimental "dog lovers," the "dog-detesters," and the "dog interested." He is now fifteen, having a life span closer to that of humans than to canines, and has become large and strong, with an accompanying self-respect that has violent undercurrents, for he is prepared to kill any human who attacks him. At the same time he develops sexual relations with a red setter bitch. The other side of his nature is described with typical Stapledonian humor. He keeps up with local events by reading the wall posters in the town (as does the canine protagonist of Mikhail Bulgakov's *The Heart of a Dog*), accurately counts loose change when shopping, and writes a letter to Plaxy, which he stamps and mails in the village. This chapter is important for its establishment of the pastoral theme, to be contrasted later with Sirius' experiences in Cambridge and London.

Chapters six and seven similarly develop the two sides of Sirius' nature. He sees Plaxy during school holidays, but they are drifting apart. Sheep work bores him, and he spends much solitary time reading and in general developing a passion for learning. One of two direct appeals to H.G. Wells is made here (73): "Taxing his eyesight, he even plunged into Wells' *Outline of History* and *The Science of Life*." In the evenings he talks with Thomas about his future and his humanness, and the continual search for himself. He speculates about humankind and has contempt for their frequent insincerity. The dog in him finds Plaxy both attractive and disgusting. Eventually he takes more responsibility for his sheep work. Stapledon provides detailed descriptions of sheep handling. This third canine influence, if we are to believe Stapledon's acknowledgment page (6), is: "Mr. J. Herries McCulloch's delightful study, *Sheep Dogs and Their Masters*." But Sirius kills a ram and a pony, and Plaxy has to coax him out of his wild wolf mood.

Up until now this is the most detailed treatment of the discord theme, where wolf nature and human nature are at odds. From this point, and for the next six chapters, the novel takes a new direction. Having established Sirius' origin, upbringing, and the chief conflicts in his character, Stapledon goes on to describe the super-dog's experiences with a variety of human types, just as in *The Golden Ass* or *Black Beauty*. Sirius is taken to Cambridge, followed by a bodyguard because an attempt had been made to kidnap him. He visits the library, the university, and meets various academics.

Like Voltaire's character Candide, Sirius looks critically at what he finds — overfed and neurotic pet dogs, the academics' vanities matched by the clumsiness of their hands (an ironic point considering Sirius's own regretted lack of them) — but he is drawn into the soft life. He ruminates about human selfishness, thinking of them (104) as "an imperfectly socialized species, as its own shrewder specimens, for instance H.G. Wells, had pointed out." Basil Davenport (x) mentions the allegorical flavor of *Sirius,* but does so by employing technological terms, missing the societal implications that Stapledon was driving at: "The whole of Sirius, the dog with an intelligence strictly canine in nature but human in power, might be an allegory of the same thing" [i.e. Homo sapiens having floundered into a mechanized situation too difficult to handle]. But Sirius' own life grows out of balance as he loses physical condition while satisfying an insatiable sex drive with a succession of bitches supplied in the laboratory. Disenchantment follows.

In Chapter nine, "Sirius and Religion," Stapledon changes his narrative style to accommodate mystical experiences, described in a diary kept by Sirius. Both Western (St. John of the Cross) and Eastern (Vedanta) works become Sirius' reading matter. This is a prelude to the next chapter where Sirius visits London and accompanies a tolerant priest, the Reverend Geoffrey Adams, on his parish rounds. The three worlds of North Wales, Cambridge and London are in contrast, especially the crushing poverty of the working classes in London. This chapter, in which Sirius sings in church, is pivotal to the novel by bringing together both Stapledon's satirical view of the Christian church and his great respect for the mystical experience. It is one of the carnivalesque moments in the novel.

There follows a sudden shift in the eleventh chapter to another breakout of Sirius' wolf nature, paralleling the onset of the Second World War. Sirius returns to his sheep work in the lake country of Cumberland under a master whose cruel treatment of both him and a Collie provoke Sirius into killing the man. Subsequently Sirius is reunited with the Pughs and continues with farm work. A highlight of the chapter titled "Farmer Sirius" is the super-dog's unsuccessful attempts to train pups in the hope that one will grow to become his intellectual peer and companion. This is the happiest period of the dog's life. Because of wartime cutbacks, Sirius is no longer involved in laboratory work, and he feels remote from the conflagration, as perhaps Stapledon did at that time. He discusses Marxism and Communism with Plaxy, who tells of her plans to marry Robert.

The ingredients for tragedy have been laid, and the dog's life speeds towards a conclusion. The churchman Geoffrey, with whom Sirius shared many discussions about religion, is killed in the London bombing, and Thomas Trelone dies similarly when he and Sirius are caught in an air raid while passing through Liverpool. Sirius makes a long trek from Birkenhead to Trawsfynydd and is reunited with Elizabeth. The cross-country trek is an important ingredient in many animal fantasy stories, symbolizing, I think, the quest of the human psyche for meaning and enlightenment. There follows Stapledon's compassionate description of Sirius sorting through Thomas' personal effects and grieving over his death (chapter fourteen).

While Sirius is now emotionally his own master, he receives excessive attention from Elizabeth in substitution for her loss of Thomas, until Elizabeth herself falls ill and dies. At this point Sirius and Plaxy hear about the sinking of a cruiser, which they believe carried Plaxy's brother Maurice. A similar misadventure happened to Olaf's and Agnes' son David six months after the publication of *Sirius* (Crossley 314). David survived. Sirius and Plaxy rent the Pugh's cottage at Tan-y-Voel and work hard in the fields. The Rev. Owen Lloyd-Thomas visits and says it is unseemly that Plaxy and Sirius should live together. Plaxy laughs it off. Sirius remarks (165) that the minister "smells as if he were in love with you." They have unwittingly made an enemy of this venal priest, who in his sermons foments hostility in the village against them.

At this point ("Strange Triangle") we come full circle to the meeting in the first chapter when Robert joins Plaxy and Sirius. Robert's proximity intensifies what was latent in the love triangle. Sirius roams the moors in one of his wild moods, and, while he is away (172), "There was human love-making in the cottage that day." By this time Sirius acknowledges that Plaxy needs human love. The short chapter goes some way towards resolving the twin themes of jealousy and sexual love, and is arguably the climax of the novel. But it is in the final chapters that the two sets of discords come together: the love triangle and village hostility.

All is well, though uneasy, between the threesome until Plaxy is called up for military service. This breaks their alliance against the villagers, weakening Sirius' human support. He lives with the Pughs and continues shepherding. A village girl claims that Sirius attempted to rape her, and a village man tries to shoot him. Once again Sirius roams wild on the moors, killing sheep. Plaxy returns and searches for him in order to coax him out of his wild mood. They hide from the searchers in his lair, where Sirius admits to eating part of a man, until they are discovered by a search party's dog. Sirius kills the animal, but is shot and dies in Plaxy's arms.

The novel closes on a mystic note that has epic resonance. Plaxy sings a requiem in the musical style invented by Sirius. It is one of the few moments (187–188) where Stapledon touches upon the cosmic theme that saturates his earlier work:

> And under the power of his music she saw that Sirius, in spite of his uniqueness, epitomized in his whole life and in his death something universal, something that is common to all awakening spirits on earth, and in the farthest galaxies. For the music's darkness was lit up by a brilliance which Sirius had called "colour," the glory that he himself, he said, had never seen. But this, surely, was the glory that no spirits, canine or human,

> had ever clearly seen, the light that never was on land or sea, and yet is glimpsed by the quickened mind everywhere.
>
> As she sang, red dawn filled the eastern sky, and soon the sun's bright finger set fire to Sirius.

The closing lines evoke Homeric images (37): "As soon as Dawn with her rose-tinted hands had lit the East...." At least two critics make this connection. Robert Philmus (74), in an acerbic judgment on Leslie Fiedler, refers in general to the "whole species [that] loom up in the mists of Stapledonian time like Homeric shapes." Arthur Swanson (292), more specifically in a comparison between *Odd John* and *Sirius,* notes the dread felt by humanists over the thought of ascending to a "higher" state that might preclude spirituality, an anxiety that begins early in Western thought with works such as *The Iliad.* In its high-mindedness, tragic unfolding, and sympathetic characterization of the protagonist, *Sirius* has an epic score. This is Stapledon at his best.

Stapledon devotes a lot of attention to detail in his portrayal of Sirius and Plaxy growing up together as child and pup — developmental stages familiar in human child rearing, but they have poignancy when they are applied to a young dog. Sirius experiences toilet training, handling wooden blocks, the acquiring of speech, and difficulties a dog's eyes have in recognizing forms and colors, and learning to read and write. He has to cope with childhood jealousies, as, for example, the disciplinarian drubbing he receives from the super-sheep-dog Gelert. An inventory of Sirius' possessions, his "toys," comprise with some exceptions the sorts of objects a human child might possess (55): "a rubber bone, a lump of gleaming white quartz, a sheep's skull, several picture books ... more books and music, his three writing gloves and several pens and pencils." Stapledon inventively shows how a dog with a human brain and self-awareness might cope with the impediments of his canine form. The holding of a pencil inserted into a rubber ball that can be grasped by a dog's mouth for writing is particularly ingenious.

As well as the obstacles encountered in his early years, the young pup has several advantages, such as finer hearing, and sensitivity to the human voice and the underlying emotions it reveals. Smelling or scent, cognition, poetry, and love of music become metaphors (76) for religious ecstasy: "Sometimes I manage to follow a trail of thought quite well for a long time, in and out, up and down, but always with my mind's nose on the trail." In some respects (23), this super-sheep dog is portrayed almost as more than human:

> Sirius was more persistently inquisitive and at times passionately constructive. His behaviour was in many ways more simian than canine. The lack of hands was a handicap against which he reacted with a dogged will to triumph over disability.

On the other hand (77): "The mind — is *me*. I'm not human, but also I'm not canine." (Nor is he simian.) Self-referral in this apparently naive mode is part of Olaf Stapledon's own presentation of self, as when denying imputed links to Communism. When he was facing an American audience following one of his last public appearances in 1949, not long before his death, Stapledon said: "I am not a Communist. I am not a Christian. *I am just me.* I am, however, a socialist" [Crossley 378, my emphasis].

For Sirius, poetry is another means of exploring his self and "spirit." The rough notes Sirius writes (99) for his projected books "reveal a mind which combined laughable *naiveté* in some directions with remarkable shrewdness in others, a mind moreover which seemed to oscillate between a heavy, self-pitying seriousness and a humorous detachment and self-criticism." Stapledon might have been describing himself.

Sirius' youth mirrors that of most humans. He has sexual adventures, including jealousies assuaged when he and Plaxy reaffirm their love for each other. His bravery against a dog bully introduces the more adult element of murder. Adolescent emotional turmoil arrives in conjunction with his "awakening mind," and he begins to ask why he was made. Kinnaird (2088) notes that

> Sirius, therefore, does not merely grow up, he grows as a character; and this growth consists in the emergence of his unique animal personality from an illusory humanity. In this respect *Sirius* is true science fiction while so many animal stories ... are not.

The acquiring of language (24) particularly marks Sirius out: "The dog's development of true speech ... was a sure sign of the fully human degree of intelligence." But it goes beyond this to include intellection, a staple ingredient in the novel. The super dog's quest for self— a burning sense of enquiry into what he is — is one of the overarching themes. Kinnaird (2088) puts it this way:

> It is the constant disparity between the human thought-language of the dog and his less than human adequacy in dealing with the correlatives of his thought in the physical world, and especially in dealing with that reality as it is mediated by his man-derived hopes and expectations, that defines Stapledon's projection of his theme: the body-mind conflict.

This conflict is played off against the other thematic discords of the love triangle between Sirius and two humans, his human nature versus his canine nature, wilderness and the city, and the reciprocated love of Plaxy both as *eros* (physical or sexual love) and *agape* (companionable and intellectual love). Tragedy results from these sets of oppositions, triggered by a clash between the dog's wolf nature and a brutality offered by humans that scarcely differs from that of a beast. As Leslie Fiedler (12) says:

> Stripped of technological trimmings and sf conventions, Stapledon's stories reveal themselves as a series of variations of quite ancient mythic themes ... man as the eternal victim of an eternal conflict between his animal inheritance and his spiritual aspirations. Nowhere does he portray the latter more dramatically than in *Sirius*.

Weakness in characterization but strength of ideas are common factors in science fiction, as noted earlier, but Stapledon's characterization of Sirius is one of the exceptions that stands head and shoulders above that of many other authors.

Like Victor Frankenstein in Mary Shelley's novel, Thomas Trelone (129) allows scientific objectivity to cloud his human feelings: "Thomas was always surprisingly insensitive about the psychological aspect of his great experiment; or perhaps not insensitive but unimaginative." His achieved ambition for the dog (52) is that Sirius become "one of the world's great animal psychologists ... working with my crowd at Cambridge." But aside from planning Sirius' life along Spartan lines, Trelone decides as an experiment to raise his daughter Plaxy and Sirius together. Sirius says to Plaxy (48), with a touch of Stapledonian humor: "You're a bitch of the species *Homo sapiens*, that Thomas is always talking about as though it was a beast in the Zoo."

Eventually, as in Victor Frankenstein's case, Trelone feels remorse over his experiment, saying at one point (78), "It's my fault that you are more than a dog. It's my meddling that woke the 'spirit' in you, as you call it." But there is a key difference. Unlike Victor Frankenstein, Trelone (92) does not abandon his creation: "I don't think I ever *really* realized that if things went wrong with *this* experiment I couldn't just wash my hands of it all, and start again..." Instead, Trelone continues to support Sirius in many ways, several times covering for his sheep-killing, and on one other occasion for the killing of a man. Kinnaird (2087) makes the same point: "Trelone, unlike his prototype in fiction, the scientist-hero of *Frankenstein*, is acutely aware of his responsibilities in providing for his creature's psychological adaptation to human society." Trelone has not "sold his soul, in order to gain scientific fame," as he is accused of (147) by the village gossips, and a strong bond of love exists between Trelone and Sirius.

Humor, Ecstasy and the Carnivalesque

Although tragic themes of sexuality and conflict between the spiritual and base nature drives the novel, there is an underlying good humor. Barbara Bengels (60) writes, "The comic element in *Sirius* exists in many forms throughout the novel, from the irony of man's indiscretions before his dog, to the childish whimsy of the urination ritual Sirius and Plaxy share." Stapledon is fond of punning, for example; lack of hands = handicap; and "doggedness" we read in other animal allegories. Sirius is not only named after the Dog Star, he is also "serious" by nature. Stapledon often employs levity when the dog is speaking weightily, and is himself serious when Sirius is joking. Love, discord and irony are closely interwoven. Bengels (57, 61), too, does not miss Stapledon's allegorical intent, pointing out

> the man-dog relationship where the dog is infinitely the more sympathetic and certainly as capable of illuminating man's strengths, foibles, and latent bestiality.... By focusing on a dog instead of on a human in his later novel, Stapledon has said more about mankind.... In being driven to bestiality, Sirius has nevertheless achieved a kindred humanity for he is the beast—and the man—in us all.

The titles of the books Sirius plans to produce (98–99) are another source of puns: *The Lamp-Post, A Study of the Social Life of the Domestic Dog* and *Beyond the Lamp-Post*. As well as prose literature, poetry is equally to Sirius' taste. Browning, Hardy and (the early) Eliot are mentioned, the last two associated (73) in the dog's mind with "the poetry of self and universe." An important feature of poetry is its auditory quality—poetry is usually intended to be read aloud—appropriate from a dog's outlook. Towards the end (167), when tragedy is soon to strike, "Sirius still took a deep delight in listening to prose and poetry read aloud." By contrast (86–87), when Plaxy studies literature at Cambridge she finds it "scientific in temper." There is thus another set of oppositions: poetry and science. The rationalization helps Plaxy to reconcile her interests in the arts with her father's wishes that she study medicine, but the remark is perhaps Stapledon's reproach of academic literary analysis.

Another means of exploring the ecstatic is through music, an occasion for more play on words at one level but with deeper ramifications. The pun is modeled on the readiness of many dogs to howl in resonance with certain kinds of musical instruments; but when Sirius sings in church, enunciating English words in a canine cadence, Stapledon lifts the carnivalesque mood so created beyond mere humor to a spiritual plane. Similarly, Sirius' act of cocking his leg at gateposts and in church is invested not only with religious experience but also with irony—that is, carnivalesque humor. When the dog sings in church, however, it is a moving episode and one of the high points of the novel. Yet, at the same time, the style of Sirius' earnest rationalizations (125–126) sounds very much like Stapledon once again poking fun at himself:

> It [music] could never speak directly about the objective world, or "the nature of existence"; but it might create a complex emotional attitude which might be appropriate to some feature of the objective world, or to the universe as a whole [Sirius' words].... The church was then flooded with Sirius' music. Geoffrey seemed to hear in it echoes of Bach and Beethoven, of Holst, Vaughan Williams, Stravinsky and Bliss, but also it was pure Sirius.

Music is also a good vehicle (73) for establishing the alien facet of Sirius' nature:

> Vast tracts of literature meant nothing to him, save as verbal music, because his subconscious nature had not the necessary human texture to respond to them emotionally, nor had he the necessary associations in his experience.... Music was ever for Sirius a more satisfying art than poetry. But it tortured him, because the texture of his own musical sensibility remained alien to the human.

Stapledon is making associations with what we popularly fancy as the psychic powers of animals, dogs and cats. Kinnaird (2088) says:

> In presenting his hero's passion for music ... Stapledon is mixing scientific truth with primitive superstition; he is taking advantage of the belief that dogs are "psychic," that they not only hear and smell things beyond man's perception but can also sense spiritual reality (ghosts and demons especially).

We often find this metaphor in other animal allegories, such as in Simak' s *City* where the Dogs are attuned to the cobbly worlds.

In a minor register of discord, Sirius experiences frustration because he wants to contribute to the human world in which he lives. Once again Stapledon writes (107) with tongue in cheek when he depicts Sirius' inner voice:

> Grandiose fantasies assailed him. "Sirius, the unique canine composer, not only changed the whole character of human music, importing into it something of the dog's finer auditory sensibility; he also, in his own incomparable creations, expressed the fundamental identity-in-diversity of all spirits, of whatever species, canine, human or super-human."

There is as much about spirit and the mystic life in Sirius' quest for understanding as it was for Stapledon, and, in many instances (84), spirit is antithetical to science, just as it is in Mary Shelley's masterpiece: "He felt his spirit washed by the blood of the quarry, washed clean of humanity with all its itching monkey-inquisitiveness, all its restless monkeying with material things and living things and living minds."

There is a reflection of Stapledon's own background reading in philosophy when Sirius discovers "the literature of mysticism" in Christian works such as Saint John of the Cross or Eastern Vedanta. Lin Yutang's phrasing (17), "the world soul and the individual soul," in his introduction to "Hymns from the Rigveda," for instance, reads very like something Stapledon might have said. First published in 1944, Yutang's anthology *The Wisdom of India* probably came too late for Stapledon to have read in time to be influenced in his composing of *Sirius*. But there were, of course, other translations of these earliest of "nature hymns" that Stapledon must have seen. Mostly Stapledon uses Christian imagery and worship. The metaphor of blood becomes another pun appropriate for a robust sheep dog — it also has carnivalesque overtones — but it has deeper significance (113) when tied into the opposing wolf theme:

> What appealed to him most was one of the hymns, sung with immense gusto. "Washed in the blood of the lamb," was its theme.... He vaguely and quite irrationally felt it as unifying all the tenderness of his life with all the wolf in him.

This recurring mix of religious figures of speech with colloquial humorous asides, especially in puns, has a lot in common with Bakhtin's theory of Carnival and the inverting of the profane over the sacred on which that theory rests.

Sexual Love Between Species: Stapledon and Women

In its combination of humor and tragedy, *Sirius*, of all Stapledon's novels, moves the sympathy of readers. Yet underlying the love story of Sirius and Plaxy is a theme not all commentators are comfortable with addressing. Patrick McCarthy (67–68) remarks, "There are suggestions that that love takes the form of sexual relations between Plaxy and Sirius," and he goes on to relate it to "the physical embodiment of a spiritual bond," which I agree is what Stapledon is getting at. Sam Moskowitz (272–273) alludes obliquely to bestiality when he observes that Sirius is "adult reading with distinct allegorical applications to the world's racial situation." By interpreting sexuality in *Sirius* in ethnic terms — implying difficulties in cross-cultural marriage or making a more general point about race relations?— Moskowitz takes a narrow view that neglects deeper implications.

The sexuality between dog and woman that Stapledon more than hints at worried his editor, who requested him to make certain cuts before the volume went to print. Naomi Mitchison records Stapledon writing to her following the publication of *Sirius* by Secker and Warburg. Methuen had rejected the manuscript on the grounds that it was obscene, and Mitchison (37), writing in 1981, remarks, "In fact the published version had been cut rather hard; it would doubtless have passed now." But while Mitchison is correct about the censorship, Crossley (3) finds evidence that the cuts were substantially less drastic. Crossley sets four texts side by side: the finished version in print, the manuscript received by Secker and Warburg, "a late manuscript" Stapledon gave to his typist, and a first draft in pencil carrying two working titles: "The Beast and Beauty" and "Odd Dog." The last-named manuscript was a personal gift from Stapledon to one of his close women friends, Evelyn Gibson, who stated in an attached note: "Olaf gave me the pencilled draft as a keepsake. He said that he had drawn on our tangled relationship, & transmuted it, and that he had based Plaxy on me" (Crossley 9).

Crossley's meticulous research (8–9) reveals that Stapledon quietly subverted his publisher's censoriousness, bringing into greater prominence "the satirical contrast between human and canine mores," making it a funnier book, expanding rather than cutting passages, and, in general, producing a better polished work. Hence, censorship, if not taken too seriously, can serve an author. Stapledon introduces the carnivalesque into cross-species sexuality just as he does for religious uplift versus the wolf nature of the protagonist. He introduces the carnivalesque in his relationship with publishers.

Perhaps the strongest reason why *Sirius* succeeds in such a forbidden zone is that one of the most personal and trusting kinds of relationship that can be had between humans is treated with sensitivity and good humor, when such a love between human and canine involves more than physical love. It can be added that mundane human relationships with dogs are often of a personal and trusting nature too. Brian Aldiss (198) observes: "Love is a rare thing in Stapledon's world; here, reaching across species, it finds the warmest and most touching expression, to live on even when the mutated dog is killed." Kinnaird (2089–2090) says this "marriage" between Sirius and Plaxy is "delicately treated." Although there remains "some degree of instinctive revulsion," it is necessary to the story that Plaxy, who is Beauty in the archetypal fairy tale upon which *Sirius* is modeled, commits her love to Sirius "*before* she knows that he is an enchanted prince" (here touching on the Frog-Prince fairy tale as well, and so mixing his metaphors). Using a Jungian model, Kinnaird refers to Plaxy as Sirius' *anima*, releasing him "from hatred of man into a brief wholeness of being," which is all that the militaristic civilization in which they live will allow. Kinnaird's reference to Plaxy discovering that Sirius is a handsome prince seems a little obscure because Plaxy's love for Sirius throughout the novel shows that he was always special to her. There is no sudden metamorphosis from frog to prince. The relationship grows through developmental stages. But the novel does end with an epiphany experienced by them both. Plaxy's last words to Sirius are "Our spirits fit," and Sirius's final words, "Plaxy-Sirius — worth while," prefigure the closing metaphors for Sirius' spirit: the dawn and the bright Dog Star after which he is named.

If one compares Peter Goldsworthy's less satisfying novel *Wish* with *Sirius*, I suggest that both works effect a balance between satire and tragedy, and thereby succeed in creating distance between the reader and the subject through defamiliarization, as well as eliciting sympathy. Goldsworthy distances himself and the reader from the sexual act (and, to an extent, from spiritual and companionate love too) by depicting John James in a mostly unsympathetic light while giving the genetically altered gorilla Wish a one-dimensional character. By contrast, Stapledon pays more attention to the characterization of his key players and draws them largely sympathetic for the reader while not omitting their faults. Indeed, vulnerability makes them attractive protagonists. To draw again on Barbara Bengels' (59–60) affectionate and witty critique of the bestiality theme:

> We *feel* the pathos of Sirius who wishes to love Plaxy and to fulfil his potentialities.... Sirius ... is the very essence of love, and it, in part, destroys him.... Love between two species can be seen as wholly tragic, but Stapledon has maintained a lighter touch here.

Robert Philmus (107) identifies that lighter touch as a "Stapledonian quality," called "niceness" by Brian Aldiss, but which Philmus prefers to describe as "decency, generosity, and honesty."

However, there is another, perhaps unexpected, facet of Stapledon's complex character.

At one point in his story Sirius fears that he is slipping into "moral decay." During the time of scientific research at Cambridge (102), "a note of sadism crept into his love-making. Once there was a terrible commotion because in the very act of love he dug his teeth into the bitch's neck." And when Sirius and Plaxy (53) discuss their love for each other in earlier times,

> "Even if I [Plaxy] fall in love with someone and marry him some day, I shall belong to you. Why did I not know it properly until today?" He said, "It is I that am yours until I die. I have known it ever so long — since I bit you." Looking into his grey eyes and fondling the dense growth on his shoulder, she said, "We are bound to hurt one another so much, again and again. We are so terribly different." "Yes," he said, "but the more different, the more lovely the loving."

Later in the novel (145): "Sadistic little bitch!" Sirius cries as Plaxy pulls his ears, "Sweet cruel bitch!" Leslie Fiedler (12) extrapolates from such passages, saying they have sado-masochistic undertones:

> Odd John, and the dog, Sirius, are both multiple murderers.... There is in all this more than a hint of a streak of sado-masochism in Stapledon, verging (it seems to me) on the pathological—as well as a suggestion that he, too, like certain of his characters is a man divided against himself.

David Pringle (77–78), while finding "small beer" factual errors in Fiedler's treatment, on the whole supports this reading and echoes Fiedler:

> It seems to me that the sado-masochistic element is very obviously present in Stapledon's fictions, manifest not only in the great dyings already referred to, but in the constant association of "ecstasy" and pain.... The persistence with which he returns to such motifs of physical torment is remarkable.

We could make similar observations about the violence and cruelty in Paul Linebarger's fiction, as in "The Dead Lady of Clown Town."

Fiedler does not get off so lightly, however, at the hands of Robert Philmus (72–73), who claims he has a "profound distaste for Stapledon." (On the other hand, Pringle notes, with approval, Fiedler's admission that he wept at *Sirius*' ending.) Philmus criticizes Fiedler for "misinformation and misleading assertions," for not attempting "to interpret Stapledon in Stapledon's own terms," for "derogatory rumors" surrounding the publication of his (Fiedler's) book, and labels the work "regressive criticism." So intent is he on this hatchet job that Philmus allows no room to consider the issues of sadism/physical torment, and, in his turn, is open to challenge for not addressing that theme. Perhaps Philmus is unwilling to do so. The dark side of Stapledon's writing is as legitimate an object of literary enquiry as any other.

A tragic element of Sirius' and Plaxy's love is certainly the pain it brings. It seems likely that Stapledon is using physical pain as a metaphor for spiritual anguish. There is a continual cross-over between physical and emotional subjects, so we find that amid his overpowering sexual desires (the physical), Sirius' quest for self-understanding (the emotional and intellectual) continues. He can say (145), somewhat patronizingly, of the bitch Mifanwy, who is one of his companions during the happiest period of his life back on the farm, "Though she's so deadly stupid, she really has the rudiments of a soul." It is characteristic of Stapledon's dense writing that in the paragraph preceding Sirius' remark about Mifanwy a mix of ambiguous themes meld together, followed by speculation as to whether dogs and other animals have souls.

Sirius' remark about Mifanwy comes immediately after a flirtatious wrestling match with Plaxy, romping that would otherwise be normal among many dogs and their humans. The element of familiarity is present. Dogs (and cats) have long tactile associations with humans as companions. They share with us hearth and home and, let us face it, beds. There is an expression from outback Australia, the "three dog" night, when referring to an especially cold time. The great apes, though anthropomorphic and more closely related to humans genetically, do not usually stand in the same relationship. In popular experience, we pat and stroke our animal companions, and they, in turn, share our body warmth and lick us. Most readers with dog companions, or who have observed them often enough, will know that a male dog understands very well the gender of his human mistress who, in his tightly knit hierarchical world, is alpha female to (usually from his point of view) alpha male. Those who are fortunate enough to be owned by a male dog know that they can at times be embarrassing.

One explanation for the presence of cruelty in *Sirius* is that Stapledon's public world was experiencing social and political upheavals — the two world wars and poverty, for instance — while at the same time his private world was troubled. Through the novel, Stapledon is expressing personalized remorse over a secret. The nature of that secret is revealed by Evelyn Gibson's note to Stapledon's penciled manuscript: that Stapledon was allegorizing a real-life *menage à trois* in which he himself was implicated. Whether Stapledon also had sado-masochistic tendencies is probably not the point.

Crossley (385) tells us that Stapledon was twice unfaithful to Agnes, first with Evelyn Gibson and then with a woman identified as "N." Agnes knew both women, and, indeed, at one point Stapledon wanted an open marriage between himself, Agnes and N. But the strain on them all was too great, "wrecking both love and friendship," and Stapledon reluctantly gave up the idea. Robert Philmus (108) explains this "insensitive treatment at times, of the three women in his life" as a mark of immaturity — "innocence" he calls it — adding, a little unkindly, that Stapledon's "mental evolution" was "unusually gradual and protracted." There can be other explanations. Stapledon was in his fifties and may have been experiencing what we call now the "mid-life crisis." There is also the man's intense physical energy. Crossley (223) shows a photograph of Stapledon climbing a Cumbrian cliff wall at the age of fifty.

What seems clear is that Stapledon was deeply troubled by his infidelities. Crossley's (11) strong implication that he made the writing of *Sirius* a means of self-catharsis is persuasive: "In having Sirius killed off by moral vigilantes at the end of the novel and restoring Plaxy to Robert, he allegorized his own reluctant abandonment of an extramarital love, his surrender to moral convention, and his return to the woman he had loved for forty years."

Stapledon characterizes Plaxy as sometimes part animal and part human, and at other times possessing supernatural qualities. The animal with which she is most often compared is the cat, and, appropriately enough, her mystery is likened to that of a witch (who traditionally has cat familiars) or nature-spirit. Robert (49) describes her as "at once human and 'para-human,' so that she seemed to me not so much cat as fay. She was at once cat, fawn, dryad, elf, witch." The imagery recurs (158, 172). Plaxy is "'scarcely human,' though cat-like and fey," and "inwardly not human at all but some exquisite fawn-like beast, or perhaps a fox or dainty cat transformed temporarily into the likeness of a woman." The words "fay" and "fey" have slightly different meanings, the first as "fairy" and the second as "otherworldly" or "elfin" (*OED*), both connoting the Fates or being fated.

This is probably more than Stapledon's perception of woman as mystery. It is an ingredient in the "love and discord" that characterizes Plaxy's relationship with Sirius and, in a less obvious way, with Robert, perhaps also with her father. It also serves as a distancing mechanism between the reader and the underlying theme of sexual relations between human and beast. What better metaphor to employ than the pun of dog and cat?: "It was her latent antagonism to Sirius that had turned that manner cat-like" (49). This may be read in terms of Plaxy's humanness coming to the fore; also as relatively normal conflict in a person's individuation, the search for independence from others who are (too) close. Upon Thomas Trelone's death, when Robert talks about Plaxy's relationship with her father (162), we are told:

> Suddenly she gave up her work and practically broke off relations with her lover in order to join her life with the strange being who was her father's most brilliant creation. Does it not seem probable that the underlying motive of this decision was the identification of Sirius with her father?

In its emphasis on inter-species love, *Sirius* has something in common with Paul Linebarger's novella "The Dead Lady of Clown Town" and Goldsworthy's *Wish*. Like all of us, Sirius is a mix of contradictory traits. Intelligent and self-respecting, he walks (62–63) "with a proud tail." He is magnanimous, his fine spirit calling for Robert's respect. Yet (43) he is "at heart a timid creature who rose to a display of boldness only in desperation or when the odds were favourable." As other commentators suggest, we might not be far wrong in extrapolating from this characterization of an allegorical dog hero to Stapledon himself.

CHAPTER 10

Companionate and Erotic Love 2: *Wish*

Sexuality between human and non-human is a relatively unique theme, but Peter Goldsworthy, when he writes explicitly on it in his novel *Wish* (1995), is not the first to have done so. Where sexual relations between humans and beasts are concerned, we can go back to Greek mythology and tales of erotic exploits between humans and gods. The story of Leda and the Swan comes to mind. In the present era, this theme of sexual and companionate relationships and needs between the human and non-human can be traced back through a number of science fiction and fantasy works to the great nineteenth century myth of Mary Shelley's *Frankenstein*. When writing about animal-human sexuality there is a fine line between establishing reader sympathy towards the protagonists while at the same time using narrative techniques that distance the reader from their actions, because bestiality is a strong social taboo (not the last, however, because whenever a "last taboo" is declared, a new one is soon invented). Tragedy is one way of establishing distancing; humor is another.

According to the *Who's Who of Australian Writers* (256–257), Peter David Goldsworthy was born in 1951 in the South Australian town of Minlaton. Holding Bachelor of Science and Bachelor of Medicine degrees from the University of Adelaide, he is in that envious position of being able to earn a living in medicine while pursuing writing: poetry, screenplays, short fiction, and novels. He is described (probably by himself) as a humorist and satirist, and, in the blurb for his novel *Honk if You Are Jesus* (1992), as a mixer of "sci-fi, medical marvel, satire and romance." His writing has earned him several awards (for example, the Commonwealth Poetry Prize in 1982 and the Bicentennial Literature Award in 1988). His major works include *Readings from Ecclesiastes* (1982), *Archipelagoes* (1982), *Zooing* (1986), *Bleak Rooms* (1988),

This Goes with This (1988), *Maestro* (1989), *This Goes with That: Selected Poems 1970–1990* (1991), *Magpie* (co-authored with Brian Matthews, 1992), *After the Ball* (1992), *Little Deaths* (1993), and *Keep It Simple, Stupid* (1996). By this reckoning, *Wish* (1995) is Goldsworthy's eleventh book, published at the age of forty-four. Since then, he has written two novels: *Three Dog Night* (2003) and *Everything I Knew* (2008).

"Wish" is the designated name of one of the work's two principal characters, a female gorilla descended from the western lowlands subspecies *Gorilla gorilla gorilla*, originally named Eliza by the couple raising her. She is dubbed Wish by John James — the other chief protagonist — because of her repeated use of that sign: crossed fingers in Auslan, the Australian signing language used by the profoundly deaf through which Wish's minders and John communicate with her. This double meaning, wish as name and as substantive, is the dominant motif of the novel.

In order to communicate the Otherness of Wish, Goldsworthy uses sentences broken by commas, interrupted by parentheses, often staccato — a conversational, stream of consciousness mode. The novel makes frequent use of tactile, olfactory and gustatory imagery. Scent and taste are employed to communicate emotion and mood. Language in the broader sense as more than speech is another important motif. One of the novel's themes is the difficulty of communication between different sorts of people, between the deaf and non-deaf among humans, and between humans and non-humans (animals), also between words and non-verbal communication. They are pairings in juxtaposition.

There is frequent recourse to extra-verbal modes of communication, principally poetry and music, but also intertextual forms such as television, film, and scientific treatises, both real and fictionalized, that allow for parody. John James' growing understanding of Wish and eventual love for her is expressed in poetic terms — either through a direct appeal to poetry as "symbolic utterance" (109) or the creation of actual poems, as in those written by one of the other chief protagonists, the animal liberationist Stella Todd: "...I sniff the Sniff/ of Two Legs opening White Door:/ the Cold Kennel where Meat lives" (63). Compare this with Gummidge the cat's naming of his human compatriots "Old Horsemeat" and "Kitty-Come-Here" in Fritz Leiber's diverting short story "Space-Time for Springers," where the giving of nicknames to humans by sentient animals is a parody of the human predilection for applying unusual names to animals.

These animal poems help to establish a sympathetic mood in the reader before the meeting with Wish. Stephen Muecke (47) observes, "Literature often heightens its medium through poetic intensifications," but then puzzlingly claims that Goldsworthy does not need poetic intensifications "because he is doing something different ... his is the double play of the language of words and the language of signs." The suggestion that Goldsworthy has no need for poetic tropes I think misses the point. Goldsworthy, throughout the novel, consciously employs "poetic intensifications" that are part of the "language of words" in a stylistic policy that helps the novel move. The novel would lack some of its power without the poetic touches.

Wish/Eliza's first "spoken" communication — witnessed by John in a video recording and really a signed or mimed act — is described by John (109) as a poem: "To the best of my knowledge Eliza had spoken the first symbolic utterance — the first poem — ever created by another species." Similarly (117), John hails Wish's use of the "wish" sign as "a beautiful touch, an improvised variation, another poem which moved me." Poetry as "symbolic utterance" is important to the story because it demonstrates in Wish what is commonly taken to be a characteristic that defines humanness: the ability to communicate in abstracts with symbols. Music is not alluded to so often, but when it is, Goldsworthy, through his character John (203), clearly associates it with the rhythms of poetry: "As she closed her eyes and rocked her head in time, I realized that the main sense of those sweet songs was in the melodies; the words needed no translation."

The narrative plot within which these stylistic modes operate is relatively straightforward. John James, a large overweight fellow who is something of a misanthrope since his divorce from Jill, is asked by Stella Todd and her partner Clive Kinnear to teach Auslan to their young charge Eliza. Eliza turns out to be a genetically altered gorilla. John renames her "Wish," and as their lessons in communication proceed, a bond of affection grows between the two, which culminates with them having sex. This occurs in Book Three and, appropriately enough, is the episode that marks the climax of the novel. Book Four is the dénouement in which they are discovered by Clive, who begins court proceedings against John — not from moral outrage, however, but with the motive of making Wish's case a *cause célèbre* for animal rights, especially those of an intelligent, self-aware animal.

It is this duplicity that brings tragedy upon them rather than John's moral lapse. Wish is removed to the Adelaide zoo, where, in despair, she suicides by hanging. Stella leaves Clive, and John becomes further estranged from his ex-wife and daughter Rosie. But a reconciliation of sorts is hinted at between Stella and John when the former visits John in his minimum-security prison; also between John and the now-dead Wish in a final touch of the numinous (299):

> A breeze stirred somewhere; I heard the shiver of the treetops, the sweepings of approaching debris across the carpark, then saw the wind catch and embroider and then divide the rising column of smoke, two fingers which briefly tangled, as if crossing index and middle, before joining again in a single smooth column rising upwards into the blue.

Compare the trope in James Joyce's (218) *Ulysses* (1922/1971), cited in Kingsley Amis (443):

> Kind air defined the coigns of houses in Kildare street. No Birds. Frail from the housetops two plumes of smoke ascended, pluming, and in a flaw of softness softly were blown.

The Client Ape

As Stephen Muecke (47) observes (unnecessarily), "Once he had the idea for this new work, Goldsworthy had to establish fictional plausibilities." Human glands and the hormones they produce are a common factor in stories of this kind. Wish was "biologically engineered," as the subtitle says, by the removal of the embryonic adrenal glands, an operation facilitating growth of the brain because the inhibitor of such growth, cortisone, is no longer present. There is a negative payoff, for without doses of corticosteroids daily, such an animal would soon die (226–228). This is another tragic element, that the genetically changed animal is usually incomplete. Victor Frankenstein's Creature — the debt that Goldsworthy and many others owe to Mary Shelley — is fashioned from a patchwork of human parts culled from graveyards. In her case, Wish possesses an ape-like body but with a gracile, almost human visage.

Wish the novel raises questions about social and ethical justifications for animal experimentation, dramatized in its climactic section by a debate between John and Terry, the scientist who originally took Eliza/Wish from the Melbourne laboratories. Partly disaffected with the project after becoming emotionally attached to Wish, Terry, however, retains the scientific point of view. One goal of the project is "to produce primates that could perform a range of intelligent tasks" (228), or, as John James instantly rejoins, produce "slaves for the assembly line!" — a common theme that harks back to Aldous Huxley's *Brave New World* (1932) and Čapek's *War with the Newts*. But there is a broader motive. "Think of the implications for human intelligence," says Terry (230) in an echo of Clive's thoughts expressed sixty-five pages earlier: "We can learn much by looking at ourselves through her eyes" (165). The search for an understanding of our selves underpins western science, a view that suggests a general truth, that we must always know ourselves in relationship to some other phenomenon. But is this motive any more redeeming than that of creating a labor pool? What can make this quest go awry is to forget the importance of the emotional life.

Characteristics that make us human include self-awareness, an apprehension of consequences, a tendency to speculate about the meanings of death and life, and the experiencing of "human" emotions such as anxiety, fear, and love in all permutations. These appreciations come indirectly in the novel and not from a thoroughgoing characterization of Wish herself. In *Wish* the theme of a consciously aware Other questioning the world in which they have been born is muted and presented mostly through John James' thoughts, in his debates with Clive and Stella (and with some of the minor characters), in his conversations with Wish, and in his interpretations of those conversations and Wish's actions. Wish, in this light, is an innocent, a naïf protected from most of the harsh realities of the world. One of the strengths of the novel lies in her reactions to the real world — revulsion upon learning that humans eat animals, or anxiety about death (both good examples of defamiliarization that help us look anew at such issues). Wish rebels, but at a restricted level, as when she signs her dislike of Stella's badgering (109). The tragedy for Wish lies in her increasingly conscious awareness of, and exposure to, human cruelties, to which she finally succumbs. As John James says, Wish "still had an important lesson to learn, perhaps the most important: that the stupidity and cruelty of her cousin species, Homo sapiens, was limitless" (290).

Together with Wish's innocence, another central ingredient for tragedy lies in her quest for self. Wish is very nearly human in physiology: "She was almost adult sized, but her face was surely not the face of an adult gorilla. Her forehead was less protruding, her head disproportionately larger and more rounded — a child's big head" (99). And Wish's chief desire is to become more human. One of the most harrowing episodes in the novel is her attempt to shave her body hair, motivated in part by jealousy on seeing Stella and John in bed together.

John James recognizes anthropomorphism in the photographs in Clive's (C. Francis Kinnear's) book *Primate Suffrage*, noting that they appear to have been selected "for cuteness — to find some human essence in the apes, a kinship with which the reader might identify" (89). This invented book, a parody on scientific discourse, helps to introduce another theme important for the novel's development. Goldsworthy takes the arguments of animal liberation rhetoric to their logical conclusion when Clive, in a television interview, says pedantically, "The rights of a particular individual of that species are far more important — far more tangible.... The client ape should be fully acquainted with the pros and cons and allowed to make an informed decision" (79). This parodies not only scientific prose but also the jargon of the social worker.

Wish is, in Clive's words, "outside human culture, looking in"; and to Clive this has the valuable scientific implication — as we have seen — that we can learn a great deal about ourselves through her eyes because Wish is "free from the preconceptions, the acculturation" (165). This is fallacious because Wish has already learned much more about human culture than Clive and Stella realize, as John discovers. In an extension of Clive's earlier point, John's argument is that just as the deaf should participate in the outside world while retaining their unique (Sign) language (139), so too should Wish be allowed similar outlets. In this respect, the two protagonists have compatible positions, although they are opponents on other issues. There is then only a relatively short step to the next freedom: "If Wish deserved human rights, she deserved human pleasures" (214). "If she is entitled to human rights, those rights should, I would have thought, include the right to *fuck*" (251), says John.

This brings us to companionship (by which I mean spiritual love or *agape*) and sexuality (sensual love) — hand in hand with John James' growing insights into Wish's intellectual capacities and her inner emotional life. There is a further twist when Wish, the object of study, begins to ask John about himself (168) — akin to the experience common among anthropologists when interviewees ask questioners about them, joke with them, and even take their photograph in a sort of carnivalesque overturning of roles. It reflects the curiosity of an enquiring, and therefore intelligent, mind. Wish jokes with John, she takes him into a high tree, into her natural environment, and shows him sketches attached to the wall of her room. At this point John feels "an odd sensation: of tables turned, of *my* artwork being scrutinised, searched for psychological clues" (171). Wish's drawings of John reflect the reality of his large bulk, as would a photograph. Perhaps, too, the psychological phenomenon called transference is taking place. John responds: "Wish's growing puppy-love, adoring even when she was teasing me, added immensely to the pleasure of those days" (181).

John falls in love with Wish because "we shared more than language; we also shared the nearest thing to a natural relationship in her life" (238). But is this a rationalization? At the psychological level, John realizes, "My deepest need was for tenderness, for intimacy" (244). This is said after the fact when, standing in the shadows of Wish's room before going to her, John overturns a joke made at his expense by Terry: "I felt, for once in my life, beautiful: a giant of a man, a human silverback, in full sexual rut" (239). Wish's love is a powerful boost to John's self-esteem. The novel, in my opinion, depicts John's quest for self as much as, or even more than, that of Wish.

Distancing

In literature, the search for self, for companionship and sexual happiness can generate challenging and uncomfortable insights. That is one reason why such stories are written. But the same argument explains why not many really good tales are extant. In the better works, to question what is human touches on archetypal cultural images. A writer treads unstable ground when depicting characters engaged in what the law calls bestiality, one of society's great taboos. Part of Goldsworthy's success in circumventing this limitation is stylistic. As Michael McGirr (51) says of Goldsworthy's writing in general: "The progression ... is so logical ... that it is difficult to count back and find the precise point at which moral chaos got in under the brick veneer." But how successfully the theme of moral chaos is handled depends on more than literary skill; its effectiveness can be made or broken by the prevailing mood in society. Goldsworthy can write explicit sexual passages, and get them published, because present day sociosexual mores admit greater tolerance towards such descriptions:

> I lay down on the bed and wrapped my arms about Wish, but awkwardly, trying to keep the lower half of my body out of actual contact. She rolled suddenly onto her back and pulled me on top of her, the force of her great arms gentle, but irresistible. For the first time our lower halves came in contact, which meant the end of my resistance. I wanted suddenly to be inside her — not because of the thrill of a forbidden sexual act, but simply because I loved her [240–241].

Stephen Muecke (48) observes: "Goldsworthy is working in a society where the heterogeneity of desire is celebrated, and rapacious Man is no longer considered the centre of his long-suffering world." That statement is a bit sweeping and needs some modification. The ideologues for human dominance are still among us, but what Muecke says is certainly true inasmuch as a writer can get away with more in the 1990s, up to a point, than one could fifty years earlier.

Would Goldsworthy's novel have met with resistance if it had dealt too sympathetically with its characters? For they do not, in my opinion, elicit a wholly sympathetic reader response.

I think Goldsworthy succeeds because he employs several distancing techniques that make it possible to confront the idea of bestiality. He does it, however, less subtly than Stapledon in *Sirius*. While Wish herself is presented sensitively, our knowledge about her is relatively little. On the other hand, our knowledge of the dog Sirius is proportionately biographical. A great deal of Goldsworthy's work is about different kinds of hypocrisy masked beneath scientific rationalism or obscured by ignorance and misunderstanding. I felt that the soapbox was not far, especially in the somewhat contrived scientific debates between human protagonists. Most commonly, a lack of sufficient feeling, a dearth of emotion, lies at the heart of these. It is a contretemps between two Jungian functions of the psyche, thinking and feeling, the first articulated by Clive and Terry, the second dramatized by John James and Wish. Stella comes somewhere in between, at first joining in the experiment with Clive but redeemed towards the end when she rejects Clive's scientific ideology. This thinking versus feeling model is reflected also in the two sub-plots: John's conflicts with his deaf parents — a hostile and authoritarian father, a mediating and more affectionate mother — also conflicts with the studied reasonableness of his ex-wife Jill.

These functions are played out on the novel's center stage in the relationships between John, Clive, Stella, and Wish. The relationship between Clive and Stella towards Wish is characterized by paternalism. To Clive, Wish is a scientific object of study, a project; for Stella, Wish may be a surrogate child. Paradoxically, these preoccupations cause them to lose sight of the quality of feeling in Wish's almost-human nature: "To both of them, Project Wish came first, even at the expense of Wish's happiness" (189). Clive is depicted as measured, over-controlled, prissy (29), qualities about which Stella often confronts him so that it becomes a marital game: "They were playing their favourite game again: spot an emotion" (190). At one point Stella says, "Clive tends not to see what she [Wish] feels — only what she says.... Clive doesn't believe in emotions " (128). John, above all, sees himself in opposition to these people, perhaps to the world. He is dominated not only by feeling but also by a degree of intuition derived from his unique childhood: using Auslan, watching for subtle physical clues in people, their body language. This is the yardstick by which he measures others.

There appears also to be some arrogance in John's dealings with those around him. He constantly compares his skill at Sign and greater sensitiveness towards other's feelings with the hypocrisies and double-dealing that he believes are contained in the spoken word. My reaction was at first to be intrigued by the descriptions of Auslan, illustrated throughout the book by line sketches, only to grow disaffected by John's chauvinism. Was this Goldsworthy's intention? Since Roland Barthes had people believing that the author was dead, maybe less attention has been given to author intention. Privately John derides the efforts of all attempts by others to learn the direct, sublime but difficult mode of communication that is Auslan. He makes that commonest of insider claims noted by Irving Goffman years ago: "Others will never really understand," an outlook that is essentially self-defeating.

At bottom, John James is characterized as a misanthrope. He is large and awkward, acutely aware of his bulk and operating predominantly at the level of feeling and the sensual. He is highly susceptible emotionally to the tactile and the olfactory — his earliest attraction towards Wish triggered by her not unpleasant musky smell — to such an extent that he is greatly dependent on those senses, perhaps too dependent.

He escapes from the cares of the world by donning a wet suit and floating in the still waters of the Glenelg beach front, and later in the dam at Stella and Clive's farm immediately prior to having sex with Wish. The physical setting shifts back and forth from the South Australian Adelaide suburb of Glenelg to the Hills (where I used to live), between John James's home and that of Wish. This imagery of the sea as a natural float tank with cleansing properties and overtones of returning to the womb is a recurring motif, altering the novel's pace between the conflicts of interpersonal debate and moments of quietude (e.g. 209). The image spills over at one point when towards the end of his conversation with Terry — before Terry chides him with the joke about being a silverback — there is a return to the floating, swimming motif, a cetacean image, with a suggestion, too, of post coital *triste*, though John and Wish have not yet coupled: "The day had been long, a heavy surf of emotions and ideas; I was exhausted, but not unpleasantly, beached in a tranquil aftermath" (233).

Essentially, John and Wish are outsiders. John especially is beyond the pale after he commits the offence of bestiality. Being outsiders applies to other characters. John's parents are outsiders because of their hearing disabilities. Clive, Stella and Terry have gone against the scientific establishment by taking Wish from the laboratories, and in their espousal of the scientific method they are also "deaf" to the emotional life. Wish is denied the rights of a conscious, self-aware, thinking and questioning being because physiologically she is not human.

For tragedy to work, there must be a degree of reader sympathy towards the recalcitrant character, even someone like Macbeth, sufficient to allow the reader to suspend judgment. Being outsiders helps evoke the reader's sympathy. Clive is well-meaning, Stella is warm and somewhat lost in her partnership with Clive, John's parents evoke sympathy, and is there not always some residual sympathy for an overweight person? What in the end makes the tragedy most poignant is society's attitude that dismisses John's offence as a bad joke. He can be dismissed as harmlessly eccentric (293) by comparison with the pedophiles sharing jail with him (the current social taboo)—precisely because he has transgressed with a nonhuman: "Finally, I was a joke, and therefore Wish also was a joke, consigned, again, to the inhuman world, and perhaps even to the inanimate" (294).

The most striking distance-setting strategy is that after Goldsworthy has depicted explicitly sexual acts between a human and a nearly-human ape he introduces mythopoeic imagery with an economy characteristic of his writing, as when Wish thanks John in Sign using all her limbs: "Her four hands, waving like those of some dark Hindu goddess, seemed at that moment the most beautiful thing I had ever seen" (242). This has an archetypal power but is communicated with a light touch combining the animal popularly regarded as "less-than-human" and a goddess that is "more-than-human." The dictionary definition of anthropomorphism includes the religious or numinous, and it may not be too far-fetched to see in *Wish* an appeal to mythology, namely the identification of Woman with nature, with the evocation of goddesses from religions that existed many hundreds of years before Christianity.

Imagery of woman's mystery permeates the novel. Stella, for example, is introduced in vaguely Earth Mother terms: "She had a comfortable thirty-something face, plenty of laugh-lines, a broad lopsided smile" (27). As a large-breasted "comfortable" woman she is a muted human reflection of Wish, and, like Wish, she attempts to seduce John, though unsuccessfully. Wish is human in her sentience, yet mysterious in her animal nature. The recurring images of the sea (the Gulf) and the Hills, well known metaphors for the feminine and the masculine principles, may be no accident. In Jungian phraseology, the sea is John's *anima*, and the Hills (or trees) represent Wish's *animus*. One of the novel's messages is that modern humans have lost the old pre-scientific union they once had with the intuitive, religious mysteries. The tragic love between John James and Wish represents allegorically the separation in our psyches of reason from feeling, nature from culture, scientific from religious mysteries.

Concerning authorial voice, are tales of this kind best told from the standpoint of the sentient animal or from that of human protagonists? It is partly a question of style. *Wish* would have been quite a different novel had it been told from the point of view of Wish herself, but that is a tall order. To attempt a sustained development through an alien mind would test the skill of any writer. Stapledon did it admirably in *Sirius*, and Tess Williams in *Sea as Mirror* (2000). Goldsworthy tells the story of Wish in the first person from John James' viewpoint, and most of the novel traces the development of character through the relationships between John and Wish, John and his parents, John and his ex-wife, John and his boss, John and Stella and Clive, John and the police. The central character is John James, not Wish. This allows some distancing from Wish herself, though there are plenty of incidents to illustrate her mixed human-alien character. Goldsworthy is no Stapledon.

To try too hard to create an alien viewpoint might be to create a clever text but one that becomes indecipherable to many readers. I think that to understand the Other we need to apply a process of "translation" or "appropriation"—though not in the pejorative sense used by many critics influenced by postcolonial studies and political correctness—by bringing concepts into our language that were once alien, or very nearly so, and banging them together. We do this all the time, and not always with fidelity to the meaning or spirit of the original. Take, for example, the appearance of the word "mantra," a buzzword in journalistic commentaries. Goldsworthy does something similar by using the unfamiliar language of Auslan, which, from Wish's signed utterances, becomes stripped down into "broken English." In this manner it may be possible in our literary imaginations to comprehend an alien viewpoint.

Humor is an important factor, and having one-dimensional characters is another way of creating distance. On satire, Muecke (48), for example, identifies "'signs' of political correctness" in the characters of Stella and Clive. McGirr (51) points out that the use of nicknames (which appear often in joking relationships) tends "to reduce characters to a single dimension." Also, when Goldsworthy has John James reading (that is, parodying) press reports about bestiality, he is alluding to well-recognized topics for carnal humor: the shepherd and his sheep or the woman and her large dog. But there are poignant edges to the satirical touches aimed at present-day morés. We are never far from tragedy. John feels that the note of amusement in the press reports is unfair to animals because "They are as much victims as any human victim, a crime against them is as serious as any human crime" (240).

Making the stigmatized the butt of jokes is both a means of handling the jokers' unease in the face of difference (which means that we will always have joking of this kind), and a means of excluding the stigmatized, whether they are human or animal. This is where the counter-pointing of a fictional animal possessing human intelligence against the real world experiences of the profoundly deaf comes into play. A common stereotype about even the partially deaf is that such individuals possess below-average intelligence, the real reason behind this misconception being that they often miss the auditory cues that a hearing person catches with little difficulty. The 1990s appeared to be a decade of greater knowledge of, and tolerance towards, difference, though compassion and political correctness are uneasy bed-persons. Political correctness may throw a veil over hypocrisy. This is another of Goldsworthy's messages.

What places *Wish* in the ranks of science fiction and fantasy is that it rehearses such questions as those raised by James Gunn (6–7) almost twenty years ago:

> In the first forty years of the twentieth century science fiction began to ask questions that had never before been asked: Will humanity progress or regress? Will its social forms change? Will humanity survive?

Muecke (28) says, "A main point of the book is that ideal humanity is no longer the most important thing to strive for, but rather one has to rethink humanity as just one among many forms of life, and as still in a process of change as it encounters its Others." Maybe so, and perhaps the "rethinking of humanity" might extend to non-physical (meta-physical) "human" qualities: combinations of spiritual and sexual love, plus a union between scientific and spiritual views. These are not really new ideas. They are traditionally eastern, as symbolized by Goldsworthy in his description of Wish as Hindu goddess.

When an earlier version of this chapter was published (Shaw 2000b), friends said that after reading the review they were not inclined to read the book. Other reviewers were more damning. Trevor Kettlewell (2007) gives the novel a rating of B+/F: B+ meaning "Solid. Or maybe OK but with some very good bits"; the F denoting the work as "Vile. Appalling dross, offensive, deeply flawed: As ever well written but ultimately a deeply offensive theme." The sticking point is bestiality. Kettlewell, in what Martin Amis (74) calls "an extra-literary response" to nastiness in novels, writes:

> It's too much for me.... Goldsworthy has written a fine book [but] he's never going to sell me bestiality as potentially acceptable, either in reality, or even as a purely fantastical idea merely for a potent literary work.... If he's stating this theme as anything more than a novel idea, he differs from this popular stance in his preparedness to take such a conviction to one of its more disturbing moral conclusions.... If there really is no difference, there is nothing morally wrong with a person having consensual sex with an animal.

Kettlewell adds, however, "I don't think he's so much interested in being the champion of bestiality as using it as the real weapon to confront double standards."

A slightly different point of view comes from an unnamed reviewer for the Literature, Arts, and Medicine Database (2005), who, while finding the novel weird, "whimsical and engaging," sees the main theme as "of course, the varieties of communication," and the satire of the tale centering upon the animal rights movement, with Clive as possibly a satirized Peter Singer and John "the tragicomic anti-hero."

Wish is balanced between tragedy and satire with touches of parody. Its chief theme, the "hook" by which the author attracts the reader, is a sexual relationship between a human male and a nearly human female gorilla. If sensual and sexual love was the only factor at work, the novel might stray towards the genre of pornographic literature. But Goldsworthy overcomes this hazard by suggesting the principle of spiritual love, with its emphasis on mutual respect and companionship. His narrative techniques raise the relationship between Wish and John James to a mythopoeic level, appealing to the poetic and the numinous, plus the employment of distancing mechanisms like presenting most characters in an often satiric, less than sympathetic light. This saves the novel from crassness or banality. Readers are challenged, on the one hand, by a questioning of accepted scientific truths, and, on the other hand, by the flouting of a moral taboo.

CHAPTER 11

"It Had Been Such a Nice Rabbit!": *City*

Because of how it developed, Clifford Simak's *City* can be appreciated either as a novel or as separate stand-alone short stories. *City* is a collation of nine short stories that were first published in various issues of *Astounding Science Fiction*. Most were written in the mid–1940s: "City," "Huddling Place," "Census" and "Desertion" in 1944; "Paradise" and "Hobbies" in 1946; "Aesop" in 1947; and "Trouble with Ants" in 1951 (retitled "The Simple Way" in 1952). Almost all stand in their own right, and many, such as "City," "Huddling Place," and "Desertion," appear frequently in anthologies. The ninth addition, "Epilog," was published more than twenty years later in 1973 under special circumstances. It was not, of course, included in the first book version when that came out in 1952. "Epilog" is the weakest offering in the series.

Simak invents a family line, the Websters, to carry the series of stories through a chronology of more than 12,000 years. The first story, "City," is set in 1990. "Huddling Place" opens with the funeral of Nelson Webster (2034–2117), father of Jerome Webster, grandfather of Jerome's son Thomas, in which Simak (47) introduces in "the family roll" the founders of the Webster dynasty,

> starting with William Stevens, 1920–1999. Gramp Stevens [of "City"], they had called him, Webster remembered. Father of the wife of that first John J. Webster, who was here himself—1951–2020. And after him his son, Charles F. Webster, 1980–2060. And his son, John J. II, 2004–2086.

In the next tale, "Census," 300 years have passed. In "Aesop" it is 10,000 years since Jon Webster closed Geneva, and almost 12,000 years have passed when we come to "The Simple Way." "Epilog" takes place in an even more remote future when the Dogs have left the Earth and Jenkins remains as caretaker of the old Webster house. This evocation of antiquity and the long passage of time is reinforced by Simak's choice of names for the Dogs — Nathaniel, Ebenezer, Joshua, and Homer (Classical and Old Testament), and similarly for some robots (Joshua, Hezekiah), in contrast to the "doggish" names of their successors: Tige, Rover, and Bounce.

The novel's title appears something of a misnomer because most of the action that follows the short story "City" takes place in a rural setting at the old Webster house. The city as an entity appears rarely, in "Hobbies" and once again in the penultimate chapter, "The Simple Way," where one episode is set in the enclosed city-become-mausoleum of Geneva. Instead, the first of the stories describes the demise of the generic city where human decentralization into country areas has become a fact of life.

Simak worked on many other themes as well as the pastoral. David Pringle (15–29) identifies twelve, all of which we find in *City* and "The Big Front Yard":

> I have isolated a dozen themes that intertwine throughout Simak's work ... 1. The Old Man, 2. The House, 3. Listening to the Stars, 4. The Neighbour, 5. The Alien, 6. The Pastoral, 7. Animals, 8. The Evils of the City, 9. Servants, 10. The Frontier, 11. Bartering, 12. The Artifact.

"City" opens with Gramp Stevens (the old man) watching an automated lawnmower at work, a motif (the artifact) with which the story ends. Ole (a neighbor) tells Gramp about his plan to sell naturally grown food in opposition to the fashion of hydroponics. Gramp is visited by Mark, another neighbor, with plans to move to a ten-acre country estate (the pastoral). After their farewell, Gramp walks to the old Adams place (the house) where he meets Adams' grandson. The scene shifts to another character, John Webster, who is asked by a squatter, Levi Lewis, to intercede with the council over their threat to burn down the squatters' houses (one of the evils of the city). Webster confronts the council but quits in disgust (the council is another city evil). Later he has an interview with Mr. Taylor of the "Bureau of Human Adjustment," who offers him a job helping others adapt to the social changes taking place. Webster again meets Levi, who says the squatters, led by Gramp, are preparing to fight back using guns from the museum (the artefact again). Webster bursts in on the Mayor. Shooting begins outside, and the big gun explodes but without injuring anyone. Gramp arrives with the young Henry Adams, who says he has bought the property. Adams demands they extinguish the fires, dissolve the city charter, and establish a park under the control of Webster, to which they accede (a form of bartering/negotiation).

Not all the themes are present in this first tale of small-town politics. There is little or no mention of animals, aliens, servants, or listening to the stars, but this is soon remedied in the next of Simak's tales, "Huddling Place." A lesser theme missed by Pringle is violence, which goes no further than scuffles and punching, though shooting occasionally occurs, as in "City." Other themes Pringle misses include the all-important idea of the dynasty, soon to be embodied in the Webster family, and psychic or metaphysical powers, such as telepathy or the ability of the Dogs to sense the cobbly worlds. There is a gradual shift through the stories from human politics to elements found more often in the animal romance.

The theme of "Huddling Place" is that it is not cultures but persons who invent certain ideas, institutions or artifacts, not without cross-fertilization from other persons in other cultures, and that when such opportunities are lost, the repercussions can be far-reaching, even tragic. The older man, Jerome Webster, is the protagonist. Sitting in front of the fire at home, Jerome drinks a whiskey handed to him by his robot butler Jenkins, and mentally rehearses (for the reader) the circumstances leading up to the present point in human history. Over the years people have resettled into the countryside to take up new manorial lives, while others set out on expeditions to distant stars, like Jerome's own son. People communicate by means of a machine that, in a touch of prescience, suggests today's "virtual reality" technology. It can "transport" one anywhere in the world, or out of it. Using this device, Jerome's old friend, the Martian philosopher Juwain, asks why he has never returned to Mars, which now has human settlements.

Later, as Jerome Webster bids farewell to his son, departing with the Alpha Centauri expedition, he abruptly experiences agoraphobia and retreats to the fireside safety of his home. In the physical form of Juwain (51) we meet the first real alien of *City*:

> He turned slightly and saw the elaborate crouching pedestal, the furry, soft-eyed figure of the Martian squatting on it. Other alien furniture loomed indistinctly beyond the pedestal, half guessed furniture from that dwelling out on Mars.
>
> The Martian flipped a furry hand toward the mountain range.

These conversations finely illustrate the cultural differences between the two species. Says Juwain (52–53):

> "My people do not make good doctors. They have no background for it. Queer how the minds of races run. Queer that Mars never thought of medicine — literally never thought of it. Supplied the need with a cult of fatalism. While even in your early history, when men still lived in caves–."
>
> "There are many things," said Webster, "that you thought of and we didn't. Things we wonder now how we ever missed. Abilities that you developed and we do not have."

"Abilities ... we do not have" introduces not only this story's conflict but also the central conflict behind all the tales and, by rolling them together, the novel as a whole. In "Huddling Place," news comes a season later that Juwain is dying from a brain disease while on the brink of a new philosophical breakthrough. Webster is persuaded, much against his inclination, to leave for Mars to assist his ailing friend. He packs and awaits the arrival of the spaceship, but it does not appear. At dusk Jenkins tells him a ship arrived earlier but he sent it away. Like a computer (which he is, essentially), the robot has taken literally Jerome's request, not to be disturbed. In subsequent stories we learn that Juwain died before he could disclose his philosophic breakthrough.

In the third story, "Census," we meet the Dogs for the first time. Richard Grant is the census taker of the title. The initial conversation between Grant and Nathaniel sets the scene and introduces the main protagonists: more Webster descendants, the Dog Nathaniel, a mutant human named Joe, and the ants. Bruce Webster is a Victor Frankenstein figure who, through surgery, gives the Dogs speech so that they may become new companions for Man. The science of this is not told in detail. The mutant theme is developed — mutant humans, mutant ants — and the Dogs receive their "human contract." Jenkins the robot butler continues to serve the Websters.

Three hundred years have passed since humans drifted into the wilds, and the government that Grant represents is concerned about a hidden population of mutant humans. There has been no news from the Alpha Centauri expedition. Grant ponders on the mutants and the loss of the Juwain philosophy. Nathaniel visits him and sleeps at the end of his bed. The next day in the woods Grant meets the mutant Joe, who repairs his atomic gun for him. The day after their strange encounter, Grant observes that the ants are pulling small carts and have chimneys protruding from their hill. He recognizes the danger to men and Dogs, and suspects Joe's intervention. In a subsequent meeting with Joe he learns that the mutant has no interest in human needs, such as race preservation, and when Grant shows Joe the papers containing Juwain's unfinished philosophy, Joe, who appears to understand the philosophy, refuses to hand them back. Instead, in an apparently irrational action, he kicks over the anthill. Grant attempts to shoot Joe but is knocked unconscious and comes to with Nathaniel licking his face. Grant tells Nathaniel that if humans become like Joe the Dogs may have to carry on alone. Nathaniel promises to pass the word to the pups through the generations.

"Desertion" is shorter and has virtually no internal connecting links to the other stories, but it does have several of the earlier themes. Perhaps for this reason it is often anthologized. Simak provides a technological explanation for the ultimate disappearance of humans from the earth, apart from the exploration of the stars. The only way in which people can set foot upon Jupiter, with its crushing gravity and poisonous atmosphere, is to have their bodies converted into forms that sustain life. But those who venture out do not return. In order to uncover the mystery, Kent Fowler and his dog Towser pass through the converter, and, as new creatures called Lopers, man and dog find themselves in healthy bodies experiencing marvelous feelings of well-being, with heightened senses and intelligence. They have their first conversation together as true peers, compare notes, and race each other to a waterfall of ammonia cascading down a cliff of oxygen. Like those who had gone before, they decide not to return to their original forms, deserting their human/canine world. Simak is exploring the old question of what it means to be human by posing the idea of conversion to other life forms. "Desertion" introduces the reader to an extra-terrestrial wilderness more preferable than the technological installation for dog and man become Lopers. Humans and Lopers are so different, gifted with differing abilities, that understanding is almost impossible between them.

Fowler does return temporarily, however, in "Paradise" because he feels it his duty to tell the others about the metamorphosis. Towser remains behind because he is too old to be reconverted safely. The world Fowler re-enters is changing. A hundred and twenty-five years have passed since the last murder. The robot Jenkins is now almost 1,000 years old. Another in the Webster dynasty, Tyler Webster, tells Fowler that his news will mean the end of the human race. It is a mark of each Webster protagonist that they feel guilt over some issue. Tyler thinks of his family as a jinx on humanity. The mutant Joe explains to Tyler (135) that the secret of Juwain's philosophy is "an ability to sense the viewpoint of another." This form of empathy and tolerance will enable every person to understand and accept the other, and advance humankind's evolution by thousands of years at a stroke. The ability is imparted to all by mutant trickery through a message imprinted on the brain by colored lights from toy kaleidoscopes and neon signs (still part of the technology of this distant future). But it is a "Catch 22" situation. "Paradise" on Jupiter is a danger because everyone will desire to forsake their human forms by going there; but application of the Juwain Philosophy via the mutant's kaleidoscope will enable humans to understand (empathize with) Fowler's report, and many will take that option.

By the time we read "Hobbies," this has come to pass. Men have left the earth; the Dogs are carrying on as predicted by Richard Grant in "Census"; some humans remain in suspended animation in the city of Geneva. This is now a pastoral world revolving almost exclusively around animals. The Dogs have a farming community; the pups bring in the cows. Inseparable robot companions compensate for the Dogs' lack of human hands. Ebenezer's companion robot is Shadow. Ebenezer succumbs to his old canine instincts by chasing a rabbit, but this exuberance is broken by the intervention of a wolf that kills the rabbit. This introduces the theme of wild wolf nature, as in Olaf Stapledon's *Sirius*. Ebenezer's disappointed exclamation—"*It had been such a nice rabbit!*" (Simak's emphasis)—is a statement of friendly intentions: he liked the creature and was chasing it in play. (Terriers do that.) Meanwhile, in Geneva, Jon Webster stands in a dusty vault (152) at "the foundation of empire." There is a Wellsian evocation of the almost deserted city that has not gone unremarked by Tweet (516), who refers to *City* as "this sad, nostalgic book reminiscent of Campbell's 'Twilight' (1934) or the end of H.G. Wells's *The Time Machine* (1895) and other early science fiction works that capture the same exquisite sense of loss."

Here, too, is Simak's rare mention of a woman, Jon Webster's wife Sara, who awaits him before taking the Sleep. Humans who have chosen to remain on earth periodically enter into suspended animation as a means of avoiding the boredom of their lives. The same theme appears in Cordwainer Smith's Instrumentality series, including "The Dead Lady of Clown Town," except that in Linebarger's future for humanity, those who become bored opt either for euthanasia or for the hazards that reintroduced diseases bring. Later Jon Webster dictates a section of his book via a "thinking cap," describing the elimination of government, crime, economic pressure, and the decline of human effort. There is regret (162): "*The root of it all. If the families had stayed together. If Sara and I had stayed together*" (Simak's emphasis). He continues an internal monologue on Sara's painting of the Webster House in North America, while Ebenezer reports to Jenkins about the wolf.

Subsequently, Ebenezer meets Jon Webster in the old house and tells him he listens for the cobblies, while Jon thinks about his son living in the wild with bows and arrows, a "hobby" that he and a group of other young people take up. Ebenezer removes Jon's warts, and Jon wonders about the Dog's powers. Jenkins explains (181) how the Dogs, with their psychic powers, "try to make friends with the animals and ... watch the wild robots and the mutants," the first intimations of the Dogs' brotherhood of animals concept. He adds that Man could still give leadership, but Webster, back in Geneva, believes that mankind has failed. He activates the defense mechanism sealing off the city from the world and takes the Sleep "forever," reasoning that the Dogs need to be left to work out their own civilization for themselves.

"Hobbies" is a long story, and by now Simak's world has grown strange: the Dogs with their robots and the other woodland animals; wild robots, wild mutant humans, the ants, a band of young humans, a small number of world-weary humans in Geneva sealed in Sleep, and the cobblies, nightmare creatures from another dimension. The Dogs are beginning to tame the wild creatures, and hunting (killing) is no longer allowed. The reluctance of some animals to make the change is shown with gentle irony. Are they so very different from humans?

The episode in which Jon Webster cradles Ebenezer in his arms is one of the most touching in the book: alliterative, subtly repetitive, with long vowels to communicate the comfort and peace felt by Ebenezer, a blend of words evoking strength, gentleness and a sense of security: striding, strong hands, lifted, overpowering, strong (repeated), tight; in juxtaposition to crawl, water, croon, stroke (172). It is the theme of the human as god.

> God had come.... Ebenezer tried to rise, tried to crawl along the floor, but his bones were rubber and his blood was water. And the man was striding toward him, coming in long strides across the floor.
>
> He saw the man bending over him, felt strong hands beneath his body, knew that he was being lifted up. And the scent that he had smelled at the open door — the over-powering god-scent — was strong within his nostrils.
>
> The hands held him tight against the strange fabric the man wore instead of fur and a voice crooned at him — not words, but comforting...
>
> Webster's hand came up and stroked Ebenezer's head and Ebenezer whimpered with doggish happiness.

Themes presaged in "Hobbies" are developed in "Aesop," and this, originally the penultimate story/chapter until Simak decided to add "Epilog" twenty years later, is the climax of the book. Appropriately, the title alludes to the Classical teller of fables, for the chapter is packed with allusions to myths and fairy stories: Br'er Rabbit, Peter and the Wolf, "Who Killed Cock Robin?" The Dogs are referred to consistently with a capital D, the Mutants with capitalized M. Jenkins is now 7,000 years old. The animals' caves and dens have lighting. But Jenkins stays in the old Webster House alone with his memories. The Dogs have forgotten about Men. Through their own psychic gifts, they have found that one cannot travel back in time, for there is no past. Time (193) is "Like two dogs walking in one another's tracks." They remain on the lookout for the cobblies, malicious creatures which old-world dogs as well as Dogs had always been able to sense, from whom it was their self-appointed task to protect humans (a theme in some of the short stories surveyed earlier). The main theme of "Aesop" is the old (human) problem of killing, which has two outcomes. The first is overpopulation of the Dogs' world because there is no longer killing between animals. The second is a reoccurrence of killing. While talking with Lupus the wolf and Fatso the squirrel, Peter — who is one of the woodland cave people — demonstrates his bow and arrow, and, to everyone's consternation, kills a robin. In order to hide the evidence, Lupus eats the bird.

Word comes from the Dog Joshua that one of the cobblies has entered their world, and Fatso the squirrel reports Peter's shooting of the robin. Jenkins decides to wear his new body, given by the Dogs as a birthday present, and to ask the Mutants for help. The new body gives him greater sense perception and strength. Jenkins expects the Mutants to have progressed further than the robots and the Dogs, and wonders whether he was right in misting over the Dogs' memories of men. He discovers that the Mutant's castle has been empty for a long time and that certain rooms lead into other worlds, to one of which presumably they have migrated. Meanwhile, a cobbly ("shadow") stalks Peter and Lupus (208) with "slavering expectancy and half cringing outland terror." It kills Lupus but retreats in the face of Peter's projected hate. Jenkins comes upon Peter confronting the cobbly and telepathically catches the spell the creature is frantically trying to remember in order to escape to its own world. Later, at a Webster picnic (Jenkins' birthday celebrations), Jenkins in a game has the human boys and girls guess what he is thinking, for they have telepathic powers. It is the cobbly's escape spell, the repeating of which transfers the young humans into that other world. The presents Jenkins gives in return contain seeds and fishhooks for their new lives. He feels compassion for what awaits the cobblies at the hands of the humans.

"Aesop," as the title suggests, is the most allegorical of Simak's tales. As well as the question it poses about over-population, common to science fiction, the story is a twist on the theme of parallel worlds. The shooting of the bird draws upon a fairy tale archetype. Humankind and hatred are virtually synonymous in the confrontation between Peter and the cobbly, balanced against love when Peter stays to mourn for and bury Lupus. The wolf, we remember, represents the wild and is the evolutionary forerunner of the dog, as well as a prominent character in fable.

What Simak devised as the eighth and final story of the series, "The Simple Way" — originally titled "Trouble with Ants" — picks up on the main themes of the previous story in its first episode by reintroducing us to Man, Dogs (and other animals), Mutants, Robots, cobblies, and ants. Isolated individuals among the animals, such as Archie the raccoon, resist the Dogs' pressures for them to become part of their new civilization. Jon Webster lies in Geneva in the Sleep. It is 10,000 years since he closed the city. Jenkins the robot, once the Dogs' mentor, lives in a parallel world. The ants have learnt how to manufacture minute robots (harbingers of nanotechnology). The Dogs are organizing a lottery for animals interested in going to other worlds (231):

"just extensions of the Earth." Andrew the robot tells Homer that the Dogs had to start afresh. Jenkins communicates telepathically with Jon Webster, asking what Men did about ants. The solution, that men used to poison them, calls for chemistry, which the Dogs do not have, and for killing, which goes against the grain. Jenkins decides it is better to lose the earth than to return to those old practices.

The repetition of themes by Homer, Jenkins, and Jon Webster is no doubt intentional. Maybe there is too much recapitulation in Simak's desire to tie together the loose ends. Simak is attempting to impart the passage of time (almost 12,000 years), the city theme, and the problems that can arise when the moral law against taking life is observed scrupulously. "The Simple Way" is an ironic title, with an echo of the Nazi's "final solution." It may have been Simak's intention that the story have no real closure, but in my opinion it is the weakest of the tales, with the exception of the one that came later. Perhaps Simak said all he wished to say in "Aesop."

"Epilog" (1973) is not particularly well composed in comparison to the earlier tales, and Simak himself (240) had mixed feelings about writing it:

> The saga, I told myself, was complete as it stood; I also was sceptical about how competent a job I could do on a ninth City story, more than twenty years after I had written the others. After all, I knew I was a different writer than the younger man who had fashioned the tales.

Sadly, he was right. Like "The Simple Way," it is repetitious. The touch of the ants' hilltop leg—symbolizing the kick delivered by the mutant Joe that provided the evolutionary trigger for ant development—is a novel idea, but a lot is lacking otherwise. The story is thin (and not divided into episodes), but perhaps it served the purpose of doing homage to John W. Campbell as Simak desired. Ironically, Clareson (372) reports that Campbell rejected the earlier tale, "The Trouble with Ants," "because there had been enough dog stories."

Jenkins walks across the meadow, stepping carefully between the grass tunnels of the mice that, aside from the ants, are the only animals to have remained. The Dogs have departed to one of the cobbly worlds, leaving the Earth to the ants. Jenkins has been caring for the Webster House alone. The ants, in the meantime, have built over the entire planet, leaving Webster House in a grassy courtyard. A crack appears in the ants' wall. As he had discovered on entering the Mutants' castle, Jenkins finds no sign of life. Further into the building he comes upon a dead robot. There is no explanation. He speculates that the cause of the ants' decline was their first protective dome, for their world became too circumscribed. He speculates about the possibility of intelligent life evolving from the seas as the ants' building continues to break up. A spaceship lands. The "wild" robot Andrew, who had spoken with Homer in the previous story, emerges and invites Jenkins to join them because they have work to do, and Jenkins debates whether by now he has paid his debt to the Websters. He is no longer needed on Earth and walks to the ladder where Andrew awaits him. Jenkins is now more or less human and has human emotions. He laughs when he sees the ants' emblem of a kicking foot, and sits in a chair like a man. But when he departs he cannot cry.

Simak was forty years old when "City," "Huddling Place," and "Census" were published, and forty-seven when "The Simple Way" appeared. He was sixty-nine when he wrote "Epilog," twenty-two years later and fifteen years before his death. If *City* was written initially from disillusionment, as Simak (1) says in 1976, the ninth and final tale of the "saga" is couched in an even darker mood. Roald Tweet (517) says that Simak's writing entered into "a period of decline" by the late 1960s, so "Epilog" is to be read in that context. Mary Weinkauf's profile (496) on Simak is generous: "As his world experienced the cold war, racism, ecological deterioration, and loss of faith, Simak responded with works that were at once good SF adventures and parables." Though not perhaps "good," "Epilog" meets one criterion for a parable — if, with Baldick, (159) we interpret it as "an allegory illustrating some lesson or moral." At the interface between the world and the person, Tweet (ii) cites Simak's own words:

> Looking back at the disillusion out of which the city stories were written, *now deepened* by the atomic devastation of Hiroshima and Nagasaki, Simak suggests that "Perhaps, deep inside myself, I was trying to create a world in which I and other disillusioned people could, for a moment, take refuge from the world in which we lived" [my emphasis].

The theme of this rather indifferent effort is security, one of the themes for the novel as a whole; another is the non-interference of one species by another. The motif of the old house remains, and in Jungian psychology we are reminded that houses and rooms are dream symbols for the individual's psyche or self, sadly, an attenuated self by the time Simak reached old age. "Epilog" leaves us an empty world. The ants are extinct. Presumably Geneva still stands and some humans remain in Sleep. The rest of what once were human are swimming in the ammonia pools and gamboling in the oxygen fields of Jupiter, enjoying lives of intellectual fulfillment. Robots, not humans, are exploring the cosmos. But what happened to Alan Webster's expedition mentioned in "Census?" The Dogs are in one of the cobbly worlds; so too are humans descended from the band of young hunters. Where then are the Dogs who engage in literary criticism of the tales?

The Dogs' Critique

The strategy that helps *City* work as a novel is a parody of critical literary debate between canine scholars about the authenticity of the tales. It is cleverly and engagingly done. The debates serve as connecting links between the stories, what Tweet (515) calls "narrative bridges," all the more important because some stories on their own appear to have few, if any, links with the others. The notes to the tales, if brought together, would form a short story in themselves as a science fiction dog's colloquy (with a sidelong acknowledgment to Cervantes). They add an element of mythologizing to *City* the novel, and in mood reflect the good-heartedness attributed to Simak. They are also a means of bringing into prominence Simak's main themes.

The canine Editor's Preface (5) makes use of the dramatic formula of newly discovered literary fragments that may throw light on a controversy: whether the oral tales told to the pups ("when the fires burn high and the wind is from the north"—that is, the north American winter) have any basis in fact; namely, that Man (humankind) did exist and had a close association with the Dogs of old. It is a poetic opening, moving because it elicits in the reader deep-seated feelings about origins that are both mythological (legendary to the Dogs) and religious (humans as gods), and are the objects of speculation among animals with which we have strong emotional ties. By this means Simak introduces from the start three themes uppermost in his mind: cities, war, and the family. The first two concepts are meaningless to the Dogs of this far future world, and the third is extended to the idea of a community of all animals.

The critical protagonists in "Notes on the First Tale" ("City") are Tige, Bounce, Rover and an unnamed narrator. Bounce represents a skeptical view that the tales are "the clever improvisations of an ancient storyteller to support an impossible concept." Rover (9–11) similarly identifies the stories as "an ancient satire, of which the significance has been lost," replete with symbolism and "almost pure myth," primitive in nature, too, because "such concepts as war and killing could never come out of our present culture." The narrator disagrees with Rover on the relatively minor point of the story's myth-content. Tige, on the other hand, argues against mainstream criticism by maintaining that the tale is to be read literally, that it reflects the breakdown of human culture, and may be part of a larger work of epic proportions. Colloquialisms and terminology in the legends are baffling, though human children are recognizable as pups. A city is an impossible concept; so too the notions of war and killing. Ironically, Simak is setting the stage for developing the very tropes over which the Dogs are arguing, for the novel is all of those things: satire, symbol, myth, entropy (the diaspora of human society), cultural misunderstandings (Juwain), anti-war and anti-killing.

In "Notes on the Second Tale" ("Huddling Place"), Tige extends his argument by positing Jenkins as the legend's "real hero." This "puppish favorite" is thought by Tige to be the "mechanical device by which human thought continued to guide the Dogs long after Man himself was gone." Bounce, however, rules out this theory, saying it is merely a romantic story device. On the robots' genesis — they are familiar(s) to the Dogs in both senses of the word — Bounce believes that although present-day Dogs can no longer build them, earlier Dogs must once have done so, and in the doing created robots that could build others like themselves, problem-solving "in a typically Doggish manner." Once again cultural differences come into play, for to the Dogs (43–45) the stars are nearby lights in the sky, and space travel "no more than an ancient storyteller's twist on the cobbly worlds," of which the Dogs have always known. Hence more themes are added. Jenkins appears in almost all the tales. Space travel and the cobbly worlds are two extra-terrestrial realms forming a distant backdrop to the pastoral settings around the old house and the city of Geneva.

In the notes to the third tale ("Census"), the Dogs (67–68) discuss the characters. The appearance of the first Dog, Nathaniel, prompts a chauvinist response in the narrator (or Bounce — it is not clear). Nathaniel, they speculate, may be an actual historical figure because he is mentioned in many other stories. Otherwise, the tales go against canine logic and become less believable, for "no Doggish storyteller would have advanced the theory of mutation, a concept which runs counter to everything in the canine creed." The themes of human shortcomings, futility and guilt — "the human race placed little value upon stability" — cannot be understood. What the Dog commentators do not accept is the idea that they are created through human intervention. The regular appearance of the Webster family appears to support Tige's contention that the stories are of human origin, but the narrator (or Bounce) argues that their presence is a storytelling device "used to establish a link of continuity in a series of tales which otherwise are not too closely linked." Simak must have been aware of this lack of fit in some of his tales and may have been parodying himself. Rover continues to see no more than myth and "an ancient attempt to explain racial origins ... an explanation which amounts to divine intervention." The arguments parody one of the overarching themes of science fiction: what is it to be Doggish (that is, human)?

When we come to the fourth tale ("Desertion"), the line between Tige and the other critics remains drawn. Towser (102) finds much that is "inconsistent with the essential dignity of our race" and the equating of other planets with the cobbly worlds. The narrator calls it myth, in the sense perhaps of untruth, because, as Simak was aware, "Desertion" does not easily fit in with the series. But, from another point of view, it is pivotal because it becomes a convenient means of removing humans from their home planet. Thomas Clareson (72) notes that internal evidence in "Desertion" shows none of the "narrative ties" present in the stories leading up to it; yet the book hinges on the tale because it provides an explanation for the voluntary demise of humankind.

In "Paradise," the fifth tale, Rover's view (118) is that "Man is set up deliberately as the antithesis of everything the Dogs stand for," that it is "a sociological fable." Humans are unstable, preoccupied with mechanization, and unsure of what goals they desire; whereas, it is implied (117), Dogs possess "a culture based on some of the sounder, more worthwhile concepts of life." In the "Notes on the Sixth Tale" ("Hobbies") this is reinforced by a reiteration (145) of "the hallmarks of Doggish storytelling"—that the world of the Dogs has a "deeper emotional value." There are discordant elements, such as Ebenezer's worship of Man as God, which to the canine critics "has certain disturbing overtones." But references to the Dogs' storytelling by the fires, their first contacts with the cobbly worlds, and the idea of a brotherhood of animals, Tige sees as confirmation of his theory. Rover's opposing view is that the hypothetical story "brings to a logical conclusion a culture (imaginary) such as Man developed."

"Aesop," the seventh tale, is identified as a literary fragment concerning the early brotherhood of animals. Jenkins' steps to expunge the memory of humankind so as to allow the Dogs to develop their own civilization unhindered are explained by Tige as "a deliberate conspiracy of forgetfulness" with a less altruistic motive "to save Doggish dignity." In the end, as the narrator (188) says, "The entire controversy surrounding the legend can be boiled down to one question: Did Man exist?" The eighth and at the time final tale, "The Simple Way," weaves together elements from the earlier tales too cleverly to be believed by a canine mind. The narrator thinks it a fraud, and, in any case, it is impossible to find archaeological evidence because the ant world known to the Dogs is closed. There are no canine discussion notes in "Epilog," the ninth tale.

In his interview with Walker (59–60, 64), Simak says:

> I have asked at times what the purpose of life may be; I have tried to probe into the real meaning of intelligence, and I have at times wondered about the inevitability of death.... I have suggested that our intellectual capacity may be a tool designed ... to bring about a complete understanding of the universe, if not by us humans, then by some other race of beings who

> evolve from us.... Any purpose achieved by any life is a triumph for all life and all life must be given credit.... If there is despair and pessimism in my later work, it was not so intended and I was not aware of it when I wrote. I think that what has happened is that I have lost some of the exuberance and easy optimism of my youth.

The Dogs' notes to the tales are the most obviously allegorical passages in the novel and, in the way by which they make fun of scholarly debate, I suggest have carnivalesque elements. Turning narrative on its head by characterizing civilized Dogs engaging in critical literary debate, just as humans do, is a touchstone of the allegorical approach. Part of Baldick's (5) definition says that "allegory involves a continuous parallel between two (or more) levels of meaning in a story, so that its persons and events correspond to their equivalents in a system of ideas or a chain of events external to the tale." By such means we gain insights into human intellectual enquiry, including the conceptual blinkers that lead us to ignore or gloss over material not to our liking.

Poking fun at western scientific/scholarly investigation through parodying it is frequently found in animal allegories. Allegorically, we are the Dogs of *City*. Tige is the familiar scholarly rebel whose theories are profoundly unsettling to his peers. Simak has neatly done a variety of things, not least to establish connecting links between the stories, some of which he admits do not sit comfortably within the framework of the series. He places the novel within several frames: some 12,000 years for its action, and a longer, indeterminate time for the Dog civilization that has inherited the legends on one of the parallel worlds. The approach allows the novel greater depth. It is more than the sum of its parts, while at the same time several of its parts — the better short stories — stand on their own. We are not told specifically, but one might guess from the last debate that Tige, Bounce and the others are research staff in the literature department of a university on one of the cobbly worlds.

Science and Sentiment

In what Clute and Nichols (1109) call a pastoral novel in which humans leave the cities, "aided by a benign technology," the science and technology of *City* is surprisingly rich, though it comes indirectly. Simak's prophetic powers are limited, but he comes very close to some of our *fin de siècle* developments. The world of "City" (the short story) has entered an atomic age to replace the use of fossil fuels; the family aeroplane and helicopter replace the motorcar; wood is superseded by plastic; there are robotic lawnmowers that malfunction. "Huddling Place," set in 2117, has potential interstellar travel, "robots in place of serfs" (50), human settlements on Mars, and a communicating device that reminds one of the fad for virtual reality. In "Cęnsus" we have genetic or surgical engineering ("surgery and grafting") in the uplift of the Dogs (77), mutated humans, an atomic gun, and the beginning of an industrial revolution among the ants. The list goes on: a machine that converts humans (and a dog) to a new form on Jupiter, the Mutant's kaleidoscope (and the anachronism of the neon sign), the enclosed city of Geneva (with suspended animation), automated machines like the "thinking cap," the Mutant's castle, the improvement of the robotic form so that robots become almost human, and, in the last lines of the final chapter, a return to the spaceship.

The Dogs, who are the subject of this animal allegory, have a new dispensation, explained along fictional lines with which we are by now familiar. Richard Grant's meeting with Nathaniel has resonances of Robert's first meeting with Sirius in Stapledon's "fantasy." Step one (69) explains/introduces speech:

> The words were there. There was no doubt of it. Almost like human speech, except they were pronounced carefully, as one who was learning the language might pronounce them. And a brogue, an accent that could not be placed, a certain eccentricity of intonation.

Step two (76) expatiates on doggish intelligence, as Thomas Webster does:

> A dog has a personality. You can sense that in every one you meet. No two are exactly alike in mood and temperament. All of them are intelligent, in varying degrees. And that is all that's needed, a conscious personality and some measure of intelligence.
>
> They didn't get an even break, that's all. They had two handicaps. They couldn't talk and they couldn't walk erect and because they couldn't walk erect they had no chance to develop hands. But for speech and hands, we might be dogs and dogs be men.

So step three provides substitutes for hands in the form of personal robots.

The brotherhood between two different minds, both created by humankind, is for most of the novel between the Dogs and the robots, not between Dogs and Man. Yet the philosophical ideal of a companionable union between Dogs and humans is one of Simak's two overarching themes. It is best expressed in Thomas Webster's briefing (76–77) to the census-taker, an ideal that relates also to the human–Martian union of minds in the story of Juwain:

> Thus far Man has come alone. One thinking, intelligent race all by itself. Think of how much farther, how much faster it might have gone had there been two races, two thinking, intelligent races, working together. For, you

> see, they would not think alike. They'd check their thoughts against one another. What one couldn't think of, the other could. The old story of two heads.
>
> Think of it, Grant. A *different* mind than the human mind, but one that will work with the human mind. That will see and understand things the human mind cannot, that will develop, if you will, philosophies the human mind could not [Simak's emphasis].

The other overarching theme is the disappearance of the humans, either through the Sleep, through a diaspora into space, or by metamorphosis into non-human beings. This is the direction that *City* ultimately takes, the demise of humankind in its present form, perhaps an evolutionary advance to be desired. Simak (97–98) critiques his own era by reiterating those values he feels make us human, as do other writers using the animal fable. His values are essentially social and what the Mutants are said to lack:

> The need of one human being for the approval of his fellow humans, the need for a certain cult of fellowship — a psychological, almost physiological need for approval of one's thought and action. A force that kept men from going off at unsocial tangents, a force that made for social security and human solidarity, for the working together of the human family.... It had led to terrible things, of course — to mob psychology, to racial persecution, to mass atrocities in the name of patriotism or religion. But likewise it had been the sizing [stiffening, a culinary metaphor] that held the race together, the thing that from the very start had made human society possible.

City is packed with themes such as this. Some are contradictory or at best ambiguous, and have made a few critics unhappy. David Pringle (18) agrees implicitly with Bounce's position that the stories are written to support an impossible concept. Pringle finds a conservative "cosiness" behind Simak's tales, those elements of security and reassurance already noted. To Pringle (21, 26), Simak is a liberal in the small-l American sense: "a genuine conservative within a revolutionary genre [science fiction and fantasy, allegory, the carnivalesque], an enemy in the camp of progress," whose robots make him uneasy because they are suspiciously like Uncle Toms. One of the grounds for his opinion (18) is the element of gentleness and a negation of violence in Simak's work; and City *is* an anti-war, anti-killing novel where

> his imagination is rooted in what Northrop Frye calls the last phase of romance.... One gets a sense of all passion spent: there is very little violence — indeed, very little *action* — in Simak's stories [emphasis his].

However, consonant with Tige's view that the stories represent the breakdown of human society, Simak does not avoid brute confrontations, though he does not paint such extreme pictures of violence as Linebarger does in "The Dead Lady of Clown Town" and the other Instrumentality stories, or Stapledon in *Sirius.* While *City* is a novel of ideas and not action, it has its moments, such as the fracas over council control in "City," the blow to the face in "Census," and the fight between Peter and the cobbly in "Aesop." If not violence, there is the danger, indeed monstrousness, of the cobbly worlds, the loneliness and apparent failure of the human attempt to travel between the stars, and the strangeness of a world made empty by ants.

That *City* is a novel of ideas flies in the face of another of Pringle's (17) criticisms when he says that Simak

> can concoct involved plots with the best of them (vide *Time and Again*)—but there is no sense of intellectual play in his writing, of the juggling of concepts and points of view, of the "mind-blowing" quality that is supposed to be of central importance to science fiction.... His seriousness is moral rather than cerebral (which factors go a long way towards explaining his popularity). Like such widely differing authors as Heinlein and Bradbury, Simak is primarily an emotional writer, even if his emotions are of that quiet kind usually dubbed "sentimental."

This view concurs with Bounce's critique that the tales are romantic storytelling devices. Pringle is half right, because Simak is not as "mind-blowing" as Paul Linebarger or as mischievous as Karel Čapek. But is not a converting machine for a new physical form on Jupiter mind-blowing enough? And there *are* different points of view, as expressed by the different Webster characters, and by Juwain, the Dogs, the other animals, the Mutants, and the robots. Simak *does* juggle with different concepts: space travel, metamorphosis, parallel worlds, suspended animation, evolution, and animal (Dog) intelligence. He succeeds in imparting a sense of wonder, which is a hallmark of science fiction, and it is a heady mix when emotions, the romantic and sentiment, are added.

John Dean supports Pringle and Bounce. He cites (75) Pringle's remark about Simak's conservatism, and castigates Simak for creating a "pastoral-and-wilderness mix in *City* [as] a masculine dream-world which has abandoned society and government, sex and sexual tensions," pointing out the scarcity of women in the stories. (It's a little like Rover's view that the stories are sociological fables.) He says also that Simak's "wilderness is flaccid and false," that there are no confrontations with cats, no earthquakes or other forms of natural disaster, no discomforts such as mosquitoes (he misses Towser's fleas in "Desertion"), and that Simak's narrative strategy is deplorable. It sounds very like an ideological confrontation between romanticism and realism, especially when Dean the realist (70) says that:

> Wilderness is not pastoral. They are radically different visions of nature. The literature of wilderness aims at locating the original character, the primal reality, of nature. Pastoral is "the landscape of an idea."

This is a giveaway, for *City* is a novel of ideas, and it is carping to criticize Simak for that. To be fair, Dean (68–69) makes an exception of *City* elsewhere, to some extent contradicting himself in the claim that "for once, Simak doesn't opt out for the octogenarian pastoralism which he so loves." But Dean's remark in the same paragraph that Simak elicited an Edgar Allan Poe landscape on Jupiter and not a pastoral environment is a little off the point, considering that, in their new bodies as Lopers, man and dog are in an idyllic and more or less pastoral setting.

For feminists, however, Simak might represent another dead white male, as Dean (74) implies, in contrast to Paul Linebarger, whose chief protagonists are often female. In *City* the only woman protagonist other than Sara entering the Sleep (104) is the "prim, school-teacherish" Miss Stanley of the Jupiter dome. David Pringle (50) notices this neglect of women too, but observes that "love between man and woman is of no importance in Simak's fiction, but the memory of such love has its sentimental place." I recognize this as regret in Jon Webster's soliloquy about his wife Sara.

Clifford Simak in daily life appeared happily married — if we accept Gordon Dickson's testimony. Perhaps, like many middle-class American men of his era, he did not feel comfortable when characterizing women. Point-scoring seems too easy in the deconstructive search for silences in a text, criticizing authors for not writing what the critic prefers, although there are bases for these critiques (aside from furthering the careers of those who write and publish commentaries and book reviews). I believe we should always refer back to the writer, for whether or not we accept an author's intentions, it is important to take them into account. Simak (1–3) says that

> *City* was written not as a protest (for what good would protest do?) but as a seeking after a fantasy world that would serve as a counterbalance to the brutality through which the world was passing.... It has been said that the tales were an indictment of mankind.... I can see now that they were.... At the time I wrote *City* I felt there were other, greater values than those we find in technology ... the city is an anachronism we'd be better off without.... So, on the face of it, I find that I still stand on the same ground on which I stood when I wrote the tales thirty years ago ... my job at the time, as it is today, is not to ride a white charger, but to write stories that have some entertainment value.... *City*, by and large, has gained a wider and more enduring acceptance than anything I have ever written.

The double meaning in Ebenezer's exclamation, "*It had been such a nice rabbit!*" appears a faithful reflection of the complexities and ambiguities in

City, a novel that can be received in more than one way. The rabbit is not for eating but for companionship, the novel not for analysis but for entertainment. Does *City* depict the decline of humankind or their evolution into new forms, either Jovian Lopers or Mutants like Joe? How realistic is the ideal that humans and Dogs live in intellectual symbiosis with one another against the actuality that the Dogs forge their own culture and civilization? What price individual eccentricity and the choice to remain outside the ordered social world of the Dogs, a minor theme exemplified by the recalcitrant raccoon and the field mice (the latter appear never to leave the planet)? What does it mean to be human, when a robot (Jenkins) discovers within himself human emotions and the "wild robots" take up the challenge of travelling to the stars that humankind renounced?

There is an aesthetic appeal in Simak's style that makes many stories in *City* moving and satisfying to read. *City* contains allegory, parody, and some elements of the carnivalesque in the ways by which so many accepted ideas and practices are inverted, mostly gently in comparison to the violence in the works of Linebarger, Stapledon and Čapek, or Čapek 's boisterousness, or the *canus agonistes* of Stapledon's character Sirius.

CHAPTER 12

Crafted Tales: "The Dead Lady of Clown Town"

As a stylist, and for the subtlety of his thought experiments, Paul Linebarger (alias Cordwainer Smith) is a challenging read. Linebarger is a sensitive and humane author who takes as his broad theme the inhumanity towards non-humans of those who consider themselves human. The setting is in a far future where the political and social order is controlled by an authoritarian aristocratic oligarchy collectively named the Instrumentality of Mankind. An accompanying theme is the amelioration of neglect and prejudice through love, an age-old spiritual antidote to inhumanity. It is not difficult to translate these themes and the tales to which they are attached into allegories of race relations, the Second World War and the Cold War years, although critics note that these are not the only themes in Linebarger's writing, or the most dominant. The pleasure a reader may take in Linebarger's narrative style comes not from moments eliciting the carnivalesque as, in *Sirius* or *War with the Newts*, so much as from a realization that one must read carefully, for Linebarger writes in a style that at first appears simple but on closer examination is complex and demands attention. The engaging though complex style is a pleasure to read.

A psychologist and Orientalist, Linebarger comes from a unique background, very different from the journalism professed by many of the others in this survey. Earlier I noted two qualities in Linebarger's writing — a complex "mind-blowing" intellectual play, and his frequently sympathetic depiction of women characters. The latter are often major protagonists, if not heroes, and represent the Jungian archetype of the *anima* so obviously that they cannot be ignored. Moreover, many are animal in origin (though human in form), which situates Linebarger's works well within the category of science fiction and fantasy stories that have their roots in the tradition of the animal fable.

Linebarger must have been aware that he was conjuring with archetypes. Those qualities are explicit in his characterizations of D'joan ("Dog Joan"), the dead lady Panc Ashash, and C'mell ("Cat Melanie") in three of his tales. (The Lady May in "The Game of Rat and Dragon" is a clearly identifiable *anima* figure too.) In Linebarger's/Cordwainer Smith's world, as Jane Hipolito (1557) says:

> Earth represents humanity's divided consciousness, split between the pragmatic, rational thinking which dominates Western civilization and the intuitive, emotional thought processes which Westerners have traditionally associated with women, (some) animals, and the inscrutable Orient.

They stand in opposition to qualities such as obstinacy, coldness and inaccessibility, attributable to the *animus* or "man within." These qualities are communicated by the "dragons" of one story, the Instrumentality of Mankind in the other two tales, and in antagonists such as the cruel Lord Femtiosex in "The Dead Lady of Clown Town." The *anima* figures in Cordwainer Smith's stories are expressions of love, often unrequited but no less intense, and close personal relationships between individuals set against impersonal powers and frequently cruel persons who wield and uphold those powers. The world/galactic order under the Instrumentality of Mankind is a dystopian order, but the goal of renewed humanization is utopian in spirit. It includes bringing cloned animals, the underpeople, and robots into the fold of humanity.

The three stories that best illustrate the subject of animal and human connectedness within the allegorical mode in Linebarger's writing are those already mentioned: "The Game of Rat and Dragon," (1955) discussed in chapter 5; "The Ballad of Lost C'mell" (1962); and "The Dead Lady of Clown Town" (1964). The tales are psychologically complex and difficult to interpret because of the rich poetic and literary allusions they contain, both oriental and western. Critics have noted Linebarger's use of traditional Chinese storytelling techniques as one of the most important features of his writing. The tales, for these reasons, have a fineness of touch which, although different in style from that of his contemporary Clifford Simak, places Linebarger in the same category as Simak, perhaps also Olaf Stapledon.

Paul Linebarger was a devoutly religious man who in his science fantasy sought to reconcile ambiguities in science and religion, and in human nature and morality. As Pierce (xv–xvi) says:

> He was a social and psychological thinker, whose experience with diverse cultures gave him peculiar and seemingly contradictory ideas about human nature and morality.... "The God he had faith in had to do with the soul of man and with the unfolding of history and of the destiny of all living crea-

> tures," his Australian friend Arthur Burns once remarked; and it is this exploration of human — and more than human — destiny that gives Smith's work its unity.

That phrase, "more than human destiny," reminds one of Clifford Simak's evolving robots, Dogs, and other animals. The "underpeople" and the robots in Linebarger's stories aspire to humanness. Linebarger deals with a time scale as vast as Simak's 12,000 years-plus in his Instrumentality series, of which "The Game of Rat and Dragon," "The Ballad of Lost C'mell" and "The Dead Lady of Clown Town" form parts — "a vast historical cycle taking place over some fifteen thousand years," observes Pierce (xvi). As M.H. Zool (126) says, Linebarger's tales "examine authority, religion and free will through conflicts spanning millennia of future history."

The Dead Lady

The theme of unselfish love pitted against the subjugation of the underpeople at the hands of the Instrumentality of Mankind is more fully developed in "The Dead Lady of Clown Town" than in "The Ballad of Lost C'mell" or "The Game of Rat and Dragon," although love is the chief theme of all three stories. In Cordwainer Smith's fictional chronology, the Rediscovery of Man predates and hence prefigures the events described in "The Ballad of Lost C'mell."

At eighty-five pages in ten parts, "The Dead Lady of Clown Town" ranks as a novella. Such a length, unlike "The Ballad of Lost C'mell," allows for *three* heroines. The first is the psychic healer Elaine. Her tragedy (but Smith would say her triumph too) is to be created by the eugenics machine with skills that are no longer needed in a dispensation where most diseases are vanquished. The second, D'joan (or "Dog Joan"), is a character, says Pierce (124), based loosely upon Joan of Arc. D'joan's tragic death focuses the story on her, and there is a tendency for the reader to miss the significance of the third character, also tragic but for different reasons, the "dead lady" Panc Ashash. Cordwainer Smith makes her central by naming the tale after her. Panc Ashash, we are told by Pierce, are Hindi words meaning "five-six," but the name's significance, if any, is obscure. Pierce does not speculate.

Clown Town is the quarter (ghetto) where the underpeople live. Terry Dowling (36) provides a synopsis:

> By losing herself among the renegade underpeople of Clown Town on Fomalhaut III, the already-lost witch-girl Elaine joins D'joan, Hunter, and the Lady Panc Ashash, and is able to help "bring mankind back to humanity"

> (B/141) by giving the Instrumentality a valuable insight into its own decadence and nearsightedness. D'joan loses her own life to win "*real life*" (B/150) for all who seek a way through love. Elaine wins nobility and understanding, and "the world's great age begins anew" (B/137) [Dowling's in-text references are from *The Best of Cordwainer Smith*].

Dowling omits the fate of Panc Ashash. This character appears to be given very little attention by the critics, although, as the story suggests, she is a central figure.

Part one of "The Dead Lady of Clown Town" introduces scientific explanations for events that are to follow, a common storytelling ploy in science fiction that dates back as far as the novels of H.G. Wells. The machine that automatically fertilizes human embryos malfunctions and creates Elaine. Comparisons with Aldous Huxley's *Brave New World* are inevitable. Linebarger would almost certainly have read that classic. The second chapter begins with the characterization of Elaine and closes with her choice to descend the steps into the old city, upon which the newer city of Kalma is built. Chapter three tells of her first meeting with the dog girl D'joan, but its true focus is the dialogue between Elaine and the "dead lady" Panc Ashash. In chapter four Elaine meets the underpeople, is told that her "lover" is approaching, and is led deeper into the underground chambers. Chapter five covers Elaine's meeting with Hunter, at the end of which the three minds of Elaine, D'joan and Hunter meld telepathically. In the sixth chapter the telepathic melding not only results in D'joan becoming human ("Joan" and dog no longer), but her being "printed" with the memories of past underpeople of accomplishment. This chapter introduces violent action in a knife attack against Joan and Elaine by the jealous buffalo-woman Crawlie, whereupon Elaine heals Joan with her medical skills. Crawlie is killed by the snake woman, and, as the underpeople begin to realize that they too are people, Joan and Elaine in chapter seven lead them to the city street above to begin the revolution against the Instrumentality.

This "revolution" consists of no more than the underpeople appearing openly in the streets and proclaiming their common humanity and love for the "real people" above ground. As Smith (183), in the role of narrator, says ironically, the revolution "lasted six minutes and covered one hundred and twelve meters." In chapter eight the trial begins under the lords and ladies Arabella Underwood, Goroke, Limaono and Femtiosex, and by so doing (188) establishes a history-turning precedent: "Perhaps they are people. They must have a trial." (In *War with the Newts*, one measure of being human is to be subject to taxes and the law.) The trial leads inevitably to the execution of Joan and the underpeople in chapter nine, the climactic chapter which depicts scenes that might well come from stories of war atrocities. In this dramatized critique against brutality (197), we see "the face of a weeping child, bewildered by hurt and shocked by the prospect of more hurt to come." It is not one of the underpeople, however, being put to death, but a soldier carrying out the deed. Linebarger is showing us the effects of cruelty on the perpetrators themselves.

Through the compassion of the dead Lady Panc Ashash and her advice to Joan, a precedent is established for a future reconciliation between humans and their creations, the underpeople. In the novella's dénouement (208), Elaine and Hunter have their minds "cleansed" of the memory of "the wild political gamble of the dear dead Lady Panc Ashash," whose robot body is shattered into crystals by a soldier at the commencement of the purge. But by having been the architect of the rebellion, she has planted the seed of compassion, first among the human witnesses of Joan's immolation, then in the regret and shame of the Lords and Ladies of the Instrumentality. In the long run it is love that conquers, though the lives of the initiators are lost or their personal memories erased.

The Crafting of the Tales

In his crafting or hammering out of the three tales, Cordwainer Smith consciously uses Eastern literary models. Some critics note this without going into further detail. John Pierce (xix) observes:

> Oriental narrative techniques, especially in "The Dead Lady of Clown Town" and "The Ballad of Lost C'mell," are prominent in the later stories. So is the sense of myth, whereby the just-mentioned stories are supposedly explanations of popular legends.

Elsewhere Pierce (12) remarks upon Linebarger's "odd narrative techniques and poetic word-rhythms." Gary Wolfe (506–507) says, "Other of his stories are *supposedly* based on Chinese narrative techniques" (my emphasis); and Wolfe and Williams (61), writing a few years later, see Linebarger as "closer to medieval historians and romancers such as Chrétien de Troyes or Geoffrey of Monmouth, or to the ancient Chinese historians and storytellers with which he was so familiar." Linebarger experimented with other modes of narrative, about which several critics comment, but first the Oriental influences.

David Hawkes (15–46), in his introduction to one of the best known Chinese novels of manners, *The Story of the Stone* (alternatively *A Dream of Red Mansions*), talks about such authorial ploys as the inclusion of songs (and poems), dream imagery, allegorical openings, third person commentary about future plot developments (one might add, in Linebarger's case, allusions to other related stories), psychological insight, sophisticated humor, the importance of inner experience, mythopoeic "devices," painting and drama, the techniques of professional (oral) storytelling, symbolism, word-plays and puns, authorial ebullience, and a play-off between the concepts of reality and illusion. The last-named can be seen perhaps in the double senses of playfulness, suggesting Roland Barthes' choice of the word *jouissance*, and plot development (the play's the thing).

A reading of Thomas Cleary's introduction (1–38) to a quite different work, Sun Tzu's *The Art of War*, yields a complementary checklist of Chinese narrative techniques that include the use of what Cleary calls "psychological nuances," a sensitivity to structure through allegory and imagery, ambiguity and paradox, an elicitation of reader participation, the telling of a story from multiple points of view, the painting of elaborate imagery in order that viewpoints interpenetrate and are transformed (with hints that in time and with thought they will produce further insights — a Confucian idea), and works of literature taken as "visualization models" that can awaken the reader to a better understanding of human nature and the human condition (a Taoist concept).

Virtually all the elements in these two considerable lists are found in Linebarger's *oeuvre*, and are also present to greater or lesser extent in other tales of science fiction and fantasy inspired by the animal fable. They are complementary, if not the same, in the typologies found by Slater, Čapek, Tolkien and others discussed in chapter 1.

"The Ballad of Lost C'mell" is another story of unrequited love between man and animal — between the human Jestocost and the cat girl C'mell. Unlike the more traditionally Western storytelling structure of "The Game of Rat and Dragon," "The Ballad of Lost C'mell," from its title onwards, introduces us to Chinese narrative forms that have an oral storytelling flavor. For example, there is commentary about future developments both within the plot and within a wider historical frame:

> She won her tricks against the lawful and assembled Lords of the Instrumentality (315).
>
> Even she did not realize that the romance would sometime leak out into rumour, be magnified into legend, distilled into romance. She had no idea of the ballad about herself (327).
>
> The story became known a few generations later, when the Lord Jestocost had won acclaim for being the champion of the underpeople and when the authorities, still unaware of E'telekeli, accepted the elected representatives of the underpeople as negotiators for better terms of life; and C'mell had died long since (315).

Beginning with the narrator (315, 316, 336), who, as storyteller, has an omniscient aspect, like that of the all-seeing author in other types of fiction, the tale proceeds through two different points of view: that of Lord Jestocost, then of C'mell, their inner thoughts mediated by the narrating (authorial) voice:

> She was a girlygirl and they were true men (narrator).
> Jestocost liked the morning sunshine (Jestocost).
> Her heart cried out, *It was you* ... (C'mell).

Moreover, the inclusion of songs or poems (315) is an overt theme-setting device:

> She got the which of the what-she-did,
> Hid the bell with a blot, she did,
> But she fell in love with a hominid,
> Where is the which of the what-she-did?

This "mythopoeic device" serves also as a metaphorical (allegorical) opening, with wordplay, ambiguity and paradox — the excerpt above is all of these — that becomes explicable from the tale's context. The first and last lines are teasers, alliterative word puzzles that appear to be a play on C'mell as witch, for her role is not dissimilar to that of Elaine in "The Dead Lady of Clown Town." The blot is likely to denote the trance-state or confusion into which Jestocost is thrown, also the screening of their infiltration from the minds of the other executive officers of the Instrumentality. The "which of the what-she-did" may be no more than the outcome expressed in a pun on the witch idea.

The literary style of "The Dead Lady of Clown Town" is even more derivative of Chinese models than that in "The Ballad of Lost C'mell." The same framing of the story is present through narrative asides (130, 137, 166, 187, 190):

> "Much later, when people made songs about the strange case."
> "The story has begun."
> "Most of you have seen paintings or theatricals based upon this scene."
> "The mixup came much later."
> "You all know about the trial."

The same touches of the orient are present in the naming of many characters, either directly (such as the Lady Goroke [Japanese] and Panc-Ashash [Indian] or indirectly, in repetition and allusions to personal qualities: Charlie-is-my-darling (a Scottish ballad), Crawlie, Baby-baby, the Hunter. Another oriental motif is the concept of destiny or chance, whereby an apparently trivial, "innocent" choice (such as the opening of a door) can lead to unforeseen future events of revolutionary import.

Moving to western traditions of storytelling, the chthonic *Alice's Adventures in Wonderland* imagery of secret doors leading into subterranean worlds is one of the first comparisons that springs to mind. Compare also Clifford Simak's houses and doors opening into other dimensions, as in *Way Station*, "The Big Front Yard," and *City*. Critics have seen these and similar thematic and stylistic devices at work. Karen Hellekson (128), for instance, refers to Linebarger's predilection for "exploding legends," saying, "Smith constantly keeps the legend or myth rooted in the reality of what actually happened, contrasting the two throughout his narratives." Gary Wolfe (186) writes that "The stories are sprinkled with neologisms, references to other stories, direct addresses to the reader, and bizarre concepts introduced with a minimum of exposition"—which is a touch of the carnivalesque. Wolfe adds, "Smith consistently imparts to these tales a flavor of dim legend and oral history" (188), with "larger than life" characters engaging in exploits of such heroism that they culminate in "vast historical consequences," while at an interpersonal level they are "often cursed by an unfulfilled and unrealizable love." In an article written two years later on "The Game of Rat and Dragon," Wolfe (507) also says, "What stands out most are the memorable characters of near-mythic proportions, the romantic legends he weaves, and the oddly nostalgic style, reminiscent of oral history or folktales, in which he writes."

Johan Heje (147) likewise observes the switching of narrative viewpoints from that of omniscient chronicler to the first person and back again as "a distancing device that is a significant characteristic of some of Smith's later works." Heje (150) also notes that *Norstrilia* (1975)—the novel Smith wrote as a sequel to "The Ballad of Lost C'mell" and "The Dead Lady of Clown Town," and in which he traces C'mell's continued adventures—started out as a "picaresque cat story" that very quickly threatened to become "a political allegory." I think Smith did not want to over-simplify his story because, as Heje notes, he desired to take the theme further to encompass questions about humanity's survival, and this in turn could not be done "without a sense of history, without myths, without religion."

In other words, Cordwainer Smith was consciously mythologizing while crafting his tales, and he drew upon all the traditions of which he had intimate knowledge, the European (English, French, German) as well as the Oriental (Chinese, Japanese, Indian). The result is an entirely engaging mind-play that holds the reader's attention and, in its carnivalesque manner, challenges the reader's assumptions.

Critics of the Instrumentality stories concern themselves with a number of principal themes. One is that of utopian societies, where it should be remembered that dystopias are never far away. Wolfe and Williams (68) write on the prelude to the slaughter of the underpeople, a context in which their humanness is made clear:

> Utopia demands the rediscovery of humanness — hate, pain, fear and all. That is, it demands *acht*: the double meaning of "Take care." *No* feeling is Cordwainer Smith's hell.

Compare this with John Pierce's (xviii) summation:

> Under the ruthless benevolence of the Instrumentality, a bland utopia takes shape. Men are freed of the fear of death, the burden of labor, the risks of the unknown — but deprived of hope and freedom. The underpeople, created to do the labor of mankind, are more human than their creators. The gift of vitality, seemingly, has been lost, and history come to a stop.

Another theme is the juxtaposition of romance against political realism, race relations and dehumanization. As Wolfe (188) notes:

> The growing sterility and excessive standardization of life during the Instrumentality's decadent phase suggests the leisure society that began to develop in the United States after World War II, and the systematic oppression of the underpeople suggests the racism which permeated that society.

Some critiques, such as that of Darko Suvin (205), contain an *ad hominem* touch:

> I have all kinds of doubts about Cordwainer Smith, because he was ideologically a very strange person. He was a CIA expert on psychological warfare, for Asia especially — a specialist on Indonesia, China, and whatever. Nonetheless, or because of that, I think he is very representative of American ideology, especially today.... I'm not saying that Cordwainer Smith is the same as Reagan; as Marx said, Rousseau is not the same as a normal petit bourgeois.

An ambiguous statement of Linebarger's (278) may stand in his defence:

> The things which are most important to me are *for the record* such things as the North Atlantic Pact, the development of the UN, the security of constitutional liberty, the avoidance of World War III, or victory in it if it comes, my duties as a Reserve officer, my responsibilities as a professor, my work in psychological warfare.... That's what I tell other people and what I try to tell myself. It's not *me*.

It's a little like Stapledon's claim — I'm just me — when refuting criticism about his socialism. Note the ambivalence in the ironic phrase "what I try to tell myself."

Concerning relationships between animals and humans, it appears to be generally held that Linebarger writes in favor of a union or reconciliation between the two, although he can also betray ambiguity in his treatment of this theme. As Heje (151) says:

> In Smith's science fiction animals are not monsters, not enemies of humankind; generally they are its helpers ... it is one of the axioms of Smith's future world that the potential of animals is vastly superior to what any computer ... can achieve.... The highly developed underpeople in Smith's later fiction are despised, but also feared by humans as a threat to human supremacy. Their extrasensory capacities make them the superior species, in certain respects at least, even in societies of human telepaths.

Underlying these views is what Jane Hipolito (1555) calls a "basic antithesis between logical positivism and intuitive spirituality." Or, as Karen Hellekson (128) writes, "In 'Dead Lady,' Smith shows metaphorically that it isn't biology that makes humans human. Rather, it is a quality within people themselves; it is love." Against which we might place Terry Dowling's (28) caveat recalling us to the harsh realities in many of Linebarger's tales: "We have yet to see the true emancipation of the underpeople, and this reminds us that there are not always simplistic, spectacular transformations in any society, no matter how enlightened." In a point which harks back to my opening comment about the difficulty of reading Linebarger, Gary Wolfe (506–507) observes:

> Smith was a Christian, a romantic, and a shrewd political theorist.... All of these strains come together in his fiction, giving it a complexity and depth of meaning that are sometimes confusing to readers encountering one of his stories for the first time.

Complexity in narrative form, a thematic dichotomy between logical positivism and intuitive spirituality, and harsh realities that beg to be reconciled are the hallmarks of Paul Linebarger's work.

Linebarger and Women: Ria *(1947) and "The Dead Lady of Clown Town"*

Linebarger's relationships with women, it seems, were never comfortable, a mix of unease and empathy, and these can be described, and to some extent explained, through what we know about his personal life and what is revealed in the two mainstream novels he wrote with women protagonists. The novel *Ria*—written under the pseudonym of Felix C. Forrest—contains several passages that touch on themes and tropes that appear more fully realized in Linebarger's later works. Very early (6) there is a reference to finding the enemy as an animal within, and killing it with light, a pivotal motif in "The Game of Rat and Dragon." In this case it marks the beginning of Ria Regardie Browne's quest to identify and assuage her inner, unconscious guilt about an incident that took place earlier in her life and for which she believes herself to have been the catalyst.

As in many of Linebarger's stories, the inner worlds of his protagonists are the focus, often explicated in the form of the quest, which is one of the most common themes of the folk tale, as we know from Vladimir Propp and others. The inner lives are reflections of and catalysts for outer events, sometimes events that turn violent. In "The Dead Lady of Clown Town" there is the climactic killing of the underpeople and the burning alive of D'joan. In *Ria* it is the death by suicide of the character Brautigam who is hopelessly in love with an urbane sophisticated young woman to whom he was introduced by Ria, who is likewise sophisticated but not as wise in the world of the erotic as the other woman.

Animal characters predominate in Linebarger's fiction. The underpeople and other animal-human clones, such as C'mell and D'joan, are major presences in "The Dead Lady of Clown Town" and "The Ballad of Lost C'mell." In *Ria* the animal contact is a cat named Sardanapal, the name a Greek form for Assurbanipal (669–640 B.C.), the Assyrian king who was patron of the arts and letters at the height of that empire, a classical allusion characteristic of Linebarger. This feline in Ria's life stands (or walks) as a representation of the ungraspable or inscrutable, and thereby symbolizes the unconscious. Ria Regardie Browne (6) speculates that the cat "really was the incarnation of a scientist from Mars," a familiar fantasy. It suggests the character of the Martian philosopher Juwain in Clifford Simak's *City* that Linebarger might easily have read (either as novel in full or as an isolated short story in 1944) more than a decade before the publication of *Ria.* The cat Sardanapal reappears at certain points in the story. Its violent death at Brautigam's hands — the killing of a creature he loves — suggests an unsuccessful attempt on Brautigam's part to wipe the subconscious/unconscious from his mind.

There are elements in Ria's fictional biography that echo circumstances in Linebarger's real life. Ria (9) is an American woman raised in Japan and Germany, "and God knows where." This lends the novel a sense of geographic dislocation that must have been close to Linebarger's experience, aided by a sense of temporal dislocation because its structure is based on the flashback. The flashback is one of Linebarger's favorite narrative devices, just as "The Dead Lady of Clown Town" — using the narrative style of the fairy tale — is told by a narrator living at a future epoch long after the legendary events about Elaine, D'joan and the dead Lady Panc Ashash. Linebarger likes temporal inversions.

Another archetypical image (20) is that of the mysterious door: "Somehow, at the tail-end of the memory, the recollection included a door, warmed, stiff, boarded, and her own feeling that her feet had no choice but to carry her toward that inescapable door." Again (93), at the end of part one of three, "The Memories of Ria": "Unconsciously Ria had chosen the way she knew best: the steep long flight of steps which was more like a shaft than a tunnel, going straight down through the Black Forest and coming out at the top of Grafinnenallee." Compare this against the passage wherein Elaine approaches the door to the below ground city of the underpeople in "The Dead Lady of Clown Town" (133):

> She walked from Waterrocky Road toward the bright esplanade of the Shopping Bar. She saw a forgotten door. The robots could clean near it but, because of the old, odd architectural shape, they could not sweep and polish right at the bottom line of the door.... The civilized rule was that prohibited areas were marked both telepathically and with symbols.... But everything which was not prohibited, was permitted. Thus Elaine had no right to open the door, but she had no obligation not to do so. She opened it—
>
> By sheer caprice.
>
> Or so she thought.

Memory, recollection, the unconscious, the forgotten, and caprice are elements that own strong psychic values. Linebarger evokes imagery using such elements over and over again in his writing.

In *Ria* there are two brief allusions to the idea of an "instrumentality." In the penultimate chapter there appears the phrase "the instrumentality of her intelligence" when Ria tries to express a compassionate side to her nature, though not one of nurturing or heroism. On her way to visit Brautigam, who she will discover in emotional extremis after killing Sardanapal, Ria feels brave until she draws closer to the house (223): "While this dread flashed across her mind, once again compassion and curiosity went to work, using the instrumentality of her intelligence to defeat the deeper forces of her intuition." This is ironic, for Ria flees, and one wonders how compassion can not be seen as an out-working of intuition, for compassion and curiosity, like intuition, are subjective states of mind and, in my opinion, are closely related (although they are not the same). Ria's character is one of potentiality. She does not achieve the heroic and healing sacrifices that are the lot of women in "The Dead Lady of Clown Town." At the very close of the novel, however, Ria experiences a sort of epiphany (241–242) when many years later the recollections flow through her mind as she falls asleep:

> She felt that she stood somewhere in the lower part of her own tremendous skull, and that she listened to the fluent deep roar of a resounding bronze instrument of some kind—something metallic, something which sounded like the instrumentality of man, not like the unplanned noises of nature

> and the sea.... "I know what that is, that big gong. That's me, my own life ... echoing."

Such a closing has similarities with the epiphany experienced by Sirius and Plaxy as the intelligent dog lies dying.

The religious images are intentional. Bronze instruments, for example, are Old Testament tropes and are found, too, in Tibetan Buddhism. This aspect of Linebarger's writing has often been remarked upon. James Jordan (4) reminds us that Linebarger had an Episcopalian (Anglican) High Church background, and that in the Christian tradition the word instrumentality refers to the priest giving the sacrament as "the 'instrumentality' of God," adding: "Linebarger's Instrumentality of Mankind is a kind of benevolent humanism that functions like a secular church, like the communist party, in overseeing human development." Gary Wolfe (186) says:

> The real purpose of his Instrumentality seems to be to provide a symbolic world through which he could explore the issues that mattered most to him: romance, nationalism, psychology, bigotry, morality, and the ways in which these issues are interconnected.

Alan Elms (282) points out in a footnote that to infer Linebarger approved of the Instrumentality would be mistaken. He is using it to tell some very important principles.

A way of seeing Linebarger's women protagonists, then, is to cast them in romantic/heroic and nurturing roles. These archetypes are not prominent in the psychological novel *Ria,* though certainly they appear in Linebarger's science fiction and fantasy. In *Ria,* it is not the eponymous heroine who has this role, though Ria is a romantic of sorts; it is the world-knowing old woman Miss Pidgin, an important but relatively minor character who warns (75) that Brautigam is "a Wrong One." She has a sibylline role that casts her as a forerunner of the dead lady Panc Ashash. Ria's strong aversion to Miss Pidgin means that she does not appreciate the warnings until many years after the events surrounding Brautigam's savage killing of his beloved cat Sardanapal, followed by his self-mutilation (stabbing the hand that cut the cat's throat). In "The Dead Lady of Clown Town," the two symbolic figures of the heroic/romantic and the nurturing are more clearly drawn, the first in the character of D'joan, who is modeled on Joan of Arc, and the second in the characters of Elaine the healer and Panc Ashash, the Dead Lady herself. Ria Regardie Browne belongs to what Wolfe and Williams call the "mundane hero" type.

Gary Wolfe and Carol Williams, in "The Majesty of Kindness" (56), identify several character types in *Ria* that were to become more prominent in Linebarger's style and the development of his themes in later work. While Linebarger creates "glamorous, romantic heroes and heroines," such as C'mell, from among the many women in his stories, he also uses "mundane heroes" who attempt to break out of the pattern of their lives. They are never wholly good nor wholly evil, but are mixtures of those qualities, like most of us. This "pattern-breaking," Wolfe and Williams say, is characteristic of Linebarger's heroes in his science fiction. A second character type is the person who exerts the power of life and death over their fellows, particularly in respect to underlings, whether man or woman. Lord Jestocost in "The Dead Lady of Clown Town" is such a one. Another sort of character is the risk-taking "romantic" hero or heroine who seeks to overcome strong forces ranged against them, such as D'joan, Elaine or Hunter in "The Dead Lady of Clown Town."

A fourth character type is the kind who "will endure and prevail" by doing mundane but important tasks and solving problems. "The dear dead Lady Panc Ashash" is just such an archetypical nurturing being, which is probably why Linebarger named the novella after her. It is due to her quiet work with the underpeople over generations that the heroic D'joan the dog woman and Elaine the witch/healer are brought together, and together plant the seed for the "human" rights of the underpeople that comes to fruition in future generations.

Linebarger's characters are not without very particular suffering. D'joan is immolated by the soldiers. Elaine and Hunter have their minds altered so they will have no memory of the events in which they were key participants, after which they lead idyllic lives as shepherds. The dead Lady Panc Ashash, whose personality/mind had endured for centuries within a computer matrix, becomes truly dead when the machine is disassembled. Linebarger's preference for qualities such as those of Panc Ashash is demonstrated by his choice of her as eponymous heroine rather than choosing D'joan or Elaine.

Psychological Warfare (1948)

The harsh realities of life represented in depictions of pain and death in the Instrumentality stories may have their roots in Linebarger's own health problems, but more than that. They might also be explained, again partially, by his professional work for the Pentagon during the Second World War and the Cold War years that followed, revealed in his seminal study *Psychological Warfare*, written under his own name. In that work we find again a blend between uneasiness and sensibility, a leavening of hardnosed realpolitik with compassion, although the last-named is more subtle.

Knowledge of some aspects of this work adds an unusual perspective to his science fiction and fantasy writing, and helps us to understand it. In the introduction to his definitive text on psychological warfare (vii), prepared for the United States military, Linebarger says that he worked for five years as civilian and army officer, rubbing shoulders with the Joint and Combined Chiefs of Staff, and planning from that level down to the hands-on preparation of leaflets for use by the United States forces in China. (They resemble leaflets printed in Arabic inviting Taliban fighters to defect, shown on national television in January 2002; similarly for the Iraq invasion in March 2003.)

Linebarger's position is ambiguous. The textbook *Psychological Warfare* contains an underlying irony. For instance (vii):

> I have tried to avoid making this an original book, and have sought to incorporate those concepts and doctrines which found readiest acceptance among the men actually doing the job.... From all these people I have tried to learn, and have tried to make this book a patchwork of enthusiastic recollection.

Linebarger knew the sorts of minds with which he was dealing, both oriental and occidental, and for the latter I suspect he held certain contempt.

There are other qualities in *Psychological Warfare* that interconnect the three very different genres in which Linebarger makes his name. The most telling, especially in relation to "The Dead Lady of Clown Town," include the concept of "organized lawful violence" versus "organized persuasion by non-violent means," and the associated idea of planning or organization; the use of colloquialisms, including such words as "nightmare," "monstrous," and "terror"; and the role of the media in propaganda, especially the medium of television. Similar ideas are still fashionable in Pentagon minds. See, for example, the doctrine of "rapid dominance" or "shock and awe" enunciated in 1996 by Ullman and Wade of the National Defense University of the United States (Wikipedia 2009).

The text of *Psychological Warfare* is structured along the lines of a standard report. It is divided into four parts: definition and history of psychological warfare (six chapters); analysis, intelligence, and estimate of the situation (three chapters); planning and operations (four chapters), and psychological warfare (Psy War) after World War II (three chapters). Linebarger (1) makes an implicit distinction between military science, founded upon "the application of organized lawful violence" (in Chapter 1), and propaganda (38), founded on the principle of "organized persuasion by non-violent means" (Chapter 2 on "The Function of Psychological Warfare"). In both cases, for the concepts to work there has to be a lot of planning and organization. The distinctions between military science and propaganda — that is, psychological warfare (the latter can also be seen as part of the former)—serve to emphasize an uneasy union of violence and cruelty with non-violence and compassion. This ambiguity is also found in Linebarger's fiction and has been remarked upon by others. It appears in *Ria* and in "The Dead Lady of Clown Town."

Perhaps surprisingly for what might be at first glance a potentially dull bureaucratic report, Linebarger allows himself some freedom in style. The colloquial and the evocative go hand in hand with the historical frameworks and descriptions of strategies: "Psychological strategy is planned along the edge of nightmare"; "The Boers ... [set] off a mad uproar and [made] the world press go crazy with excitement" (1); "Hitler's queer, terrifying strategy for the period 1936–1941" (24); "Propaganda had grown into ideology" (41); "the world was convulsed by monstrous new religions" (79), meaning Nazism and Communism; and so on. It may be an example of a person freed up by writing fiction, transferring elements of literary style to the different genre of the research report. By writing in that way, Linebarger made a potentially dull text readable. As he implies in the earlier citation, this is intentionally ironic—he draws upon and reflects the mood of the military people for whom he was writing. Such colloquialism and the use of emotive language is a hallmark of his fiction. It fills "The Dead Lady of Clown Town," as it does many others of his short stories.

Linebarger (48) gives pride of place to the communication media, television in particular. Communication and propaganda are central to his definition of psychological warfare, and the media are their instrumentalities, the big guns: "*Media*—that is, the actual instrumentalities by which propaganda is conveyed—are the ordnance of psychological warfare" (Linebarger's emphasis). Presentation through the media (116) becomes propaganda when it is put to specific purposes; the truth or untruth of a matter is not the issue. Indeed, in times of peace the propaganda (126–127) is pitched "against the war-making capacity of the audience." This observation has particular application to the climactic scenes of "The Dead Lady of Clown Town."

The Immolation of D'joan

A group of underpeople quit the subterranean passages (182) and emerge into the public street, led by Elaine the healer, Joan, and the Lady Panc Ashash, "dog and dead woman championing the procession." D'joan is now simply Joan because the underpeople and the robots have become human. The unusual procession is evocative of carnival. But it is carnival that becomes carnage, where the animals die joyously at the hands of the soldiers and robots of the Instrumentality. Subversion begins among the bystanders as Joan and other underpeople embrace them or take their hands, and continues (186) with a confrontation between the Dead Lady Panc Ashash and a robot sergeant:

> Read my brain. I am a robot. I am also a woman. You cannot disobey people. I am people. I love you. Furthermore, you are people. You think.... You are making a choice. You. That makes you men.

Upon this insight, the sergeant and his thirteen foot soldiers self-destruct because (187) they had voluntarily disobeyed their original orders: "They had done something with no human command at all."

Some members of the Instrumentality begin to be swayed. Lady Arabella Underwood (188) concedes the point: "Perhaps they are people. They must have a trial," a thought that is broadcast telepathically and creates future history, remembering that the events occur in an almost legendary bygone era. But Lord Femtiosex countermands her and sends in real human troops to do what the robots had failed to do. The human soldiers carry out their orders, but with great psychic cost to themselves. The soldier who kills the rat woman (197) and her children has

> the face of a weeping child, bewildered by hurt and shocked by the prospect of more hurt to come.... Poor man. He must have been one of the first men in the new world who tried to use weapons against love. Love is a sour and powerful ingredient to meet in the excitement of battle.

Here is a practical application, within the literary mode, of a key generalization found in *Psychological Warfare* (211) about influencing the morale of troops, where Linebarger says:

> Two separate types of psychological reaction are to be sought in the enemy soldier's mind. The first consists of a general lowering of his morale or efficiency even when he is not in a position to perform any overt act, such as surrendering, which would hurt his side and help ours.... The second type of action is overt action (surrendering, deserting his post of duty, mutinying) which can be induced only if the appeal is expertly timed.... The propaganda must not meet the soldier's loyalty in a head-on collision but must instead give the enemy soldier the opportunity of rationalizing himself out of the obligations of loyalty.

The robots rationalized themselves out of their obligations by self-destructing. For the soldiers who massacred the group of underpeople it was harder. Linebarger does not spare the reader from images that are found in such novels as Eric Maria Remarque's *All Quiet on the Western Front* (1929), which Linebarger would have surely read. The violent killing of certain of the underpeople is delivered in harrowing detail. A rat woman and her seven babies are clubbed and stamped to death; a bear man named Orson has his face blown apart; Joan is immolated by a flame-thrower.

Linebarger mixes clinical news reportage with the violence, made stronger because the "trial" of the underpeople is described in flashback through television broadcasts and audio recordings. It is, in fact, summary execution, because as animals they are deemed not worthy of trial. Femtiosex attempts to make Joan's death appear like that of a "primitive canine" by using his telepathic powers to suppress the human in her. But this has the opposite effect on the bystanders from what is intended, because they draw closer to the burning woman in compassion. Then Hunter (205) distracts Femtiosex's mind with an erotic illusion, allowing Joan as she dies to send a last telepathic message to the world in tropes evocative of the New Testament: "Love asks nothing, does nothing.... Love is knowing yourself and knowing all other people and things."

The massacre scene and the burning of Joan have within them several aspects of the carnivalesque. There is a carnival-like atmosphere, with a procession. The underpeople and some of the chief protagonists — Joan, a dog woman; Elaine, a real woman with the powers of a healer/witch; and Panc-Ashash, a robot — express to varying degrees their love for the human bystanders and the military robots and human soldiers. Panc-Ashash is a steadying influence. She orchestrates the revolution after hundreds of years of planning within her computer-derived mind. There are inversions of power in which soldiers become frightened children, robots self-destruct, and the Lord Femtiosex has his plans thwarted (by Hunter in one instance and by the Lady Arabella Underwood in another instance). Like Saint Joan on whose legend "Dead Lady" is partially modeled, D'Joan/Joan delivers an epiphany of universal love before she dies.

This is one of the most common of animal-human manifestos, one that we meet with time after time in other works inspired by the animal fable, as well as in most of the short stories and novels covered in the first chapters. As Joan says (192) to the soldiers about to kill her:

> Should we be strange to you, we animals of earth that you have brought to the stars? We shared the same sun, the same oceans, the same sky. We are all from Manhome. How do you know that we would not have caught up with you if we had all stayed at home together? My people were dogs. They loved you before you made a woman-shaped thing out of my mother. Should I not love you still? The miracle is not that you have made people out of us. The miracle is that it took us so long to understand it. We are people now, and so are you. You will be sorry for what you are going to do to me, but remember that I shall love your sorrow, too, because great and good things will come out of it.

The pleasure a reader may take in Linebarger's narrative style comes not from moments like those of the carnivalesque in *Sirius,* or parody (as in *War with the Newts*), so much as from the realization that one must read carefully, for Linebarger writes in a style that at first appears simple but on closer examination is found to be complex. This comes from Linebarger's intrinsic play on words and the use he makes of tropes from folk tales with their bases in the oral traditions of different, and largely sophisticated, cultures.

Paul Linebarger's writing is multi-layered in the three genres through which he expressed his ideas — in the mainstream novels *Ria* and *Carola,* in the official Pentagon report *Psychological Warfare,* and in his science fiction and fantasy short stories and novellas. The novels and science fiction short stories draw upon techniques of storytelling that have come via animal fables and folk tales. "The Dead Lady of Clown Town" is constructed as a legendary tale with many touches of the oral tradition. It is a fine example of poetic prose.

CHAPTER 13

Good for Reading

As in a parade, there have passed before us numerous examples of writing using elements from the animal fable, a lineage that stretches beyond Classical Greece to corresponding traditions in ancient India, China and the Middle East that influenced storytelling in the West. A complementary way of looking at authorial choices is to suggest that many related themes keep bobbing up in human artistic endeavor because of their perennial importance, and so they become grist for a variety of good minds. What this research into some aspects of the animal fable demonstrates is how universal in humor, satire, parody and, above all, the carnivalesque are the two apparently opposite states of levity and the serious. The mind and paws of an animal protagonist are metonyms for the distinction between the inner world (mind) and the external world (paws).

Coleridge (397–398) wrote about his

> plan of the *Lyrical Ballads*, in which it was agreed that my endeavours should be directed to persons and characters supernatural, or at least romantic; yet so as to transfer from our inward nature a human interest and a semblance of truth sufficient to procure for these shadows of imagination that willing suspension of disbelief for the moment, which constitutes poetic faith.

The dog Sirius, the "Dear Dead Lady" Panc Ashash, Andrias Scheuchzer, and the dog Ebenezer are "shadows of imagination." By giving them human speech and feelings, Stapledon, Linebarger, Čapek, Simak and a host of other writers invest such characters with "human interest." They become real for us when we read the stories, while at the same time we know they are the authors' inventions. It is the magic behind all fiction writing — that the unreal becomes for a time real in our minds — and is "romantic" writing in Baldick's sense (193) because it appeals to "emotional directness of personal experience and ... the boundlessness of individual imagination."

Translated into science fiction terms, this appears akin to the concept of "a sense of wonder." "What if" dogs or salamanders could speak and think like humans; what if there were self-aware robots, androids or animal-human clones with intelligences rivaling and even surpassing that of humans? The stories we read wherein such characterizations are invented give us an inkling of what it might be like to live in those worlds of the imagination; and because the fictional animal worlds are in contrast to the world we know, they help make us more aware of the state in which we live, holding a mirror in which we see ourselves and our own relations to the animal world, for good or ill.

Those contrasts may be growing problematic with time, as we begin to learn more about the hard science of our state of being, while the animals disappear. This is especially pertinent in the West, where the Biblical anthropocentrism of more than a thousand years — that humankind hold dominion over the beasts — is still accepted. It is an ideology that tends to blind us to our biological and social kinship with animals. Setting this right is one of the reasons why people like Stapledon and Linebarger write their stories, among other motives. Čapek, in the end, is striking a blow against Nazism, but he begins with an agenda for animal rights. Simak suggests that not only may the city become irrelevant, but that humankind, too, might disappear. In order to transmit these sorts of messages, many of them unpalatable, these writers choose elements from the animal fable as part of their authorial armory.

At the close of the previous chapter I referred to Paul Linebarger's writing as of poetic prose. Les Murray (166) suggests that while poetry may delight and weaken or sway the tough-minded — or, as he says, the "'realistic' spirits" among us — it will not on its own convince them. Murray is using the term poetry in its broadest sense to include prose works. However, he adds that in the end, poetry does convince because it represents "the principle which controls reality." I think that what helps turn certain prose into prose poetry is the composer's use of stylistic techniques found in "real" poetry. The "poetic" tricks of repetition, and the usages and tropes of the fairy tale, I suggest belong to this prose-to-poetry category. So, too, do the applications of the carnivalesque, parody and other forms of humor. In other words, the best in fairy tales and in humor are examples of prose poetry in Murray's sense.

Several paths might have been taken to illustrate these ideas. Animal novels for a young readership, such as *Wind in the Willows* (Mole, Ratty, Toad), *Winnie the Pooh* (plush bear, Piglet, Eeyore), *The Water-Babies* (fish), or *The Book of the Dun Cow* (barnyard animals, a weasel and a motherly mouse), might have been explored. Some of those works receive glancing acknowledgment in this book. Another approach might have been to consider extraterrestrial animal intelligences pitted against human minds — for example, C.J. Cherryh's leonine Hani, or Anne McCaffrey's feline Hrruban in *Decision at Doona* (1969); also terrestrial animals transplanted into extraterrestrial environments, like the dolphins and apes in David Brin's Uplift War series; or sentient animals in terrestrial alternative histories, such as the dinosaurs and humans of Harry Harrison's Eden series; or Gaspode the talking dog and the multiplicity of other mythical creatures (werewolves, vampires, dwarfs, trolls and elves) in Terry Pratchett's Discworld series. The last-named parodies and satirizes human civilizations, and just about everything else human and non-human. I have not applied the rule limiting the choice too stringently. The underpeople of "The Dead Lady of Clown Town," whose forbears are from earth ("Manhome"), are now "brought to the stars" in the world of the Instrumentality (Smith 192).

I might have chosen works from a particular era, such as Classical Greece (*The Golden Ass*), or from Medieval literature, like the tales of La Fontaine. A particular species might have become the focus: dogs, dolphins, apes or cats. Apes were popular protagonists of the late nineteenth century, and still are. For example, Will Self's hilarious *Great Apes* or Peter Goldsworthy's flawed novel *Wish*. In the end, the thirty-year era spanning the Second World War became the fulcrum, a choice seduced by the Dogs of *City* and *Sirius*, and by Linebarger's stimulating writing, but there is an overflow of works influenced by the animal fable, novels and short stories written in both ante-bellum and post-bellum decades.

I think that speculative writing today is substantially different from that of past eras because of the evolution of "science fiction" alongside the older genre we call fantasy and the even more ancient fable. They share elements that can be inventoried with confidence to yield a paradigm — that is, "a set of concepts, etc. *shared by a community* of scholars or scientists" (Macquarie Dictionary, my emphasis). A paradigm results from a shared set of ideas, of sets of identifiable factors about which there is general agreement.

Maya Slater on La Fontaine identifies several related factors: diversity with duality, pessimism with light-hearted irony, subversion, a variety of layers and shifts in perspective, the intention to both instruct and entertain the reader, moral or cautionary instruction, the use of allegorical characters, the tradition of using animals as characters to emphasize the points being made, the use of wit and humor in the making of serious and unsettling points, and the skilled crafting of the written or spoken tale. Karel Čapek, on the fairy tale, considers: narration (story-telling); narrative epic continuity, detours and deviations; the repetition of themes such as obstacles, questions and tasks (cf. Vladimir Propp's motifs for fairy-tale plots); heroic deeds and adventures; and a range of motifs such as the gift, serendipity, or the magic spell.

Tolkien, also writing about the fairy tale, covers many of the same points: the unreal and incredible, the realm of Faerie (including dragons, elves, trolls, and so on); purposes such as adventure, satire or morality; the satisfaction of deep human desires; a desire to be part of a community of all living creatures; beasts speaking like humans; beasts as the principal characters; the three faces of the Mystic, the Magical and the Mirror of pity and scorn towards humans; the creation of different worlds into which the reader enters, suspending disbelief; sentiment, imagination, art and fantasy; a sense of renewal, called "Recovery" by Tolkien that also suggests defamiliarization; escapist aspects; good catastrophes — that is, plot turnings that lift the heart (the happy ending); and finally, the seriousness of tales of Faerie contrasted against the mocking satire of the *Conte,* two sorts of tale, however, that are closely paired.

Roland Barthes gives us *jouissance*: playfulness, together with loss, discomfort and unsettlement for the reader. Shklovsky considers laughter as a corrective, and the experiencing through it of contradictory realities and impiety, and defamiliarization. Todorov emphasizes the permission of licence, the safety valve idea (Aristotle's catharsis). Robert Darnton states that relationships of animals with ceremonies are satisfying for the reader/observer. Freud points out that jokes and the comic have psychological and social functions; the liberating element in humor; caricature and the manifestation of ugliness in the comic; the qualities of joking, such as juxtaposing ideas that contrast with one another, the pairing of bewilderment with illumination (insight); that jokes give us pleasure because they short-circuit expected logical thought; and that the doing of this through technical methods, such as play on words, help us rediscover the familiar. The carnivalesque linked to many of these qualities can be identified following Mikhail Bakhtin's thesis about the root of Carnival in medieval times.

The biographies of a cluster of authors provide an accompanying set of perspectives, standing midway between world events that influenced their personal lives, and their writing, which sets out to interpret and comment on those events and, indirectly, on their lives. Hence, as noted in the beginning, many authors are impelled to express the anxieties of their socio-cultural milieux in their fiction, especially in times of war or a similarly grave social upheaval. As David Lodge says (114) in reference to mainstream authors such as Milan Kundera or Salman Rushdie, "All these writers have lived through great historical convulsions and wrenching personal upheavals, which they feel cannot be adequately represented in a discourse of undisturbed realism." This counts equally well for authors in science fiction and fantasy, such as Karel Čapek or Will Self. Modernist fiction — characteristic of that era — necessarily includes confrontations with violence, nihilism and despair, and a corresponding fascination with, and fear of, the unconscious. This, I think, remains true of the present decade (see Will Self), as it was in the mid-twentieth century when many of the tales were written. That is, post-structuralism (and whatever will come next) concerns much the same issues.

Narratives such as those in science fiction and fantasy inspired by the tradition of the animal fable or folk tale are "good to read" because they entertain and, at the same time, instruct, often by making us uneasy. They entertain by challenging the reader in a variety of ways. At the beginning I said they give pleasure but also defamiliarize the reader, elicit *jouissance* and provoke laughter while exploring important moral questions by means of a variety of narrative forms whose beginnings can be traced to the animal fable. On the whole, entertainment and instruction are complementary, but they receive varying emphases in the hands of different authors whose treatment broadly takes into account public issues and personal preoccupations, with an emphasis on narrative form and its satisfactions, together with parody and satire.

The paradigm is constructed around folkloric principles related to the animal fable (as well as to the fairy tale genre in general). But elements of the animal fable cannot be applied as fully, if at all, to other genres. The detective or mystery story has its own paradigm. We do not find much *jouissance* or the carnivalesque in Conan Doyle's Sherlock Holmes mysteries, for example, or in Agatha Christie, although Andrea Camilleri's Inspector Montalbano series might be an exception. The Hound that haunted the Baskerville family is unlike the enquiring Dogs of Clifford Simak's *City.* Nor are those elements present in any force in the Gothic genre, as represented by Mary Shelley's *Frankenstein* or its offshoots. Edgar Allan Poe, as far as I am aware, does not employ images using the carnivalesque. Pits and pendulums may have an unsettling quality, but they fall short of Carnival gaiety. On the other hand, intellectual pleasure in solving a detective story mystery is associated by Karel Čapek (106) with terms very similar to that of *jouissance*: "the mad, tormenting, voluptuous pleasure of the intellect in solving problems: the passionate need of the brain to crack the hard nuts of problems artfully posed."

Melodrama of the sort performed in nineteenth century stage plays may be an exception because it has, by definition, a sort of exuberance and usually a moral ending. Modern love romances or bodice-rippers similarly may have elements of the carnivalesque; it is unlikely, however, that they have a strong instructional component or are particularly unsettling. But parodies and satires of all those genres may partake of the twin aspects of the carnivalesque and serious social issues. One of the functions of parody and satire, of humor generally, is to instruct us subtly in right behavior — that is, what is approved in our society. But at the same time parody and satire challenge that status quo.

In any well-produced writing, whether it is in the tradition of "high" literature or "low," there is a balance between the elicitation of friendly and comfortable feelings and serious and discomforting emotions experienced by the reader. A crime novel does not allow much comfort, but it can be intellectually rewarding through the puzzles it raises to be solved before the last page, even if we scan ahead and know the outcome. Similar reward can be found in tales drawing upon the animal fable, where, as David Lodge (144) says, "Part of the pleasure of this kind of fiction is that our intelligence is exercised and flattered by interpreting the allegory."

The themes of inversion, overturning, ribaldry and joyous play, with the sobering reality of tomorrow just round the corner, fit into this pattern. Namely, we enjoy reading even mediocre or popular stories (such as in the Mills and Boon category) — as much as for well-done literature — because they present amusement, divertissement, possibly *jouissance* (cf. erotica), and perhaps even the elicitation of the numinous (though I doubt that a Mills and Boon story will supply that quality). This comes about while at the same time offering serious themes to make us thoughtful — proving instructive, providing unsettling insights, and raising moral issues. That is, we like being sobered and shocked by a story almost as much as entertained by it, hence the popularity of the crime thriller. The shock indeed is the entertainment because of the cathartic value it has (for example, the apparently wide readership for novels about serial killers). But, as I have said, I doubt whether *jouissance* has much of a role to play.

For these reasons, the science fiction works using the tradition of the animal fable are "good to read."

We choose animal protagonists because they are familiar to us, though perhaps superficially. Human cultures have long been intermeshed with the cultures of animals — domestic species such as dogs and cats, and animals of the wild. We have close emotional ties with some species. We tend to ascribe human qualities to them, collectively and even more as individuals. Those associations mean that animals are a useful vehicle through which a storyteller communicates a wide range of messages — to entertain, instruct and cause the hearer/reader to laugh, and to make the reader/hearer uncomfortable as well. Introducing animals into a story as major characters makes the story different. Moral tales — and searching for the "moral" of a tale in many instances — call for certain forms of narrative technique that, at their best, produce a story satisfying for the audience. Some of those questions I raised earlier, such as what it means to be human, have answers here. Are we alone in the cosmos? No, because there are animals who share our lives with us and stimulate our imagination, as I am sure we do for them.

Bibliography

Abbot, Joe. "The 'Monster' Reconsidered: *Blade Runner*'s Replicant as Romantic Hero." *Extrapolation*, 34.4 (1993): 340–350.

Abrams, M.H. *A Glossary of Literary Terms.* Fort Worth: Harcourt Brace Jovanovich, 1988.

_____. *The Norton Anthology of English Literature, Volume 2.* New York: Norton, 1986.

Aldiss, Brian W. *Billion Year Spree: The History of Science Fiction.* London: Corgi/Transworld, 1973.

_____. "General Editor's Foreword." *Last and First Men: A Story of the Near and Far Future.* Olaf Stapledon. Harmondsworth: Penguin, 1930/1987, pp. 7–10.

_____, and David Wingrove. *Trillion Year Spree: The History of Science Fiction.* London: Victor Gollancz, 1986.

Amis, Kingsley. *The Golden Age of Science Fiction.* London: Hutchinson, 1981.

_____. *New Maps of Hell.* London: New English Library, 1960.

Amis, Martin. "Introduction" (1992). *Lolita.* Vladimir Nabokov. Everyman's Library, London: Random House, 1955/1992, pp. v–xxiii.

_____. "Kith of Death: Angus Wilson." *The War Against Cliché: Essays and Reviews 1971–2000.* London: Vintage Books, 2001.

_____. "Nabokov: His Life in Part by Andrew Field." *Observer*, August 1977. *The War Against Cliché: Essays and Reviews 1971–2000.* London: Vintage Books, 2001, pp. 245–247.

_____. "Nabokov's Grand Slam." *Atlantic Monthly*, September 1992. *The War Against Cliché: Essays and Reviews 1971–2000.* London: Vintage Books, 2001, pp. 471–490.

_____. "Part II *The Lost World* by Michael Crichton." *Sunday Times*, October 1995. *The War Against Cliché: Essays and Reviews 1971–2000.* London: Vintage Books, 2001, pp. 219–223.

_____. "*Ulysses* by James Joyce." *Atlantic Monthly*, September 1986. *The War Against Cliché: Essays and Reviews 1971–2000.* London: Vintage Books, 2001, pp. 441–446.

Andersen, Hans Christian. *Andersen's Fairy Tales.* London: Blackie and Sons, ND, pp. 162–166.

Anderson, Alan. "Strokie." *Science Fantasy*, 13.37 (1959): 103–112.

Anderson, Poul. *Brain Wave.* London: New English Library, 1954/1977.

_____, David Hartwell, and Stephen King. "In Memoriam: Fritz Leiber." *Nebula Awards*, 28. Ed. James Morrow. New York: Harcourt Brace Jovanovich, 1994, pp. 95–103.

Annas, George. "Dolphin Mission." *Analog*, 49.7 (1979): 103–111.

Apuleius, Lucius. *The Transformations of Lucius: Otherwise Known as The Golden Ass* (Trans. Robert Graves). London: Penguin, 1950/1990.

Arbur, Rosemarie. "Teleology of Human Nature for Mentality?" *The Intersection of Science Fiction and Philosophy.* Ed. R.E. Myers. Westport: Greenwood, 1983, pp. 71–91.

Aristotle. "On the Art of Poetry." Ed. T.S. Dorsch. *Classical Literary Criticism.* Harmondsworth: Penguin, 1965.

_____. *Poetics* (Trans. by Malcolm Heath). London: Penguin, 1996.

Ash, Brian. *The Visual Encyclopedia of Science*

Fiction. London: Pan Books, 1977, pp. 197–8, 201, 213.
Asimov, Isaac. *The Hugo Winners.* Harmondsworth: Penguin, 1962.
_____, Martin Greenberg and Charles Waugh. *Flying Saucers.* New York: Ballantine, 1982, p. 106.
_____, _____, and Joseph O. Olander. *Microcosmic Tales: 100 Wondrous Science Fiction Short-Short Stories.* New York: Daw Books, 1980.
Ash, Brian. *The Visual Encyclopedia of Science Fiction.* London: Pan Books, 1977.
_____. *Who's Who in Science Fiction.* London: Sphere Books, 1976.
Ashley, Mike. *The History of the Science Fiction Magazine Part Two, 1936–1945.* London: New English Library, 1975.
Atkins, John. "*Animal Farm.*" *George Orwell: A Literary Study.* London: Calder & Boyars, 1971, pp. 221–232.
_____. *George Orwell: A Literary Study.* London: Calder & Boyars, 1971.
Atwood, Margaret. *Curious Pursuits: Occasional Writing 1970–2005.* London: Virago, 2005.
Babylon online dictionary "Effoliation," 1997–2007. http://www.babylon.com/definition/effoliation/English
Bailey, K.V. "On Clifford D. Simak." *Foundation: The Review of Science Fiction,* 21 (1981): 64–67.
_____. "A Prized Harmony: Myth, Symbol and Dialectic in the Novels of Olaf Stapledon." *Foundation: The Review of Science Fiction,* 15 (1979): 53–56.
_____. "Time Scales and Culture Cycles in Olaf Stapledon." *Foundation: The Review of Science Fiction,* 46 (1989): 27–39.
Bakhtin, Mikhail. *The Dialogic Imagination: Four Essays.* Ed. Michael Holquist (Trans. M. Holquist and Caryl Emerson). Austin: University of Texas Press, 1981.
_____. "From Discourse in the Novel." *Modern Literary Theory: A Reader.* Eds. Philip Rice and Patricia Waugh. London: Edward Arnold, 1992, pp. 197–205.
_____. "From the Prehistory of Novelistic Discourse." *Modern Criticism and Theory: A Reader.* Ed. David Lodge. London: Longman, 1988.
_____. *Rabelais and His World* (Trans. Helen Iswolsky). Bloomington: Indiana University Press, 1984.
_____. *Speech Genres & Other Late Essays.* Ed. Caryl Emerson and Michael Holquist (Trans. Vern W. McGee). Austin: University of Texas Press, 1986/1996.
Bakis, Kirsten. *Lives of the Monster Dogs.* London: Hodder and Staughton, 1997.
Baldick, Chris. *The Concise Oxford Dictionary of Literary Terms.* Oxford: Oxford University Press, 1990.
_____. *The Oxford Book of Gothic Tales.* Oxford: Oxford University Press, 1992.
Barron, Neil. *Anatomy of Wonder: A Critical Guide to Science Fiction.* New York: Bowker, 1981.
Barthes, Roland. *The Pleasure of the Text* (Trans. Richard Miller). Oxford: Basil Blackwell, 1990.
Baudelaire, Charles. "Of the Essence of Laughter" (1855). *Selected Writings on Art and Literature* (Trans. P.E. Charvet). London: Penguin, 1972/1992, pp. 140–161.
Benford, Gregory. *Against Infinity.* London: Victor Gollantz, 1983.
_____, and Gordon Eklund. *Find the Changeling.* London: Sphere Books, 1980.
Bengels, Barbara. "Olaf Stapledon's 'Odd John' and 'Sirius': Ascent into Bestiality." *Foundation: The Review of Science Fiction,* 9 (November 1975): 57–61.
Bergson, Henri. *Laughter* (1900). *Comedy.* Ed. W. Sypher. New York: Doubleday Anchor, 1956, pp. 61–190.
Bishop, Michael. *Nebula Awards 24: SFWA's Choices for the Best Science Fiction and Fantasy 1988.* San Diego: Harcourt Brace Jovanovich, 1990, pp. 140–146.
Blain, Virginia, Patricia Clements and Isobel Grundy. *The Feminist Companion to Literature in English.* London: Batsford, 1990.
Bleiler, E.F. *Science Fiction Writers: Critical Studies of the Major Authors from the Early Nineteenth Century to the Present Day.* New York: Scribner's, 1982.
Blish, James. *Nebula Award Stories 5.* London: Victor Gollancz, 1970.
Bloch, Robert. *The Best of Fredric Brown.* New York: Ballantine, 1977.
Bloom, Harold. *Shakespeare: The Invention of the Human.* London: Fourth Estate, 1998.
_____. *The Western Canon: The Books and School of the Ages.* London: Papermac, 1994.
Boucher, Anthony. "John Shepley." *The Best from Fantasy and Science Fiction.* Ed. An-

thony Boucher. New York: Ace Books, 1959, p. 152.

Bradbury, Ray. "Emissary." *The Stories of Ray Bradbury Vol. 1.* London: Granada, 1980, pp. 568–77.

Branham, Robert. "Stapledon's 'Agnostic Mysticism.'" *Science-Fiction Studies,* 9.3 (1982): 249–256.

Brin, David. *Startide Rising.* Toronto: Bantam, 1983.

_____. *The Uplift War.* Toronto: Bantam, 1987.

Broderick, Damien. "Introduction." *Alien Shores: An Anthology of Australian Science Fiction.* Eds. Peter McNamara and Margaret Winch. North Adelaide: Aphelion Publications, 1994, pp. 1–5.

_____. *Strange Attractors: Original Australian Speculative Fiction.* Sydney: Hale & Iremonger, 1985, pp. 7–13.

Brooks, Peter. *Reading for the Plot: Design and Intention in Narrative.* Cambridge, MA: Harvard University Press, 1992.

Brown, Fredric. "Star Mouse" (1942). *The Best of Fredric Brown.* Ed. Robert Bloch. New York: Ballantine, 1977, pp. 157–178.

Brown, Terence. "Introduction." *Dubliners.* James Joyce. London: Penguin, 1992, p. xl.

Bryant, Edward. "Jade Blue." *Magicats!* Eds. Jack Dann and Gardner Dozois. New York: Ace, 1984, pp. 147–162.

Bulgakov, Mikhail. *The Heart of a Dog.* New York: Harcourt, Brace & World, 1968.

_____. *The Heart of a Dog* (Trans. Michael Glenny). London: Harvill (HarperCollins), 1989.

_____. *The Master and Margarita* (Trans. Michael Glenny). London: Harvill Press, 1967/1993.

Bullock, Allan, and Oliver Stallybrass. *The Fontana Dictionary of Modern Thought.* London: Fontana/Collins, 1977.

Bunyan, John. *The Pilgrim's Progress.* London: Blackie & Son, 1678 & 1684.

Burgess, Michael. *Reference Guide to Science Fiction, Fantasy, and Horror.* Englewood, CO: Libraries Unlimited, 1992.

Burns, Arthur. "Paul Linebarger." *Exploring Cordwainer Smith.* Ed. Andrew Porter. New York: Algol Press, 1975, pp. 5–11.

Campbell, James L., Sr. "Olaf Stapledon." *Science Fiction Writers: Critical Studies of the Major Authors from the Early Nineteenth Century to the Present Day.* Ed. E.F. Bleiler. New York: Scribner's, 1982, pp. 91–100.

Campbell, Joseph. *The Portable Jung.* Harmondsworth: Penguin, 1971/1981.

Camus, Albert. *The Myth of Sisyphus and Other Essays* (Trans. Justin O'Brien). London: Hamish Hamilton, 1973.

Cao Xueqin. *The Story of the Stone: A Chinese Novel in Five Volumes, Volume I "The Golden Day"* (Trans. David Hawkes). Harmondsworth: Penguin, 1973, pp. 15–46.

Čapek, Karel. *Dashenka or the Life of a Puppy: Written Drawn Photographed and Endured by Karel Čapek* (Trans. M. & R. Weatherall). Great Britain: George Allen and Unwin, 1933.

_____. "Holmesiana, or About Detective Stories." *In Praise of Newspapers: and Other Essays on the Margin of Literature.* London: George Allen and Unwin, 1951, pp. 101–122.

_____. *In Praise of Newspapers: and Other Essays on the Margin of Literature.* London: George Allen and Unwin, 1951.

_____. *Tales from Two Pockets* (Trans. Paul Selver). London: Faber and Faber, 1932.

_____. *War with the Newts* (Trans. Ewald Osers). London: George Allen and Unwin, 1936/1985.

_____, and Josef Čapek. *R.U.R and the Insect Play.* London: Oxford University Press, 1923/1975.

Carr, Terry, and Carol Carr. "Some Are Born Cats." Eds. Jack Dann and Gardner Dozois. *Magicats!* New York: Ace, 1984, pp. 123–136.

Casillo, Robert. "Olaf Stapledon and John Ruskin." *Science-Fiction Studies,* 9.3 (1982): 306–321.

Caute, David. "Introduction." *Penguin Island.* Anatole France (Trans. Belle Notkin Burke). New York: Signet/New American Library, 1908/1968, pp. v–xvi.

Cervantes (Miguel de Cervantes Saavedra). "The Deceitful Marriage" (1613/1615). *Exemplary Stories* (Trans. C. A. Jones). London: Penguin, 1972, pp. 181–193.

_____. "The Dogs' Colloquy" (1613/1615). *Exemplary Stories* (Trans. C.A. Jones). London: Penguin, 1972, pp. 195–252.

Chambers Biographical Dictionary. Edinburgh: W. & R. Chambers, 1993, p. 10153.

Chandler, A. Bertram. "Giant Killer" (1945). *Isaac Asimov Presents the Golden Years of Science Fiction.* New York: Bonanza Books, 1954/1982, pp. 264–312.

Charvet, P.E. "Introduction." *Selected Writings on Art and Literature.* Charles Baudelaire (Trans. P.E. Charvet). London: Penguin, 1972/1992, pp. 7–32.

Chaucer, Geoffrey. "The Nun's Priest's Tale." *The Canterbury Tales* (Trans. Neville Coghill). London: Penguin, 1977, pp. 214–231.

Chekhov, Anton. "Kashtanka" (1887). *The Cook's Wedding and Other Stories* (Trans. Constance Garnett). New York: Macmillan, 1972, pp. 175–204.

Cherryh, C.J. *The Pride of Chanur.* New York: Daw Books, 1981.

Christopher, John. "Socrates" (1951). *Stories for Tomorrow: An Anthology of Modern Science Fiction.* Ed. William Sloane. London: Eyre & Spottiswoode, 1955.

Clareson, Thomas D. "City." *Survey of Science Fiction Literature.* Ed. Frank N. Magill. Englewood Cliffs, NJ: Salem Press, 1979, pp. 369–373.

_____. "Clifford D. Simak: The Inhabited Universe." *Voices for the Future.* Ed. Thomas D. Clareson. Bowling Green, OH: Bowling Green University Popular Press, 1976.

_____. "The Emergence of Science Fiction." *Anatomy of Wonder: A Critical Guide to Science Fiction.* Ed. Neil Barron. New York: Bowker, 1981.

_____. *Voices for the Future: Essays on Major Science Fiction Writers, Vol. 1.* Bowling Green, OH: Bowling Green University Popular Press, 1976.

_____, and Thomas L. Wymer. *Voices for the Future, Volume Three.* Bowling Green, OH: Bowling Green University Popular Press, 1984.

Clark, Katerina, and Michael Holquist. *Mikhail Bakhtin.* Cambridge, MA: Harvard University Press, 1984.

Clarke, Arthur C. "Moondog." *Galaxy Magazine*, 20.4 (1962): 188–194.

Cleary, Thomas. "Translator's Introduction." *The Art of War.* Sun Tzu (Trans. Thomas Cleary). Boston: Shambala, 1988, pp. 1–38.

Clute, John. "Karel Čapek 1890–1938." *Science Fiction Writers.* Ed. Everett F. Bleiler. New York, 1982, pp. 583–589.

_____. *Science Fiction: The Illustrated Encyclopedia.* Surry Hills, NSW, Australia: Readers' Digest Press, 1995.

_____, and Peter Nicholls. *The Encyclopaedia of Science Fiction.* London: Orbit, 1993.

Coleridge, Samuel Taylor. "Biographia Literaria." *The Norton Anthology of English Literature.* Ed. M.H. Abrams. New York: Norton, 1986, pp. 397–398.

Collodi, Carlo. *The Adventures of Pinnochio* (Trans. M.A. Murray). New York and London, 1883/1892.

Cook, Kenneth. *Play Little Victims.* Rushcutter's Bay, NSW, Australia: Pergamon, 1978.

Corona, Laurel Ann Weeks. *Man into Beast: The Theme of Transformation in American and European Fiction from the 1860s to the 1920s.* Ph.D. Thesis, University of California, Davis, 1982.

Cotton, G.B., and Alan Glencross. *Cumulated Fiction Index 1945–1960.* London: Association of Assistant Librarians, ND, pp. 26 ("animals"), 72 ("cats"), 150 ("dogs").

Cranston, Maurice. "Introduction." *The Social Contract.* Jean-Jacques Rousseau. Harmondsworth: Penguin, 1968, pp. 9–43.

Crawford, Hal. "Gorilla Goes Ape on the Net." *The West Australian, Bits & Bytes,* Tuesday, April 28, 1998, p. 6.

Crichton, Michael. *Congo.* London: Random House (Arrow), 1993.

Crick, Bernard. *George Orwell: A Life.* London: Penguin, 1980/1992.

Crossley, Robert. "Censorship, Disguise, and Transfiguration: The Making and Revising of Stapledon's *Sirius.*" *Science-Fiction Studies*, 20 (1993): 1–14.

_____. *Olaf Stapledon: Speaking for the Future.* Syracuse, NY: Syracuse University Press, 1994.

_____. "Olaf Stapledon's 'Letters to the Future.'" *The Legacy of Olaf Stapledon: Critical Essays and an Unpublished Manuscript.* Eds. Patrick A. McCarthy, Charles Elkins and Martin Harry Greenberg. New York: Greenwood Press, 1989, pp. 99–120.

_____. "Politics and the Artist: The Aesthetic of Darkness and the Light." *Science-Fiction Studies*, 9.3 (1982): 294–305.

_____. *Talking Across the World: The Love Letters of Olaf Stapledon and Agnes Miller, 1913–1919.* Hanover and London: University Press of New England, 1987.

Crow, John, and Richard Erlich. "Mythic Patterns in Ellison's *A Boy and His Dog.*" *Extrapolation*, 18.2 (1977): 162–166.

Crowley, John. *Beasts.* London: Futura, 1976.

Culhane, John. "Characters Drawn to Nature," in "The Making of Bambi: A Prince

Is Born," *Bambi* (2-Disc Special Platinum Edition DVD) (1942), March 2005.
Culler, Jonathan. "Foreword." *The Poetics of Prose.* Tzvetan Todorov (Trans. Richard Howard). Ithaca, NY: Cornell University Press, 1977, pp. 7–13.
Dann, Jack, and Gardner Dozois. *Future War.* New York: Ace Books, 1999.
_____. *Magicats!* New York: Ace Books, 1984.
Darnton, Robert. *The Great Cat Massacre and Other Episodes in French Cultural History.* London: Penguin, 1984.
Darrieussecq, Marie. *Pig Tales: A Novel of Lust and Transformation* (Trans. Linda Coverdale). London: Faber and Faber, 1997.
Davenport, Basil. "The Vision of Olaf Stapledon." *To the End of Time.* Olaf Stapledon. New York: Funk and Wagnalls, 1953, pp. viii–xvi (Reprinted, Gregg, 1975).
Davidson, Avram. "The Tail-Tied Kings." *Galaxy Magazine,* 20.4 (1962): 51–57.
Dean, John. "The Science Fiction City." *Foundation: The Review of Science Fiction,* 23 (1982): 64–72.
_____. "The Uses of Wilderness in American Science Fiction." *Science Fiction Studies,* 9 (1982): 68–81.
De Botton, Alain. *The Art of Travel.* London: Hamish Hamilton/Penguin, 2002, p. 238.
DeCamp, L. Sprague, and Catherine Crook de Camp. *The Science Fiction Handbook.* Philadelphia: Owlswick Press, 1975.
De Lint, Charles. *Greenmantle.* London: Pan, 1982.
Del Ray, Lester. "The Faithful" (1938). *The Road to Science Fiction #2: From Wells to Heinlein.* Ed. James Gunn. New York: New American Library, 1979, pp. 429–437.
De Maupassant, Guy. "The Horla" (1887). *Selected Short Stories.* London: Penguin, 1971, pp. 313–344.
Dick, Philip K. *Blade Runner* (*Do Androids Dream of Electric Sheep?*). New York: Ballantine, 1968.
_____. "The Little Movement" (1952). In *Beyond Lies the Wub Vol. 1: The Collected Stories of Philip K. Dick.* London: Grafton Books, 1987, pp. 37–46.
_____. "Roog" (1953). *The Best of Philip K. Dick.* New York: Ballantine, 1977, pp. 11–16.
_____. "Roog" (1953). In *Beyond Lies the Wub Vol. 1: The Collected Stories of Philip K. Dick.* London: Grafton Books, 1987, pp. 31–36.
_____, and Roger Zelazny. *Deus Irae.* London: Sphere, 1976/82.
Dickens, Charles. *Hard Times.* Oxford: Oxford University Press, 1982, pp. 399–408.
Dickson, Gordon R. "Dolphin's Way." *Analog* (1964). *In the Bone: The Best Science Fiction of Gordon R. Dickson.* New York: Berkley Publishing Group (Ace), 1987.
_____. "In Memoriam: Clifford D. Simak." *Nebula Awards 24: SFWA's Choices for the Best Science Fiction and Fantasy 1988.* Ed. Michael Bishop. San Diego: Harcourt Brace Jovanovich, 1990, pp. 140–146.
DiPrete, John. "WAY STATION by Clifford D. Simak." *Science Fiction Review.* 39m (1981): 47.
Dissertation Abstracts International, 46.6 (1985.): 1617–1618\-A.
Dorman, Sonya. "Man and Beast." *Analog* (1977): 169–170.
Dorsch, T.S. *Classical Literary Criticism.* Harmondsworth: Penguin, 1965, p. 39.
Dowling, Terry. "Lever of Life: Winning and Losing in the Fiction of Cordwainer Smith." *Science Fiction: A Review of Speculative Literature,* 4.1 (1982): 9–37.
Dozois, Gardner, Jack Dann and Michael Swanwick. "Afternoon at Schrafft's." *Magicats!* Eds. Jack Dann and Gardner Dozois. New York: Ace, 1984, pp. 255–263.
Dundes, Alan. "Introduction to the Second Edition." *Morphology of the Folktale* (Trans. Laurence Scott 1st ed., Louis Wagner, 2nd ed.). Vladimir Propp. University of Texas Press, 1968/1979, p. xi.
Dupont, Denise. *Women of Vision: Essays by Women Writing Science Fiction.* New York: St. Martin's Press, 1988.
Eagleton, Terry. *Literary Theory: An Introduction.* Oxford: Basil Blackwell, 1983.
Edwards, Malcolm. "William Tenn 1920–." *Science Fiction Writers.* Ed. Everett F. Bleiler. New York, 1982, pp. 525–530.
Ellison, Harlan. "A Boy and His Dog" (1969). *Best SF Stories from New Worlds 8.* Ed. Michael Moorcock. London: Panther, 1974, pp. 7–47.
_____. "A Boy and His Dog" (1969). *Nebula Award Stories 5.* Ed. James Blish. London: Victor Gollancz, 1970, pp. 15–64.
Elms, Alan C. "The Creation of Cordwainer Smith." *Science-Fiction Studies,* 11.3 (1984): 264–283.
_____. "Origins of the Underpeople: Cats,

Kuomintang and Cordwainer Smith." *Fictional Space: Essays on Contemporary Science Fiction.* Ed. Tom Shippey. Atlantic Highlands, NJ: Humanities Press, 1991, pp. 166–93.

Ettin, Andrew V. *Literature and the Pastoral.* New Haven: Yale University Press, 1984, pp. 52–57.

Fast, Howard. "The Mouse" (1969). *Flying Saucers.* Eds. Isaac Asimov, Martin Greenberg and Charles Waugh. New York: Ballantine, 1982.

Fiedler, Leslie A. "Introduction." *Odd John: A Story Between Jest and Earnest.* Olaf Stapledon. London: New English Library, 1978, pp. 7–13.

_____. *Olaf Stapledon: A Man Divided.* New York: Oxford University Press, 1983.

Filmer, Kath (ed). "Introduction." *Twentieth Century Fantasists: Essays on Culture, Society and Belief in Twentieth Century Mythopoeic Literature.* London: Macmillan, 1992, pp. 1–7.

Firchow, Peter. *Aldous Huxley: Satirist and Novelist.* Minneapolis: University of Minnesota Press, 1972.

Fisher, Margery. *Who's Who in Children's Books: A Treasury of the Familiar Characters of Childhood.* London: Weidenfeld & Nicolson, 1975.

Forrest, C. Felix. *Ria.* Minneapolis: Jwindz Publishing, 1947/1987.

Foster, Alan Dean. *Cachalot.* London: New English Library, 1980.

Foucault, Michel. *The Archaeology of Knowledge.* London: Tavistock, 1972, pp. 3–17, 62–65, 135–140.

Foyster, John. "Cordwainer Smith." *Exploring Cordwainer Smith.* Ed. Andrew Porter. New York: Algol Press, 1975, pp. 10–17.

_____. "John Foyster Talks with Arthur Burns." *Exploring Cordwainer Smith.* Ed. Andrew Porter. New York: Algol Press, 1975, pp. 18–23.

France, Anatole. *Penguin Island* (Trans. Belle Notkin Burke). New York: Signet/New American Library, 1908/1968.

Franklin, H. Bruce. *Robert A. Heinlein: America as Science Fiction.* Oxford: Oxford University Press, 1980, pp. 92–95 [on "Jerry Was a Man" (1947)].

Freud, Sigmund. "Humour" (1928). *Sigmund Freud Collected Papers, Volume V.* Ed. James Strachey. London: Hogarth Press, 1950/1971, pp. 215–221.

_____. "Jokes and Their Relation to the Unconscious" (1905). *The Standard Edition of the Complete Psychological Works of Sigmund Freud, Volume VIII.* Ed. James Strachey (Trans. James Strachey, in collaboration with Anna Freud). London: Hogarth Press, 1960/1978, pp. 9–15, 117–158, 181–236.

Frye, Northrop. *Anatomy of Criticism: Four Essays.* Princeton, NJ: Princeton University Press, 1957/2000.

Gard, Ron (ed.). *The Critical Muse: Selected Literary Criticism.* London: Penguin, 1987.

Garnett, David. *Lady into Fox & a Man in the Zoo.* London: Chatto & Windus, 1922/1960, pp. 1–91.

Garrett, Randall. "A Little Intelligence." *Magicats!* Eds. Jack Dann and Gardner Dozois. New York: Ace, 1984, pp. 215–244.

Geis, Richard. "CITY: A Selection, 'Aesop,' Is Read by the Author, Clifford D. Simak, Caedmon TC 1649," *Science Fiction Review*, Vol. 9, No. 4, Winter 1980, p. 17.

Ghidalia, Roberta. "Friends?" *Microcosmic Tales: 100 Wondrous Science Fiction Short-Short Stories.* Eds. Isaac Asimov, Martin H. Greenberg, and Joseph O. Olander. New York: Daw Books, 1980, pp. 221–225.

Gillie, Christopher. "Culture and Consciousness: The Twentieth Century English Novel." *Bloomsbury Guide to English Literature.* Ed. Marion Wynne-Davies. London: Bloomsbury, 1989, pp. 113–135.

Goldin, Stephen. "Way Station." Magill, Frank, N. (ed.). *Survey of Science Fiction Literature*, Vol. 5, Englewood Cliffs, NJ: Salem Press, 1979, pp. 2429–2432.

Goldsworthy, Peter. Official home page. http://www.petergoldsworthy.com/.

_____. *Wish: A Biologically Engineered Love Story.* Sydney: Angus & Robertson, 1995.

Goulart, Ron. "Groucho." *Magicats!* Eds. Jack Dann and Gardner Dozois. New York: Ace, 1984, pp. 77–93.

Gould, J., and W.L. Kolb. *A Dictionary of the Social Sciences.* London: Tavistock, 1964.

Gould, Stephen Jay. "The Monster's Human Nature." *Dinosaur in a Haystack: Reflections in Natural History.* London: Penguin, 1997, pp. 53–62.

Grahame, Kenneth. *The Wind in the Willows.* London: Methuen, 1908/1954.

Grant, Michael. "Introduction," The *Transformations of Lucius: Otherwise Known as The Golden Ass.* Lucius Apuleius (Trans. Robert Graves). London: Penguin, 1950/1990, pp. vii–xviii.

Gunn, James. "The Alchemists Gather." *The Road to Science Fiction #2: From Wells to Heinlein.* New York: New American Library, 1979, pp. 426–9.

_____. *Alternate Worlds: The Illustrated History of Science Fiction.* New Jersey: Englewood Cliffs, 1975.

_____. *The New Encyclopedia of Science Fiction.* New York: Viking, 1988.

_____. *The Road to Science Fiction #2: From Wells to Heinlein.* New York: New American Library, 1979, pp. 1–16.

Gutwirth, Marcel. *Laughing Matter: An Essay on the Comic.* New York: Cornell University Press, 1993.

Hall, H.W. *Science Fiction and Fantasy Reference Index, 1878–1985: An International Author and Subject Index to History and Criticism.* Detroit, MI: Gale Research Company, Book Tower, 1987.

Handford, S.A. (trans.). *Fables of Aesop.* Harmondsworth: Penguin, 1954.

Harkins, William E. *Karel Čapek.* New York and London: Columbia University Press, 1962.

Harris-Fain, Darren. *H.G. Wells and the Modernist Revolution.* Ph.D. Thesis, Kent State University, 1992.

Harrison, Harry. *Return to Eden.* London: Grafton, 1988.

_____. *West of Eden.* London: Granada, 1984.

_____. *Winter in Eden.* London: Grafton, 1986.

_____, and Leon Stover. *Apeman, Spaceman: Anthropological Science Fiction.* US, 1968.

Hawkes, David. "Introduction." *The Story of the Stone: A Chinese Novel by Cao Xueqin in Five Volumes, Volume I "The Golden Days."* Harmondsworth: Penguin, 1973, pp. 15–46.

Hawthorn, Jeremy. *Studying the Novel: An Introduction.* London: Edward Arnold, 1993.

Heje, Johan. "On the Genesis of Norstrilia." *Extrapolation,* 30.2 (1989), pp. 146–155.

Hellekson, Karen. "Never Never Underpeople: Cordwainer Smith's Humanity." *Extrapolation,* 34 (2), Summer, 1993, pp. 123–130.

Hillegas, Mark R. *The Future as Nightmare: H.G. Wells and the Anti-Utopians.* New York, 1967.

Hipolito, Jane. "Norstrilia." *Survey of Science Fiction Literature, Vol. 4.* Ed. Frank N. Magill. Englewood Cliffs, NJ: Salem Press, 1979, pp. 1555–1559.

Hoban, Russell. *The Mouse and His Child.* London: Faber and Faber, 1969.

Høeg, Peter. *The Woman & the Ape* (Trans. Barbara Haveland). London: Harvill Press, 1996.

Holmes, Richard. *Coleridge: Darker Reflections.* London: Flamingo HarperCollins, 1998.

_____. *Sidetracks: Explorations of a Romantic Biographer.* London: HarperCollins, 2000.

Holquist, Michael. "Introduction." *Speech Genres & Other Late Essays.* Mikhail Bakhtin (Trans. Vern W. McGee; ed. Caryl Emerson and Michael Holquist). Austin: University of Texas Press, 1986/1996, pp. ix–xxiii.

_____. "Prologue." *Rabelais and His World.* Mikhail Bakhtin (Trans. Helen Iswolsky). Bloomington: Indiana University Press, 1984, pp. xiii–xxiii.

Homer. *The Odyssey* (Trans. E.V. Rieu). Harmondsworth: Penguin, 1954, p. 37.

Horne, Donald. *An Interrupted Life.* Sydney: HarperCollins, 1998.

Huizinga, Johan. *Homo Ludens: A Study of the Play Element in Culture.* London: Paladin, 1949/1971.

Hunter, Jeffrey. *The Animal Court: A Political Fable from Old Japan* (Trans. from Ando Shoeki, *Hosei Monogatari*). New York: Weatherhill, 1992.

Huxley, Aldous. *After Many a Summer.* London: HarperCollins, 1939/1994.

_____. *Ape and Essence.* London: HarperCollins, 1949/1994.

Ihab Hassan. "The Culture of Postmodernism." *Theory Culture and Society,* 2.3 (1985), pp. 119–131.

Ikin, Van. "The March of the Talking Nebulae." *Science Fiction: A Review of Speculative Literature,* 4.2 (1982), pp. 74–75.

The International Encyclopedia and Atlas. London: Macmillan, 1979, p. 194.

Jacobs, Eric. *Kingsley Amis: A Biography.* London: Hodder and Staughton, 1995.

Jakes, John. "The Highest Form of Life." *Amazing Fact and Science Fiction,* 35.8, August (1976), pp. 6–16.

Jakobson, Roman. "Linguistic and Poetics."

Language in Literature. Eds. Krystyna Pomorska and Stephen Rudy. 1987, p. 66f.

Jakubowski, Maxim, and Edward James. *The Profession of Science Fiction: SF Writers on Their Craft and Ideas*. London: Macmillan, 1992.

James, Henry. "From Honoré de Balzac, *Galaxy*, December 1875." Ed. Ron Gard. *The Critical Muse: Selected Literary Criticism*. London: Penguin, 1987, pp. 88–94.

_____. "The Story-Teller at Large: Mr. Henry Harland. Comedies and Errors, *Fortnightly Review*, April 1898." Ed. Ron Gard. *The Critical Muse: Selected Literary Criticism*. London: Penguin, 1987, pp. 333–334.

Jasper, David. "Foreword." *Twentieth Century Fantasists: Essays on Culture, Society and Belief in Twentieth Century Mythopoeic Literature*. Ed. Kath Filmer. London: Macmillan, 1992, pp. ix–xi.

Johnson, Stephanie. *The Whistler*. St. Leonards: Allen & Unwin, 1998, p. ix.

Jolly, John. "The Bellerophon Myth and *Forbidden Planet*," *Extrapolation*, 27.1 (1986), pp. 84–90.

Jones, C.A. "Introduction." *Exemplary Tales*. Cervantes. London: Penguin, 1972, p. 14.

Jordan, James B. "Christianity in the Science Fiction of 'Cordwainer Smith.'" *Contra Mundum*, 2 (1992).

Jotcham, Nicholas. "Introduction." *Carmen and Other Stories*. Prosper Mérimée. Oxford: Oxford University Press (World Classics), 2008, pp. vii–xxv.

Joyce, James. *Ulysses with Ulysses: A Short History by Richard Ellmann*. Harmondsworth: Penguin, 1922/1971.

Jung, Carl. *Memories, Dreams, Reflections*. London: Flamingo, 1961.

_____, et al. *Man and His Symbols*. New York: Dell, 1964.

Kafka, Franz. "A Report for an Academy" (1917). *Stories 1904–1924* (Trans. J.A. Underwood). London: Futura Macdonald, 1981, pp. 219–228.

_____. "A Report for an Academy." *The Transformation ("Metamorphosis") and Other Stories*. London: Penguin, 1992, pp. 187–195.

_____. "The Transformation." *The Transformation ("Metamorphosis") and Other Stories*. London: Penguin, 1992, pp. 76–126.

Kavan, Anna. *Ice*. London: Picador/Pan, 1967.

Kaveney, Andrew. "The Instrumentality of Mankind by Cordwainer Smith." *Foundation: The Review of Science Fiction*, 18, pp. 92–93.

Kaveney, Roz. "New New World Dreams: Angela Carter and Science Fiction." Ed. Lorna Sage. *Flesh and the Mirror: Essays on the Art of Angela Carter*. London: Virago, 1994, pp. 171–18.

Keesing's Contemporary Archives. "Weekly Diary of Important World Events with Index Continually Kept Up-to-Date." Vol. II (1934–1937). London: Keesing's Publications Ltd., est. 1931.

Kerr, Philip. *Esau*. London: Vintage, 1996.

Kessel, John. *Easy Accommodations*. Ph.D. Thesis, University of Kansas, 1981.

Kettlewell, Trevor. "Wish." Trevor Kettlewell's Book Reviews. April 2007. http://people.aapt.net.au/~trevorkett/home.htm

Keyes, Daniel. *Algernon, Charlie, and I: A Writer's Journey*. Orlando, FL: Harvest, 1999.

_____. "Flowers for Algernon" (1959). Ed. Eric S. Rabkin. *Science Fiction: A Historical Anthology*. Oxford: Oxford University Press, 1983, pp. 371–401.

King, Vincent. *Candy Man*. Newton Abbot, Devon: Science Fiction Book Club, 1972.

Kingsley, Charles. *The Water Babies*. Oxford: Oxford University Press, 1863/1995.

Kinnaird, John. "Sirius: A Fantasy of Love and Discord." *Survey of Science Fiction Literature*. Ed. Frank N. Magill. Vol. 5. Englewood Cliffs, NJ: Salem Press, 1979, pp. 2085–2090.

_____. "Stapledon." *Twentieth Century Science-Fiction Writers*. Ed. Curtis Smith. Surrey: Macmillan, 1981, pp. 516–7.

Kipling, Rudyard. *The Jungle Book*. London: Macmillan, 1894/1951.

_____. *Just So Stories*. London: Macmillan, 1962, pp. 129–143.

_____. *The Second Jungle Book*. London: Macmillan, 1895/1950.

_____. "The White Seal." *The Jungle Book*. London: Macmillan, 1951, pp. 127–159.

Knight, Damon. "*Books*: New Maps of Hell," *The Magazine of Fantasy and Science Fiction*, 18.6 (1960), 84–86.

Kotzwinkle, William. *The Bear Went Over the Mountain*. London: Black Swan, 1996.

_____. *Doctor Rat*. New York: Bantam, 1971/1977.

La Faille, E.E. "Pawprints Across the Galaxy:

Dogs in Science Fiction," *Kliatt Young Adult Paperback Book Guide*, 18.6 (1984), pp. 2–3, 76.

Lafferty, R.A. Past *Master.* New York: Ace Books, 1968.

La Fontaine, Jean de. *Selected Fables.* Ed. Maya Slater (Trans. Christopher Wood). Oxford: Oxford University Press, 1995.

Lawler, Donald. "War with the Newts (Valka S. Mloky)." *Survey of Science Fiction Literature.* Ed. Frank N. Magill. Englewood Cliffs, NJ: Salem Press, 1979, pp. 2424–2428.

Lefanu, Sarah. *In the Chinks of the World Machine: Feminism and Science Fiction.* London: Women's Press, 1988.

Le Guin, Ursula K. *Buffalo Gals and Other Animal Presences.* London: Penguin (ROC), 1987/1994.

_____. *Dancing at the Edge of the World.* London: Victor Gollancz, 1989.

_____. "Schrodinger's Cat," *Magicats!* Eds. Jack Dann and Gardner Dozois. New York: Ace, 1984, pp. 67–76.

Leiber, Fritz. *The Best of Fritz Leiber.* London: Sphere, 1974.

_____. "Kreativity for Kats," *Galaxy*, 19.4 (1961), pp. 63–73.

_____. "Space-Time for Springers" (1958). *The Best of Fritz Leiber.* London: Sphere, 1974, pp. 208–21.

Leunig, Michael. *Leunig's Carnival of the Animals.* Sydney: Pan Macmillan, 2000. [Accompanying CD: Camille Saint-Saens (comp. 1886) *Carnival of the Animals*, performed by the Australian Chamber Orchestra, directed by Richard Tognetti; Leunig's text narrated by Peter Garrett].

Lévi-Strauss, Claude. *Structural Anthropology, Volume 2* (Trans. Monique Layton). Harmondsworth: Penguin, 1973.

_____. "Structure and Form: Reflections on a Work by Vladimir Propp." *Structural Anthropology, Volume 2* (Trans. Monique Layton). Harmondsworth: Penguin, 1973, pp. 115–145.

Linebarger, Paul. *Psychological Warfare.* Infantry Journal Press, 1948.

Literature, Arts, and Medicine Database. "Goldsworthy, Peter. Wish." New York University, 1993–2009. Last Revised 08/15/05. http://litmed.med.nyu.edu/Annotation?action=view&annid=12393

Lodge, David. "After Bakhtin." *After Bakhtin: Essays on Fiction and Criticism.* London: Routledge, 1990, pp. 87–99, 189–190.

_____. *The Art of Fiction.* London: Penguin, 1992.

_____. *Consciousness and the Novel: Connected Essays.* London: Secker & Warburg, 2002.

_____. "Milan Kundera, and the Idea of the Author in Modern Criticism," *After Bakhtin: Essays on Fiction and Criticism.* London: Routledge, 1990, pp. 154–167, 193.

_____. *Modern Criticism and Theory: A Reader.* London: Longman, 1988.

_____. *20th Century Literary Criticism: A Reader.* London: Longman, 1972/1995.

Lomax, William. "The 'Invisible Alien' in the Science Fiction of Clifford Simak," *Extrapolation*, 30.2 (1989), pp. 133–145.

Lorey, Dan [alt.fan.furry]. Novels List. Internet, March 20, 1995. http://www.usenet.com/newsgroups/rec.arts.sf.written/msg29923.html

Lundwall, Sam J. "The Heart of a Dog (Sobatje Serdtse)," *Survey of Science Fiction Literature, Vol. 2.* Ed. Frank N. Magill. Englewood Cliffs, NJ: Salem Press, 1979, pp. 956–959.

MacAvoy, R.A. Damiano. Toronto: Bantam, 1983/1985.

Machiavelli, Nicolo. *The Prince and the Discourses* (Trans. Luigi Ricci). New York: Random House, 1950, p. 64.

Magill, Frank, N. *Survey of Science Fiction Literature,* 5. Englewood Cliffs, NJ: Salem Press, 1979.

Mahabharata (Trans. C. Rajagopalachari). Bombay: Bhavan's Book University, 1966.

Mandelbaum, David. "The Study of Life History: Gandhi," *Current Anthropology*, 14.3 (1973), p. 181.

Marquis, Don. *Archy & Mehitabel.* London: Faber and Faber, 1931.

Martin, Mick, and Marsha Porter. *Video Movie Guide 1990.* New York: Ballantine, 1989.

Mattingly, Robert. "Discovering a New Earth" (1980), *Microcosmic Tales: 100 Wondrous Science Fiction Short-Short Stories.* Eds. Isaac Asimov, Martin H. Greenberg, and Joseph O. Olander. New York: Daw Books, 1980, pp. 29–32.

Matuska, Alexander. *Karel Čapek, an Essay* (Trans. Cathryn Alan). London: George Allen and Unwin, 1964.

May, Keith M. *Aldous Huxley.* London: Elek Books, 1972.

McCarthy, Patrick. A. *Olaf Stapledon.* Boston: Twayne, 1982.

_____. "Stapledon's Microcosm of Community." *Science-Fiction Studies*, 15.2 (1988), pp. 237–239.

_____, Charles Elkins, and Martin Harry Greenberg. *The Legacy of Olaf Stapledon: Critical Essays and an Unpublished Manuscript.* New York: Greenwood Press, 1989.

McDonald, Ian. "Floating Dogs," *Future War.* Eds. Jack Dann and Gardner Dozois. New York: Ace Books, 1999, pp. 69–94.

McGirr, Michael. "Strange Talk," *Eureka Street*, 6.2 (1996), p. 51.

McIntosh, J.T. *The Fittest.* London: Transworld, 1955/1961.

McKinley, Marlene. "Viewing 'the Immense Panorama or Futility and Anarchy That Is Contemporary History' in the First Six Novels of Charles Williams," *Twentieth Century Fantasists: Essays on Culture, Society and Belief in Twentieth Century Mythopoeic Literature.* Ed. Kath Filmer. London: Macmillan, 1992, pp. 71–91.

McKinney, Richard. "On Roger Zelazny and Clifford Simak," *Foundation: The Review of Science Fiction*, 13 (1978), pp. 61–63.

McNamara, Peter, and Margaret Winch. *Alien Shores: An Anthology of Australian Science Fiction.* North Adelaide: Aphelion Publications, 1994.

Mérimée, Prosper. *Carmen and Other Stories* (Trans. Nicholas Jotcham). Oxford: Oxford University Press (World Classics), 2008.

_____. "Lokis," *Works of Prosper Merimee.* Ed. George Saintsbury. New York: Bigelow, Brown, 1905, pp. 3–74.

Merle, Robert. *Day of the Dolphin* (Trans. Helen Weaver). Harmondsworth: Penguin, 1967/1973.

Merril, Judith. "Books," *The Magazine of Fantasy and Science Fiction*, 29.4 (1965), pp. 92–97.

Miller, Walter M., Jr. *Conditionally Human* (1952). London: Victor Gollantz, 1964.

Milling, Jill Langston. *The Ambiguous Animal: Evolution of the Beast-Man in Scientific Creation Myths.* Ph.D. Thesis, the University of Texas at Dallas, 1985.

Mills, C. Wright. *The Sociological Imagination.* Harmondsworth: Penguin, 1970, p. 248.

Mitchison, Naomi. "Wonderful Deathless Ditties" (1981), *The Profession of Science Fiction: SF Writers on Their Craft and Ideas.* Eds. Maxim Jakubowski and Edward James. London: Macmillan, 1992.

Morgan, Chris. "Cordwainer Smith," *Science Fiction Writers.* Ed. Everett F. Bleiler. New York: Scribner's, 1982, pp. 519–524.

Morrow, James. *Nebula Awards 28.* New York: Harcourt Brace Jovanovich, 1994.

Morton, Peter. *The Vital Science: Biology and the Literary Imagination, 1860–1900.* London: George Allen & Unwin, 1984.

Moskowitz, Sam. *Explorers of the Infinite: Shapers of Science Fiction.* New York: World, 1963.

_____. "Introduction," "Olaf Stapledon: The Man Behind the Works," and 'Peace and Olaf Stapledon," *Far Future Calling.* Philadelphia: Oswald Train, 1979.

_____. "Karel Čapek," *Science Fantasy*, 46.16 (1961), pp. 100–112.

_____. "Olaf Stapledon: Cosmic Philosopher," *Darkness and the Light.* Olaf Stapledon. Westport, CT: Hyperion Press, 1963.

_____. "Olaf Stapledon: Cosmic Philosopher," *Explorers of the Infinite: Shapers of Science Fiction.* New York: World, 1963, pp. 261–277.

_____. "The Saintly Heresy of Clifford D. Simak," *Amazing*, 36.6 (1962), pp. 86–97.

_____. "The Sons of Frankenstein," *Science Fantasy*, 11.34 (1959), pp. 76–86.

_____. "The Strange Case of Murray Leinster," *Amazing Fact and Science Fiction*, 35.12 (1961), pp. 104–116.

_____. "The Wonders of H.G. Wells," *Science Fantasy*, 11.34 (1959), pp. 72–82.

Muecke, Stephen. "Goldsworthy's *Wish*," *Australian Book Review*, 178 (1996), pp. 47–48.

Murray, Les. "Embodiment and Incarnation: Notes on Preparing an Anthology of Australian Religious Verse" (1987), *The Paperbark Tree: Selected Prose.* Manchester: Carcanet Press, 1992, pp. 251–269.

_____. "Eric Rolls and the Golden Disobedience" (December 1982), *The Paperbark Tree: Selected Prose.* Manchester: Carcanet Press, 1992, p. 166.

_____. "A Folk Inferno" (1988), *The Paperbark Tree: Selected Prose.* Manchester: Carcanet Press, 1992, pp. 317–328.

Myers, R.E. *The Intersection of Science Fiction and Philosophy.* Westport: Greenwood, 1983.

Nabokov, Vladimir. *Lolita*. Everyone's Library, London: Random House, 1955/1992.

Nance, Guinivera A. *Aldous Huxley*. New York: Continuum, 1988.

Narayan, R.K. *A Tiger for Malgudi*. Harmondsworth: Penguin, 1982.

Natov, Nadine. *Mikhail Bulgakov*. Boston: Twayne, 1985, pp. 1–21, 38–48, 125.

Newby, Jonica. *The Pact for Survival: Humans and Their Animal Companions*. Sydney: ABC Books, 1997.

Nicholls, Peter. *The Encyclopedia of Science Fiction*. London: Granada, 1979.

_____. *Explorations of the Marvellous: The Science and the Fiction in Science Fiction*. Glasgow: Fontana/Collins, 1978.

Norton, Andre. "All Cats Are Gray," *Zoo 2000: Twelve Stories of Science Fiction and Fantasy Beasts*. Ed. Jane Yolen. New York: Seabury Press, 1973, pp. 107–117.

_____. *Star Man's Son: 2250 A.D.* London: Victor Gollantz, 1952/1968.

Olander, Joseph D., and Martin Harry Greenberg. *Robert A. Heinlein*. Edinburgh: Paul Harris Publishing, 1978, pp. 42–43.

Olivelle, Patrick. "Introduction," *The Pancatantra: The Book of Indian Folk Wisdom*. Oxford: Oxford University Press, 1997, pp. ix–xlv.

Orwell, George. *Animal Farm: A Fairy Story*. Harmondsworth: Penguin/Secker & Warburg, 1945/1967.

Owen, D.R. (Trans.). *The Romance of Reynard the Fox*. Oxford: Oxford University Press, 1994.

Ower, John. "'Aesop' and the Ambiguity of Clifford Simak's *City*," *Science Fiction Studies*, VI (1979), pp. 164–167.

Pancatantra: The Book of Indian Folk Wisdom (Trans. Patrick Olivelle). Oxford: Oxford University Press, 1997.

Panshin, Alexei. *Heinlein in Dimension*. Chicago: Advent, 1968, pp. 44–47.

Parrinder, Patrick. *Science Fiction: A Critical Guide*. London: Longman, 1979, pp. 90–109.

Pearson, Roger (Trans.). "Introduction," *Candide and Other Stories*. Voltaire. Oxford: Oxford University Press, 1990, pp. vii–xxxix.

Philmus, Robert M. "Kindred Spirits: Robert Crossley on Olaf Stapledon," *Science-Fiction Studies*, 22 (1995), pp. 106–112.

_____. "Undertaking Stapledon," *Science-Fiction Studies*, 11 (1984), pp. 71–77.

Pierce, John J. "Cordwainer Smith: The Shaper of Myths," *The Best of Cordwainer Smith*. New York: Ballantine, 1975, pp. xi–xix, 124.

_____. "Treasure of the Secret Cordwainer," *Science Fiction Review*, 12.3 (1983), pp. 8–14.

Piper, H. Beam. *Fuzzy Sapiens*. London: Futura, 1964/1977.

_____. *Little Fuzzy*. London: Futura, 1962/1977.

Pirkova-Jacobson, Svatava. "Introduction to the First Edition," *Morphology of the Folktale*. Vladimir Propp (Trans. Laurence Scott 1st ed., Louis Wagner, 2nd ed.). University of Texas Press, 1968/1979, pp. xx–xxi.

Pohl, Frederik. "Slave Ship," *Galaxy*, Installment 1, 38, ND, pp. 84–127.

_____. "Slave Ship," *Galaxy*, Installment 2, 39, ND, pp. 64–107.

_____. "Slave Ship," *Galaxy*, Installment 3, 40, ND, pp. 88–127.

_____. *The Way the Future Was*. New York, 1978.

Porter, Andrew. *Exploring Cordwainer Smith*. New York: Algol Press, 1975.

Pringle, David. "Aliens for Neighbours: A Reassessment of Clifford D. Simak," *Foundation: The Review of Science Fiction*, 11/12, 1977.

_____. "Olaf Stapledon: A Man Divided, by Leslie Fiedler," *Foundation: The Review of Science Fiction*, 19 (1983), pp. 76–79.

Proffer, Ellendea. *A Pictorial Biography of Mikhail Bulgakov*. Ann Arbor: Ardis, 1984.

Propp, Vladimir. *Morphology of the Folktale* (Trans. Laurence Scott 1st ed., Louis Wagner, 2nd ed.). University of Texas Press, 1968/1979, pp. ix–xxii, 19–65, 119–127.

Putnam, Samuel (Trans.). *The Portable Rabelais*. Canada: Viking Press, 1946/1967.

Rabkin, Eric S. "Composite Fiction of Olaf Stapledon," *Science-Fiction Studies*, 9.3 (1982), pp. 238–248.

_____. *Science Fiction: A Historical Anthology*. Oxford: Oxford University Press, 1983, pp. 371–401

Ramayana (Trans. C. Rajagopalachari). Bombay: Bhavan's Book University, 1965.

Reed, Kit. "Piggy," *The Magazine of Fantasy and Science* Fiction, 21.2 (1961), pp. 60–72.

Remarque, Erich Maria. *All Quiet on the Western Front*. London & Sydney: Bodley Head/Pan Books, 1929/1987.

Reynolds, Mack. "Dog Star," *Microcosmic Tales: 100 Wondrous Science Fiction Short-Short Stories*. Eds. Isaac Asimov, Martin H. Greenberg, and Joseph O. Olander. New York: Daw Books, 1980, pp. 102–104.

Rice, Philip, and Patricia Waugh. *Modern Literary Theory: A Reader*. London: Edward Arnold, 1989/1992.

Rose, Lois and Stephen. "Humanun: What Manner of Men Are We?" *The Shattered Ring: Science Fiction and the Quest for Meaning*. Richmond, VA: John Knox Press, 1970, pp. 41–69.

_____. *The Shattered Ring: Science Fiction and the Quest for Meaning*. 1970.

Rubin, Rick. "The Interplanetary Cat," *The Magazine of Fantasy and Science Fiction*, 21.5 (1961), pp. 24–28.

Russell, Bertrand. *Wisdom of the West*. London: Macdonald, 1959, pp. 192, 215, 237.

Saintsbury, George. *Works of Prosper Mérimée*. New York: Bigelow, Brown, 1905.

Saki (H. H. Munro). "Tobermory," *The Chronicles of Clovis*. Harmondsworth: Penguin, 1911/1986, pp. 16–24.

Salten, Felix. *Bambi*.

Sandison, Alan. "Introduction," *Kim*. Rudyard Kipling. Oxford/New York: Oxford University Press, 1987, pp. xxviii–xxix.

Sargent, Pamela. "Out of Place," *Magicats!* Eds. Jack Dann and Gardner Dozois. New York: Ace, 1984, pp. 51–65.

Satty, Harvey. "Introduction," *Nebula Maker*. Olaf Stapledon. London: Sphere Books, 1976, pp. vii–x.

Saunders, Ian. *Open Texts, Partial Maps: A Literary Theory Handbook*. The University of Western Australia, Centre for Studies in Australian Literature, 1993.

Searles, Baird, et al. *A Reader's Guide to Science Fiction*. New York: Avon, 1979.

Selden, Raman. *A Reader's Guide to Contemporary Literary Theory*. Hertfordshire: Harvester Wheatsheaf, 1989.

Self, Will. *Great Apes*. London: Bloomsbury, 1997.

_____. "Scale," *Grey Area*. London: Penguin, 1993, pp. 89–123.

Selver, Paul. *Masaryk: A Biography by Paul Selver*. London: Michael Joseph, 1940.

Shaw, Bruce. "Agape, Eros and the Zoophilous: An Appreciation of Peter Goldsworthy's *Wish*," *Science Fiction: A Review of Speculative Literature*, 15.2 (2000b), pp. 27–38.

_____. "The Animal in Comic Riot," *Australian Journal of Comedy*, 7.1 (2001a), pp. 71–92.

_____. "Animal Fables and Bakhtin's Carnival," *Australian Journal of Comedy*, 6.1 (2000a), pp. 99–131.

_____. "Clifford Simak's *City* (1952): The Dogs' Critique (and Others')," *Extrapolation*, 46.4 (2005), pp. 488–499.

_____. "Fables," *The Greenwood Encyclopedia of Science Fiction and Fantasy: Themes, Works, and Wonders*. Ed. Gary Westfahl. Westport: Greenwood Press, 2005, pp. 272–274.

_____. "The Heart of a Dog by Mikhail Bulgakov," *Science Fiction: A Review of Speculative Literature*, 151.2 (2009) (forthcoming).

_____. *Mind and Paws: The Carnivalesque in Tales of Science Fiction & Fantasy (1936–1964) Inspired by the Tradition of the Animal Fable*. Ph.D. Thesis, English Department: Flinders University, 2003.

_____. "Surdity and the Canine Mind: *The Whistler* by Stephanie Johnson," *Science Fiction: A Review of Speculative Literature*, 16.1 (2001b), pp. 57–60.

_____. "The Tibetan 'Wheel of Life' Versus the Great Game in Kipling's *Kim*," *The Kipling Journal*, 69.276 (1995), pp. 12–21.

_____, and David Stewart. "Thoughts on the Structure and Iconography of Kim," *The Kipling Journal*, 71.283 (1997), pp. 12–17.

Shelley, Mary. *Frankenstein or the Modern Prometheus*. London: Penguin, 1818/1992.

_____. *The Last Man*. Oxford: Oxford University Press, 1994.

Shelton, Robert Fredrick. *Forms of Things Unknown: The Alien and Utopian Visions of Wells, Stapledon, and Clarke*. Ph.D. Thesis, University of California, Berkeley, 1982.

_____. "The Moral Philosophy of Olaf Stapledon," *The Legacy of Olaf Stapledon: Critical Essays and an Unpublished Manuscript*. Eds. McCarthy, Patrick A., Charles Elkins and Martin Harry Greenberg. New York: Greenwood Press, 1989, pp. 5–22.

Shepley, John. "Gorilla Suit," *The Best from Fantasy and Science Fiction*. Ed. Anthony Boucher. New York: Ace Books, 1959, pp. 152–161.

_____. "The Kit-Katt Klub," *The Magazine of Fantasy and Science Fiction*, 22.4 (1962), pp. 57–67.

Shippey, Tom. "Introduction," *The Oxford Book of Science Fiction Stories.* Oxford University Press, 1993, pp. ix–xxvi.

_____. *The Oxford Book of Science Fiction Stories.* Oxford University Press, 1993.

Shklovsky, Victor. "Art as Technique" (1965), *Modern Criticism and Theory: A Reader.* Ed. David Lodge. London: Longman, 1988, pp. 16–30.

Silverberg, Robert. *Mutants.* London: Corgi, 1974.

Simak, Clifford D. "The Big Front Yard" (1958), *The Hugo Winners.* Ed. Isaac Asimov. Harmondsworth: Penguin, 1962.

_____. "Census," *Astounding Science Fiction,* 1944, p. 2.

_____. *City.* London: Methuen, 1952/1980, pp. 240–255.

_____. *City.* New York: Ace Books, 1952/1976.

_____. "Desertion" (1944), *The Oxford Book of Science Fiction Stories.* Ed. Tom Shippey. Oxford: Oxford University Press, 1993, pp. 115–126.

_____. "Room Enough for All of Us," *Extrapolation,* 13 (1972), pp. 102–105.

_____. *They Walked Like Men.* New York: Doubleday, 1962 (Manor Books Inc., 1972).

_____. *Way Station.* New York: Macfadden, 1963.

Slater, Maya. "Introduction," *Selected Fables.* Jean de La Fontaine (Trans. Christopher Wood). Oxford: Oxford University Press, 1995, pp. vii–xxvii.

Slesar, Henry. "My Father, the Cat," *Magicats!* Eds. Jack Dann and Gardner Dozois. New York: Ace, 1984, pp. 95–104.

_____. "Speak," *Microcosmic Tales: 100 Wondrous Science Fiction Short-Short Stories.* Eds. Isaac Asimov, Martin H. Greenberg, and Joseph O. Olander. New York: Daw Books, 1980, pp. 183–185.

Sloane, William. *Stories for Tomorrow: An Anthology of Modern Science Fiction.* London: Eyre & Spottiswoode, 1955.

Smith, Cordwainer. "The Ballad of Lost C'Mell" (1962), *The Best of Cordwainer Smith.* Ed. J.J. Pierce. New York: Ballantine, 1975, pp. 315–337.

_____. *The Best of Cordwainer Smith.* Ed. J.J. Pierce. New York: Ballantine, 1975.

_____. "The Dead Lady of Clown Town" (1964), *The Best of Cordwainer Smith.* Ed. J.J. Pierce. New York: Ballantine, 1975, pp. 124–209.

_____. "The Game of Rat and Dragon" (1955), *The Best of Cordwainer Smith.* Ed. J.J. Pierce. New York: Ballantine, 1975, pp. 67–83.

_____. *The Instrumentality of Mankind.* New York: Ballantine, 1979.

_____. "Mother Hitton's Littul Kittons" (1962), *The Best of Cordwainer Smith.* Ed. J.J. Pierce. New York: Ballantine, 1975, pp. 257–282.

_____. *Norstrilia.* London: VGSF, 1975.

Smith, Curtis C. "Diabolical Intelligence and (Approximately) Divine Innocence," *The Legacy of Olaf Stapledon: Critical Essays and an Unpublished Manuscript.* Eds. McCarthy, Patrick A., Charles Elkins and Martin Harry Greenberg. New York: Greenwood Press, 1989, pp. 87–98.

_____. "Horror Vs. Tragedy: Mary Shelley's *Frankenstein* and Olaf Stapledon's *Sirius,*" *Extrapolation,* 26.1 (1985), pp. 66–73.

_____. "Olaf Stapledon's Dispassionate Objectivity," *Voices for the Future: Essays on Major Science Fiction Writers.* Ed. T. D. Clareson. Bowling Green, OH: Popular Press, 1976, pp. 44–63.

_____. *Twentieth Century Science Fiction Writers,* 2nd edition. Chicago, 1981.

_____. "William Olaf Stapledon: Saint and Revolutionary," *Extrapolation,* 13.1 (1971), pp. 5–15.

Smith, George O. "History Repeats," *Astounding Science* Fiction, 15.8 (1959), pp. 72–82.

_____. "Understanding," *Galaxy Magazine,* 26.1 (1967), pp. 137–182.

Smith, Marion Kay. *Whence, Whither, and Why: Science Fiction's Conceptions of the Origin and Destiny of the Human Species.* Ph.D. Thesis, the University of Texas at Austin, 1986.

Smith, Vincent. *Musco—Blue Whale.* Sydney: Harper & Row, 1978.

Sontag, Susan. "The Imagination of Disaster," *Against Interpretation.* London: Vintage, 1961/1994, pp. 209–225.

_____. "Writing Itself: On Roland Barthes," *Where the Stress Falls: Essays.* London: Jonathan Cape, 2001, p. 71.

Soyka, David. "Frankenstein and the Miltonic Creation of Evil," *Extrapolation,* 33.2 (1992), pp. 166–176.

Stapledon, Olaf. *Last Men in London*. London: Methuen, 1932/1978.
_____. *Nebula Maker.* London: Sphere Books, 1976.
_____. *Odd John: A Story Between Jest and Earnest.* London: New English Library, 1978.
_____. *Odd John and Sirius: Two Science-Fiction Novels by Olaf Stapledon.* New York: Dover, 1972.
_____. "Preface," *Last and First Men: A Story of the Near and Far Future.* Harmondsworth: Penguin, 1930/1987, pp. 11–13.
_____. "Preface," *Star* Maker. Harmondsworth: Penguin, 1937/1972, pp. 7–9.
_____. *Sirius: A Fantasy of Love and Discord.* Harmondsworth: Penguin, 1944/1973.
Stiglitz, Beatrice. *Meditations D'un Agnostique Pascalien: Essai Sur "Le Miroir des Limbes" [Mirror Limbo] S'Andre Malraux* (French text). Ph.D. Thesis, City University of New York, 1981.
Stirling, John. *The Bible: Authorized Version.* London: The British & Foreign Bible Society, 1955, p. 2 [Genesis 1: 24–26].
Strachey, James. *Sigmund Freud Collected Papers,* V. London: Hogarth Press, 1950/1971.
Sun Tzu. *The Art of War* (Trans. Thomas Cleary). Boston: Shambala, 1988.
Suvin, Darko. "Karel Čapek, or the Aliens Amongst Us," *Metamorphoses of Science Fiction.* New Haven, CT: Yale University Press, 1979, pp. 270–283, 308–309.
_____. *Metamorphoses of Science Fiction.* New Haven, CT: Yale University Press, 1979.
Swanson, R.A. "The Spiritual Factor in *Odd John* and *Sirius,*" *Science-Fiction Studies,* 9.3 (1982), pp. 249–256.
Sypher, W. *Comedy.* New York: Doubleday Anchor, 1956.
Takayuki Tatsumi. "An Interview with Darko Suvin," *Science-Fiction Studies,* 12.2 (1985), pp. 202–220.
Taylor, Angus. "Comment," *Foundation,* 16 (1979), pp. 24–25.
Tenn, William. "Null-P" (1951), *Spectrum I: A Science Fiction Anthology.* Eds. Kingsley Amis and Robert Conquest. London: Pan, 1961, pp. 125–136.
Thomas, Elizabeth Marshall. *The Hidden Life of Dogs.* London: Weidenfeld and Nicolson, 1993.
Thompson, Francis. "The Hound of Heaven" (1893), *Poems of Francis Thompson.* Ed. Terence L. Connolly. New York: Appleton-Century-Crofts, 1932/1941/1960, pp. vii–xxiv, 77–81, 349–371.
Todorov, Tzvetan. *The Fantastic: A Structural Approach to a Literary Genre* (Trans. Richard Howard). Cleveland/London: Press of Case Western Reserve University, 1973.
_____. *Genres in Discourse* (Trans. Catherine Porter). Cambridge: Cambridge University Press, 1990.
_____. *The Poetics of Prose* (Trans. Richard Howard). Ithaca, NY: Cornell University Press, 1977. [Ch. 6, "An Introduction to Verisimilitude"; Ch. 15, "How to Read?"]
_____. "The Typology of Detective Fiction" (1966), *Modern Criticism and Theory: A Reader.* Ed. David Lodge. London: Longman, 1988, pp. 157–165.
Tolkien, J.R.R. "On Fairy-Stories." *The Monsters and the Critics: And Other Essays.* London: HarperCollins, 1983, pp. 109–161.
Tremaine, Louis. "Historical Consciousness in Stapledon and Malraux," *Science-Fiction Studies,* 11.2 (1984), pp. 130–138.
_____. "Olaf Stapledon's Note on Magnitude," *Extrapolation,* 23.3 (1982), pp. 243–263.
_____. "Ritual Experience in Odd John and Sirius," *The Legacy of Olaf Stapledon: Critical Essays and an Unpublished Manuscript.* Eds. Patrick A. McCarthy, Charles Elkins, and Martin Harry Greenberg. New York: Greenwood Press, 1989, pp. 67–85.
Tubb, E.C. "The Captain's Dog," *Nebula Science Fiction,* 35 (1958), pp. 3–22.
Turner, A.K. "Chronology," *Exploring Cordwainer Smith.* Ed. Andrew Porter. New York: Algol Press, 1975, pp. 28–30.
Tweet, Roald D. "Clifford Simak," *Science Fiction Writers: Critical Studies of the Major Authors from the Early Nineteenth Century to the Present Day.* Ed. E.F. Bleiler. New York: Scribner's, 1982, pp. 513–518.
Tymn, Marshall B. "Masterpieces of Science-Fiction Criticism," *Mosaic,* XIII.3–4 (1980), pp. 219–222.
_____. *The Science Fiction Reference Book.* Mercer Island, WA: Starmont House, 1981.
_____. "The Year's Scholarship in Fantastic Literature: 1987," *Extrapolation,* 29.3 (1988), pp. 235–284.
Versins, Pierre. *Encyclopedie de L'Utopie des Voyages Extraordinaires at de la Science Fiction.* Lausanne: L'Age d'Homme, 1972.

Voltaire. *Candide and Other Stories.* Oxford: Oxford University Press, 1990.

Von Franz, Marie-Louise. "The Process of Individuation," *Man and His Symbols.* Eds. Carl G. Jung et al. New York: Dell, 1964, p. 161.

Vonnegut, Kurt, Jr. *Sirens of Titan.* Coronet, Hodder and Stoughton, 1959/79.

Waldren, Murray. "Unfulfilled by the Feast," *The Weekend Review*, February 15–16, 1997, p. 7.

Waley, Arthur. "Introduction," *Monkey.* Wu Ch'eng-en (Trans. Arthur Waley). London: Unwin, 1942/1979, pp. 7–8.

Walker, Paul. *Speaking of Science Fiction: The Paul Walker Interviews.* New Jersey: Luna, 1978.

Wallace, F.L. "Big Ancestor," *Galaxy*, 25 (1954), pp. 104–127.

_____. "Bolden's Pets," *Galaxy Science Fiction*, 34 (ND), pp. 70–87.

Wallace-Crabbe, Robin. *Dogs.* Pymble, NSW: Angus & Robertson, 1993.

Wangerin, Walter, Jr. *The Book of the Dun Cow.* London: Allen Lane, 1980.

Warrington, John. *Everyman's Classical Dictionary 800 B.C. to A.D. 337.* London: Dent, 1961.

Watt, Donald. *Aldous Huxley: The Critical Heritage.* London: Routledge and Kegan Paul, 1975.

Waugh, Evelyn. *Brideshead Revisited: The Sacred and Profane Memories of Captain Charles Ryder.* Harmondsworth: Penguin, 1945/1984.

Webster, Roger. *Studying Literary Theory: An Introduction.* London: Edward Arnold, 1990.

Weinbaum, Stanley G. *A Martian Odyssey.* London: Sphere Books, 1974.

_____. "Proteus Island" (1936), *A Martian Odyssey.* London: Sphere Books, 1974, pp. 277–309.

Weinkauf, Mary S. "Simak, Clifford D(onald)," *Twentieth Century Science Fiction Writers.* Ed. Curtis C. Smith. Chicago, 1981, pp. 495–497.

Weinstein, Lee. "Quest of the Three Worlds by Cordwainer Smith," *Science Fiction Review*, 8.5 (1979), p. 51.

Welch, Robert. *George Orwell Animal Farm.* York Notes, UK: York Press Longman, 1980.

Wellman, Manly Wade. "The Witch's Cat," *Magicats!* Eds. Jack Dann and Gardner Dozois. New York: Ace, 1984, pp. 187–204.

Wells, H.G. *The Invisible Man.* London: Pan, 1987.

_____. *The Island of Dr Moreau.* London: Pan/Heinemann, 1896/1977.

Who's Who of Australian Writers. Port Melbourne: D.W. Thorpe, in association with the National Centre for Australian Studies, 1995.

Wikipedia: The Free Encyclopedia. "Comedic Device," August 2008a. http://en.wikipedia.org/wiki/Comedic_device

Wikipedia: The Free Encyclopedia. "Eucatastrophe," November 2008b. http://en.wikipedia.org/wiki/Eucatastrophe

Wikipedia: The Free Encyclopedia. "Robert Darnton," March 2009. http://en.wikipedia.org/wiki/Robert_Darnton

Wikipedia: The Free Encyclopedia. "Svetan Todorov," March 2009. http://en.wikipedia.org/wiki/Tzvetan_Todorov

Wikipedia: The Free Encyclopedia. "Vladimir Propp," March 2009. http://en.wikipedia.org/wiki/Vladimir_Propp

Wikipedia: The Free Encyclopedia. "Shock and Awe," March 2009. http://en.wikipedia.org/wiki/Shock_and_awe

Williams, Tess. *Sea as Mirror.* Sydney: HarperCollins, 2000.

Willis, Connie. "The Last of the Winnebagoes," *Isaac Asimov's Science Fiction*, 12.7 (1988), pp. 18–72.

_____. "The Last of the Winnebagoes," *Nebula Awards 24: SFWA's Choices for the Best Science Fiction and Fantasy 1988.* Ed. Michael Bishop. San Diego: Harcourt Brace Jovanovic, 1990, pp. 206–261.

Wilson, A.N. *C.S. Lewis: A Biography.* London: HarperCollins, 1990.

Wilson, David Henry. *The Coachman Rat.* London: Robinson, 1984/1989.

Wilson, Richard. "Just Call Me Irish," *Microcosmic Tales: 100 Wondrous Science Fiction Short-Short Stories.* Eds. Isaac Asimov, Martin H. Greenberg, and Joseph O. Olander. New York: Daw Books, 1980, pp. 56–60.

Wolfe, Bernard. "The Bisquit Position," *Again, Dangerous Visions Book 1.* Ed. Harlan Ellison. London: Pan Books, 1972, pp. 334–354.

Wolfe, Gary K. "The Best of Cordwainer Smith," *Survey of Science Fiction Literature, 5.* Ed. Frank N. Magill. Englewood Cliffs, NJ: Salem Press, 1979, pp. 186–190.

_____. *The Known and the Unknown: The Iconography of Science Fiction.* Ohio: Kent State University, 1979, p. 204.

_____. "Mythic Structures in Cordwainer Smith's 'The Game of Rat and Dragon,'" Science-*Fiction Studies*, 4.2 (1977), pp. 144–150.

_____. "Simak, Clifford Donald," *Twentieth Century Science Fiction Writers.* Ed. Curtis C. Smith. Chicago, 1981, pp. 495–507.

_____. "Smith, Cordwainer," *Twentieth Century Science Fiction Writers.* Ed. Curtis C. Smith. Chicago, 1981, pp. 506–507.

Wolfe, G.K., and C.T. Williams. "The Majesty of Kindness: Dialectic of Cordwainer Smith," *Voices for the Future 3.* Ed. Thomas D. Clareson. Bowling Green: Popular Press, 1984, pp. 52–74.

Wolfe, Peter. "Tolstoy's *War and Peace*: A Flawed Masterpiece?" Postgraduate/Staff Seminar, September 6, English Department, Flinders University of SA, 1995.

Woodcock, George. *Dawn and the Darkest Hour: A Study of Aldous Huxley.* New York: Viking Press, 1972.

Wright, A. Colin. *Mikhail Bulgakov: Life and Interpretations.* Toronto: University of Toronto Press, 1978.

Wu Ch'eng-en. *Monkey* (Trans. Arthur Waley). London: Unwin, 1942/1979, p. 1.

Wymer, T.L. "Cordwainer Smith: Satirist or Male Chauvinist," *Extrapolation*, 14.2 (1973), pp. 157–162.

Wynne-Davies, Marion. *Bloomsbury Guide to English Literature.* London: Bloomsbury, 1989.

Yolen, Jane. "Introduction," *Zoo 2000: Twelve Stories of Science Fiction and Fantasy Beasts.* New York: Seabury Press, 1973, pp. 9–12.

Yutang, Lin. *The Wisdom of India.* London: Michael Joseph, 1944/1956, p. 17.

Zelazny, Roger. *The Dream Master.* Ace Books, 1982.

Zinner, Paul E. *Communist Strategy and Tactics in Czechoslovakia, 1918–48.* London: Pall Mall Press, 1963.

Zool, M.H. *Bloomsbury Good Reading Guide to Science Fiction and Fantasy.* London: Bloomsbury, 1989.

Index